CW00879658

R. Barri Flowers is an ...
crime, thriller, mystery an...
three-dimensional protagoni...
twists and turns, and heart-pounding climaxes. With
an expertise in true crime, serial killers and characterising
dangerous offenders, he is perfectly suited for the
Mills & Boon Heroes series. Chemistry and conflict
between the hero and heroine, attention to detail and
incorporating the very latest advances in criminal
investigations are the cornerstones of his romantic
suspense fiction. Discover more on popular social
networks and Wikipedia.

USA Today bestselling author **Kacy Cross** writes romance
novels starring swoonworthy heroes and smart heroines.
She lives in Texas, where she's seen bobcats and beavers
near her house but sadly not one cowboy. She's raising
two mini-ninjas alongside the love of her life, who cooks
while she writes, which is her definition of a true hero.
Come for the romance, stay for the happily-ever-after.
She promises her books 'will make you laugh, cry and
swoon—cross my heart.'

Discover more at millsandboon.co.uk

HIDING IN ALASKA

R. BARRI FLOWERS

COLTON AT RISK

KACY CROSS

MILLS & BOON

All rights reserved including the right of reproduction in whole or in part in any form. This edition is published by arrangement with Harlequin Enterprises ULC.

This is a work of fiction. Names, characters, places, locations and incidents are purely fictional and bear no relationship to any real life individuals, living or dead, or to any actual places, business establishments, locations, events or incidents. Any resemblance is entirely coincidental.

This book is sold subject to the condition that it shall not, by way of trade or otherwise, be lent, resold, hired out or otherwise circulated without the prior consent of the publisher in any form of binding or cover other than that in which it is published and without a similar condition including this condition being imposed on the subsequent purchaser.

® and ™ are trademarks owned and used by the trademark owner and/or its licensee. Trademarks marked with ® are registered with the United Kingdom Patent Office and/or the Office for Harmonisation in the Internal Market and in other countries.

First Published in Great Britain 2025
by Mills & Boon, an imprint of HarperCollins*Publishers* Ltd
1 London Bridge Street, London, SE1 9GF

www.harpercollins.co.uk

HarperCollins*Publishers*
Macken House, 39/40 Mayor Street Upper,
Dublin 1, D01 C9W8, Ireland

Hiding in Alaska © 2025 R. Barri Flowers
Colton at Risk © 2025 Harlequin Enterprises ULC

Special thanks and acknowledgment are given to Kacy Cross
for her contribution to *The Coltons of Arizona* series.

ISBN: 978-0-263-39704-8

0325

This book contains FSC™ certified paper and other controlled
sources to ensure responsible forest management.

For more information visit: www.harpercollins.co.uk/green

Printed and Bound in the UK using 100% Renewable Electricity at
CPI Group (UK) Ltd, Croydon, CR0 4YY

HIDING IN ALASKA

R. BARRI FLOWERS

In memory of my cherished mother, Marjah Aljean, a devoted lifelong fan of Mills & Boon romance and romantic suspense novels, who inspired me to excel in my personal and professional lives. To H Loraine, the true love of my life and very best friend, whose support has been unwavering through the many terrific years together, as well as the many loyal fans of my romance, suspense, mystery and thriller fiction published over the years. Lastly, a nod goes out to my great Mills & Boon editors, Denise Zaza and Emma Cole, for the wonderful opportunity to lend my literary voice and creative spirit to the Mills & Boon Heroes series, as well as Miranda Indrigo, the wonderful concierge, who serendipitously led me to success with Mills & Boon Heroes.

Prologue

Giselle Kinard had always assumed she was smart enough to choose the right person to be in a solid relationship with. Boy, had she been wrong. How could she have been so blind? Justin Buckner was anything but the right man to build a future with. Much less become her fiancé.

At the age of twenty-eight, she was still dealing with the recent deaths of her parents, both succumbing to illnesses one soon after the other. Feeling vulnerable, Giselle had thought she was ready to move on when she'd met Justin at her studio in Chesapeake, Virginia, where she was a dance instructor. She had been interested in dancing from a very young age, when her mother had made her take ballet lessons. This would ultimately lead to her receiving a bachelor of arts degree from the dance program at Old Dominion University in Norfolk, Virginia.

Two years older, Justin Buckner was very good looking, tall, golden haired, blue eyed and in great shape. He'd been charming, sure of himself, a successful financial planner and very easy to teach how to ballroom dance. Not to mention he'd been as single and available as she'd been and eager to get involved with the right woman.

Was it any wonder that she'd been swept off her feet by him? They had only been dating for six months when Justin had asked Giselle to marry him, declaring his strong love for her. Though she'd hesitated to say yes, sensing something was off with him, she'd ultimately gone against her instincts and put her trust in the man, and agreed to marry him.

But the more time they'd spent together—mainly in his huge waterfront estate with magnificent views of the Elizabeth River—the more Giselle had begun to pull away from him before they could walk down the aisle. As she'd lost sight of who she was under his thumb, she'd seen the dark side of Justin. He'd become possessive, domineering, controlling, jealous, irrational and, frankly, dangerous. She'd hated it when he'd warned her more than once, "Don't test me, Giselle!"

She viewed that as much more than just a veiled threat. Especially when he'd outright cautioned her that were she to ever leave him, he would go after everyone Giselle knew, one by one, saving her for last but certainly not least.

She believed he meant business and would sooner see her dead than allow her to walk away from the life he felt was meant to be for them as husband and wife.

But even that intimidation was not enough for Giselle to go through with a doomed marriage that she knew would be very wrong. At least for her.

Leaving Justin and getting a restraining order to keep him at a safe distance was not an option. At least not a viable one. How many times had she read about a woman being murdered by her current or former partner after he'd blatantly disregarded a protection order and come after her?

Giselle was determined not to end up another statistic of a domestic-related homicide while Justin possibly ended up using his family's money and influence to beat the rap. Then another woman or more potential victims could wind up in his crosshairs down the line.

That was when she made the decision to run. Some place where he would never find her. With the lease to her apartment up, the few things she had already placed in storage and plans to ditch her red Toyota Camry, she was set to make her escape. Having stashed away some money, including a small inheritance from her parents, she could afford to leave everything behind, painful as it was, and start over.

Giselle could only hope that by putting time and distance between them, Justin would get past her ending their engagement—including leaving the diamond engagement ring he'd given her and a key to his house on the granite countertop in the gourmet kitchen while he was out—and stop looking for her.

Maybe then she would be able to return home and reclaim her life.

Or was that too much to hope for, given the vindictiveness Giselle knew was intrinsic in his nature, were they to ever lay eyes on one another again?

She didn't take time to have any second thoughts before going into hiding.

JUSTIN BUCKNER WAS incensed when he came home from work and spotted the engagement ring and house key on the kitchen counter. It told him everything he needed to know but didn't want to believe.

Giselle had left him. Left their relationship before it ever became official in two months.

Did she really think it would be so simple to walk away from what they had?

He had sold his parents on Giselle. Even when they'd believed she wasn't good enough for him, he'd believed otherwise. They were perfect together. She would be a great mother to their children. No matter that she needed his guidance when Giselle managed to step outside the line that he'd set from time to time, only for him to steer her right back on track as he wanted.

He wasn't about to let her slip from his grasp and take up with someone else. Not in this lifetime.

Defeat wasn't in his DNA. At least when it came to his choice for a lifelong partner.

Giselle was that woman. He'd known it the moment he'd laid his blue eyes upon her, smitten with Giselle's dark-haired, green-eyed beauty, with a slender body to match.

She was his and only his. Sooner than later, she would realize that.

But only after he taught her a costly lesson so that she would get the message loud and clear. Once and for all.

Getting on his cell phone, Justin called Giselle, only to get her voice mail. He demanded that she pick up but was ignored. His nostrils flared at this sign of disobedience.

He checked the GPS tracker he'd installed on her phone and saw that she was at her apartment.

Storming across the walnut hardwood flooring in his great room, Justin disregarded the custom-made furnishings and was out the door.

Moments later, he was driving away from his property in a blue BMW 430i coupe. He tried Giselle again on his cell, but she wouldn't answer him. Why would she put him in a position of having to punish her for this brazen act of disloyalty?

Did she really think that by simply ditching her ring it would be over between them?

Not hardly.

Think and think again.

No one left him. And lived to talk about it.

Unbeknownst to Giselle, this had happened once before.

His last girlfriend, Jenna Sweeney, had made the foolish mistake of trying to end their relationship.

He'd made sure she'd paid the price with her life.

Unless he could get Giselle to come back on her own and promise to never pull a stunt like this again, she would suffer the same fate.

It took him a few minutes to get to her apartment complex on Ferris Drive. Had it been up to him, she would have moved into his place by now—he'd given her a key to show how serious he was about this. But she'd refused to do so till after they were married.

He had gone along with this, though now he wondered if he should have applied more pressure to get married instead of waiting.

When he got out of the car, Justin never bothered to look for Giselle's vehicle in the parking lot, figuring it was out of his view. Instead he headed straight for her second-story apartment. Using his own key that she had given him, he opened the door and went inside.

To his surprise, he saw that the place was empty. He checked his cell phone GPS tracker. It indicated that her device was at that location. He called it and realized that the phone was in a trash can in the small kitchen.

"That bitch," Justin muttered angrily, hating himself for underestimating Giselle. *Run, but you can't hide forever*, he thought.

He would find her—if it was the last thing he ever did. And she would never know what had hit her.

Until it was too late.

Chapter One

Taller's Creek, Alaska.

The quaint town of less than five thousand inhabitants, located in the Kenai Peninsula Borough, was about as far away from Chesapeake, Virginia, as could be.

That was certainly how Giselle Kinard had seen it as she had settled in there comfortably at the age of thirty-one, believing she had successfully evaded her ex-fiancé, Justin Buckner. He had refused to take no for an answer when she'd wanted to end their relationship and any plans for marrying him, once his true colors had come out in plain and frightening view.

It had been nearly three years since her brazen escape. First she'd bounced around a few states in the Lower 48— going to Atlanta, Georgia; then Huntsville, Alabama; then San Antonio, Texas and Oakland, California. But she'd felt she was constantly looking over her shoulder, sure Justin would track her down, working odd jobs to survive before making her way to Alaska eighteen months ago.

It seemed the perfect escape. Taller's Creek was tucked away in the Gulf Coast Region and offered her the refuge Giselle had sought. There were enough interesting things to see and do to keep her from getting bored, while staying safe at the same time.

She had moved into a cozy little one-bedroom apartment with lots of windows on a dead-end street in a wooded area by Teary Lake, furnished it with secondhand but attractive contemporary furniture, adopted a Burmese kitten and gotten a job at a bookstore as a sales associate. Though she'd loved her old job and had been good at it, she didn't dare continue to be a dance instructor while on the run, certain that this would be something Justin would be looking for in his quest to find her.

Over time she had made a few friends, who thankfully didn't ask too many questions. Taking no chances, she didn't use social media under her name, went out of her way to avoid being photographed by anyone and resisted contacting people from her past life for fear that it could put them in harm's way. Or lead Justin to locating and coming after her.

So far, so good, Giselle told herself as she got ready for work on this mid-July Saturday morning, slipping into a purple button-up chiffon shirt, jeans and flats. She had dyed her long hair blond and cut it into a shoulder-length shag style with curtain bangs.

Maybe her ex-fiancé had more pressing issues to deal with than discovering her whereabouts and making good on his threats, she considered, moving across the hardwood flooring while glancing at the mostly closed vinyl shutters on the windows. About a year or so ago, she had used a computer at the library to look him up and had been surprised—or maybe not so much—to see that Justin was under federal investigation for bilking many of his clients out of amounts that went into the hundreds of thousands of dollars.

But checking on this periodically, Giselle was disappointed to see that the investigation seemed to have stalled, in spite of the indication that it was still ongoing. She wondered if Justin might be able to somehow worm his way out of going to prison. If so, it would mean that he would continue to pose a danger to her.

At least in theory.

Or was it more than that?

Though she had nothing more than a feeling at this point, something deep within Giselle sensed that she still wasn't entirely out of the woods yet where it concerned Justin.

Or had she allowed him to get into her head way too much, with no contact since the day she'd walked away from the nightmarish life she'd had—and would have had beyond that—with him?

She fed her rambunctious kitten, Muffin, who had been abandoned before Giselle had come to her rescue, then she grabbed her crossbody bag and headed out the door.

Moments later, she was behind the wheel of her silver Honda CR-V and on the road. Giselle took in the sights and sounds of Taller's Creek, amazed by its geographically diverse surroundings that included great beaches, kettle lakes, mountains and wetlands.

A stone's throw from Soldotna, Taller's Creek, alongside Owen Bay, sat on the western side of the Kenai National Wildlife Refuge, a nearly two-million-acre wildlife habitat preserve with an abundance of wildlife, such as black and brown bears, caribou, Dall sheep, eagles, mountain goats, moose, trumpeter swans and wolves.

She'd taken up birdwatching as a hobby, with various land birds, shorebirds, seabirds and waterfowl getting her attention. Beyond that, as an active person, she loved to hike, jog, cross-country ski and river float whenever she could.

Honestly, Giselle wasn't sure if she would ever be ready to give this up. Though she occasionally grew homesick and missed being a dance instructor (but didn't dare make it easier to be found), with her parents gone and no friends

Justin had allowed her to get close to, Giselle felt she was in a good place right now.

Until proven otherwise.

She reached the Taller's Creek Books building on Milton Lane, parked in the back and went inside. The independent bookstore was practically a landmark, having been around for half a century, and had gone through several owners. The current owner, Jill Kekiwi, a sixty-five-year-old widow, had bought the place twelve years ago to keep her busy after retiring from her schoolteacher job when her husband had died. She had hired Giselle on the spot, sensing her need for employment and believing her to be a good fit for the midsized bookseller that had two other full-time sales associates, Wesley Abbott and Ellen Ebsen, and one part-timer, a college student named Sadie Pisano.

"Morning," Jill greeted her cheerfully as Giselle walked up to her.

"Good morning." She flashed her teeth at the medium-sized woman with white hair in a chopped pixie style and brown eyes behind browline glasses.

"Don't get too relaxed. There's a customer waiting for you..."

"Really?" Giselle turned around and saw her friend, Neve Chenoweth, standing by the counter, holding a stack of books. "I'm on it," Giselle told her boss.

Jill smiled. "Good to know."

Giselle walked over to Neve, whose brown eyes were buried in one of the books, and got her attention. "Hey."

Neve, who was African American, Giselle's same age and five feet, seven inches tall, had short brown hair in a feathered cut with blond highlights. She looked up and said, "There you are."

"Here I am." Giselle grinned at the US Air Force veteran,

who had chosen to remain in Alaska after being honorably discharged. "Sorry to keep you waiting, but aren't you supposed to be hiking this morning?"

"Yep," Neve admitted, dressed for the excursion. "But I wanted to drop by and pick up some books to deep dive into later."

"I see." Giselle took them from her and sat them on the counter before going to the other side to ring up the purchase. "Well, you've come to the right place—and thanks for allowing me to be your sales associate."

Neve laughed. "What are friends for, right?"

"Right." Giselle got her credit card. "Maybe next time we can go hiking together." As they had on other occasions when she had the time to be adventurous and work up a good sweat.

"Sure," Neve agreed. "Whenever you're ready, let me know."

Giselle put the books into a bag and was about to ask Neve if she was back on the market after dumping the last guy she had been seeing but decided not to go there. It would invariably result in being asked about her own love life, which to Giselle had admittedly been pretty much nonexistent since moving to Alaska. She had gone out with someone every now and then but mostly chose to keep to herself and not get too serious about anyone for fear of history repeating itself in being attached to a controlling, unstable and dangerous man. "Here you go," she said, handing her friend the bag.

"Thanks." Neve eyed her. "So, what are you doing tonight?"

"Not much," Giselle had to admit. "Probably catch up on some chores, watch television."

"I have a better idea," she said, smiling. "A few of us are meeting up at the Owl's Den. Why don't you come?"

As she had no good reason to reject the idea of hanging out with friends at a popular bar in town, Giselle agreed. "Count me in."

"Cool." Neve licked her lips. "I'll call you later."

"I'll call you first," she countered.

"Okay."

Neve walked away, and Giselle watched for a moment as she walked out the door. She barely noticed the tall man wearing a hoodie and loose clothing who followed Neve from the store. Other than the fact that it didn't appear as though he had purchased any books.

Giselle didn't give it much thought as another customer came up to the counter.

QUINCY LANKARD SAT in a swivel seat of a black leather office chair at his wooden workstation as an investigator assigned to the regional major crimes unit of the Alaska Bureau of Investigation on Kalifornsky Beach Road in Soldotna, Alaska. A branch of the Alaska Department of Public Safety's Alaska State Troopers, the ABI had been his employer ever since he'd gotten his bachelor's degree in criminal justice from the University of Alaska Fairbanks ten years ago.

An Alaskan Native and member of the Eyak, he was honored to represent Indigenous peoples of the state in law enforcement, wanting to make sure that justice was served equally to anyone who violated the law. At thirty-two, a few months removed from turning thirty-three, he was still single and childless, much to the chagrin of his parents and younger and married sister, Olivia, who had two great kids.

Though he, too, hoped to someday find that right person to walk down the aisle with and become the mother of his children, Quincy was not desperate enough to rush into something he'd only end up regretting. Everything in life would come at the right time, he firmly believed. That included marrying the woman of his dreams and going from there.

He turned his focus to his latest investigation. A home invasion in Soldotna had turned deadly, with the fifty-three-year-old homeowner, Abigail Tavares, the victim. The ABI, in conjunction with the Anchorage Police Department, had tracked down the home invader in Anchorage, Alaska, one hundred and twenty miles away. Matthew Fife, a twenty-six-year-old with an extensive criminal history, had been charged with first-degree murder and burglary.

Quincy had personally slapped the cuffs onto the suspect and was glad to have him off the streets. While savoring that victory for a moment, a 911 call came in from the Soldotna Public Safety Communications Center, the dispatch center for the Kenai Peninsula Borough.

"We have a report of a dead female found near the Pippen Trail," the dispatcher said somberly.

"That's not good..." Quincy muttered musingly, his brown-gray eyes hardening. He immediately suspected that the deceased person was Neve Chenoweth, a thirty-one-year-old hiker who had been missing for two days now. An AST search and rescue team had been sent to the area in Taller's Creek after cell phone pings had indicated that the woman's phone was in the vicinity. So, was this her? And how had she died?

Not wanting to jump the gun, Quincy kept all options on the table. He noted that a year ago a male hiker had been found dead in the same area, and it had been ruled an accidental fall down a gulley. Though he suspected something similar might have happened here, Quincy was duty bound to investigate any death of an otherwise healthy individual as suspicious until proven otherwise.

After briefing the lieutenant who headed the command staff on the situation, Quincy rose from his desk, a solid six-feet, four-inch frame in full uniform. He was wearing a felt campaign hat above thick, trimmed dark hair, a ballistic vest and a body camera. A loaded Glock 22 40 S&W caliber handgun sat in his tactical thigh holster. He headed out, steeling himself for the grim discovery.

After climbing into his white Ford Police Interceptor Utility SUV, Quincy drove away from the regional MCU and headed northeast on Kenai Spur Highway toward Taller's Creek. He wondered what the last thoughts had been of the deceased hiker, assuming there had even been time to take stock of her life and where she'd wanted it to go. Maybe she could still get somewhere on the other side.

When he arrived on the scene at the Pippen Trail on Klatton Road, Quincy exited his vehicle and made his way past search personnel before meeting up with Search and Rescue Coordinator Gabe McAuliffe.

Nearly as tall as him but thinner, with blond hair in a high-and-tight cut, the fortysomething Gabe furrowed his brow and said sourly, "We've located Neve Chenoweth... Sorry it came to this."

"Me too," Quincy replied, having already anticipated such. "Where is she?"

"This way..."

He followed Gabe down a trail through a forested area and onto a side trail above Owen Bay, where Quincy spotted the body. It was invisible from the main trail and lying awkwardly. Neve Chenoweth was African American, tall and slender. Her short, feathered hair was reddened with blood, as her head lay atop a large rock.

Gabe uttered, "I'm guessing that she tripped accidentally while jogging, hit her head and was out like a light."

"Maybe," Quincy said thoughtfully. He could imagine some other scenarios. Such as someone hitting her from behind. Or perhaps she'd been suicidal and deliberately followed those dark impulses. "We'll see what the State Medical Examiner's Office has to say."

"Right," Gabe agreed. "Aside from that, there's the difficult task of family and friends having to come to terms with the reality that Neve is gone."

"Yeah, there is that." Quincy pinched his nose, knowing this was the hard part. Especially when, presumably, no one had seen this coming. Or had someone?

THREE HOURS LATER, Quincy entered Taller's Creek Books. As part of his investigation, pending the autopsy report, he wanted to reach out to Neve Chenoweth's friends in hopes of getting a complete picture of her last hours of life. Maybe give him a different perspective to lean on for the deceased, whom he'd discovered had been originally from Syracuse, New York, where much of her family lived, and had served in the US military.

He took note of the slender woman in her early thirties who was putting books on a shelf in the children's section. *That must be her*, he thought instinctively and headed her way.

"Hi," Quincy said, getting her attention. "Are you Giselle Kinard?"

"Yes," she spoke softly.

He could tell she was gorgeous without needing to look too hard. She gazed at him with the loveliest, though clearly saddened, green eyes he had ever seen. They were on a nice heart-shaped face, along with a dainty nose, full lips and a small cleft in her chin. Her shaggy blond hair rested on her shoulders, and he liked the bangs. She was wearing a ruffled short-sleeve rose-colored blouse, black straight-leg pants and brown loafers.

"I'm Trooper Quincy Lankard with the Alaska Bureau of Investigation," he told her. "We're looking into the death of Neve Chenoweth."

"You are…?" She batted her eyes, ill at ease.

"It's just routine," he tried to reassure her. "Though it appears her death was a tragic accident—which the autopsy should confirm—the ABI still has to sign off on that. As I understand it, you were one of Ms. Chenoweth's friends. And furthermore, the time line indicates that she purchased some books here shortly before she went hiking—"

On that note, Giselle's legs seemed to give out on her, prompting Quincy to gladly come to her rescue, holding her steady. He liked the way she felt in his arms—soft and supple—while wondering curiously if there was something in particular that could have triggered this reaction to his news.

Chapter Two

If she was being honest about it, Giselle had to admit that it felt surprisingly natural to be in the powerful arms of the good-looking trooper. Were the circumstances different, she could imagine it being something that she could get used to in a hurry. As it was, they were in the middle of a bookstore, and he had merely reflexively come to her aid before Giselle's legs gave out from beneath her and she went sprawling embarrassingly down to the floor.

Giselle wasn't quite sure why she reacted that way. Yes, she was still reeling at the news from a little earlier that her friend Neve Chenoweth had been found dead by the Pippen Trail. The speculation was that it was likely accidental. Trooper Quincy Lankard seemed to believe that would prove to be the case.

So why had she freaked out at that moment?

If you even think about ever leaving me, Giselle, just know that you'll pay for it in ways you can't even imagine. I'll go after everyone you care about...or cares about you, even a little...one by one. Saving you for last.

Her ex-fiancé Justin Buckner's chilling words replayed in Giselle's head. Could he have found her and made his threat come true?

"Are you all right?" Trooper Lankard asked in a deep

voice, still holding her close to his rock-hard body as though never wanting to let her go.

"I'm fine," she stated, making herself believe this to be true as Giselle extricated herself from his arms and made sure her legs wouldn't buckle again.

"You sure about that?" He trained deep brown eyes shaded in gray at her with mild concern.

"Yes." She colored while quickly sizing him up. Aside from being very tall in comparison to her height of five-seven with his uniform seemingly showing off every muscle in his body, she guessed the handsome trooper to be in his early thirties, like her. He had a square face and strong jawline with a straight nose and round chin that was smooth shaven. Though he was wearing a blue campaign hat, she could see that he had rich black hair cut short in a military style and could imagine running her hands through it.

"I just had a moment," she tried to explain. "Losing a friend like that so suddenly has been difficult to process—"

"I understand," he said in a sympathetic tone of voice. "Why don't we sit and talk..." He angled his eyes toward a nearby set of velvet accent reading chairs.

Giselle nodded. "Okay."

She walked ahead of him, and they sat down at the same time before Trooper Lankard stretched his long legs out and asked gently, "So, how long have you known Ms. Chenoweth?"

"About a year and a half."

"Do you know if she ever suffered from PTSD?" He waited a beat, then said, "I understand that Ms. Chenoweth was a Tactical Air Control Party specialist with the US Air Force before her discharge."

"Neve never mentioned that she'd experienced PTSD," Giselle responded, while wondering why it would matter in any event if her death had truly been an accident. "But that doesn't mean she didn't choose to keep it to herself."

"True. I can dig deeper here with the military if it becomes necessary in the investigation, but that likely won't be the case," he stressed, then leaned back and scratched his chin thoughtfully. "Any indication that Ms. Chenoweth was suicidal…?"

"What?" Giselle's brow furrowed, surprised that he would even go there. "Are you suggesting that Neve killed herself?" she snapped.

"Nothing of the sort." His voice dropped an octave. "I have no reason to believe that we're looking at a suicide here, based on what we know thus far. Just trying to cover the bases as a prelude to closing the case. Sorry if you took umbrage to the question."

Maybe I was a bit over the top or too defensive, Giselle told herself regretfully. The trooper had every right to want to know what Neve's state of mind might have been before her death. Even if the notion that she would take her own life was absurd.

"It's okay." Giselle softened her voice. "I know you're just doing your job. In any event, the answer is no, Neve was in no way suicidal. She loved life too much to want to leave it the way that she did."

"Figured as much," he said coolly. "Anyone who likes to hike has to enjoy living and being in touch with nature."

"Yes, that pretty much describes the Neve I know— knew," Giselle said, still trying to come to terms with thinking of her in the past tense.

"All right." Trooper Lankard flashed a crooked grin. "One more question and I'll get out of your hair, figuratively speaking." He paused. "Did she always go hiking alone? I'm only asking because even for experienced hikers, partnering up with someone is always a good idea—if only to be able to call for help should one or the other have a problem. That could have made the difference between life and death—"

Giselle agreed on the face of it, wishing she had accompanied her friend to the Pippen Trail. On the other hand, accidents did happen as part of life. Maybe there was nothing that could have made a difference in the outcome. Unless it was proven that Neve's death had been no accident after all.

"Neve often hiked alone," Giselle informed the trooper. "She liked exploring Alaska on her own. But she wasn't opposed to hiking with others, including me. If only that had been the case this time…" Giselle shuddered at the thought that Neve had had to die with no one around to offer comfort.

"You can't blame yourself," he said firmly. "I'm sure she wouldn't want you to. We all make choices that we can't always run away from and just have to deal with them, for better or worse…"

That comment struck a nerve with Giselle. She had made the choice to run away from the life she'd had in Virginia. And had to live with the consequences—mainly leaving everything behind and not being able to look back for her own safety. Fortunately, things had fallen into place for her up to this point. So long as she didn't count the fact that one of the first people who had befriended her upon arriving in Taller's Creek was now dead—reminding Giselle that bad things could still happen, even when you least expected it.

She realized that Trooper Lankard had stood up and moved closer to her. "I'd better let you get back to stocking children's books on the shelves," he spoke evenly. "Thanks for your time."

"No problem." Giselle quickly got to her feet, meeting his

warm eyes. At the mention of children, she couldn't help but wonder if he had any. Somehow it seemed like the trooper would make a good father. At the very least, she could tell that he took his job seriously. Even if he had to deal with such tragedies as death. Impetuously she said to him, "In case you're interested, we're having a candlelight vigil at eight p.m. tonight at the Pippen Trail, to honor Neve's life."

"I'll be there," he said, as if not needing to give it a single thought.

"Okay." Giselle smiled at him, feeling like he truly cared about people. He was the type of person she could imagine, at least in theory, getting to know better outside of his official capacity. Or would that be unwise, after her nightmarish relationship with Justin? "See you then," she told the trooper simply, masking the eagerness to do just that.

"You will," he promised and tipped the brim of his hat courteously, then walked away.

No sooner had Quincy Lankard left the bookstore and Giselle was contemplative as she returned to stocking shelves when Wesley Abbott, one of the other sales associates, came over.

In his midforties and gangly, with brown hair in a spiked mohawk and blue eyes behind wire-rimmed glasses, Wesley stated curiously, "Saw you talking to the state trooper. What was that all about?"

"He's looking into the death of my friend, Neve Chenoweth," Giselle answered, holding a new children's book in her hands. By now, she was sure that everyone in Taller's Creek had heard about the tragedy, including Wesley, whom she hadn't spoken to since learning the news herself.

"Yeah, I'm sorry about that." He touched his glasses. "Do they still believe it was an accident?"

"As far as I'm aware," she replied, knowing that they

were waiting for the autopsy report to make it official. "As an ABI investigator, Trooper Lankard is questioning people Neve knew as part of the routine in order to close the case."

"I see." Wesley was holding two hardcover copies of a just-released spy novel. "Well, if you ever need someone to talk to about what happened to your friend, I'm a good listener."

Giselle batted her lashes. Was he actually coming on to her? Or legitimately concerned about her peace of mind? Though she didn't know him all that well, in spite of working at the same bookstore for months now, last she'd heard he was in a committed relationship with the Norwegian woman he lived with. Had that changed?

Giselle smiled thinly. "I'll keep that in mind."

He nodded and walked away. She turned back to the shelf she was working on, knowing it was a good distraction. Even if it was hard to get what had happened to Neve out of her head. Perhaps the vigil would serve as a means to not only pay her respects but help her try to get on with her life, which had already seen more than its fair share of challenges to overcome.

THE CANDLELIGHT VIGIL was held at the Pippen Trail as a way to meet the tragedy of Neve's passing head-on. Honoring her memory near the spot where her death had occurred was in line with Neve's adventurous spirit and, to Giselle, a suitable send-off to her friend, wherever she landed next.

The site, which had a memorial cross, flowers and mementoes, was attended by several people who'd been closest to Neve and whose friendship Giselle had inherited as a result. These included Kimberly Herrington, a twenty-five-year-old artist who was just starting to make a name for herself in the local art scene; Seth Lombrozo, in his forties and a residential architect; Ethan Gladstone, a fiftysomething caterer; Jacinta Cruz, a thirty-year-old local documentary producer; Pablo Wersching, in his late forties and a dog-kennel owner; and Yuki Kotake, a fashion designer in her thirties. Some others Giselle didn't recognize, but she was happy to see that they were there to show the love and respect Neve so richly deserved.

Noticeably absent was Trooper Quincy Lankard. Giselle wondered if he had forgotten the time. Or had he ever truly intended to attend the vigil? Perhaps something else had come up, she considered while holding a candle in memory of her friend.

"Hey." Giselle heard the deep, recognizable voice over her shoulder. She turned to face Quincy Lankard, who locked eyes with her. He was dressed casually in a dark red pocket polo shirt, slim jeans and black Chelsea boots. His short dark hair was on full display and was parted on the side.

"You came," she said happily.

"Yeah. I wanted to be here to pay my respects to Ms. Chenoweth, fully honoring the dead as she makes her way to the spirit world."

"Nice to know." Giselle imagined that this appreciation for the bridge between life and death was in his DNA. As it was in hers, to one degree or another. "I'm sure that Neve would welcome your appearance, Trooper Lankard."

"I'm not on duty. Please—call me Quincy," he insisted.

"Okay." She smiled at him. "So long as you call me Giselle."

"Deal." He stuck out a hand, inviting her to shake it. She obliged and felt a tingle as their palms pressed together. Had he felt this too? "Good to see you again, Giselle," he said equably, "albeit under sad circumstances."

"Yes, it is sad," she agreed, adding, "but it's also meant

to be a joyous occasion to the extent it can be—to remember the amazing life Neve had, though cut short."

"Glad to be a part of it and representing the Alaska Department of Public Safety, albeit off the clock."

Giselle nodded, then they turned and watched as some of Neve's friends spoke about her. When it came around to Giselle, she, too, said kind words about her late friend and couldn't help but wonder why such accidents happened to good people. She supposed that this was simply one of life's cruelties. It could happen to anyone if they were in the wrong place at the wrong time. She could only be thankful that it appeared as though death had come quickly for Neve, so she hadn't been left to suffer.

All that was left was for Neve to be returned to her family in Syracuse for a proper burial.

QUINCY WAS ALWAYS MOVED when people gathered to pay their respects to a fallen friend. Or family member. He'd certainly been there more times than he cared to admit on both fronts. As an AST, part of the community and a relative. He recalled losing his grandfather, Thayer Lankard, when Quincy had only been ten years old. Heart attack that his grandfather had never seen coming till it had been too late to prevent.

Then there was losing his best friend from high school, Grant Sackett, who'd died when his motorcycle had flipped on a dirt road. He'd been just twenty-two years old at the time.

But as Quincy watched the candlelight vigil for Neve Chenoweth and even said a few words in her memory as an outsider who was still able to feel the emotions that hung in the Alaska air like a dark cloud, he had to admit that it was the chance to spend more time with Giselle that motivated him most to attend.

Aside from being a real looker who'd caught his eye from the start, she impressed him as someone he wouldn't mind getting to know better. If she were willing. And available. But at the moment, she was huddled with other friends of Neve's, commiserating over her tragic loss. Respectfully, Quincy chose to slip away quietly, knowing there would be another opportunity to see Giselle in the future while not wanting to take away from her need to grieve a death that appeared to be nothing more than a terrible accident.

He headed home and looked forward to confirming this when the autopsy report came out tomorrow. In the meantime, he was happy to be able to return to his place to chill, knowing that there was more to life than the demands of his job and its connotations that were not always pleasant. That included being able to look at himself in the mirror and feeling that he had a hell of a lot to offer someone who wanted to join him in whatever journey lay ahead. Giselle suddenly entered his thoughts in that regard. He was aware that was putting the cart ahead of the horse but had no problem with fantasizing about it.

Quincy pulled up to his four-acre wooded property on Keystone Lane. The residence itself was a two-story, four-bedroom log home with a Kenai River frontage. He had purchased it five years ago, once it had become clear to him that he would likely be based in Soldotna for as long as he wished. Living there alone was another story altogether, and one he wanted to rectify sooner than later with a family to share it with.

He left his vehicle and headed inside the house. Spacious with an open concept, most of the features were solid wood, including a plank vaulted ceiling and maple hardwood flooring. A combination of double-hung and picture windows were everywhere, with woven wood shades. There was a gas fireplace in the great room, along with log furniture, and the midcentury-modern kitchen had a quartz epoxy countertop and contemporary appliances.

Quincy went to the kitchen and grabbed a can of beer from the stainless-steel refrigerator. He opened it and took a drink before checking his phone. There was a text message from his sister, Olivia. She was reminding him that his nephew Todd's fifth birthday was next week—in case he wanted to buy him a birthday present.

Quincy laughed. *Talk about pressure*, he thought with amusement. He loved Todd as his own son. Of course, he was happy to continue to spoil him, along with his six-year-old sister, Krista. At least as long as there were no kids of his own to dote over instead.

It occurred to Quincy that a couple of children's books would make a perfect birthday gift for Todd. He wondered what Giselle could recommend. If nothing else, it would give him an excuse to see her again, with the nature of Neve Chenoweth's death more or less a done deal.

He texted Olivia back, assuring her that he hadn't forgotten his nephew's birthday, before finishing off the beer and heading upstairs for a shower.

JUST DOWN THE Kenai Spur Highway on Angler Drive, in the Kenai Peninsula Borough of Alaska, sat an isolated one-story, two-bedroom farmhouse nestled in a wooded area, separated from nosy neighbors. At least this was how Justin Buckner saw it, making it the perfect location for him to set up shop as part of his plans. He had rented the place a little more than a week ago, after discovering at long last just where his ex-fiancée, Giselle Kinard, had ended up.

It had taken him almost three years to find her. Might have been sooner, but she had apparently just managed to elude him for parts unknown when he had tracked her to Oakland, California.

Damn her.

He walked back and forth across the worn hardwood flooring as if nothing better to do. The place had come furnished with rustic furniture and had picture windows. It was a far cry from his old spacious waterfront digs that had been a good fit. Till she'd left and everything had fallen apart.

He'd lost everything dear to him, starting with Giselle. His business had gone up in flames, figuratively and quite literally, and he was up a creek without a paddle. He'd had to get out of Dodge and do whatever he needed to keep his head above water.

And all with one central goal—get back what was owed him. That began with Giselle. She would pay dearly for leaving him high and dry. But not before others in her orbit paid the ultimate price first. Such as the pretty hiker he'd pushed to her death. And had made it appear to be an accident.

Just as he'd promised Giselle, should she ever decide to bolt and keep him from marrying her and having the life with her that he'd fantasized about for the past three years.

Drip. Drip. Drip.

One deadly step at a time.

He would save her for last. Make her sweat. And sweat. And worse.

Then finish her off—watching with satisfaction as her life was taken away.

Only then could he reclaim his own life and find someone else worthy of him to share it with.

Justin smoked the weed he was holding, feeling its nice effects as they worked their way into his system while continuing to pace. He thought about his ex-fiancée, his thick brows knitting with resentment. Revenge was on his mind.

Couldn't come soon enough. But patience was necessary, even against his eagerness to get this over with. Some things couldn't be rushed. This was one of them. Especially when playing with her psyche was so satisfying in and of itself.

Payback was a bitch, as the saying went.

Giselle would get the full brunt of it. Before she breathed her own last breath. Just like his previous ex, Jenna Sweeney, after she'd crossed him. And hadn't lived to talk about it for very long. He'd made sure she'd been put somewhere that they could never find her.

Justin took another puff on the joint and laughed as dark thoughts filled his head naughtily.

Chapter Three

Giselle was up bright and early for a Tuesday-morning jog on the empty street. She was wearing a purple cap and light summertime jogging clothes with white sneakers. Running was one of her favorite pastimes that she had continued when relocating to Taller's Creek.

I can't let Justin rob me of everything precious in my life, Giselle told herself stubbornly as she spied a moose in the short distance, seeming just as observant of her. It was but one of the fascinating things she had become accustomed to experiencing since moving to Alaska.

Though she could hardly say the same thing about Quincy Lankard, Giselle admittedly liked what she'd seen of the trooper thus far. Unfortunately, before she could've maybe tapped into that a bit more last night, he had disappeared from the candlelight vigil without even saying goodbye. Had that been his way of letting her know that he had fulfilled his obligation to Neve, assuming he saw it in that regard? Or had he bowed out gracefully out of respect to her and so as not to overstay his welcome among those who'd known her friend?

I'm probably overthinking it, Giselle thought as she rounded the corner and headed back to the apartment. She would like to become better acquainted with Quincy, but only if she could do so without seeming over eager. Or having him pry too much into her past life, which she was in no hurry to have to relive. At least the parts that had anything to do with her ex-fiancé.

When she got inside the apartment, Muffin wasted little time in cozying up to her, obviously looking for some attention. "Okay, you win," she told the kitten, scooping her up into her arms and cradling her. "But only for a minute or two," she warned, knowing she needed to get ready for work. Muffin seemed more than happy to take what she could get, closing her eyes and purring happily.

An hour later, Giselle was in the bookstore putting up a display for a new science-fiction title with sales associate Ellen Ebsen. In her midtwenties and rail thin with long natural red hair in an A-line cut and big blue eyes, Ellen was vivacious and totally smitten with her girlfriend, Tatiana, whom she couldn't stop talking about.

"She's such a good person and makes me feel good about myself," Ellen gushed as she lined up a stack of books perfectly on the table.

"That's nice to hear," Giselle said enviously. She could only dream about having someone in her own life who could accept her for who she was rather than try to make her into someone else. Or threaten to ruin her life if she didn't capitulate.

"Does he want to come in or not?" Ellen asked, making a face.

Giselle looked at her, confused. "Who?"

"The man gawking in the window."

Facing that direction, Giselle's heart skipped a beat as she caught sight of a tall male who turned away at that moment. But not before she got a glimpse of his face. She recognized it. Or at least thought she did.

Justin? a voice in her head rang loudly. Had he found her? At last?

"What's wrong?" Ellen asked, concern in her tone. "You look like you've just seen a ghost!"

It might be better if I did, Giselle thought, unnerved. The dead couldn't hurt you. She blinked and then looked at the window again. The man was gone. Had it just been her imagination that it was Justin instead of someone simply innocently checking out the bookstore? That imagination had gone off the charts on different occasions during her time away from Justin.

Would he really look exactly the same way after three years? Like the face emblazoned in her memory as if seared there permanently, along with the sandy-colored, wavy hair in a midlength cut?

If Justin was truly in Taller's Creek, Giselle was sure he wouldn't hesitate to make his presence known as part of his sick process of tormenting her. Wouldn't he?

She regarded Ellen and admitted, "I thought I saw someone I recognized from among the living." Giselle twisted her lips thoughtfully. "But I was apparently mistaken."

"Happens to us all." Ellen shrugged indifferently. "Guess he decided not to come in after all and see if there was a book or two he might have been interested in."

"Guess not." Giselle glanced again at the window, wondering if the man might have rematerialized. Nothing doing. She supposed he'd just been passing by and might have only looked inside the bookstore haphazardly before going on his way. As for Justin, he was most likely still in Chesapeake, probably having charmed some other vulnerable woman to obsess over as his prospective bride or current wife.

Giselle tried to erase the thought out of her mind as they finished putting the display together and moved on to other duties.

JUSTIN COULD ALMOST feel the fear inside Giselle as she'd spotted him checking her out through the bookstore window. It was his intention to shake up his ex-fiancée a bit, mess with her pretty head as one step in the ultimate punishment she had coming to her. But before she could truly come to grips with the notion that what she was seeing wasn't merely a figment of her warped imagination but the real deal, he quickly averted his face and moved away from the window and out of her view.

Justin laughed with self-satisfaction as he moved briskly down the sidewalk. He wasn't about to make this exercise in terror easy for Giselle. Let her sweat it out. And sweat some more. Till she was dripping with perspiration and a fast-beating heart. That was the least of what she deserved for dropping out of his life, catching him off guard, leaving him wanting for much more from his ex than what he'd been given from her.

And he would have it. This wasn't the end of it. Not by a long shot. But he was clever enough to get under her skin while maintaining a low profile. Till it was time to make his presence felt again.

Until then, he was more than content to see just what it was that had drawn Giselle to Alaska. And Taller's Creek, in particular.

Justin chuckled musingly and crossed the street to get to his car.

QUINCY WAS STANDING over his desk as he read the autopsy report from the Alaska Department of Health State Medical Examiner's Office on Neve Chenoweth. According to Chief Medical Examiner Rhonda Ullerup, MD, Ms. Chenoweth had died as a result of an epidural hematoma caused by her head hitting a large rock. The death was ruled as accidental.

That didn't come as a surprise to Quincy, having expected as much. Still, part of him couldn't help but wonder if an experienced hiker with a military background would be so careless as to allow herself to trip or fall with a fatal outcome. Of course, the alternative was that her death had been due to other circumstances. Suicide seemed to be all but ruled out, with no indication that she'd been suffering from depression or PTSD. There was no reason to expect foul play. Till there was one.

"Sorry for her loved ones," remarked Alaska Bureau of Investigation Trooper Alan Edmonston, who had handed him a copy of the report. Alan, who was in his early forties, tall and solidly built with blue eyes and shaven bald beneath his campaign hat, shrugged resignedly. "It happens…"

"I'm sorry too." Quincy sighed, hating to admit that this type of thing in Alaska was par for the course, for better and far too often worse. "At least I'll be able to give them some closure," he reasoned. That included Giselle, whom he found himself wanting to get past this as quickly as possible. So that they might be able to have a do-over in getting to know each other, without Neve's tragic death hanging over them.

"That's all we can do," Alan said. "While being grateful we get to do this, go home ourselves and live to see another day."

"At least you have someone to go home to," Quincy remarked, knowing that Alan had been happily married to his high school sweetheart, Minnie, for two decades and counting. But this was hardly the time for Quincy to start feeling sorry for himself. He had too many blessings to count for that. And at least one prospect over the horizon.

"Your time will come," Alan told him, as though without a doubt. "In the meantime, enjoy your freedom while you can. Don't rush it, in spite of all the joy that comes with marriage."

Quincy wasn't quite sure how to interpret his words. "I'll try to remember that," he said, while more than willing to hedge his bet for marriage and family over the lonely life of a bachelor.

They talked briefly about a case of attempted assault in the process of a robbery that Alan was investigating while Quincy awaited his next assignment, before he headed out for Taller's Creek Books. There he planned to update Giselle on the official cause of Neve Chenoweth's death. And take the time as well to pick up some books for his nephew's birthday gift.

HE FOUND THE lovely woman he was looking for pointing a petite, red-headed female teenager in the right direction before Quincy watched Giselle take note of him standing there.

"Hey," he said, offering her a crooked grin.

"Hey." She smiled back softly and lost this as Giselle uttered inquiringly, "Where did you go last night? One moment you were there—the next you were gone…"

"I could see that you were pretty busy with the vigil, and I didn't want to intrude upon that, so I slipped away." Now Quincy wondered if that had been a mistake.

"You weren't intruding," she insisted, while admitting, "but I was caught up in the moment, so I completely understand why you left. Thanks for showing up, anyway."

"I was happy to do so." He met her eyes coolly. "In fact, one of the reasons I'm here now is to let you know that the autopsy report came in on Neve."

Giselle's thin brows lifted tensely. "Oh…?"

Without going into the morbid details, Quincy said, "As expected, it was concluded that the death was an accident." He watched what appeared to be relief wash across Giselle's face.

"I'm glad to know that it wasn't the result of something nefarious."

He cocked a brow curiously. "Did you think it could have been?"

"No," she spoke hastily. "It's just nice to have the cause of Neve's death official."

Quincy decided to take her word for it, even if he sensed there might have been something more to the story. "Okay."

Giselle eyed him interestedly. "You said that was one of the reasons you came to the bookstore. Was there another?"

To see you again, he told himself in all candor but responded smoothly, "Yes, my nephew, Todd, will turn five next week. Thought I'd pick up a few books for a birthday present. And while I'm at it, may as well grab some books for my six-year-old niece, Krista, so she doesn't feel left out. I was hoping you could recommend some?"

Giselle's eyes lit up. "Of course. I'd be happy to help you out there," she gushed.

Quincy followed her to the children's section, where Giselle presented him with a number of great choices, leaving it up to him to make the final decision on which books to purchase. After he did just that and paid Giselle for them, he got down to what was really on his mind, asking her, "So, are you seeing anyone these days?"

She appeared caught off guard by the question, making him wonder if it was wholly inappropriate, but she recovered quickly, stating, "Actually, I'm not." She paused, musing. "Are you?"

He grinned. "I'm pretty single at the moment—never been married either." *Maybe that could change on both fronts*, he thought, feeling even more emboldened. "Would you like to grab a bite to eat sometime?"

Giselle gazed at him encouragingly. "I'm on lunch break in ten minutes. We can grab a bite at the café across the street, if you're game?"

"Definitely," he told her without preface. "I'll go get us a table and wait for you."

"All right." She smiled genuinely. "See you in a few."

Quincy tipped his hat to that effect and walked off, looking forward to delving more into the woman behind the beautiful face.

GISELLE WAS ADMITTEDLY a little nervous as she entered Juanita's Café. She hadn't been on a real date in longer than she cared to remember. Was this a date? Or more of a friendly lunch?

She took a *wait and see* approach on that, welcoming the opportunity to get to know the ABI investigator better as Giselle spotted Quincy at a table by the window and was waved over.

He stood as she approached, sporting a handsome grin. "Hey."

"Hi." She smiled back, noting he had taken his hat off and put it on a corner of the table.

"I took a chance and ordered us both lattes," he said confidently.

"A latte is good," she voiced her approval as they both sat across from each other and Giselle took a sip of the drink.

"So, what's good on the menu?" Quincy asked, correctly presuming that she was a regular there.

She had no trouble responding. "The halibut sandwich is great and comes with coleslaw."

"Sounds good to me," he said, and they both ordered.

A short while later, they were eating and Giselle was still trying to decide what to say and what not to regarding her past life when, as expected, Quincy said curiously, "I'm guessing that you're not from Alaska?"

She laughed. "Is it that obvious?"

He laughed back. "No, but most people I run into seem to have relocated here from elsewhere, for one reason or another. Apart from that, I'm picking up a mid-Atlantic accent. Correct me if I'm wrong."

"You're not," Giselle confessed, impressed, though she had long believed she had no accent at all. "I'm from Virginia," she told him simply.

"Ahh." Quincy nodded satisfyingly as he bit into his sandwich. "Where in Virginia?"

I knew he would go there, Giselle thought. Had he been to the state? "Chesapeake," she responded, feeling comfortable enough to do so with him.

"Long ways from home," he commented. "How did you end up in Taller's Creek, if you don't mind my asking?"

"I don't," Giselle decided, without going into uncomfortable details. "After breaking up with my ex-fiancé three years ago, I felt a change was in order."

Quincy cocked a brow. "You were engaged?" he interjected before she could finish her thoughts.

"Yes." She didn't shy away from this now that she had chosen to mention that much. She hoped he didn't view this as a negative somehow. "Seemed like the right thing at the time—till I realized it would never have worked in the long run for many different reasons." She paused considerately. "Anyway, after bouncing around for a bit, I wound up in Alaska, which seemed interesting. With no other strong ties holding me back, I figured, why not?" She knew it wasn't quite that simple but wasn't ready to go there just yet, if ever. "I've been in Taller's Creek for a year and a half. It suits me."

"I can see that." Quincy peered at her admiringly. "Well, however it went down, I'm glad you're here."

"Thanks." Giselle blushed. "How about you? I'm guessing that you grew up in Alaska?"

"Good guess." He smiled again and dug his fork into the coleslaw. "Yeah, I've been here my entire life," he said matter-of-factly. "I'm a member of the Native Village of Eyak, an Alaska Native tribe."

"Cool," she said, piqued to learn more about his heritage later. "How long have you been with the Alaska State Troopers?"

"For about a decade now. Or since I've been out of college." Quincy took another bite of his sandwich. "It's been interesting, to say the least."

"I'm sure it has been." Giselle smiled as she imagined what type of cases and persons he must have come across in his line of work. "You've probably encountered a little of everything," she deduced, finishing off her coleslaw.

"Yeah, you could say that," Quincy conceded. "Some good, some not so much. Comes with the territory."

"I see." Giselle looked at him with a smile and wondered why some lucky woman hadn't already snatched him up. Maybe it was just because the right woman hadn't come into his life. Just as the right man hadn't come into hers. Certainly, that hadn't been the case with Justin. Far from it. Someone such as Quincy might be more to her liking. Or was she getting ahead of herself, his strong appeal notwithstanding?

"What other work have you done besides being an employee at a bookstore?" he asked knowingly, gazing at her.

Giselle sensed that he could see right through her, to some

degree. She saw no reason to deflect from the truth in this instance. "I used to teach dance lessons after college," she told him evenly. "And also did my fair share of odd jobs to make ends meet, here and there." She felt her low lip quiver while considering the sacrifices she'd been forced to make in her life. "Anyway, I'm fine with being a bookstore sales associate at this point. As an avid reader, it gives me the opportunity to be around books."

"I like to read too, when afforded the time." Quincy dabbed his mouth with a napkin. "Mostly westerns, spy novels and some literary stuff."

"That's great," Giselle said, smiling. "I prefer historical novels, mysteries and cozies, but I'll pretty much read anything if it can hold my attention."

"Yeah, same here," he suggested and finished his latte.

She did the same while thinking that this was a nice start to opening herself up to the possibility of getting involved with someone again. Or at the very least, letting down her guard a bit after what Justin had put her through.

Before leaving the café, Giselle took the liberty of buying some freshly made blueberry cupcakes to pass out to the staff at the bookstore, knowing they would appreciate the gesture.

Quincy walked her across the street and said by the door of the bookstore, "It was nice hanging out with you."

"You too."

"Hope we can do it again sometime."

She smiled softly. "I'd like that."

He grinned at her. "Can I get your number?"

"Yes," she agreed. "Hand me your phone."

Quincy dug it out of his trousers and gave her the cell phone.

Giselle punched her number into his Contacts list. "There," she said, giving it back to him.

"Thanks," he said and called her. She grinned, taking the cell phone out of the back pocket of her linen pants. "Now you have my number, too."

She blushed. "Cool."

"Well, I've probably kept you long enough. I'll let you get back to it."

"All right." Giselle waited a beat while pondering whether or not to leave it at that. She decided to be courageous in wanting to see him again, sooner than later, tossing out, "Would you like to come to dinner—at my place?"

He didn't hold back in replying, "Sure. Just tell me when."

"How about tomorrow night at, say, seven?"

"I'll be there," he promised.

"I'll text you the address," she told him before they said their goodbyes.

Giselle went inside the bookstore feeling a mixture of excitement and nervousness in putting herself out there again after the disastrous experience she'd had with Justin, leaving her pessimistic where it concerned romance. But something told her that Quincy was cut from a whole different cloth and she had nothing to fear from him. And everything to look forward to.

Chapter Four

Giselle Kinard was still very much on Quincy's mind as he worked out at the Soldotna Gym on Kenai Spur Highway after work that evening. He'd enjoyed having lunch with her and getting to know more about her. He hoped to build on that now that they had a second date tomorrow. The fact that they had met under less-than-ideal circumstances wasn't as important as meeting at all and using this as a stepping stone to wherever it led. In his mind, that very well could be a magical place when all was said and done.

Quincy finished lifting weights as part of his routine for staying fit before heading to the treadmill, where he continued his workout. He was curious about Giselle once being engaged, sensing there was more to the story, but would leave it up to her to reveal in her own time if she wanted to. His main takeaway from it was the *better safe than sorry* suggestion he'd read in her words. Though he'd never come close to walking down the aisle with anyone as of yet, he'd been around and dated long enough to know that using instincts to avert disaster was the best way to go in the long run. Whatever had gone wrong between Giselle and her ex-fiancé, Quincy was just glad that she happened to be available here and now, as he was, and would go from there.

After finishing the exercise session, he took off his

sweaty workout clothes, showered and put on his uniform in the locker room before heading to his car and an empty house to go to.

ON WEDNESDAY MORNING, while on duty, Quincy got the word from the AST's Southcentral Area-wide Narcotics team about a suspected bootlegging operation at a house on Blanden Street in Taller's Creek and a raid about to go down. He headed to the scene as part of the overall investigation. Though the ABI's regional major crimes unit was principally focused on cases involving serious crime against persons—such as homicides, suicides, sexual assaults, robberies, officer-involved incidents where deadly force was used and suspicious or unexplained deaths—they also took very seriously any and all illicit trafficking of liquor in the state. Unfortunately this practice was all too common in Alaska these days, as far as Quincy was concerned, and could hardly be ignored, with bootlegging often correlating with crimes of violence and property crimes in the area.

He reached the destination and rendezvoused with other troopers and investigators from the Taller's Creek Police Department before the operation got underway. In executing search warrants for the two-story residence and two vehicles, a GMC Sierra 1500 AT4 and a Chevrolet Silverado 2500 HD, the team came away with more than they bargained for.

Along with seventy-five bottles of illegal alcohol, confiscated were five hundred counterfeit M30 fentanyl pills, two-hundred-plus grams of methamphetamine, more than twenty firearms and an undetermined amount of hard cash. An adult male and female, both in their early thirties, were arrested without incident at the residence and faced a slew of charges.

"That went well," Quincy remarked to a SCAN team investigator after securing his weapon back in its holster, in that they had put at least one bootlegging operation out of business, with no one getting hurt in the process.

"Knock on wood," Kelly Reppun, fiftysomething and nearly six feet tall with curly crimson hair, quipped. "You never know what's around the next corner in this line of work."

"I hear you." He eyed her in earnest. "Guess we'll all have to cross that bridge when we get to it."

"Yeah, we will," she agreed with a smile as the successful raid began to wind down.

Quincy was happy to move on, heading toward his vehicle, unsure what was next on his plate. He used that ironic thought to contemplate his dinner date tonight with Giselle. Something told him that he would love whatever she had planned for their meal. And just maybe, if things went his way, there might even be dessert to one degree or another to savor.

WITH THE DAY OFF, Giselle spent much of it getting her apartment in order. Not that it needed much cleaning up, as she was always tidy. But sprucing it up just a bit for her date with Quincy seemed like a good idea. Now she was counting on Muffin, who could be finnicky around strangers, to behave herself.

Hope he isn't allergic to cats, Giselle told herself, not wanting there to be any unforeseen impediments to spending time with the trooper and seeing where it went. Before she headed out to the supermarket to pick up a few items for dinner, she lifted up Muffin and warned her playfully, "Now, you behave yourself this evening!"

Ten minutes later, Giselle was moving a cart down the

aisle at Safeway grocery store on Kenai Spur Highway. She was gathering all she needed for a dinner that included baked salmon coated with chopped pecans, herbed garlic potatoes, fresh spinach, and blueberry-and-raspberry cream pie. Admittedly, she was excited at the prospect of preparing a meal for someone other than herself, which hadn't been the case very often since moving to Alaska.

Maybe this could become a whole new tradition, Giselle thought with a chuckle while wondering if she could measure up to what Quincy might have been used to eating. Perhaps as a single man, he was settling for takeout and fast food and hadn't had too many homecooked meals himself of late.

When she switched to the section of the store that sold beer, wine and spirits, Giselle studied the wines, trying to guess if Quincy preferred red or white to wash down the food. She went with the white wine.

Just as she grabbed a bottle off the shelf, Giselle happened to look toward the end of the aisle. A tall man was standing there, peering at her, almost tauntingly.

Justin Buckner.

Without even realizing what she was doing till it was too late, the wine bottle slipped from Giselle's hands and crashed to the floor. The bottle shattered and, with it, the wine spilled everywhere.

As she gathered up the courage to do so, Giselle looked up, expecting her ex-fiancé to come barreling toward her like a battering ram to hurt her in any way he could.

Instead she was surprised to see that there was no one there. Where was he? Why hadn't he come after her?

Had she actually imagined seeing him? Or could this have been his way of psychologically terrorizing her?

"Ma'am, are you all right?"

The voice boomed in her ears, and Giselle turned to see a man standing there. He had a concerned look on his oblong face. His sandy-blond hair reminded her of Justin's. Even the face bore some resemblance to the person she had last seen three years ago. Could the man now before her have been the one she'd seen at the end of the aisle? Giselle realized now that he was wearing a store uniform and she had not bothered to home in on the clothing worn by the man she'd thought was Justin.

She cleared her throat and uttered embarrassingly, "I'm fine. Other than having butter fingers. The wine bottle slipped from my hand somehow..."

"That happens to the best of us," he said understandingly. "Don't worry about it. I'll get someone to clean this up."

"Thank you," Giselle told him but would definitely pay for the bottle of wine anyway. She grabbed a second bottle, this time determined to hang on to it, thanked the employee again for what she secretly now believed had been a case of mistaken identity and sidestepped the broken glass and wine as best she could before pushing her cart down the aisle.

Moving in the direction where she had imagined seeing Justin, Giselle's heart raced as she wondered if he might actually be waiting for her to emerge, so as to spring himself upon her. But when she reached the junction that was wider spaced and bordered multiple aisles, there was no sign of him.

Checking the aisle over on both sides, she was relieved to see that Justin was nowhere to be found. He hadn't somehow made his way to Taller's Creek, Alaska, to haunt her after all. The sooner she got this in her head—instead of allowing someone from her past to mess with it out of the blue—the better off she would be. And better her chances of finding romance with someone worthy of her.

Such as Quincy Lankard.

JUSTIN WAS TOYING with Giselle when he stood in front of the aisle where she was peering over bottles of wine as if they held the keys to the universe. He had followed her to the grocery store while being sure to keep his distance, so as not to spoil the mischievous fun just yet. He only wanted her to catch a glimpse of him, sure she would remember what he looked like—only to dash out of sight in the blink of an eye. Leaving her to second-guess that it was truly him, come to town to get his revenge, as promised.

It worked like a charm, as he overheard Giselle speaking with a male employee, whom Justin had spotted earlier and bore some resemblance to himself. Undoubtedly, she would assume this was the man Giselle thought she saw in the aisle. And not her worst nightmare. As he viewed himself.

Justin watched from behind a liquor display as Giselle scanned the store to see if she could spot him, apparently still not trusting herself that he had not, in fact, found her. But he wasn't quite ready just yet to give her the satisfaction—frightening as it would be—to know that she was right. When she seemed confident that he was nowhere to be found, he saw that she relaxed the strain in her pretty face and went on to pay for her wine.

He quickly exited the store, careful not to draw any attention to himself. Once outside, he breathed in the fresh Alaska air and went to his car, which he had paid for in cash.

After waiting for a few minutes, Justin spied Giselle coming out of the supermarket with her cart. She had parked her Honda CR-V just feet from his car. Her green eyes took a sweeping glance of the parking lot routinely—or perhaps hoping to spot him—but he ducked to be on the safe side. Once she got inside her car, he looked up and watched as she drove off.

He thought about following her but saw no need to tip

his hand at this point. Besides, he knew exactly where she lived, having already scoped out the place more than once. When the time was right, he would be more than happy to make his presence felt, when she least expected it.

Justin started his car and began whistling the first song to pop into his head before driving off.

QUINCY HAD TO admit that he felt like he was in high school all over again when he'd had his first date with Mona Eubank. Though it had gone absolutely nowhere, the initial enthusiasm was the same. As he drove toward Giselle's apartment in his personal vehicle, he hoped for a more promising outcome. He'd even cleaned up nicely, if he said so himself, for the dinner date—wearing a yellow Oxford dress shirt, dark blue trousers and black loafers. It actually felt good to dress up a bit as part of spending time with someone he wanted to become better acquainted with.

Arriving at Giselle's apartment building, Quincy wondered briefly if he should have brought something along with him, like wine or whatever. He was admittedly out of practice in that regard.

Next time, he told himself optimistically as Quincy emerged from the gray Subaru Forester and headed to her first-floor unit.

It took only one ring of the bell before the door opened and Giselle's beautiful face appeared before him. "Right on time," she said enthusiastically.

Knowing he had arrived late for the candlelight vigil, Quincy was determined not to miss out on any moment they could spend together. "Wouldn't have it any other way," he joked.

She smiled. "You look nice."

"Thanks." He regarded her, wearing a body-flattering

floral midi dress and espadrille wedge sandals, to go with her natural good looks, and Quincy had to say honestly, "You look even better."

"And thank you back." Giselle blushed. "Come in." He did so, and she said humbly, "This is home."

He gave the place a sweeping glance—taking in the modern though worn furniture in the living and dining room combo and small kitchen with a butcher-block countertop and slate appliances—noting everything neatly in place. "It's nice," he told her, while imagining Giselle fitting right in at his larger residence. Then movement on the floor caught his eye, and Quincy saw a Burmese kitten race along the baseboard.

"That's Muffin," Giselle said proudly.

"Hey, Muffin." He grinned at the kitten and, before she could ask, said, "I love cats. Had some when I was a boy—and dogs too."

"Cool." She flashed her teeth and watched as her kitten came toward Quincy before abruptly running away. "Muffin's unusually shy today," Giselle offered apologetically.

"I'm sure she'll come around once she sees I'm on her side—and yours," he spoke confidently.

"Good to know." Giselle smiled again. "Dinner's ready."

Quincy picked up the scent of food, prompting him to say, "Smells great."

"Hope you feel the same after eating," she teased.

"I'm sure I will," he countered perceptively. "What can I do?"

"You can open the wine, if you like." She eyed the bottle on the counter and wineglasses beside it.

"Sure thing." Quincy proceeded to do just that, while admiring her. When they literally bumped into each other in the kitchen, he felt a surge of sexual energy zip through him. Had she felt it too? He considered this as he poured the wine.

A couple of minutes later, they were sitting across from each other on cushioned chairs with oval backrests at the beveled wooden table.

"So, what do you think?" Giselle asked anxiously once Quincy had started eating.

After swallowing, he grinned, looked her straight in the eye and responded keenly, "It's delicious!"

Her features relaxed. "That's good to hear."

Quincy took it that she didn't cook very often. Or at least not for male guests. That made him feel special. A light that he was beginning to see her in too. "Do you have family in Chesapeake?" he wondered curiously.

"Not anymore." Giselle's expression dampened. "My parents both died not too long ago from illnesses. They never had any more children after I came along."

Quincy met her eyes sadly. "Sorry to hear about your folks."

"Do your parents live around here?" she asked.

"They live in Juneau," he answered matter-of-factly, slicing his knife into the baked salmon. "I try to visit whenever I can, but it's not often enough as far as they're concerned."

"I'm sure." Giselle smiled softly. She dug a fork into the herbed garlic potatoes. "I take it your nephew and niece live nearby?"

"Yeah, Todd and his sister, Krista, live in Nikiski, with my sister, Olivia, and her husband, Kenneth."

"Nice to know you can visit them at any time."

"True." Quincy lifted his wineglass and took a sip, regarding her thoughtfully. "You must miss home?" He assumed that was the case, even if she was clearly happy to put some distance between her and the ex-fiancé.

"I do, honestly," she responded, a catch to her voice. She colored. "But there was really nothing there for me anymore, so it was just a good time to move on…"

"I can respect that," he told her, even if thinking that there was more to the story that she wasn't revealing. But he wasn't about to press for more, as Quincy was just grateful that she had made the move to Alaska—allowing them this opportunity to make a connection, as though it was meant to be.

"Are you ready for dessert?" Giselle got his attention.

"Absolutely." He finished off his meal, then helped her clear the table and bring over their slices of blueberry-and-raspberry cream pie, to go with more wine.

"So, aside from reading spy novels and westerns, what else do you like to do?" she asked inquisitively, putting the fork into her mouth.

He leaned back in the chair. "I enjoy hunting, fishing, kayaking, working out—the usual things for most Alaskans…"

"Nice." She smiled. "I've never hunted and have only gone fishing on occasion, but I have kayaked," she said. "I also love to swim, jog and hike…"

Quincy watched her shoulders slump and suspected she was thinking about the accidental death of her friend, Neve. "Those are all worthwhile pastimes," he said quickly and ate more of the pie.

"I agree." She sipped her wine.

They both saw Muffin walk into the room, study them curiously and, once satisfied, make her way toward the kitchen to finish off her own meal, causing them to chuckle.

Quincy mused about her career as a dance instructor and asked interestedly, "What type of dances did you teach?"

Giselle's eyes lit up as she answered coolly, "Ballroom,

bolero, country western, foxtrot, hustle, rumba, salsa, tango, waltz—you name it."

He laughed. "Wow! Sounds like you taught everything."

She giggled. "Pretty much."

Quincy could tell that she missed dancing and was obviously good at what she did. So why not continue being a dance instructor in Alaska? Was there any reason, in particular, why she would turn her back on this for work at a bookstore?

Instead of asking her and risk being told it was none of his business, ruining the date, Quincy decided to take a different approach. He stood up and said, "I'm not much of a dancer, but if you're game, I'd love for you to show me a few moves…"

Giselle stared at the notion for a long moment or two before yielding to the challenge. She rose to her feet and said, "You're on."

Quincy watched as she grabbed her cell phone off the table and put on a jazz tune from her playlist; then Giselle took his hand and gave him a crash course in tango that morphed into a waltz. Both had them pressed together and holding each other, tapping into his libido.

"You're a natural at this," she declared, clearly in her own element.

"I'll take your word on that," he said soulfully while hoping not to step on her toes, literally, as Giselle had kicked off her sandals to dance barefoot.

Before he knew it, Quincy was kissing her. He wasn't quite sure who'd initiated the kiss. Only that Giselle's soft lips were a perfect fit for his. And vice versa. He probably could have kissed her and held her in his arms all night.

But before they went much further, Quincy did the honorable thing in wanting to make sure this was really what she wanted, and neither would have any regrets—so he pulled back. If he played his cards right, there would be plenty of time to pick up where they'd left off.

Giselle seemed to be of the same mind as she touched her swollen lips and told him, "Thank you, Quincy, for...a very pleasant evening."

He nodded, gazing at her eyes intently. "Thanks for inviting me."

By the time he left, Quincy was already looking forward to spending more time with Giselle. And all that came with the desirous territory.

Chapter Five

Giselle was still on cloud nine the next morning as she got ready for work, with Muffin observing quietly. Quincy had kissed her as they'd been doing a tango-and-waltz combination dance. Or had it been the other way around? In any event, she'd enjoyed the feel of his lips upon hers. It had been a long time since she had kissed or been kissed by anyone, hesitant to move in that direction with the specter of Justin still hanging over her like a shroud.

But Quincy had singlehandedly managed to change that and resurrect in her the feelings of wanting to be with someone again. While giving Giselle hope that he might be that person, if things continued to progress in that direction. Or, at the very least, a man that she wanted in her life in Alaska.

After putting some whitefish-and-rice wet kitten food in a bowl for Muffin and watching her devour it, Giselle left the apartment, hopped into her car and drove off. Moments later, she spotted a lynx come out from a batch of yellow cedars. The wildcat seemed to look directly at her, perhaps more out of curiosity than anything, before heading back into the trees.

Upon reaching her destination and parking in the back lot for employees, Giselle walked into the bookstore, where they had a book signing and reading by an Alaska Native author of young adult fiction scheduled for this afternoon.

Jill was standing by the checkout counter, along with Wesley. Both were admiring a dozen orange roses on a table. They turned when seeing her approaching.

"Hey," Giselle uttered uneasily. "What's with the roses?"

"Beats me," Jill said, shrugging her shoulders. "They were delivered here this morning. The card that came with them simply said, 'From a book lover.'"

"Seems to me someone has a secret admirer," Wesley suggested and held the bouquet to his nose. He eyed Giselle suspiciously. "Who do you think the lucky person is?"

"I have no idea," she answered with a snap, trying hard to maintain her composure. In fact, Giselle did have some idea. Or at least was no stranger herself to orange roses. Justin had loved giving them to her as a symbol of his hold on her, desire for her and enthusiasm for the forever relationship he'd envisioned them having. Initially she'd thought it was the sweetest thing and indicative of what at the time had seemed to be a reflection of what they could become as a couple.

But soon, she'd grown to detest the orange roses, for they'd become symbolic of his obsession with her and his brazen attempt to control her at all costs. Whatever it had taken.

Could Justin have sent the roses to let her know he was in Taller's Creek? And that she had not imagined seeing him at the bookstore window—and later at the grocery store?

The mere notion sent chills up and down Giselle's spine. Even as she tried to assess the likelihood that her ex-fiancé had managed to locate her after three years away from him.

"They smell so good," gushed Sadie, who had joined the group. In her early twenties and a marine biology major at the Kenai Peninsula College in Soldotna, she worked only two days a week for some extra income.

Giselle watched as Sadie, who was tall and thin with black hair in a lob with faux bangs, put her nose to the orange roses. "Yes, they do," she agreed from memory of the fruity fragrance.

"Whose are they?" Sadie asked, her bold blue eyes flashing.

"Apparently the bouquet is for all of us," Jill declared.

"I'll go along with that," Wesley said. "I suppose they were simply meant to brighten our day collectively."

"Maybe," Giselle muttered, mainly to herself, as she wondered if the roses were much more ominous in their intentions than any of the others could ever imagine. She contemplated the thought as they spread out to get to work.

JUSTIN DID FIFTY PUSH-UPS on the well-worn hardwood floor in his rental home, straining his muscles to the limit but determined to do so. He figured that by now, Giselle had already laid eyes on the bouquet of orange roses that he'd had delivered before she'd arrived at work. He had little doubt that it had gotten under her skin and made her pretty uncomfortable. Surely she hadn't forgotten that it had been his flower of choice to give her as an indication of his love and cherishing the long-term relationship he'd envisioned for them?

I don't think so, Justin told himself confidently as he passed the fifty mark and decided to do fifty more push-ups. He sucked in a deep breath and thought some more about his ex-fiancé. She might have bailed on him, but it would come at a huge price for her and those within Giselle's orbit. He would see to that, and then some.

Justin considered his latest step in that direction. The window was starting to close on his still gorgeous ex.

And there was nothing she—or anyone else—could do about it. He would have his revenge and had no intention of stopping what she had started until he did what was necessary to make things right.

QUINCY FOUND HIMSELF daydreaming about kissing Giselle yesterday but put that thought on hold as dispatch reported that a Taller's Creek woman had been found dead at her house by her sister, with the deceased having apparently shot herself. If true, the mere thought of someone taking her own life—particularly in such a gruesome fashion as what a bullet could do to the body—whatever the reason might have been, shook Quincy. Just as it did when any life was lost unnecessarily.

That included the accidental death of Giselle's friend, Neve Chenoweth.

He felt grateful that it hadn't been Giselle instead, as Quincy didn't want to see anything come between her and him in seeing what the future might have in store for them.

Conferring with his boss at the ABI Soldotna Major Crimes Unit, Lieutenant Ron Valdez, Quincy passed along the latest disturbing incident. "Possible suicide," he told him bleakly as they stood in the hall.

Valdez, pushing sixty, of medium build and six feet tall, with gray hair in a Caesar cut, narrowed brown eyes and muttered, shaking his head forlornly, "When will they ever learn that there's always another way to go?"

"Never soon enough," Quincy only wished he didn't have to say, but so true. As he knew the lieutenant was well aware of, after tragically losing his daughter, Margie, from Valdez's first marriage, to suicide five years ago. "I'm on my way to check it out."

Valdez nodded, and then Quincy gave him a brief update on an earlier case before heading over to Taller's Creek.

QUINCY ARRIVED AT the single-story cabin on Lenbrooke Avenue and was greeted by Taller's Creek PD Sergeant Miriam Fontaine, who had requested the ABI's assistance.

"Sergeant," he acknowledged casually while regarding the thirtysomething first responder. She was blue eyed and muscular in her uniform, with dark hair in a midlength cut. A Glock 22 40 S&W caliber service pistol sat in an open-carry waistband holster.

"Thanks for coming," she said routinely and made a face. "Looks like the victim may have died from a self-inflicted gunshot to the head. Her name is Yuki Kotake, a thirty-four-year-old fashion designer. The victim's sister, Willow Kotake, discovered the body—"

"That couldn't have been easy," Quincy muttered thoughtfully.

"When is it ever?" Miriam concurred drearily.

"Yeah." He paused. "Let's have a look…"

He followed her to the cabin while noting a white Subaru Outback and red Chevrolet Blazer in the gravel driveway along with a wooded backdrop.

Inside Quincy saw a young blond-haired female officer consoling a twentysomething slender Asian woman with short and curly brunette hair. She was bawling her brown eyes out as they sat on a black leather sofa, telling him everything he needed to know.

Or almost. He still needed to view the deceased and assess the situation.

"She's in the back room," Miriam told him.

Quincy headed across the blue carpeted floor and made his way down the hallway. He passed by a bedroom on the right and then a bathroom before arriving at the back bedroom. Stepping inside, he first took note of the platform bed that was unmade, then his eyes caught sight of the legs on the floor on the other side of the bed.

When he went around to that side, Quincy saw the victim lying flat on her back, her face turned sideways. Blood had streamed from a bullet wound to her temple, spilling onto long, straight black hair and the carpeting. She was wearing a green tank top, frayed flare jeans and was barefoot. A handgun lay near the body. He recognized it as a Walther PDP, or Performance Duty Pistol, 9mm Luger semiautomatic handgun and spotted a single shell casing against the wall.

Turning back to the deceased, Quincy studied her face further and did a double take, as it occurred to him only now that he had seen her before.

Picking up on his reaction, Miriam, who had followed him to the bedroom, asked, "What is it?"

"She was at a candlelight vigil a few days ago for Neve Chenoweth," he responded in almost disbelief.

"The hiker," Miriam said knowingly.

"That's the one." Quincy glanced at Yuki Kotake, whom he hadn't spoken to at the vigil, but Giselle had.

"Hmm. And now she's dead too…" Miram wrinkled her nose. "So sad."

"Yeah." He didn't disagree. But Quincy wondered if it went beyond that. Two friends—both of whom Giselle had known by extension—to die within days of each other. What were the odds? "The crime scene unit will process the scene," Quincy told her, both aware that any such death had to be treated with the possibility of foul play, no matter the presumed cause and nature of a death—with any physical evidence collected accordingly. "In the meantime, I'd like to talk to the victim's sister."

"Of course," Miriam agreed. "Officer Hutton can help you, if needed. Beyond that, the State Medical Examiner's Office should be here shortly to collect the body."

Quincy nodded and went back into the living room, where the officer was still trying her best to comfort the obviously distraught sister of Yuki Kotake. Though he certainly felt for her in that trying moment, what had to be done had to be done for the investigation.

Moving toward her, Quincy motioned to Officer Hutton that he needed to question Willow Kotake and watched as the officer nodded and gingerly rose up and stepped away from the young woman. Taking Hutton's place on the sofa, Quincy said softly, "I'm with the Alaska Bureau of Investigation. I'm very sorry for your loss. I need to ask you a few questions…"

Willow nodded with expectation, wiping away tears from her eyes. "I understand," she said in a shaky voice.

"How did you come to discover your sister… Ms. Kotake dead?"

"I was supposed to meet Yuki for lunch at a restaurant in Soldotna," Willow explained. "When she didn't show up or answer her cell phone, I drove over here, concerned." She wiped her nose. "I have a key to her house." Willow drew a breath. "I found Yuki in her bedroom—"

Quincy nodded respectfully. "Do you know if your sister owned a gun?"

"Yes, she purchased a gun last year for self-defense." Willow's voice dropped contemplatively. "I never thought it was a good idea."

"Was she being threatened by anyone?"

"Not that I'm aware of."

That aroused his curiosity, and all things considered, Quincy asked point-blank, "Was Ms. Kotake suicidal?"

Willow batted curly lashes, musing, then responded, "Yes, she has suffered from depression and had suicidal thoughts from time to time in her life, but she'd been taking antidepressants to control it."

"Was there something that happened recently that might have triggered shooting herself?" He needed to know.

She stared at the question for a second or two. "Last week Yuki and her boyfriend, Armand, broke up," Willow said. "They fought all the time... But Yuki still took the breakup hard and seemed to want to get back together with him, in spite of everything."

Quincy took this in. Had the attempt at reconciliation failed? Causing Yuki Kotake to take her own life? Or was there an even more ominous explanation for her death? Perhaps the ex-boyfriend had come to the cabin, used her handgun and killed Yuki in a fit of rage? Stranger things had happened in a state which had one of the highest murder rates in the entire country.

But he didn't want to get ahead of the curve in getting to the root of the fashion designer's untimely demise. At least not before the CSU investigation and autopsy were completed.

Also weighing on Quincy's mind was having to confront Giselle with yet another death of a friend in short order while wondering how she would take it.

THE BOOK SIGNING EVENT went without a hitch, as the teen-fiction bestselling author Charlotte Hawk held her seated audience captive while she read the first chapter of her new novel about an Alaska Native girl's life in Alaska during the

1930s. Giselle admired the talented writer who looked like she was barely older than a teenager herself, with soft features and frizzy raven hair in a long fishtail French braid, though she was in her early thirties.

Maybe someday I'll try writing a novel, Giselle told herself dreamily, figuring that between her love for fiction and life's experiences, good and bad, anything was possible. She even imagined coauthoring a book with Quincy, combining what each brought to the table, should things between them progress accordingly.

As Charlotte wrapped things up by signing every copy of her book that they had available and was quickly ushered out the door by her publicist for another scheduled event, Quincy was coming into the bookstore. He smiled at the author for whom he had something in common with as Native Alaskans, and Giselle felt the slightest twinge of jealousy, though she knew it was inappropriate, if not wholly unfounded. She had no right to feel the need to want to command all his attention. What was meant to be between them would occur naturally and without insecurities by either of them. Unlike in her last toxic relationship with Justin.

"Hey." Quincy's voice was even as he came up to her.

"Hey." Giselle looked up at him, feeling foolish for such silly thoughts, even as the kiss and dance they'd shared yesterday evening flashed brightly in her head.

He met her eyes solemnly. "You have a minute?"

"Yes." She sensed that there was something serious on his mind. "Why don't we step outside?" Giselle suggested, knowing she could spare a few minutes without being missed now that the bookstore had all but emptied with the Charlotte Hawk signing over.

"All right," Quincy agreed and followed her back out the door.

"What is it?" she almost hated to ask, ill at ease.

"Something bad has happened," he began delicately, "and I wanted you to hear it from me…" He sighed. "Another friend of yours, Yuki Kotake, is dead."

"What? Yuki…dead?" Giselle swallowed thickly. "How?"

"It appears as though she shot herself to death," Quincy said straightforwardly. "Her sister, Willow, discovered the body at Ms. Kotake's cabin." He paused. "I'm sorry—"

Giselle felt the color drain from her face. How could Yuki be dead, so soon after Neve?

Don't test me, Giselle!

The stark warning from Justin registered in her head.

If you even think about ever leaving me, Giselle, just know that you'll pay for it in ways you can't even imagine. I'll go after everyone you care about…or cares about you, even a little…one by one. Saving you for last.

Was this Justin's way of following through on his wicked promise? Had he somehow been involved in Yuki's and Neve's deaths, in spite of the evidence and appearances to the contrary? The mere possibility had Giselle freaking out.

"What's wrong?" Quincy asked, peering at her with concern.

Giselle forced herself to meet his steady gaze and uttered unevenly, "I think my ex-fiancé may have something to do with Yuki's death…and maybe Neve's too…"

Chapter Six

Quincy had admittedly been thrown for a loop when hearing Giselle suggest that her ex-fiancé could have been a killer of not one but two of her friends. How could she believe such a thing? Or did she know something he didn't that could somehow defy logic as well as what was generally believed to be true in the deaths of both Yuki Kotake and Neve Chenoweth?

"Care to explain?" Quincy demanded after Giselle had asked him to pause that thought till they were seated at a table at the café across the street with cups of black coffee in front of them.

She tasted the coffee thoughtfully, then said ill at ease, "I haven't been entirely forthcoming about my ex…" She drew a breath. "His name is Justin Buckner. To say that we had a contentious relationship would be a serious understatement. Justin was possessive, controlling, jealous, mean spirited, manipulative and very vindictive, as it turned out."

Giselle sipped more coffee, and Quincy felt her anguish and wanted nothing more than to comfort her. He still needed to hear just where this was going. "I'm listening," he prodded gingerly.

She sighed and continued, "I couldn't take it—him—anymore and… I ran away—"

"Ran away?" Quincy gazed at her.

"Yes." Nodding, Giselle stammered, "I was fearful of what he would do if I broke things off—or, worse, stayed and kept taking everything he was dishing out—and what I might have done in needing to defend myself or break the stranglehold he had on my life. Three years ago, not trusting the police or a restraining order to protect me, I just got up and left my entire life behind without looking back. I moved around the mainland for a while, going from one state to the next, always looking over my shoulder, knowing he would never let me go. Not without exacting some sort of retaliation that I didn't even want to imagine…" She sucked in a deep breath. "I ended up in Alaska, where I thought I might finally be free of him. Now I have to wonder if Justin has reemerged to make my life hell. And other unsuspecting lives as well."

Quincy took a moment to let this sink in. Especially the part about hiding in Alaska—Taller's Creek—from her ex-fiancé. Was it her plan to eventually head back to Chesapeake, Virginia? Was she really from there? Or was that also part of her subterfuge in staying one step ahead of an abusive and otherwise creep of a former boyfriend?

I can't allow my personal feelings of how this might impact the long-term potential between us to get in the way of the ordeal this man has obviously put Giselle through, Quincy mused as he put the coffee mug up to his lips. More important at the moment was why she would believe that her ex-fiancé could have anything to do with two local deaths that gave no indication there was foul play involved.

"I wish you had told me about the situation with your ex in relation to your living in—or hiding out—in Taller's Creek," Quincy couldn't help but say against his better judgment.

"I know," Giselle owned up to, clutching her mug of coffee. "I'm sorry I wasn't up front about that." She frowned, sipping the coffee. "It's not exactly the type of thing I wanted to share with anyone," she stressed. "I've been trying my best to put that dark part of my past behind me. I hope you can understand that."

"I can," he admitted, having seen firsthand in the course of his work with the ABI that domestic violence and psychological abuse and manipulation was real and came in many forms. Law enforcement and restraining orders, if that came at all, could only go so far against a determined aggressor. Sometimes escaping the situation was the only viable remedy in order to survive it. Clearly Giselle had reached this breaking point and done what she'd felt she'd needed to do. He could hardly criticize her for that, even if the protector in Quincy would have wanted to be there for her from the start and every step along the way.

"Thank you," Giselle uttered softly.

"So, what makes you think this Justin Buckner could be responsible for Yuki Kotake's death?" Quincy cocked a brow curiously. "Much less Neve Chenoweth's death?"

Giselle sighed, pondering it for a long moment. "Justin warned me that if I ever left him, he would find me and make me pay," she said nervously. "His exact words were, 'If you even think about ever leaving me, Giselle, just know that you'll pay for it in ways you can't even imagine. I'll go after everyone you care about…or cares about you, even a little…one by one. Saving you for last.'" She waited a beat and continued, "With two people in my orbit suddenly dead within days of one another, I'm left to wonder if Justin— even after three long years apart—has somehow found a way to do what he promised…before coming after me."

Quincy leaned forward with a jaundiced eye. "Have you seen Buckner in Taller's Creek?"

"Not exactly..." Giselle confessed.

Quincy arched a brow. "What does that mean?"

"It means that I thought I saw him once, looking in the window of the bookstore," she responded. "But then the person was gone. Another time, I thought Justin was standing at the end of an aisle at the beer, wine and liquor area at Safeway." She flushed. "But apparently it was only a store employee who resembled Justin. Or at least how I remembered he looked from three years ago. Also, someone left a dozen orange roses at the bookstore." Giselle sighed. "Though the card with them was only signed 'From a book lover,' Justin often gave me a dozen orange roses when we were together..."

"Hmm..." Quincy's tone was laced with skepticism about her ex being in town. And having anything to do with the deaths of her friends. "It doesn't exactly sound as though what you've said amounts to real proof that Buckner is in town stalking you...or worse—"

"I know. Silly, right?" Giselle flushed sheepishly. "Guess I've just allowed my imagination to run wild lately." She wrinkled her nose. "Still, even with that, I'm scared that he could have discovered my whereabouts...and he's definitely capable of inflicting bodily harm on anyone who crossed him. Especially me—"

Quincy sat back, mulling over her position and apparently valid concerns. Though she had not unquestionably laid eyes on her ex—but rather seemed to have made herself believe she had seen him—it didn't seem like something that could be dismissed. Even if she *was* mistaken. Given her difficult—and frankly, disturbing—history with the man, Quincy in no way held that against Giselle. She was only human, and it was understandable that Buckner's image would manifest itself from time to time. Or even likely misconstruing someone innocently sending flowers to the bookstore as coming from him.

But it wasn't the same thing as actually seeing her ex-fiancé in the flesh.

"So, what does Buckner do for a living?" Quincy wondered, hoping to gain some perspective as it related to his ability to travel without being missed.

"Justin's a financial planner," Giselle answered. "At least he was at the time I broke away from him."

"In Chesapeake?" Quincy regarded her questioningly, assuming she had been on the level about this part of her past.

"Yes." She met his eyes squarely. "It's where we met," she replied.

"Okay—just checking," he sought to justify his asking. "I'd be happy to look into whether or not Justin Buckner could actually be in Alaska—Taller's Creek—currently or if he has been at any time recently," Quincy volunteered, knowing that putting the notion to rest, more or less, by indicating this likely wasn't the case would give her peace of mind, if nothing else. Never mind that this might be guesswork at best, all things considered, unless Buckner was a wanted man or otherwise making it easy to track his movements.

"Thank you." Giselle's strained features relaxed ever so slightly.

"That being said, the chance that Buckner played a role in either of the deaths of your friends seems small at best," Quincy reiterated. "As we've already discussed, Neve Chenoweth's death was ruled an accident. And as things now stand, it appears that Yuki Kotake took her own life. There's no indication to the contrary, pending an examination of the firearm used, gunshot residue and the autopsy on the deceased."

"I guess I'll have to accept that," she said, running a finger along the rim of her mug. "Unless you find out otherwise."

"All right." Quincy flashed a faint smile, while recognizing that, Buckner aside, Giselle had still lost two acquaintances tragically. No sugarcoating that. Still, accidents happened. So did suicide. In this instance, both would be somewhat easier to accept than either woman being a victim of homicide. "Well, I'd better let you get back to the bookstore," he said, even if part of him would rather they spent more time together with a fresh start now that everything was out in the open with her true reasons for being in Alaska. He could only hope that she was there to stay and would not find herself running away from him.

"Probably a good idea." Giselle nodded musingly. "The last thing I need is to get fired for an unauthorized extended break."

"Wouldn't want that." *Especially if it means giving you a reason to go elsewhere*, Quincy thought. He stood, watching her do the same. "I'll walk you back."

GISELLE WAS RUNNING for her life. Her pursuer was intent upon making sure she never saw another day, so consumed was he to have her at all costs. Or see to it that she paid a price that there was no walking back from.

But it was a place that she was unwilling to go. He couldn't have her. She deserved so much better in a man. In a relationship. In the great love of her life and father of her children. Not someone who was so repugnant and obsessed with molding her into someone she wasn't. She would rather die than succumb to his unreasonable demands. No matter what personal sacrifices she would have to make.

Sucking in a deep breath, Giselle ran up the quarter-turn staircase in the waterfront mansion to the second story, the determined attacker in hot pursuit. If she could just get to the primary suite and lock the door behind her, maybe she could survive the ordeal by calling the police to come to her rescue. Only then could she ever hope to have a normal life, with a normal man to give her love to.

She raced in her bare feet across the hardwood flooring in the long hallway, nearly tripping but correcting herself from tumbling. But even losing half a step shortened the distance between her and the man who wanted her dead. Still, she forged ahead, reaching the room she'd once shared with her hunter, but seeing it now as nothing more than a prison.

Inside, she barely had a chance to take in the expensive Italian furnishings while simultaneously attempting to slam the door shut before he could stop her, when he was able to do just that.

Using his greater strength, he forced the door open, knocking her to the floor in the process. Scrambling to her feet, she ran toward the king-size bed, hoping to somehow get to the other side and maybe onto the balcony. Instead, he caught up to her, grabbed her by the hair and threw her down hard onto the dark blue comforter.

Before she could even breathe, he had climbed on top of her, where he placed large hands around her neck, his face contorted with anger like a man possessed. She tried to fight him off but to no avail, as she felt her strength fading—along with her very life.

He was strangling her to death. And there was nothing she could do about it. Other than accept her fate.

She looked into the evil eyes of death. Glaring back at her was Justin.

Giselle tried to scratch his face, but he stayed just out of reach of her flailing hands and fingernails. Before she could breathe her last breath, she managed to squeeze from her mouth that she hated him with a passion—to which he seemed to draw upon in his contorted face and sick satisfaction in achieving his ultimate objective of taking her life.

THE SCREAM THAT threatened to shatter her eardrums was, in fact, coming from Giselle's own vocal cords as she opened her eyes. It took her a moment to adjust to the darkness and surroundings to recognize that she was in the small bedroom of her Taller's Creek apartment, lying atop a cotton quilt on her sleigh bed in the wee hours of the morning.

It was only a dream, Giselle told herself, sitting up and catching her breath, feeling relieved. She still needed a moment to regain her equilibrium. Even then, she half expected Justin to emerge from the shadows and finish off what he had started in her nightmare. She froze in that instant— darting her eyes this way and that—before deciding that he wasn't there.

But Muffin was. Apparently having heard her cries of dreaming anguish, the kitten had wakened from sleeping comfortably in her kitten bed in the corner and jumped up on the bed out of concern for her and was cuddled against her.

"I'm fine, Muffin," Giselle uttered appreciatively, holding the kitten to her chest. "It was just a silly nightmare." In truth, she didn't consider it silly at all but rather a manifestation of a nightmare ex-fiancé that she hadn't been able to entirely shake, in spite of her best efforts to the contrary. The latest episode had been undoubtedly triggered by the untimely deaths of two people she'd been acquainted with—in addition to imagined sightings of Justin in Taller's Creek.

Giselle cringed while running her hand gently along Muffin's back. She regretted not having come clean with Quincy right from the start on the man she had escaped from, bringing her to Alaska. But she'd been wary of trusting anyone too soon about her past. Even a person who was employed by the Alaska Bureau of Investigation.

Now she realized that some chances were worth taking in life and that it was okay to trust her instincts. Particularly where Quincy was concerned. She could only hope he didn't hold this against her and pull back from any chance that they might be able to establish a relationship in her post-Justin life.

If only she could be certain, once and for all, that he was, in fact, out of her life for good. Perhaps Quincy would be able to give her that reassurance.

Until then, Giselle was resolved to not allow herself to be spooked by the specter of Justin. No matter how hard he had made this for her—even from a distance. Assuming that was indeed the case.

She got up in her short pajamas and, along with Muffin, went into the kitchen. Turning on the light, Giselle adjusted her eyes accordingly, refusing to think that Justin was lurking somewhere in the apartment. Waiting to attack her. As it was, there was no sign that her personal space had been breached.

She opened the refrigerator and grabbed a bottle of water for her and kitten liquid for Muffin.

After they drank, with Muffin deciding to curl up on an upholstered lounge chair, Giselle went back to bed. She imagined Quincy being beside her, cuddling, while fearing that falling asleep would result in a repeat performance of Justin trying to strangle her to death.

Instead, there was no nightmare this time around. Giselle slept peacefully, making the most of the hours she had left before starting a new day in earnest.

Chapter Seven

Sergeant Miriam Fontaine sat on a metal chair in an interview room at the Taller's Creek Police Department on Lamotte Street. On the other side of the wooden table, Armand Younis was seated. The forty-one-year-old construction worker and former boyfriend of Yuki Kotake had come in voluntarily to, as he'd put it, clear the air as it related to the fashion designer's death.

With the investigation still underway, Miriam was interested in what he had to say after the body had been discovered the day before. She regarded the beefy ex, who had a blond mane in a combed-backward style and wore square glasses over blue eyes. "Thanks for coming in," she told him, saving her the trouble of looking for him, should it have proven necessary down the line. "Sorry about Ms. Kotake... If you have any information on what happened to her, I'm happy to take your statement."

Armand nodded and said, "They say that Yuki killed herself." He grimaced. "She'd never do that," he argued.

Miriam had heard it all before. It was always easier to be in denial in these situations, even when the evidence suggested otherwise. She was guilty of this herself from time to time when tragedy hit too close to home. In this instance, Ballistics had linked the shell casing recovered at the scene and bullet removed from the victim to the Walther PDP near the body. Unless, of course, there was a strong reason for the ex-boyfriend to believe someone else could have wanted her dead.

Without giving away anything that might compromise the investigation, Miriam noted, "The firearm found near Ms. Kotake's body was legally purchased by her. Also, according to the victim's sister, Willow Kotake, she was suicidal."

"Yuki would not have committed suicide," Armand maintained, narrowing his eyes. "She loved life too much for that. Her antidepressants were working. No, someone else had to have been there…"

"There was no sign of forced entry," Miriam said, while conceding that the fashion designer could have let her killer in unsuspectingly. At least in theory. Including her ex. Was he trying to confess in a roundabout way? "Where were you when this happened?" she asked, providing him with an estimated time of death.

Without prelude, he replied confidently, "I was in Seattle, working on a project. There are plenty of people to vouch for that. I just got back this morning after hearing the news about Yuki."

Recognizing that this was easy enough to confirm, Miriam had no reason to detain him. But she would keep an open mind on the circumstances of Yuki Kotake's death till the results came in on the autopsy and gunshot residue.

THAT AFTERNOON, Quincy sat at his desk, comparing findings from the State Medical Examiner's Office and the ABI Scientific Crime Detection Laboratory regarding the death of Yuki Kotake.

According to the autopsy report, the victim had died from a gunshot to the right side of her head, causing serious damage to both her brain and skull. The manner of death had been ruled to be likely self-inflicted. With a history of using antidepressants, a forensic toxicology test was still pending but unlikely to change the basic premise on the conclusion of how she'd died.

Quincy zeroed in on the gun-residue aspect of the autopsy report. It was unclear just how much had been found on one of Yuki Kotake's hands. The GSR kit was sent to the crime lab for further analysis. Staring at their report, he saw that it indicated that particles were present on the dead woman's right hand that were indicative of gunshot primer residue. Or, in other words, the forensic evidence suggested that the victim had been holding the pistol she'd owned when one slug had gone into her head.

Looks like it was, in fact, suicide, Quincy told himself, trusting the joint evidence to that effect. This certainly seemed to throw cold water on the notion that Giselle's former fiancé had somehow engineered it to make Yuki Kotake's death appear to be self-inflicted. That said, Quincy admitted that stranger things had happened over the years in his line of work. Could this be one of them, against the odds? Would the same be true of Neve Chenoweth's accidental death as well?

After bringing Lieutenant Valdez up to speed on Yuki Kotake's tragic ending, Quincy got on the computer to do some digging on Justin Buckner. First and foremost, he wanted to see if the man had committed any crimes—especially serious offenses. Accessing the National Crime Information Center, Quincy ran a criminal history check on Buckner. He quickly discovered that Giselle's former fiancé did have a rap sheet—including arrests for assault, drug possession, fraud and threatening a police officer. None of these had resulted in conviction, as the charges had either been dropped or otherwise disappeared.

Someone must have had his back, Quincy couldn't help but think, suspicious. Just what else might he have done and gotten away with—could he be making Giselle's life a living hell when they were together, by making real or implied threats toward her physical safety, health and well-being?

Gazing at Buckner's mug shot, Quincy imagined Giselle being involved with him. He quickly dismissed the unappealing thought, rejecting the notion of competing with the man for her affections when it was obvious that Giselle wanted nothing more to do with Buckner, given the extreme measures she'd taken to get away from him.

Quincy got on the phone with the Federal Bureau of Investigation. Or, more specifically, Daniel Malaterre, a fellow Eyak member and buddy since grade school. He'd joined the Bureau nearly a decade ago and was currently the special agent in charge at the field office in Omaha, Nebraska, where Daniel lived with his wife and college sweetheart, Shania, and their newborn daughter, Connie.

Daniel answered the video call on the second ring. His narrow face appeared on the cell phone screen, along with black hair in a textured cut and brown eyes. Sporting a crooked grin, he said, "Hey, Trooper."

"Hey." Quincy grinned, remembering their days growing up. Without preface, he asked him, "Got a sec?"

"Yeah, I have a few minutes to spare." Daniel sounded like he was adjusting in his office desk chair. "What's up?"

"I need some info on a guy," Quincy told him. "Name's Justin Buckner. Lives in Chesapeake, Virginia."

"Looking for anything specific?"

"I need to know if Buckner may have taken a plane to Alaska in the last month." Quincy stood up. "Or even to the state of Washington or Canada," he added, realizing that Buckner could have driven to Alaska from one of those places, theoretically.

"What has he done?" Daniel asked curiously.

"Probably nothing in this state," Quincy admitted honestly. "It's more of a personal request, on behalf of someone who used to be engaged to Buckner and wants to be reasonably certain that he's not stalking her."

"Okay. Let's see what I can find out…"

Quincy was put on hold and waited for him to use his FBI connections to access passenger info from a travel database on bookings worldwide. It operated in real time to help the Bureau track suspects, or potential suspects, and their movements on airlines, from reservations to seat assignments and more. If Buckner had boarded a plane under his own name anytime recently, it would show up.

After a few minutes, Daniel came back on the line and said, "There's no indication that Justin Buckner has flown to Alaska, Washington, Oregon, California or Canada in the past month. Or, for that matter, anywhere else…" He took a breath. "Of course, if Buckner was traveling under an assumed name, then it might be a different story."

"All right." Quincy had no reason to believe that was the case for the time being. The more likely scenario was that Buckner was not in Taller's Creek right now, stalking Giselle, much less involved in the deaths of Yuki Kotake or Neve Chenoweth. "Thanks for checking."

"No problem. Actually, I've come up with something else on Buckner that may interest you…"

"I'm listening," Quincy said.

"He's currently being investigated by the feds—including the Securities and Exchange Commission—for wire fraud and embezzlement in relation to Buckner's business as a certified financial planner in Chesapeake."

"Hmm…" Quincy was thinking out loud. "So Buckner is in trouble?"

"I'd say so," Daniel told him. "From what I'm seeing, I'd say that an arrest is imminent."

And, in the process, likely to keep him preoccupied with trying to stay out of prison, Quincy told himself. "I'll be sure to pass that on to Giselle," he said, knowing that would ease her fears regarding Buckner.

"One other thing I've come across in the investigation…" Daniel mentioned. "Four years ago, Buckner was questioned about the disappearance of a waitress named Jenna Sweeney. But apparently nothing became of this, and it didn't go any further."

"I see," Quincy mused, wondering if Giselle knew about this Jenna Sweeney. Or if Buckner could still be a threat to Giselle, should she ever set foot outside of Alaska.

After catching up for a few minutes, Quincy disconnected from Daniel and headed out to share the latest news with Giselle.

While on his way to the park where they'd agreed to meet, Quincy got a call from his sister, Olivia. He sensed it pertained to his nephew's birthday party, which included Quincy's parents driving up from Juneau, feeling that the more than twenty-hour trip by car was well worth it.

Putting his cell phone on speaker, Quincy said in an affable tone of voice, "Hey, sis."

"Hi, Quincy." Olivia waited a beat, then said, "I know you're pretty busy, but just thought I'd remind you that Todd's birthday bash is Saturday. Hope you can make it." She added as further incentive, "Everyone will be there."

"I wouldn't miss it," Quincy told her, smiling, even if he

had missed his niece Krista's birthday party last year, as duty had called.

"Wonderful." Olivia's voice rose excitedly.

"Can't wait to see Mom and Dad," he told her, wishing there was more time to visit them in Juneau.

"They will be just as happy to see you!"

Quincy watched the road ahead of him thoughtfully. "Do you mind if I bring a guest?"

"Of course not," Olivia assured him.

"Good."

"Who's the guest…?"

"Her name's Giselle," he answered. "She works at the bookstore where I picked up some books for Todd—and got a few for Krista too while I was at it."

"How nice."

Olivia was silent for a moment, and Quincy could read her mind in wondering about Giselle, knowing that he didn't make a habit of inviting anyone to meet his family. But this time it felt right, wanting to make Giselle feel even more at home in Alaska. "I think she'd like meeting everyone," he said intuitively.

Olivia asked, "New woman in your life…?"

Quincy pondered the notion. "One can always hope," he answered candidly, realizing that they weren't quite there yet to define this as a relationship based on one kiss, satisfying as it had been.

"Yes, one can." His sister laughed understandingly. "Giselle's always welcome at our house. You, too."

Quincy grinned, taking the hint about wanting him to visit more often. Now maybe he had a good excuse to do just that, if Giselle planned to stick around and accompany him. Or would she be more likely to bolt from Alaska once her ex-fiancé had been arrested and was no longer an impediment to her life in Virginia?

GISELLE SPOTTED QUINCY at Teary Lake Park on Dakley Road. He waved to her while standing on the shore by the lake. She walked past some aspen trees toward him and wondered if he had frightening news that Justin had indeed located her and, in the process, was making his presence felt by going after people she knew.

I have to stay positive and assume that isn't the case, Giselle told herself, wanting to believe that Neve's and Yuki's unfortunate deaths were unrelated to her ex-fiancé, just as Quincy had intimated from his investigations.

"Hey." He eyed her with a handsome smile.

"Hi." She held his gaze guardedly and got right to it, asking, "What did you learn about Justin...?"

Quincy touched the brim of his campaign hat and said coolly, "Well, the good news is that as near as my FBI contact was able to determine, there's no evidence that Buckner has traveled by plane to anywhere in Alaska, much less in the vicinity of Taller's Creek in the last month or so. Same is true for the West Coast or Canada. At least using his real name. Odds are that your ex has not been stalking you or played any role in the deaths of Neve Chenoweth or Yuki Kotake—whose death was ruled by the medical examiner to be a probable suicide, when combined with her history of depression and suicidal ideation. As if that isn't enough proof," he said firmly, "gun residue found on Yuki's hand strongly suggested that she was holding the firearm that was used to kill her."

"I'm glad to hear that Justin wasn't responsible for their deaths," Giselle admitted as she glanced out at the lake and back while feeling relieved on that front, in spite of still grieving the untimely demise of her friends. "And that he isn't in Taller's Creek as a stalker—intent on intimidating me for his own sick pleasure."

"It certainly doesn't appear to be a real cause for concern," Quincy stressed again, a catch to his voice.

Giselle picked up on this as well as his emphasis on the *good news* about Justin, as though there was bad news to follow. "What else did you learn?" She hesitated to ask but sensed there was a real need to know.

He drew a breath and answered straightforwardly, "Buckner is under federal investigation for embezzlement and wire fraud regarding his work as a financial planner."

Giselle cocked a brow. "Oh, really?"

"Yeah." Quincy jutted his chin. "It appears as though Buckner has been filling his pockets, perhaps for years, at the expense of those entrusting him with their funds."

"This isn't really news to me," she said candidly. "After I'd been in Taller's Creek for about six months, curiosity—and perhaps instincts—made me do a little research online for news out of Chesapeake related to Justin. I saw that he was being investigated by the federal government for the crimes you've described. Then it seemed like the investigation had run out of steam and that Justin may have been let off the hook."

"Not by a long shot," Quincy asserted squarely. "It often takes time—in some cases, years—before the feds can build a solid enough case to put the hammer down on a suspect. That seems to be the case here, with Buckner living on borrowed time…"

Giselle took a breath. "In truth, I've always been suspicious that Justin could be stealing clients' money. Or otherwise enriching himself illegally. But I had no proof to support this feeling." Her nose wrinkled guiltily. "If only I had. It could've saved his clients from losing their money, perhaps forever, that they invested with him."

"None of what Buckner is being accused of and investigated for is your fault, Giselle," Quincy insisted, setting his jaw. "In any event, I'm told that he could be arrested soon, which would likely keep Justin Buckner out of your life—and his bilked clients—for years to come."

"Good." Giselle grinned, feeling as if she might finally be able to let her guard down in a way that had been impossible as long as Justin was free to pursue her to the ends of the earth. "Honestly, I never want to see that man again!"

"You don't have to." Quincy fixed her with a straight gaze contemplatively. "There's something else that's worth mentioning regarding Buckner—"

Do I want to know? Giselle mused, ill at ease, but uttered, "What is it?"

"Four years ago, he was questioned by the police about the disappearance of a waitress," Quincy revealed. "Apparently there wasn't enough evidence to charge him with anything, so it ended there. No word on what happened to the woman—if anything at all..."

"Hope she's all right." Giselle's voice shook with obvious concern. Knowing Justin as she did, she wouldn't put anything past him. Including being obsessed with someone else before they met. And exacting revenge upon her if the woman wanted out of the relationship. Had that occurred here? *Or am I allowing my imagination to create a crime by my ex that never happened?* she asked herself.

"Me too," Quincy told her and added, "I'm sure if there was any evidence of wrongdoing by Buckner, the authorities would have kept him on their radar."

Giselle nodded, as this made sense to her. She forced herself to block out a persistent feeling that the news of

Justin being a suspect in a woman's disappearance was a forerunner to his fixation on her and how he'd vowed to never let go of her.

She lifted her eyes to Quincy and asked, "Would you like to come for dinner tonight?"

He met her gaze. "I have a better idea. How about I invite you to dinner at my place—if you're comfortable with that?"

"I am," she responded quickly, with a reassuring smile on her face. "I'd love to have dinner at your house."

"Good. Then it's a date." He grinned back at her. "I'll text you my address."

"Okay." Giselle looked forward to them spending more personal time together and also saw it as a way to further push Justin out of her mind, once and for all. With a much better man to give her attention to.

JUSTIN HID BEHIND a large spruce tree, watching surreptitiously as Giselle talked to a state trooper in the park. He was guessing it was about him. Ironically, even if he were to reveal himself to them, Justin wasn't sure that his ex-fiancée would recognize the man she'd promised herself to.

After allowing her to catch a glimpse of him at the bookstore window and in the wine and liquor section of the grocery store, making sure the image was one that was pretty close to how he'd looked when they'd last spoken three years ago, Justin had taken steps to give himself a makeover. Gone were the golden locks covering his head, replaced with baldness that was shaven specifically to alter his appearance. And instead of being smooth shaven, as had been the preference for much of his adult life, he had deliberately gone with a five o'clock shadow to camouflage his facial features.

Similarly, he had changed his style of clothing to both fit into his new environment and throw off Giselle. His fash-

ionable designer suits and Oxford shoes had been replaced
with camp shirts, jeans and chukka boots or sneakers, de-
pending on what he was doing.

At the moment, he was wearing black sneakers, as Justin regarded Giselle and the trooper, while keeping himself
out of their line of vision. He couldn't hear what they were
saying, but the fact that Giselle was meeting with a law enforcement officer told Justin all he needed to know. Did his
ex-fiancée believe she was safe from him if she reported her
suspicions to the authorities? *If so, think again...* he thought.

Or was there more to this get-together by the lake?

Justin mused, pinching the bridge of his nose. As it was,
he'd taken extraordinary steps to stay one step—maybe
two or three steps—ahead of the law. He knew that he was
under investigation by the feds. And that he was guilty of
wrongdoing, but it was too much to pass up on when the
opportunities presented themselves as clear as day.

When his lawyer had informed him three weeks ago that
an arrest was all but imminent and that he might want to
start to get his affairs in order, Justin hadn't hesitated to for-
mulate a plan to escape. He had no desire to spend the rest
of his life in prison. Especially now that he had discovered
Giselle's whereabouts and wanted retribution for humiliating
him and stomping on his love for her like it was worthless.

He'd emptied his bank accounts, to the degree he could,
and fled Chesapeake—only telling his parents that he'd
needed to get away for a while to clear his head. He didn't
want them involved in his legal troubles any more than
necessary.

Knowing he couldn't travel safely and freely under his
own name, Justin had stolen the name of a recently deceased client, Jesse Teague, using his new identity to make
his way to Alaska.

To Giselle's hideaway.

As soon as he dealt with her, so that Giselle could never again flee to what she mistakenly believed was a safe haven, Justin planned to leave the country altogether. He would settle in a place where there was no extradition treaty with the US, such as Taiwan, Cuba or Morocco. Or maybe even Vietnam.

But not just yet.

Not when there was still work—and some play—to be done under the moniker Jesse Teague.

Justin chuckled wickedly under his breath. He continued to give Giselle and the trooper the benefit of his attention for a while longer before quietly slipping away.

Chapter Eight

Quincy had admittedly not spent as much time in the kitchen as he would have liked. At least not as a cook, having settled more often than not these days for microwave dishes and takeout. But then again, there hadn't been much of a reason to put his cooking skills to the test. Till now.

Having learned some great authentic dishes from his mother and both grandmothers, it was time he made good use of that. Giselle would give him that opportunity. Not to mention it was another chance to further their involvement with one another. He was glad she was amenable to it.

That said, Quincy was a little worried that with things apparently coming to a head with Justin Buckner's impending arrest, it might result in Giselle leaving Alaska and returning to Virginia once the dust settled. If so, where would that leave them and what Quincy had hoped might be the match made in heaven that he had longed to find with someone?

He tried not to think about it too much as he stood in the kitchen preparing the meal, which included moose steak, fondant potatoes, sweet carrots, fry bread, salmonberries and Alaskan ice cream for dessert. They would wash the meal down with red wine.

Quincy glanced down at his light blue button-up shirt and dark trousers worn with loafers before laying out dishes, glasses and silverware on the rustic red-cedar dining room table and heading back to the kitchen for final preparations. He wanted this to be a worthwhile meal and enjoyable experience for Giselle.

When she arrived like clockwork, he couldn't help but be thoroughly captivated by her. Even at a glance, Giselle was the picture of beauty, a sight for sore eyes or any other adage Quincy could think of while dressed in a yellow flutter-sleeve top, white linen pants and ankle-strap sandals. He picked up a faint citrusy scent she wore that was appealing to him.

"Hey," he said smoothly, offering a sheepish grin.

"Hey." She showed her pretty teeth.

"Come in." After she did so, Quincy greeted Giselle with a gentlemanly kiss on the cheek, as if they had never kissed on the lips before. He hoped they might pick up where they'd left off in that regard later. "Here we are…"

Gazing about the downstairs, Giselle marveled, "Nice place you have."

Downplaying it, Quincy responded honestly, "I think it's way too big for just one person."

"And whose fault is that?" she teased him, batting her lashes.

"Point taken. I'll have to work on that." He laughed. "Hope you've worked up a good appetite?"

"Starved, actually," she indicated and then sniffed. "It smells amazing."

"Should taste even better," he promised. "Coming right up. Make yourself at home."

"Okay."

Apparently that meant helping him in the kitchen and seeming as natural with it as though they were living together. The notion was something that agreed with Quincy as they sat down in rustic dining chairs kitty-corner from one another.

Giselle wasted no time in saying ardently, after tasting the moose steak, fry bread and fondant potatoes, "I love it!"

Quincy grinned, forking a carrot. "You can thank my grandma Jeanne, as this is one of her favorite meals."

"I'd be happy to." Giselle nibbled on the fry bread. "Just point me in the right direction."

"Unfortunately she passed away a few years ago," he hated to say. "But she'll always be around in spirit—and I'm certain Grandma Jeanne would've been thrilled that you're enjoying the food."

"It's hard not to," Giselle maintained while trying out the salmonberries.

Quincy sliced into his own moose steak and said, "I'm glad you like it."

Later, they had Alaskan ice cream and coffee.

"This is really good," she told him gleefully, running her tongue across her mouth.

He chuckled with amusement. "Yeah, I can see you're enjoying it."

Giselle colored. "I don't mean to make a pig out of myself."

"A pig you could never be—not even on your worst day," Quincy assured her and got a laugh out of her. After a moment or two of enjoying each other's company, he decided to bring up something that had been weighing on his mind. "So, is he why you gave up dancing when you moved to Taller's Creek?" It didn't take much to speculate that she wanted to keep a low profile—in case he used that to track her down.

As if reading his mind, she sipped her coffee and answered musingly, "Yes, as a matter of fact. I figured that if I opened up a dance studio anywhere else, Justin would surely find a way to learn about it and come after me. I couldn't afford to take the chance of that happening, so I simply had to find another way to make a living."

Quincy tasted his own coffee, frowning. "Sorry that Buckner put you in such a position where you were forced to turn away from something you loved."

"Me too." She made a face. "As much as I hate him for it, though, I have to take some responsibility for the decisions I've made—which includes being too naive at the time to see what a big mistake I was making in ever getting involved with the likes of Justin."

"We're all entitled to make a few mistakes in our lives," Quincy told her, reaching his hand out to her. "I've certainly made my fair share and have learned from them, making me a better person."

"Something tells me that you've always been a better person," Giselle said flatly, a soft smile on her face. "Especially compared to the man I wish I'd never met."

"I'd like to think so," Quincy admitted. Still, he was flattered to be thought of in such a way and more than happy to command her attention as she commanded his.

"I'd love to check out the rest of your house," she told him.

"Of course." He grinned at her, wishing he had given her the grand tour sooner. "Why don't I show you around…"

They both stood after finishing off their coffees.

AFTER LEADING THE WAY up the open riser staircase to the second story, Giselle ventured off on her own, taking in the various well-appointed rooms with their rustic furniture and picture windows, while Quincy stood in the hall patiently. When she scooted past him somewhat nervously and got to the primary bedroom with an en suite, Giselle stepped inside and took a look around. She wasn't at all disappointed as her gaze fell on the king-size wood bed, covered with a gray-and-red striped comforter.

Feeling Quincy come up behind her and breathe on her neck, Giselle felt turned on as she faced him.

"Well, what do you think?" he asked, holding her gaze.

"Do you really want to know?" Her tone was daring.

He smiled playfully. "Yeah, let me have it."

"Okay, if you insist." Giselle gathered up her nerve to match her suddenly overwhelming needs. She cupped Quincy's chiseled cheeks and planted a kiss on his hard mouth, savoring the taste of him. This made her even more desirous. She made herself unlock their lips and uttered anxiously, "What I think is… I want you to make love to me."

Quincy gave her a straight look and asked in earnest, "Are you sure that you're ready for this?"

Giselle touched her tingling lips. "If you want to know the truth, I've been ready." She wondered if he had been of the same mind but had merely been waiting for the right moment to arrive.

"So have I," he told her deeply. "I want you, too, Giselle. Badly."

The notion thrilled her. "Do you have protection?" she thought to ask, knowing that being responsible was important for both of them.

"I do." Quincy smiled. "Wait here."

"Oh, I'm not going anywhere," she promised.

Giselle watched as he went into the en suite bathroom and returned with a foil wrapper, tossing it onto the bed. It was all she needed as she began to remove her clothes, and he did the same. Exposing herself like this was unnerving, to say the least. What if he didn't like what he saw? She had

always prided herself on staying in shape and was propor-
tionate from head to toe with medium-sized firm breasts.
But some men preferred more of this or less of that. Would
she measure up for him?

As if he were reading into her thoughts, Quincy gave
her a once-over and said boldly, "You're stunning…every-
where!"

Giselle smiled, feeling reassured with the praise, and
eyed his taut nakedness and six-pack abs. "I can honestly
say the same thing about you," she confessed, her libido
rising like the tide with each passing second that they were
not in his bed.

Clearly on the same wavelength, Quincy scooped her up
into his powerful arms and carried her to the bed, setting
her down gently before climbing in beside her.

What happened next was as much a blur to Giselle as it
was satisfying beyond anything she could imagine. They
kissed passionately like there was no more tomorrow and
engaged in foreplay that had her body on fire all over and
within. She could tell that the same was true for him.

When she could stand it no more, Giselle demanded,
"Take me—now!"

"With pleasure…and then some," Quincy told her on a
breath.

He ripped open the packet and slid on the condom before
making his way between her splayed legs, atop her, where
Giselle was more than welcoming, as ready for this as her
deepest fantasies for the trooper. She came almost instantly
as he plunged deep inside of her.

But even with that sheer joy, Giselle knew that the experience could only be complete and fulfilling when they rose to
the heights of carnal pleasure together. As such, she kissed

him and moved her body in a way to encourage his own climax, which had him shuddering with its powerful release.

With a sharp gasp from his thrusts, she brought their bodies together, and Giselle had a second, even stronger orgasm and, with Quincy, rode the wave of sexual ecstasy together.

When it was over and he rolled off her, each catching their breaths, Giselle blushed and still had to admit unabashedly, "Wow! That was amazing!"

"You're telling me." Quincy laughed. "It was well worth the wait—trust me. But it's *you* that's truly amazing," he uttered, sighing.

Her lashes fluttered. "Oh, you think so?"

"I know so." He kissed her moist shoulder. "Thanks for coming into my life."

She smiled. "Actually, I think it was the other way around, if I recall correctly."

Quincy waited a beat before propping up on an elbow and saying, "So, do you plan to stick around here a while now that Buckner's about to be arrested?"

Giselle paused contemplatively for a long moment, then admitted, "I hadn't really thought about it. I only knew that as long as Justin was still operating freely in Chesapeake, I could never go back there."

"And now?"

She understood that he was trying to gauge whether or not what had just happened between them was something they could build upon. Or if it was just a flash in the pan with no legs for long-term possibilities.

Had she ever planned to return home? Or had she assumed that Justin would make that impossible, without really thinking beyond that?

But that was before you entered my life, Giselle told herself, regarding Quincy. He gave her a reason to want to stay, over and beyond having made a home for herself in Alaska the last year and a half.

"I'd like to remain here and see how things go," she told him honestly, knowing there was nothing truly awaiting her back in Virginia.

Quincy grinned, looking relieved. "Good."

Though she felt the same way, Giselle couldn't help but turn the tables on him, to see his reaction. "Do you think you would ever be willing to move from Alaska yourself?" Or were his roots there so solid that the thought of ever relocating was a nonstarter? Even if it involved matters of the heart.

Quincy stared at the question for an agonizing few seconds, after which he looked her right in the eye and answered, "I've spent my whole life living in this great state and just assumed I'd be here forever. But truthfully, with a line of work that's in demand across the country, I'd move elsewhere in a heartbeat if I had a good enough reason—" his gaze sharpened on her "—such as that special someone who made the end more than justify the means."

She beamed. "Good answer."

"Just calling the balls and strikes as I see them," he claimed.

"Hmm…" Giselle took that for what it was worth. In this instance, they definitely seemed to be on the same team insofar as being open to whatever could come their way in seeing each other. She leaned into him and kissed him, a fresh round of desire rippling through her. "Care to go a second round?" she challenged him.

He kissed her back heartily and said through her open mouth willingly, "Absolutely. Let's do this…"

QUINCY TOOK HIS TIME making love to Giselle the second time around, going the extra mile in pleasuring her in every way she expressed through her words, gasps, touches and reaction to his actions. He wanted the experience to be one that demonstrated just how good they were together. While he'd been concerned that she might bolt once Justin Buckner was in custody, these fears had apparently been unwarranted as Giselle seemed just as anxious to see where things could go between them as Quincy was. He sure as hell would not run away from a woman who checked all the boxes for him. That included being as incredible in the nude as he had fantasized about, and much more. Hopefully he could fit the bill for what she deserved in a man for an intimate relationship.

Once he knew Giselle had been thoroughly satisfied, based on her deep sighs, murmurs, urging him on and tenseness of her body before it relaxed, Quincy had no need to hold back as he let loose in reaching his own climax, enhanced by her own cries of sexual bliss. Together, they peaked at just the right time and took a few moments afterward to recover their equilibrium.

As they cuddled in his bed, Quincy remembered he had been meaning to ask Giselle something. Now was as good a time as any. "How do you feel about going to my nephew's birthday party on Saturday?" he asked, hoping she wouldn't pass on the opportunity to meet his family. "My parents will be there."

"I'd love to come," Giselle said easily, then added tentatively, "if you're sure that's what you want…?"

"I'm sure," Quincy reiterated. "It'll be fun." Not to mention it would give everyone a chance to see and talk to someone he wanted in his life.

She smiled. "Then I'm in."

"Cool." He kissed her, as if to seal the deal.

Chapter Nine

On Saturday, Giselle sat in silence in the passenger seat of Quincy's Subaru Forester as he drove to the home of his sister, Olivia, and her husband, Kenneth Wheeler, in Nikiski, just off the Kenai Spur Highway. Admittedly, Giselle was a bit nervous about meeting the family of the man she had made love to last night. In the process, he had managed to win her over in more ways than one. Or in ways that counted most in what she looked for in a partner.

Not only had Quincy proven to be as gentle in bed as he was totally attentive to her needs, but he'd succeeded in making her heart skip some beats and more. It made her eager to see how far this could go between them. Right down to considering remaining in Taller's Creek for the foreseeable future—even when Justin's arrest would give her the freedom to return to Chesapeake and pick up her life where she'd left off.

But exactly what type of life would I be heading back to? Giselle asked herself as she glanced at Quincy, who seemed to be caught up in his own thoughts as he turned onto Lighthouse Avenue. One where memories of Justin's control over her and his neurotic behavior would only haunt her? Did she really want to turn her back on the potential a relationship with Quincy offered in Alaska for an unknown future in Virginia?

The answer was no. A definitive no. She needed to see this through with the gorgeous trooper beside her and not run away from what could well become her destiny. And his, for that matter.

This included doing her best to make a good impression on those whom Quincy held dear.

He swung a left on Rozella Drive and, seconds later, pulled up to a three-level house, bordered by mature pine and spruce trees. In the driveway, there were several late-model vehicles.

"Well, here we are." Quincy broke the silence, flashing her a grin out of the corner of his mouth.

Giselle regarded him cautiously. "Are you sure it's a good thing that I meet your family right now...?"

"I'm positive," he insisted. "Trust me, they won't need any help from me to be sold on just how wonderful you are, Giselle!"

She blushed. "If you say so."

Not that she was opposed to taking this next step with him, as Giselle—with her own parents out of the picture and no siblings—wanted to feel that familial sense of belonging that she'd never felt with Justin's parents, who were as cold and distant as he was domineering and needy. They'd made it clear to her that they'd thought Justin could do better in a girlfriend, much less a fiancée. But he'd seemed to have a mind of his own in opposing them.

I only wish Justin had taken their advice and turned his attention elsewhere, Giselle told herself. It would have saved them both the trouble of being in a relationship doomed to failure. Better late than never.

On the other hand, she was trusting Quincy that his family would be more welcoming and one she could become connected to as she was starting to connect with the trooper himself.

QUINCY WAS MORE THAN HAPPY to introduce Giselle to his parents, sister, brother-in-law, niece and nephew. As expected, they all warmed up to her instantly, seeing in Giselle what he did—a woman who was not only beautiful but had a good heart and soul and cared about people. That was pretty much all he could ask for in a person Quincy wanted in his life.

But he got even more when Giselle commanded the attention of Todd, his now five-year-old nephew and his six-year-old sister, Krista. They were wide eyed and all ears as Giselle read from some of the books Quincy had bought for them and seemed as natural in so doing as if they were her own kids. This gave him a real sense of just what a great mother she would make whenever Giselle decided to have children of her own.

If I'm lucky, maybe I'll be the father of those children— however many it ends up being, Quincy told himself wistfully in the large, carpeted family room with rattan furnishings, where everyone had gathered. He noted Giselle talking with his parents, both in their early sixties and in good health, while sitting on the wicker sofa. His sister, Olivia, joined in on the conversation as her kids were playing with toys on the floor.

Quincy took a sip from the bottle of beer he was holding as he stood beside his brother-in-law, Kenneth. The thirty-three-year-old petroleum engineer was a member of the Yakutat Tlingit Tribe and six feet, six inches tall with dark long hair parted in the middle.

"Where have you been hiding her?" Kenneth asked, drinking beer.

Quincy laughed. "She's always been in plain view. I just needed the right time to bring Giselle around."

"Glad you did. Looks like she's fitting right in."

"That was the plan," Quincy admitted, marveling at just how comfortable Giselle seemed around everyone. And vice versa. He saw this as a good sign that they really could make a go of this, with family an important part of his life and culture. He only wished her own parents were still alive for him to get to know.

"How did you manage to hit it off?" Kenneth asked curiously.

"It wasn't that difficult," he told him candidly. "Just came naturally." He added for context that they had met under less-than-ideal circumstances, when needing to question Giselle about the death of Neve Chenoweth. That notwithstanding, they'd still been able to find common ground, a mutual attraction, and go from there.

"She seems like a keeper to me," his brother-in-law said flatly.

"Me too," Olivia pitched in, walking up to them. "She's wonderful!"

Quincy gazed at his twenty-nine-year-old sister, a stay-at-home mom who was much shorter than her husband but taller than most women and slender, with long and wavy cappuccino-colored hair and brown eyes. "Tell me something I don't know," he teased her.

"How about that Giselle would love to have a boy and girl of her own someday?" Olivia told him. "At the very least," she added.

"Really?" Though surprised by the specifics, Quincy

was already certain that Giselle had the maternal instincts necessary to be a great mother.

"Guess she would have gotten around to mentioning this to you the closer you become, big brother." Olivia smiled at him. "Since Mom and Dad want more grandchildren to dote over while they're still alive, this would certainly work for them—as long as you're the father. I'm just saying..."

"So you are." Quincy chuckled, while feeling the pressure of measuring up to his sister and her kids in their parents' eyes. He felt more than up to the challenge if things continued to progress with Giselle.

When he looked at Kenneth for support, his brother-in-law laughed and said, "This is a hole you'll have to dig yourself out of, one way or the other."

"Duly noted." Quincy laughed and gave him a friendly pat on the shoulder before making his way over to Giselle and his parents while hoping they weren't going overboard in giving her the third degree. Or could it be the other way around?

ON SUNDAY, Giselle went jogging down the sidewalk, with quick sprints on the street itself when there was no traffic. She kept an eye out for moose or other wildlife that might literally happen to cross her path here or there.

She thought about visiting with Quincy's family the day before and how nice everyone had been to her. It was definitely a pleasant feeling to be welcomed by those who could somehow become her own extended family. She was certainly open to the possibility, wanting nothing more than to find love and give love to someone worthy of this. Quincy seemed like he could be that person.

He sure does know how to make me feel special, Giselle told herself, realizing just how much she needed that. She'd wondered for so long if it was even possible to get involved with someone again, with the lingering thoughts of Justin a living nightmare still not far from the surface. But with Quincy, it was so much different. He got her in the most meaningful way. Just as she got him. It seemed like they could really be onto something here.

Only time would tell. And patience, both ways.

As she continued to jog, happy for the exercise and wanting more than ever to stay in shape now that there was someone in her life to keep pace with in that regard, Giselle could hear what sounded like hurried footsteps. She glanced behind her and saw a bald-headed male runner who was solidly built. He reminded her of Justin, minus the hair.

She tried not to allow her imagination to run wild once again. It had already been established that her ex was nowhere to be found in Taller's Creek. Still, the mere thought of his presence had prompted her to start carrying pepper spray when running. Just as a precaution, should she ever need it.

Picking up the pace, Giselle sensed that the man on her tail had done the same. *What's his problem?* she asked herself, unnerved. Maybe that problem was her? Was his intention to attack her in broad daylight?

As panic ensued, she sucked in a deep breath and increased her speed even more as Giselle rounded a corner and trekked down the sidewalk. Glancing over her shoulder, she saw that he was still running in her direction.

And gaining ground, in spite of her best efforts to the contrary.

When it became clear to Giselle that she would not be able to outrun him and there was no one to come to her assistance, she decided to fight for her survival and freedom from victimization.

Without breaking stride, she started to reach inside the pocket of her shorts for the pepper spray—fully intending to spray it into his face liberally at the last possible moment to be most effective in catching him off guard.

But before Giselle could put her plan into action, the man had moved onto the street as though she were slowing him down, and raced past her—never even looking her way.

False alarm.

She flushed with embarrassment as Giselle caught her breath. *He wasn't out to harm me after all*, she told herself, breathing a sigh of relief while at the same time recognizing that she couldn't allow herself to be spooked by anyone who reminded her of Justin. Or was seen as threatening, unless proven otherwise.

She pushed the pepper spray deeper into her pocket and continued the run, determined to lead a normal life in Alaska, which had been given a major boost with the presence of Quincy in it. Along with his family, which gave Giselle hope that she could still have a family of her own one day.

JUSTIN TRAILED GISELLE slowly down the street in his vehicle, making sure he kept just enough of a distance to not give himself away just yet.

He had watched with interest as she'd appeared to freak out at the thought of another runner attacking her. Fortunately, the bald-headed man had passed her by harmlessly. But not before Giselle had seemed to reach into her pocket, as if prepared to pull out something in her defense. Probably pepper spray or another weapon.

She'd aborted this when the threat by the runner had proved all for naught.

I'm guessing at least part of her feared she was being

stalked by me, Justin told himself, laughing at the notion. Though he had gone to extremes to keep his presence—and identity—under wraps, Justin was sure he had managed to keep Giselle uncomfortable at the mere possibility that he could have tracked her down years after she'd vanished from his life sneakily.

If that were the case, then he was happy that she continued to look over her shoulder, knowing he was never going to stop searching for her.

Now that he had found her, Giselle's fears that he would punish her for all but leaving him at the altar empty-handed were more than warranted.

The time would come soon that he would carry out his vengeance and she would sorely regret the mistake she'd made of getting on his bad side.

It tended to come at a very high price.

Justin's mind drifted to Jenna Sweeney, his former girlfriend, who'd never given him the chance to propose before bolting. When he'd caught up to her, the look in Jenna's eyes while he'd been stabbing her to death her had given him the immense satisfaction Justin had sought in that moment.

He looked forward to getting the same adrenaline rush once Giselle breathed her last breath of life.

Justin watched as his ex-fiancée turned another corner, en route to her apartment. Though tempted to follow her there and finish the job, instead he doubled down on patience and drove past the street, more than willing to wait for it to happen under his own terms.

Chapter Ten

"Ellen called in sick with a bad cold," Jill told Giselle when she walked inside Taller's Creek Books the following morning.

"Probably for the best." Giselle wrinkled her nose. "I'd hate to catch it."

"Me too." The bookstore owner sighed. "Unfortunately, with Wesley vacationing in Mexico with his girlfriend and Sadie a no-show for work, it's just us today."

Giselle was not all that surprised that the young college student had failed to come in with apparently no notification to that effect. After all, Sadie could hardly be considered dependable when she only put in a few erratic hours at the bookstore a week. As for Wesley, he and his love interest, Farrah, had been planning their trip, so his absence was expected. Ellen, who rarely missed a day, had chosen the wrong one to take off.

Giselle smiled at Jill and said lightheartedly, "We'll just have to suck it up and carry the load all by ourselves."

"You're right." Jill forced a grin and patted her hand. "Glad to know someone's capable of carrying their weight around here." She eyed Giselle enviously. "Not that there's much weight on your slender frame."

Giselle colored, taking this as a compliment. "I'm happy

to be of service to you," she assured her, still mindful that Jill had given her a job when it had been most needed after arriving in Alaska under stressful circumstances. "So, what's on tap for today?"

"We need to unbox some new books that came in yesterday and shelve or table them," Jill said. "Then you can assist anyone who needs help while I do some bookkeeping."

Giselle grinned. "Sounds like a plan."

Half an hour later, Giselle was halfway through rearranging a shelf of romance novels, while thinking dreamily about Quincy and first meeting him there, when her thoughts were interrupted by a customer who needed her assistance, saying to Giselle, "Excuse me..."

The woman was in her midfifties and had light blond hair in a pompadour updo while wearing rectangle-shaped eyeglasses. Giselle couldn't help but think that she reminded her of her late mother, whose hair had been a darker shade of blond and styled differently. "How can I help you?"

Turned out that the customer needed some ideas for books to ship to her son, who had recently relocated to New Zealand for a job transfer. Giselle was more than happy to give some suggestions once she was given a bit to go on regarding the son's tastes in reading.

The woman ended up choosing half a dozen titles and couldn't wait to get the books sent off. Giselle rang them up, while envious of the obviously strong love she sensed for one's child. It was something she'd gotten from her own mother and Giselle knew she would give to her own children someday, if so blessed.

And she would equally have as much love to give to their father, if he was half the man she expected him to be. Quincy filled her head in that instant, with Justin fast becoming a distant, and largely forgettable, memory.

QUINCY AND fellow armed ABI Major Crimes Unit investigator Alan Edmonston, along with members of the Child Abuse Investigation Unit, Southcentral Area-wide Narcotics investigators and Soldotna Police Department personnel, converged on a single-story commercial building on Elder Street in Soldotna. They were backed by an AST Southcentral SWAT team equipped with Geissele Super Duty AR-15 rifles and dual-purpose K-9 troopers, excelling as both scent detection and search and rescue dogs. After a monthslong statewide investigation into human and sex trafficking that went after traffickers exploiting vulnerable Alaska Native teenagers and women—including crimes of violence and child pornography—enough hard evidence had been gathered, cooperating witnesses protected and the necessity to act now to rescue victims to move forward with the operation.

The operation went nearly without a hitch, as multiple arrests were made and victims of trafficking, some drugged or otherwise in obvious distress, were located and transported to Central Peninsula Hospital on Hospital Place for evaluation and treatment before eventually being reunited with their families. Weapons and narcotics were seized from the location, along with piles of cash and laptops. The perps would be held fully accountable for the criminality they'd engaged in.

Quincy was confident in their operation, which included arrests in other jurisdictions simultaneously with a similar degree of success across the state. These types of crimes were particularly hard to stomach and had no place in Alaska or anywhere, really. He hated the thought that his niece or nephew—or even his sister, for that matter—could be swept up in the victimization, were they in the wrong place at the wrong time. Just as excruciating would be if his own future children were exposed to such predators. Or Giselle, as another innocent person, were a trafficker able to get a jump on her. Regardless of what their own future held, though Quincy remained optimistic as to what that could be, he didn't want her to be hurt.

Alan looked at Quincy while they stood near his SUV, a satisfied look on his face. "We got them."

"Yeah." Quincy nodded. "Unfortunately there will always be others to take their places," he muttered realistically. He knew that the market for human traffickers was still ripe for perpetrators to ply their illicit trade in a vast landscape where Alaska Natives were disproportionately impacted.

"And we'll keep coming after them," Alan countered determinedly.

Kelly Reppun, the SCAN unit detective, overheard them and, while walking in their direction, asked, "What other choice is there? We're all that's standing between them and those most vulnerable to exploitation."

"You've got that right." Quincy gave her a definite nod of agreement. "We do what we need to do—for them and us." It was the only way to deal with the realities of the work they did, while knowing what was being given back to the communities they served in Alaska. "The victims will get all the support they need to work their way back from the horrors they experienced."

Kelly and Alan voiced their belief in this as well before Quincy separated from them and headed to his own SUV.

No sooner had he gotten inside when a dispatch call came in about a situation in Taller's Creek. A young woman had been found dead in the bathtub of her apartment. The circumstances were as yet undetermined.

Quincy furrowed his brow, thinking, *Never a dull moment as an ABI investigator.*

He headed out to the location and hoped afterward to drop in on Giselle at the bookstore and see if she wanted to hang out later. This was something he found himself looking more and more forward to with each passing day they got to know each other. He was sure she felt the same way, filling his heart with glee at the prospect.

MIRIAM FONTAINE WOULD HAVE just as soon started her shift any other way than discover that another young person in Taller's Creek had died before her time. Sadly, this proved all too true as the police sergeant stared at the deceased female, her ashen face matted with dark hair just above the soapy water that filled the acrylic bathtub in the apartment on Harper Lane. Pink slippers were on the porcelain tiles. A broken wineglass lay nearby on the floor, its contents of red wine spilled.

She was identified as Sadie Pisano, a twenty-one-year-old student at Kenai Peninsula College. Her head had been pulled up after being submerged in an attempt to save her life, as reported by the woman's roommate. According to Cynthia Saranillio, twenty-two and also in college, after staying overnight at her boyfriend's house, she'd returned to the apartment to find Sadie unconscious. After being unable to revive her, she'd phoned 911, frantic that her friend might be dead.

Miriam had no reason to disbelieve the roommate's story at the moment, including her insistence that Pisano would not have killed herself deliberately. To Miriam, it appeared at a glance that she might have accidentally hit her head on the tub and passed out, going under the water. Alcohol consumption might have also been a factor.

Miriam couldn't help but think about the recent local deaths of other women while wondering what were the odds against such in their small community. She requested assistance from the ABI and notified the medical examiner to get some answers.

AFTER QUINCY ARRIVED at the two-story Creeklin Apartments building and made his way to unit 117, he was greeted by Miriam Fontaine, who had a dour look on her face as they stepped inside.

"What are we looking at?" Quincy asked her knowingly while glancing about the small, neat place with contemporary furnishings and beige carpet.

"We have a college student named Sadie Pisano, dead inside her tub, while taking a bath apparently," Miriam reported levelly. "No obvious signs of foul play…"

"Okay." He followed her into the bathroom and took a look at the naked woman in the tub, who might have seemed like she was asleep were it not for her deathly coloring. Quincy took note of the broken glass of wine, which he had to consider could have been spiked with a date-rape drug or laced with fentanyl to facilitate a possible sexual assault. "Who found the body?"

"The roommate—Cynthia Saranillio—upon returning this morning, after spending the night with her boyfriend, Travis Kozuki, at his place."

"Hell of a way to discover someone you live with," Quincy muttered morosely.

"Tell me about it." Miriam jutted her chin. "She raised Sadie's head from beneath the water to try to revive her—to no avail."

Quincy didn't fault her for taking this necessary action, which could have made a difference had she gotten to the dead woman sooner. "Where's the roommate now?"

"She stepped outside."

"I'd like to talk to her," he said.

The sergeant nodded and led the way, spotting the young woman sitting on the lawn, weeping, near some cottonwood trees.

Getting her attention, Miriam said equably, "This is Trooper Lankard of the Alaska Bureau of Investigation. He needs to ask you a few more questions."

Quincy regarded the roommate, who was biracial and thinly built, with black hair with blond highlights in a collarbone-length blunt cut. Her clothes were wet from the bath water. Cynthia wiped her brown eyes and gazed up at him before he said considerately, "Ms. Saranillio, can you tell me when you last saw Sadie Pisano alive?"

"About ten last night, before I left," she answered tensely.

"And what was she doing at the time?" he wondered.

"Cramming for an exam."

It was something Quincy remembered all too well from his own college days, which fortunately hadn't come to such a sad ending. He asked necessarily, in noting the apparent lack of forced entry, "Does anyone else have a key to your apartment?"

Cynthia blinked. "No, just me and Sadie," she contended.

"Was Ms. Pisano dating anyone?"

"No. She was single."

Quincy still couldn't rule out that there might have been someone in her life, unbeknownst to the roommate, who could have wished Sadie Pisano harm. "Did she have any enemies that you know of?"

Cynthia didn't need long to think about it. "I can't think of anyone who didn't like Sadie," she claimed.

"Was she suicidal?" he asked, thinking about Yuki Kotake's self-inflicted death.

"Definitely not!" Cynthia raised her voice. "It had to be an accident," she insisted, wiping her eyes again. "Sadie loved life, which makes it so hard to believe that this happened."

Quincy glanced at Miriam, whose expression was unreadable, and back. He knew the scene would still need to be processed by the Crime Scene Unit as part of any ABI probe of a questionable death, appearances notwithstanding.

"Did you have any inkling that Ms. Pisano might have been in trouble when you arrived at the apartment this morning?" he wondered curiously. "Had you tried to call her or anything and she wasn't picking up?"

"I did text Sadie before I left my boyfriend's place but got no response," Cynthia replied matter-of-factly. "I didn't think anything of it." She drew in a deep breath. "But when I got here and saw her bike, I wondered why she was still home and not at work."

"Where did she work?" Quincy asked.

"Sadie worked part-time at Taller's Creek Books on Milton Lane."

Hearing that threw him for a loop, and Miriam took note of his unavoidable reaction and asked, "What is it?"

"I know someone who also works at the bookstore," he responded musingly. *Giselle must have known Sadie*, Quincy told himself uncomfortably. Just as she'd known the two other women—Neve Chenoweth and Yuki Kotake—who had died tragically and prematurely. He didn't begin to know what to make of the timing, other than purely happenstance. Sad as that was.

The state deputy medical examiner, Joslyn Bartiromo, arrived with her team to take possession of the decedent.

Doctor Bartiromo was in her midthirties and slender, with thick brunette hair in a shoulder-length cut. She was wearing nitrile exam gloves as she'd done an initial exam of Sadie Pisano's body after the tub had been drained.

"What do you think happened here?" Quincy asked her inquisitively once the corpse had been placed in a body bag and loaded onto the transport vehicle.

Joslyn smoothed an eyebrow and answered, "My initial assessment is that the decedent drowned in the bathtub, probably by accident. And possibly involved her use of alcohol." She paused, then said deliberately, "Let's see what the autopsy concludes."

With a nod, Quincy went with the likely cause of death as not involving foul play till further notice. But that wouldn't make it any easier to have to be the bearer of bad news to Giselle. And how she might react in knowing yet another female in her orbit had died.

WHEN QUINCY WALKED into the bookstore, Giselle's heart skipped a beat. There was no denying that he was doing things to her that were both exhilarating and scary. She didn't want to be hurt again. But she also didn't want to deny herself something good—maybe very good—that could come from being involved with the ABI trooper.

She left the stack of books on the floor to shelve and met him halfway. "Hey there," she greeted him affably, resisting the urge to kiss him in that setting. Maybe later.

"Hey." He looked at her ponderingly. "Do you want to go grab a cup of coffee?"

She frowned. "I'd love to, but there's only two of us on duty today. Our part-time help, Sadie, never came in, so..."

"Yeah, about that—" Quincy clenched his jaw. "I'm afraid I have some bad news to share." He paused. "Sadie Pisano's dead."

"What?" Giselle swallowed thickly. "How?"

"She drowned in her bathtub..." He put firm hands on Giselle's shoulders, as if she would collapse. "But before you jump to more far off conclusions that Justin Buckner had something to do with this, the deputy medical examiner's preliminary cause of death is that it was an accident and that the wine Sadie Pisano was drinking at the time was likely a factor."

Giselle got this and felt a certain sense of relief. But that didn't prevent her from having a sense of dread. If only because this was yet another person whom she'd been acquainted with who'd died under mysterious—if not unlawful—circumstances, in short order.

Was this really all coincidental?

Or was there something very wrong here, in spite of the indications otherwise?

"Are you all right?" The tenderness of Quincy's words of concern did not go unnoticed by Giselle.

"I'm fine," she insisted, knowing it was incumbent upon her to show strength when faced with such terrible news. "I'll need to tell Jill Kekiwi, the bookstore owner, to let her know why Sadie was a no-show for work today," Giselle stated gloomily. "She's in her office."

"I'll go with you," Quincy insisted, "and help any way I can to answer questions she may have. Of course, I'll also assist the police, if necessary, in notifying Ms. Pisano's family about her passing."

"All right. Let's go talk to Jill."

Giselle liked that he was there for her during challenging times. This surely qualified as such. Even if Sadie's death had nothing to do with Justin and his sick obsession with her, which Giselle had to believe was now a thing of the past.

Justin strained himself while going for one hundred–plus push-ups at his rented farmhouse. It was just one of the ways

he kept himself going while hiding in plain view in Alaska.
Other ways included getting high.

Then there was cold-blooded murder.

He imagined by now that the body of his latest victim
had been discovered. It wasn't especially difficult to charm
his way into her life in secret, lulling her into a false sense
of security before snuffing out her existence and making it
seem like an accident of her own making.

Or anything that didn't point back at him.

Just like the other two women who'd happened to know
Giselle. And paid for it.

Giselle herself would be punished soon enough for thinking that escape was ever in the cards for her. Not in this lifetime. It had always been only a matter of time before he'd
found out where she'd been hiding. And dispensed the type
of retaliation that she wouldn't soon forget.

He laughed at the wicked thought before focusing on
his workout and building up the muscles on his body that
would serve him well at the end of the day in staying one
step ahead of the authorities.

And two steps or more behind Giselle. Till they had one
final face-to-face encounter.

Chapter Eleven

On Wednesday afternoon, Giselle got together with her friend, Jacinta Cruz, for a drink at the Owl's Den bar on Ninth Street in Taller's Creek. She had met the Latina award-winning producer of documentaries on Alaska culture and history through Neve. Jacinta was tall, thin and attractive, with bold blue eyes and long blond hair in face-framing flippy layers that reminded Giselle of a style hers used to be.

They sat on wooden stools at the bar, sipping margaritas while commiserating over the unexpected deaths of their friends, Neve and Yuki.

Jacinta furrowed her brow. "I still can't believe they're gone."

"I know, right?" Giselle frowned thoughtfully. "It seems unreal."

"Doesn't it always?" Jacinta agreed, tasting her drink. "They will always be a part of our lives in spirit."

Giselle believed this too, but it was hardly the same as being there in the flesh. As if this wasn't enough to stomach, she had to add to the tragedies by relaying the untimely passing of her coworker at the bookstore, Sadie Pisano.

"Sadie died while taking a bath," she said. "Apparently hit her head, went under and never came up."

"I'm so sorry," Jacinta expressed. She put her hand on Giselle's. "They say that bad things come in threes. If true, then maybe the bad karma you've had to endure has run its course."

"I sure hope so." Giselle gave a little smile and sipped on the margarita. As it was, three people dying in the prime of their lives were three too many. Or would there be more deaths to come of people she knew? She hated to even think about the notion, wanting only to get past this dark period and move on with her life.

"Okay, enough with the negativity," Jacinta said, taking a sip of her drink. "Let's move on to more positive things... such as your love life. Any news you care to share on that front? I know you haven't really been in the market for anything too serious since you arrived in Alaska..."

"Actually, I'm seeing a state trooper right now," Giselle was happy to announce, seeing no reason to keep this a secret among friends who asked.

"Seriously?" Jacinta's eyes popped wide. "Since when?"

"Since he showed up at the bookstore recently and we struck up a conversation. It went from there." Giselle spared her the details of Quincy's investigation into Neve's death that had led him to Taller's Creek Books that day.

"I'm so happy for you." Jacinta flashed her teeth. "Hope your trooper turns out to be everything you'd like him to be."

"So do I," Giselle told her and added spiritedly, "So far, so good." She knew that was an understatement. Quincy had almost proven to be too good to be true, but she saw nothing that would dampen that view of him. And only wanted to be just as desirable as a romantic partner, and more, to him. "What about you? Any prospects on the dating scene?"

she asked Jacinta, who had been married once briefly at a young age but was currently single.

"I wish." Jacinta rolled her eyes. "The good ones are hard to come by these days. But hey, if your trooper knows any single and good-looking troopers on the market, send them my way."

Giselle laughed. "Will do." From what she'd gathered from Quincy, most of his coworkers with the ABI were spoken for in one way or another. But it couldn't hurt to ask. So long as she kept him for herself—which, thankfully, he seemed more than amenable to.

After finishing her cocktail, Giselle left Jacinta at the bar and headed home to feed Muffin and do some chores. Quincy was planning to drop by for dinner and whatever else they decided to do with their time together.

JUSTIN WAITED, staying out of Giselle's line of vision—not wanting to chance her recognizing him, even with a new look, in an open setting—for her to leave the Owl's Den bar. Admittedly, a part of him had wanted to spring on her like a thief in the night, undoubtedly shaking his onetime fiancée to the core. But that would take away the element of surprise, while exposing his secret presence in Alaska prematurely.

That might not go well in the long run, as he dodged the authorities who were investigating him back in Chesapeake. He had no desire to tip them off as to his whereabouts that Justin was sure would capture their interests sooner than later.

So, instead, he remained in the shadows at a back table, sipping on a gin and tonic, gazing at Giselle as she walked out the door. *See you soon, my love—take that to the bank*, he thought sarcastically as he finished off the drink and got to his feet.

Justin coolly approached the woman Giselle had been chatting with at the bar. She was talking on her cell phone. He recognized her from the candlelight vigil he had attended to honor Neve Chenoweth, the first local and acquaintance of Giselle's that Justin had taken out and gotten away with.

Sitting on the stool beside Jacinta Cruz, he waited till the nice-looking woman had gotten off the phone before Justin put on his deceptive charm and best smile. After which he said smoothly, "Can I buy the beautiful lady another drink?" Not waiting for her to respond, he added, "I just hate drinking all by myself—"

"So do I," she told him, blushing all the while. "You're welcome to buy me a drink, if you insist."

"I do." He ordered two margaritas and hit her with a totally captivated look, then said dishonestly, "By the way, my name's Jesse Teague."

"Jacinta Cruz."

No kidding, Justin mused sardonically, as he was already on top of this, but offered sweetly, "Very nice to make your acquaintance."

QUINCY WAS AT his desk when he got the request for a video chat from Daniel Malaterre, his friend with the FBI. He accepted and said, "Hey, Daniel."

"Quincy." Daniel was all business in his expression. "Have some news on Justin Buckner I thought might be of interest to you…and your friend—"

"Okay…" Quincy tuned in for what he had to say.

"Wanted to let you know that Buckner's office and home were raided early this morning and troves of evidence confiscated as part of the investigation into him."

"That's good," Quincy couldn't help but say, knowing that putting the man out of commission would certainly be comforting to Giselle. "What about Buckner himself? Has he been arrested yet?"

Creases appeared on Daniel's forehead as he said, "Afraid not. Based on what they found—or didn't—it appears as though he may have skipped town, perhaps had an inkling that things were about to turn south for him and left in a hurry."

Quincy muttered an expletive, frowning. "Not what I wanted to hear."

"Figured as much." Daniel jutted his chin. "A warrant has been issued for Buckner's arrest and a BOLO alert has been put out for his blue BMW 430i coupe." He drew a breath. "My guess is he could be anywhere, but he won't get very far." He spoke confidently.

"What about Alaska?" Quincy asked point-blank. He thought about Giselle and the extraordinary means she'd gone through to get away from that creep. Could he have actually discovered her whereabouts? And come after her, his legal issues notwithstanding?

"Highly unlikely," Daniel stressed. "That's a long way from Virginia, and as yet, there's no reason to believe he's gone to Alaska to escape his troubles. Or expose himself by stalking an ex-fiancée."

"I'm sure you're right." Quincy was inclined to agree, all things considered. "Keep me posted."

"Sure thing."

He signed off, and Quincy mused about Buckner, wondering where he was holed up and just how long it would take for the feds to dig him out.

LATER, WHILE IN BED and after he'd pleasured Giselle and been satisfied by her in kind during their lovemaking,

Quincy cuddled her to his body and said evenly, "So, I thought you'd like to know that Buckner's house and office were raided this morning—making good on the feds' plans to go after him…"

Giselle raised her eyes at Quincy expectantly. "Justin's in custody?"

"Not yet, unfortunately," he hated to admit. "But a warrant has been issued for his arrest, and with any luck, Buckner will be behind bars before you know it." Quincy hoped that would be enough reassurance that she had nothing to be worried about.

"Okay." Giselle sighed. "The sooner, the better."

"I agree," he told her. "And I can promise you the feds feel exactly the same way. They take the types of white-collar crimes Buckner's being charged with seriously."

"Good."

Just as Quincy had taken the moment of pacification as an excuse to kiss Giselle, Muffin suddenly jumped up onto the bed, seemingly determined to command their attention.

With a chuckle, Quincy lifted up the playful kitten and said, "Looks like someone feels threatened that I'm muscling in on her territory."

"Probably." Giselle laughed. "I think there's enough of me to go around for the two of you."

Quincy grinned and said, "Try convincing her of that."

"She'll just have to learn over time," Giselle insisted, taking the kitten out of his hands. She kissed the top of Muffin's head and said, "Now, be a good little kitten and give us some space." She released her, and Muffin seemed to take the hint, hopping off the bed and racing out of the room.

"Now, where were we…?" Giselle asked Quincy in a sexual tone of voice, nibbling on his lips with hers.

"You tell me. Or, better yet, show me," he replied teasingly into her mouth, and Quincy felt his libido uptick once again, in what he felt had to be the first stages of true love. If they weren't already well beyond that point.

THE FOLLOWING MORNING at work, Quincy got the autopsy report on Sadie Pisano's death. Reading with interest, he expected it to more or less confirm the preliminary assessment of the deputy medical examiner that the death had likely been accidental drowning.

Instead, as he sat at his desk, Quincy found the official conclusion to the contrary. According to Dr. Rhonda Ullerup, the chief medical examiner, the college student had died from drowning, but she'd determined the manner of death to be a homicide. She described bruising on the decedent's arms and shoulders, consistent with being held down in the bathtub water against the victim's will.

Equally disturbing to Quincy in the report was reading that Sadie Pisano had ingested the drug GHB, which had likely made her dizzy or unconscious and contributed to her death, in spite of a lack of evidence of a sexual assault. He strongly suspected that the substance had been put in the wine she'd drunk that night, which would undoubtedly be detected by the crime lab's Blood and Beverage Alcohol Section once the Crime Scene Unit's investigation of what had actually turned out to be a crime scene had been completed.

So, Sadie Pisano was killed by someone, Quincy thought, sitting back, unnerved at the sudden turn in the dynamics. Who was the unsub? Had Sadie known her killer? Was anyone else in danger?

Since Giselle was an employee of the same bookstore Sadie had worked at, he could only wonder if there could be any logical connection that could put her at risk.

While pondering this unsettling thought, Quincy took out his cell phone and updated Taller's Creek PD Sergeant Miriam Fontaine with the news.

To say it was business as usual at Taller's Creek Books would be a real stretch. Certainly, this was the way Giselle saw it, as they were still reeling over the death of one of their own. No one really wanted to talk about Sadie's passing, but it was surely on everyone's mind. That included Wesley, who had offered to cut short his vacation to return to work, knowing they were grieving and shorthanded—but Jill had insisted it wasn't necessary. Ellen, who had overcome her cold and was back, agreed.

As did Giselle, who only wanted to keep busy and try to keep things as normal as possible but was finding that difficult, to say the least. Though she hadn't known Sadie that well, losing her, even in an accident, hurt. Especially after two other females in Giselle's circle had died prematurely.

I can't control what I can't control, she told herself while arranging books on a table.

A few minutes later, Giselle could tell when Quincy came into the bookstore that something weighed heavily on his mind. Had she become that intuitive about the man she was romantically involved with? Maybe so, which she considered to be a good thing for where this seemed to be headed. She wondered if he too felt he could read her like a book.

"There's been a development..." He spoke in a somber tone, clearly there in an official capacity.

"What is it?" Giselle met his eyes tensely.

"Maybe it's best that I speak to all the employees here at once."

Now you're scaring me, she mused, ill at ease, but said, "All right."

After stepping with him into the back room, where Jill and Ellen were talking shop while surrounded by stacks of books and boxes, Giselle got their attention and said to Ellen, "This is Quincy Lankard, with the Alaska Bureau of Investigation. He has something to say to us."

"Must be serious," Jill remarked, touching her glasses.

Quincy stood in the middle of the three of them and said straightforwardly, "Sadie Pisano's death has been ruled a homicide…"

"What?" Ellen's mouth hung open.

"It wasn't an accidental drowning?" Giselle followed in disbelief.

"Not according to the chief medical examiner," Quincy said flatly.

Jill peered at him. "Do you have any suspects?"

He eyed Giselle, and she sensed that he was reading her thoughts—or more specifically, fears resurfacing about Justin and his threats—before Quincy answered succinctly, "None as yet. But the current working theory is that Ms. Pisano may have had a stalker, either from her college environment or while working here at the bookstore. Perhaps the orange roses delivered here were meant for her. We're pursuing all angles at the moment."

Someone might have been stalking Sadie? Giselle thought. Ending with her murder? This was certainly not implausible, she believed, having assumed the roses were for herself. She should have considered that any of the bookstore employees could have been targeted and not just her.

Giselle looked at Quincy and asked curiously, "What other angles are you pursuing…?"

He pinched his nose while pondering the question. "We're looking into the possibility that it could have been a random attack. Or a crime of passion or opportunity. Even a case of mistaken identity." Quincy paused. "Though there's probably nothing to worry about, the association with Ms. Pisano through the bookstore can't be dismissed altogether, per se. As such, I would suggest that you watch your backs to be on the safe side. Till the case is solved."

Giselle stiffened at the thought, knowing that for better or worse, Quincy was giving them a clear warning that perhaps a deranged book lover was behind Sadie's death.

Or could there be more cause for concern that whoever had killed her had other ulterior motives?

Chapter Twelve

In Nobber's Hill, Virginia, forty miles outside of Chesapeake, Chad and Suzanna Zimmerman were walking their
black Cane Corso named Klay through a wooded area near
South Blebard Highway. A month removed from celebrating
their fiftieth wedding anniversary, they looked forward to
being joined by their children and grandchildren for a big
celebration to mark the occasion.

For her part, Suzanna relished the thought of being with
Chad way back when they'd been attending the University
of Virginia in Charlottesville as college freshmen—and had
become practically inseparable ever since. Now in their sev-
enties, she wondered just how long they could keep it going
before one or the other ran out of steam.

She decided it did no good to dwell on the negative. Especially when there was still so much to look forward to.

That included the companionship of their dog, who
seemed to adore them every bit as much as they did him.

Suzanna was holding the leash, giving Chad a break,
when Klay suddenly tried to break away, causing her to
nearly lose her grip. He obviously was attracted to something. Perhaps an object that captured his fancy, as was often
the case during their walks.

"You see something, Klay?" she asked curiously.

Chad noticed too and asked, "What is it, boy?" He took control of the leash and allowed the dog to get to where it wanted to go.

Suzanna, with her arthritic knees, struggled to keep up with them. But when she did get to the spot where Klay was digging his paws into the dirt, she froze as she saw something no one should ever have to see.

What was clearly the skeletal remains of a human being was being unearthed before Suzanna's horrified eyes.

QUINCY HAD REALLY hated to lay that bit of bad news on Giselle and her coworkers an hour ago. But there'd been no easy way to say that Sadie Pisano had been a victim of foul play. And that the killer was still at large.

He wanted to dismiss the notion that the victimization was related to Taller's Creek Books. Much less, Giselle in particular. But Quincy was concerned about the orange roses delivered to the bookstore by an anonymous so-called book lover. Was this a forerunner to Sadie's murder? Or entirely unrelated?

That's what I need to find out, Quincy told himself as he pulled up to Ruby's Flowers and Gifts on Lavender Way.

Stepping inside the florist shop, he approached a sixty-something female employee with short crimson hair as she was arranging a bouquet of red ranunculus and sunflowers.

She looked up at him with a smile and asked, "Can I help you with something?"

"I hope so." Quincy identified himself as an ABI investigator. "I need some information on the person who bought a dozen orange roses recently and had them delivered to Taller's Creek Books..."

"I remember that," she said matter-of-factly. "We don't get as many customers wanting to send orange roses, as opposed to red, pink or even purple. I recall that the gentleman was pretty specific in what he wanted sent to the bookstore."

"Do you remember if he used a credit card to pay for the roses?"

"He paid in cash," she said flatly.

Quincy frowned. "What can you tell me about the man?"

"Not much, I'm afraid. He was white, tall and...oh yes, I believe he was wearing a cap."

"About how old was he?" Quincy asked.

"Thirties, I'd guess but can't really say for sure. I've never been very good at guessing ages." She eyed him curiously. "What's he done?"

"Perhaps nothing," Quincy admitted. *Or maybe committed murder*, he mused. "Just routine stuff as part of an ongoing criminal investigation."

"I see. Sorry I couldn't be more help."

Me too, Quincy thought but told her, "Have a nice day."

Back in his vehicle, he pondered which angles to pursue next in tracking down who might have killed the college student. And whether or not there was more to the story than met the eye.

GISELLE SAT IN the café, nibbling on a honey-almond granola bar while sipping coffee. She was still reeling over the news that Sadie had been murdered—perhaps by someone who'd been stalking her.

Would Quincy get to the bottom of it?

Or would the killer remain on the loose, while possibly targeting others?

The thought was chilling to Giselle, but she took solace in knowing that the ABI was handling the investigation and that Quincy seemed intent on solving the crime. As well as allaying her own fears that Justin was somehow in the mix, even if he seemed to have his hands full at the moment while trying to evade the law.

Stop it, Giselle admonished herself as she took another bite of the granola bar. She lifted her cell phone from the table and saw that Jacinta had sent her a text.

Hey, met a new guy named Jesse. Cool to hang out with. Wish me luck!

Giselle grinned. She was happy for her friend and did hope that things worked out with this guy. Just as she wanted her own relationship with Quincy to blossom. Definitely seemed like they were headed in the right direction.

But then, she once believed that was the case with Justin. And look where that had gotten her.

In fact, it had gotten her to Alaska. And eventually into Quincy's bed. With him also being in her bed. It had to mean something special. Right?

Giselle sipped more coffee thoughtfully before heading back to the bookstore.

JUSTIN STOOD ABOVE the king-size bed, staring at the woman he'd just had sex with. Jacinta was naked and asleep as she lay on the crumpled sheet, having exhausted herself just as he had.

Though he'd enjoyed being with her somewhat—and other women too in recent years for consensual sex—it was only because he was fantasizing about Giselle while going through the motions and physical release. But that could only last so long. There was no substitute for the real thing.

Or, in this case, the woman who was still in his dreams. Even if Giselle had abandoned him. He hadn't abandoned her. Not really. She would be his again. At least in theory.

In reality, Giselle's utter betrayal would come at a price she could never walk away from. He wouldn't let her. How could he and live with himself?

Any more than when Jenna had betrayed him and forced a reaction from him that she'd lived to regret. Or *died* was more like it.

Justin peered at his latest bedmate. He knew this would be short-lived before it ran its course. Then he would do what needed to be done.

He felt added pressure in knowing that the feds were on his trail, having raided his office and home and put out a warrant for his arrest. By the time they figured out his whereabouts, he would be long gone, safely to someplace out of the country.

But until such time, there was Giselle to deal with. And that he would.

You'll get what's coming to you, Justin told himself single-mindedly of his ex-fiancée.

He watched as Jacinta stirred a bit before curling into a fetal position and snoring lightly. Leaving the room, Justin lit up a joint and weighed his next move in what had become a deadly game of cat and pretty mouse, where there could only be one winner at the end of the day.

ON SATURDAY, Quincy was at his desk when Daniel Malaterre phoned for a video chat, which he quickly accepted.

"Hey," Quincy said.

"Got some unsettling news for you," Daniel uttered equably, frowning. "First, we located Justin's Buckner's BMW in a long-term parking garage near Norfolk International Airport, suggesting that he's fled the state of Virginia."

"That's too bad," Quincy muttered, even if he'd already believed this to be a distinct possibility. It still riled him, though, knowing that the longer Buckner remained at large, the greater the threat to Giselle's peace of mind.

"Gets worse, I'm afraid." Daniel's brows lowered and he sighed. "Two days ago, human remains were discovered partially buried in the woods in Nobber's Hill, Virginia, about forty miles from Chesapeake. Dental records and the clothing worn were used to identify the badly decomposed adult female as Jenna Sweeney, the twenty-six-year-old waitress who vanished four years ago without a trace. Till now." He jutted his chin. "An autopsy on the skeletal remains indicated she was stabbed to death by someone…"

Before he could complete his news, Quincy's heart skipped a beat while blurting out instinctively, "Justin Buckner—"

Daniel's countenance was expressionless as he replied calmly, "A latent print found on the eyeglasses of the victim was submitted to the Bureau's Integrated Automated Fingerprint Identification System. There was a hit. The fingerprint matched Buckner's as an arrestee in the database. It was enough for the Chesapeake Police Department to issue a new warrant for his arrest for murder. There's now a nationwide manhunt underway to bring him in."

"Do you have any clue as to where Buckner might be hiding?" Quincy asked anxiously.

"Not really. We've had reports that he might have been spotted in Delaware, Massachusetts, Michigan, New York, Nebraska—even as far away as California and Nevada," Daniel said. "He may have managed to get out of the country, given that he was able to drain his bank accounts before taking off. We're checking the airlines, trains and other means Buckner could be using to stay on the run."

Quincy drew a sharp breath. "I'd hate to think that Buckner could have somehow made his way to Alaska," he expressed fearfully, musing about Giselle.

"I doubt that—but we'll catch him." Daniel leaned forward. "You worried about your friend?"

"Actually, she's more than a friend," Quincy admitted and thought, *We've gotten way past the friendship level.* He wouldn't have had it any other way. "We've been seeing each other."

"I see." Daniel smiled. "That's cool." He got serious again. "Buckner will be in police custody in no time flat," he insisted. "In the meantime, just keep an eye on your girlfriend."

"Will do," Quincy assured him before disconnecting. He sat back and considered that there was no reason at this time to hyperventilate over Buckner coming after someone he presumably hasn't seen in years to settle old scores. Especially when he had new concerns that should occupy all his attention.

Still, Quincy didn't relish the thought of having to tell Giselle that her ex was now wanted for the murder of Jenna Sweeney, in addition to his other alleged crimes. Fortunately, Giselle had been able to escape Buckner's homicidal tendencies.

To Quincy, this proved in and of itself that meeting her had been meant to be. He would be damned if he allowed anyone from her past—especially Justin Buckner—to ruin what Quincy believed he and Giselle could have to work with in the future.

GISELLE SAT ON the bench with Quincy in Soldotna Creek Park on States Avenue. The stunning 13.6-acre park was not far from his house and offered a breathtaking view of the Kenai River. As she gazed at it, Giselle thought maudlinly about the annual Kenai River Festival, a three-day summertime music event, which she'd attended last year with friends, including Neve and Yuki—enjoying live music, a beer and wine garden, delectable food and crafts, and more. She couldn't believe that they were no longer around to enjoy what life had to offer on the Kenai Peninsula and beyond.

When Quincy broke the silence and suggested they take a walk along the riverfront boardwalk, Giselle agreed, holding hands as they did so.

After a moment or two, he said tentatively, "So, I was speaking to my friend with the FBI, and he passed along some info regarding your ex-fiancé."

"Has Justin been arrested?" she asked, the thought of him being in handcuffs and no longer able to bilk clients or pose a threat to her exhilarating.

"No—not yet, I'm afraid." Quincy paused and tightened the grip of his fingers around her hand. "But there's even more reason now why that's imperative…"

"What are you talking about?" Giselle demanded, sensing he was stalling whatever was on his mind but it had to be serious.

"Human remains belonging to a female were discovered a couple of days ago in a wooded area of Nobber's Hill, Virginia," Quincy told her. "The victim was identified as Jenna Sweeney, the waitress I told you about who disappeared four years ago. She'd been stabbed to death." He took a ragged breath. "A fingerprint found on the eyeglasses the victim was wearing when buried in a shallow grave belongs to Justin Buckner—"

Giselle swallowed unevenly in meeting Quincy's eyes. "Are you saying that Justin killed her…?"

"The police and FBI believe this to be the case," he answered straightforwardly. "Another warrant has been issued for Buckner's arrest—for murder!"

Her heart skipped a beat as a number of thoughts rolled through Giselle's mind. How could she have fallen for someone capable of murder? What signs had she missed, beyond the obvious, that could have warned her not to get involved with him?

But most importantly in the present sense, she wondered if Justin had stopped at the killing of Jenna Sweeney. Or had he targeted others as well?

Such as Sadie, Giselle thought with dread. "What if Justin is here in Alaska after all?" she posed to Quincy while thinking about the sightings she imagined of her ex in Taller's Creek. "And made good on his threats to me—by murdering Sadie…?"

"I thought of that," Quincy told her candidly. "More than once. But it's still a big leap from Buckner allegedly killing someone years ago to showing up in Alaska out of the blue to kill your friend as a way to get back at you. Not sure Buckner is capable or cold-blooded enough to pull it off—all while dodging the authorities on other fronts."

"I hope you're right." Giselle calmed down. The last thing she wanted was to believe that Justin had become a serial killer as part of his vendetta against her, whom he was saving for last. Not that she would ever underestimate his ability to be cruel and callous to anyone who got on his bad side to one degree or another.

Especially her.

If you even think about ever leaving me, Giselle, just know that you'll pay for it in ways you can't even imagine. I'll go after everyone you care about…or cares about you, even a little…one by one. Saving you for last.

Giselle forced herself to erase the frightening words from

her head. She was sure that Justin would be taken into custody at any time now to be held accountable for his growing list of crimes.

"You okay?" Quincy asked, breaking through her reverie.

"Yeah." She flashed a tiny smile.

He smiled back, looking relieved. "Good."

Just then, Giselle's cell phone buzzed. She removed it from the back pocket of her jeans. There was a text message from Seth Lombrozo, the architect whom she'd met through Yuki and Neve.

After reading it, Giselle regarded Quincy ill at ease and said with a catch to her voice, "A friend of mine, Jacinta Cruz, has gone missing—"

Chapter Thirteen

Hey, met a new guy named Jesse. Cool to hang out with. Wish me luck!

Quincy read the text again that Jacinta Cruz had sent Giselle two days earlier. *So, who the hell is this Jesse?* he wondered. And was this new guy she'd met the reason that Jacinta had been missing for a day, at least—after failing to show up at a production meeting? Without calling anyone she knew with an explanation?

Does this have anything to do with the murder of Sadie Pisano? Quincy asked himself as he peered at Giselle. She was understandably fearful for her friend's safety. And since the disappearance was apparently uncharacteristic for the documentary-film producer, Giselle had every reason to be concerned. With each passing hour that Jacinta Cruz failed to demonstrate that she was alive and well, it was becoming more likely she was either being held against her will or was the victim of foul play.

But rather than dwell on the obvious, which Quincy was certain that Giselle had pondered without his help, he said to her after they had gotten into his SUV, "Do you know anything else about Jesse?"

"Only what Jacinta said in the text," she responded and took a deep breath. "Do you think he abducted her...?"

"Possibly." He started the Ford Police Interceptor. "It's also possible that, for whatever reason, Jacinta lost track of time after telling you that she enjoyed hanging out with the man."

"I hope it's as simple as that," Giselle muttered nervously. "It's just so weird—and so unlike her—that Jacinta would leave everyone hanging as to what she's up to. Especially after what happened to Neve and Yuki—"

I'm sensing that too, Quincy told himself instinctively but said calmly, "Let's not go jumping to any conclusions just yet."

"I'm trying not to, but it isn't easy to look at the glass half full, especially when Jacinta's other friends are also worried about her," Giselle argued, wringing her hands from the passenger seat.

"When did you last actually talk to her?" he wondered.

"On Wednesday afternoon... We met for a drink at the Owl's Den bar on Ninth Street in Taller's Creek."

Quincy glanced at her. "Did anyone hit on her while you were there?"

Giselle thought about it and replied, "Not when I was with her." She paused. "But I left the bar while she was still there, talking to someone from work on her cell phone."

"So, it's possible that Jacinta could have met someone— this Jesse—there and one thing led to another... Including her disappearance."

"Yeah, I suppose." Giselle looked at him. "Maybe we should ask someone at the place, as it's not too far from here."

Quincy nodded. "I was just about to suggest the same thing." As the Taller's Creek PD had yet to officially request the assistance of the ABI in this situation, he saw no reason why she couldn't accompany him there. Especially if it led to finding her friend, safe and sound. He made a right turn at the light and headed toward the Owl's Den bar.

"THAT'S THE BARTENDER who served us," Giselle pointed out when they stepped inside the bar that was mostly empty.

"Let's see what he has to say," Quincy voiced.

They approached the fiftysomething burly man with a receding, slicked-back gray hairline ending in a short po-nytail. He was stacking bottles of beer behind the bar.

"Hi," the bartender said coolly when he looked their way.

After Quincy introduced himself as working for the ABI and flashed his identification, Giselle asked, "Remember me?"

"Sure." The bartender nodded. "You and the other pretty lady came in earlier this week for drinks."

"Right—Wednesday afternoon." Giselle offered him a soft smile. "After I left, do you happen to remember if my friend—her name is Jacinta—met with anyone else…?"

"Yeah," he answered firmly, without needing to give it some thought. "A dude who had been sitting at a table by himself came over and sat next to her. They struck up a conversation and may have left together—I'm not sure."

Giselle sighed and said sharply, "My friend is missing."

The bartender cocked a thick brow. "Really?"

"Yes, and we just need to find her," she stressed.

Quincy asked him evenly, "Can you describe the man?"

The bartender pondered this and replied, "He was white, bald, maybe in his thirties and looked to be in pretty good shape."

The person described didn't ring a bell to Giselle. Not that she would expect it to, if this was the same new guy that Jacinta had texted her about. "Did you happen to catch his name?" she asked.

The bartender shook his head. "Sorry."

"How about Jesse?" Quincy prodded.

"You know, come to think of it, that might have been the name he gave her," the bartender suggested after a moment or two.

"Do you have surveillance video I can take a look at for that day?" Quincy asked.

The bartender responded sourly, "We only keep it for twenty-four hours—meaning we no longer have video from Wednesday. Sorry."

Quincy bit back disappointment and muttered, "It was worth a try."

After they left the bar, Giselle told him, "That has to be the man Jacinta is with. Or at least was with…"

"I agree," Quincy said. "The only question is is she with him voluntarily or against her will?"

Or has he killed her? Giselle had to consider with dread while wondering as well if Jacinta's mysterious disappearance could have anything to do with Sadie's death.

Two HOURS LATER, Giselle had joined some of Jacinta's other friends on the Pippen Trail, after the documentary maker had reportedly been spotted there in the past twenty-four hours in the company of a bald-headed man.

Hey, met a new guy named Jesse. Cool to hang out with. Wish me luck!

Jacinta's text flashed in Giselle's mind as she contemplated whether the man had actually meant her harm and been deceptive in his ability to charm her friend into trusting him. Giselle couldn't help but think about once being in the same boat with Justin. At least she had survived to correct her huge error in judgment.

Could Jacinta say the same? Or had her fate already been sealed?

"This feels like déjà vu," Seth Lombrozo moaned as they searched for their missing friend through the boreal forest.

"That's what I'm afraid of," Giselle admitted. She looked sadly at Seth, who was a hulking man with a full head of dark hair and a Garibaldi beard. She thought about poor Neve and how it all had ended when her body had been discovered on the trail. Would Jacinta be next?

"Let's not jump to any premature conclusions," warned Kimberly Herrington, an up-and-coming local artist, who was petite and had red hair in a butterfly cut. "Just because Jacinta was hanging out on the trail doesn't mean she didn't go elsewhere, with or without someone accompanying her."

"Kimberly's right," Ethan Gladstone, a tall caterer with a blond fade mohawk, said. "We're all just freaking out over the worst-case scenario. She may be injured out here and unable to communicate but otherwise still very much alive."

"We have to believe that's the case," said kennel owner Pablo Wersching, who was long limbed with long brown hair parted in the middle. "Or maybe Jacinta is safe and sound, can explain where she's been and will have a good laugh at all the fuss about her."

Giselle smiled at the thought. "That would definitely be the best outcome for everyone."

"You can say that again," Kimberly uttered.

Giselle wanted desperately to believe that to be true. But she couldn't shake the notion that Jacinta was in danger— or worse—with this Jesse likely the root cause. Still, she remained hopeful as they continued to move through the rugged trail and said to the group, "Let's just see what the

search and rescue operation underway discovers—or not…
assuming we come up empty-handed—"

At this point, Giselle felt that was the best they could hope
for, while knowing that Quincy had been officially brought
on by the Taller's Creek Police Department to lend his expertise in trying to locate Jacinta, dead or alive.

"THEY DON'T pay us enough for this," complained Gabe
McAuliffe, the AST search and rescue coordinator at the
command center in the quest to locate Jacinta Cruz. It included search teams on the ground, by air and an Alaska
State Troopers K-9 unit.

"The pay is less important than the end result," Quincy
countered. "Finding missing persons alive is invaluable by
its very nature." Even if it didn't always work out that way,
he firmly believed that doing their jobs to achieve the best
possible results was payment enough.

Miriam Fontaine concurred. "Until there's clear evidence
of foul play here, we have to assume that Ms. Cruz is not
dead but maybe just injured or lost and waiting to be found.
To that end we issued a BOLO for the missing woman's
orange Toyota 4Runner, which may have gone off-road."

Gabe said equably, "As always, we'll keep at it till we
have some answers—one way or another."

Quincy hoped that should this turn out to be a disastrous outcome, Giselle would be able to get past it. He knew
that she had joined some of Jacinta's friends as volunteer
searchers, desperately wanting to find her safe and sound.
Under other circumstances, he would have been right beside
Giselle, holding her hand in a show of support. But he was
needed elsewhere and was sure she understood.

Miriam received information over the radio, drawing

Quincy's and Gabe's attention as she uttered, "They've found something…"

Gabe got the word from dispatch at the same time, in which they were told that an injured brown bear had been found just off the Pippen Trail—but no sign of Jacinta. "Keep searching," he ordered keenly.

Quincy found this news to be both a relief and disappointment and said, "She's out there somewhere. We'll find her…"

Miriam twisted her lips. "Well, we better make it sooner than later," she warned. "With dangerous wildlife like brown bears to contend with in the woods, along with human predators, if she's still alive, we have to get to her."

Gabe jutted his chin. "Maybe the volunteer searcher who helped lead us to Neve Chenoweth can work his magic again—if he's among the searchers—in tracking down Jacinta Cruz."

"So, who's this miracle worker?" Quincy asked him curiously.

"Just a guy who said he had a nose for this sort of thing and was able to point us in the right direction in finding Ms. Chenoweth," Gabe said. "Never caught his name."

Quincy was thoughtful as he asked, "What did he look like?"

Gabe contemplated this for a moment. "White, thirty-something, tall and fit, with short blond hair and blue eyes," he said as someone who was adept in attention to detail in his profession.

Taking mental notes, Quincy asked, "Did you ever see him after that?"

Gabe nodded. "As a matter of fact, I did. Saw him in town." He paused. "But he had changed his look."

"How so?" Miriam asked before Quincy could.

"He had shaved his head bald and allowed some hair to grow on his face." Gabe scratched his chin. "To tell you the truth, I almost didn't recognize him, were it not for the cold blue eyes that gave the man away."

Warning bells rang in Quincy's head like an alarm. Had the man in question led searchers to a body he'd known in advance had been on the trail, as if he had left Neve there to die?

Quincy considered that the bald-headed version of the volunteer searcher matched the man named Jesse who'd been hitting on Jacinta at the bar. Were they one and the same?

Equally disturbing was the thought that he could also have been the same man who'd had orange roses delivered to the bookstore. Which had happened to be where Sadie Pisano had worked part-time, before someone had murdered her.

Is there some symmetry here? Quincy asked himself, ill at ease. Were they looking at a killer—maybe a serial killer—in their midst? Masquerading as one of the good guys?

If so, Quincy feared that this didn't bode well for Jacinta's survival, wherever she was.

Chapter Fourteen

By Sunday afternoon, the official search for Jacinta Cruz on the Pippen Trail had been pared down after an alleged second sighting of the documentary-film producer in another location at a later point in the time line. Though still considered missing under suspicious circumstances, there was a lack of hard evidence to clearly indicate she was in harm's way.

Quincy believed otherwise, especially with the likelihood that the last person Jacinta had been seen with, a man named Jesse, was apparently the one who'd found Neve Chenoweth. And might have sent flowers to Taller's Creek Books, where Sadie Pisano, the murdered college student, had worked—with her killer still on the loose. Where did this leave Jacinta?

We need to find this Jesse—and interrogate him, Quincy thought while standing in his great room staring out the window. And find Jacinta, hopefully still alive, if she was being held by him against her will. He knew that Giselle was at work, if only to take her mind off her latest friend's disappearance—till news came of her whereabouts. Unfortunately, at this point, with each passing hour that they failed to locate Jacinta Cruz, Quincy recognized the greater the chance that she was no longer alive to reunite with those in her professional and personal circles.

When his cell phone buzzed, he lifted it from his pants pocket and saw that it was a call from his mother. That usually meant both parents were calling to check on him, as they were prone to do whenever they hadn't heard from him in a while. Unless one or the other had a problem to share that his sister was not privy to or kept to herself. He suspected that it was more likely that they wanted to see how things were progressing between him and Giselle. She'd left a most favorable impression on them, and he suspected that, in their minds, the next logical step was for him to marry her and give them more grandchildren to teach about the Eyak culture and more.

While he hadn't thought quite that far ahead, Quincy had thought far enough to know that he really had fallen for Giselle and wanted things to work between them in every way possible. But he needed to know she felt entirely the same way before he took things too far to the next level.

Answering the call, Quincy said sweetly, "Hey."

He had only gotten so far with a conversation that was as predictable and amusing as Quincy had imagined it would be, when he received a call from Daniel Malaterre, giving him an excuse to cut short the chat with his folks. He hoped that Justin Buckner had been taken into custody for one less headache for Giselle to have to deal with.

After accepting the video call, Quincy watched the FBI special agent in charge's strained face appear on the screen, indicating that it wasn't the news he sought, and asked him point blank, "What do you have for me…?"

"It's not good," Daniel said with an edge to his tone of voice, as he took a breath. "After digging through Justin Buckner's confiscated files, the Bureau has been able to ascertain that Buckner has been using an alias in his efforts to evade authorities."

"Which is...?" Quincy asked impatiently.

"He's been going by the name Jesse Teague—an identity Buckner stole from one of his clients, a forty-one-year-old investor who passed away from bone cancer earlier this year."

"*Jesse* Teague," Quincy voiced, emphasizing the first name, which happened to be the name of the suspect in the disappearance of Jacinta Cruz, along with more ominous possibilities. "The name definitely means something..."

As Quincy overcame the shock that Justin Buckner might have been using the moniker Jesse Teague to escape justice while hiding in plain view, Daniel said matter-of-factly, "I suspected it would. We've been able to backtrack his movements and establish that in using this fake identification of Jesse Teague, Buckner was able to book a flight a few weeks ago to Anchorage, Alaska. There's no record that he ever left the state by plane..."

"So he is here," Quincy muttered under his breath. Giselle's instincts about her ex-fiancé were right on target. And apparently his capabilities were as diabolical as she feared. Even worse, if that was possible. "A man who goes by the name Jesse is suspected in the abduction of a local documentary-film producer," he told Daniel. "And may have also committed at least one murder in Alaska, if not more than that. I have reason to believe Jesse Teague is Buckner's alter ego."

"Wow." Daniel knitted his brows. "If what you suspect about the man is true, coupled with being wanted for a cold-case murder in Virginia, then we have ourselves a bona fide serial killer. Not to mention Buckner's serious financial crimes..."

"Yeah, he's a real piece of work." Quincy snorted as he contemplated the disturbing situation that was playing out in real time before his eyes.

"I wish we'd been able to connect the dots sooner."

"Me too." Quincy felt that was a huge understatement, considering what Buckner had put Giselle through, then and now.

"But we only know what we know when we know it," Daniel offered.

Quincy twisted his lips begrudgingly. "That's the difficult part about this," he griped. "Not being able to put the pieces together regarding a stalker and psychopath beforehand in order to stop him before so much damage could be done to Giselle and Buckner's other victims."

"Now that we do have the bead on the murder suspect possibly hiding out in your neck of the woods, we need to take him down—before he can do more harm," Daniel argued, narrowing his eyes. "Toward that end, the Bureau has already reached out to my special agent in charge counterpart with the Anchorage field office, Bonnie Rawlings, to assist you guys in the ABI in capturing the fugitive financial planner."

"Okay," Quincy said, welcoming any assistance in apprehending Justin Buckner to face justice.

"Beyond that, the FBI Norfolk field office, based in Chesapeake, that's investigating Buckner's alleged white-collar crimes and the Chesapeake Police Department, after him for murder, have also been notified as players in the game."

"We're all on the same team here," Quincy stated. "With the same goal in mind."

"Yeah." Daniel titled his head. "Until Buckner's in custody, you might want to do whatever you need to do in protecting Giselle from her stalker."

Quincy nodded. "I intend to," he promised and ended the call. He immediately called Giselle, hating the thought that Buckner could be watching her at that very moment, fully intent on carrying out his threats. Or could the fugitive have cut his losses and left the state for parts unknown to try and save himself?

"Hey," Giselle said pleasantly when answering the phone.

At least she appears to be safe at the moment, Quincy told himself and then said equably, "Can you meet me at the Owl's Den when you get off work?"

"Of course." She paused. "What's up?"

"I'll tell you when you get there," he answered evasively, believing that it was best that they discuss this in person, while at the same time, putting together a plan to protect her from Buckner and his hostile intentions toward her.

"Uh, all right," she said simply, leaving it at that. "I'm off at five. See you shortly thereafter."

"Okay."

After ending that call, Quincy phoned Lieutenant Ron Valdez, his superior at the ABI Soldotna Major Crimes Unit, and apprised him of the alarming new twist in his investigation into the death of Sadie Pisano and disappearance of Jacinta Cruz. Quincy then called Sergeant Miriam Fontaine so the Taller's Creek PD was fully informed on where things stood in the cases that suddenly had Justin Buckner as the apparent common denominator.

THE MOMENT GISELLE entered the Owl's Den bar, she felt a chill in the air. Was it her imagination? Or was something going on that was about to rock her world over and beyond the strong presence of Quincy in her life?

She spotted him at the bar where Giselle had had cocktails with Jacinta before her friend had simply vanished without explanation or indication of where she was. With the search for her on the Pippen Trail suspended, more or less, Giselle could only wonder if reaching a dead end meant that Jacinta's disappearance would be swept under the rug. Or if this was something akin to the calm before the storm.

"Hey," Quincy greeted her, lifting from his stool.

"Hey." Giselle studied his undecipherable eyes tentatively as they both sat down.

"What would you like to drink?"

"A glass of white wine would be nice."

"White wine it is." He ordered this and a beer for himself from a slim thirtysomething female bartender with dark hair in a windswept bob.

After the drinks came, Giselle gazed at Quincy's face. Her first thought was that he had bad news to share about Jacinta. Had they found her—dead?

Cringing at the notion, Giselle asked uneasily, "So, why are we here...?" Instead of having drinks in a more intimate setting, such as her place or his. "What's happened?"

Quincy tasted his mug of beer first and then, regarding her squarely, responded, "Justin Buckner is very likely in Alaska—"

"What?" Her eyes widened. "He's here...?"

"Looks that way." Quincy's brow creased. "According to my FBI source, Buckner's been operating with a stolen identity." He sucked in a deep breath. "Jesse Teague."

Hey, met a new guy named Jesse. Cool to hang out with. Wish me luck!

As Jacinta's text replayed in her head, Giselle asked, "Are we talking about the same Jesse who may have kidnapped Jacinta—or worse...?"

"I think we have to assume that to be the case when you add it all up," Quincy told her lamentably. "Buckner stole the name from a dead client and was able to use his new identity to fly to Alaska from Virginia under the radar while covering his tracks in evading the authorities."

Giselle narrowed her eyes. "Are you saying that Justin's been here since…"

"He's apparently been stalking you in Taller's Creek for at least as long as you believed he was," Quincy told her straightforwardly.

"Unbelievable!" Her voice shook as Giselle mused about the warning bells that had been triggered from her earlier sightings of Justin, who was apparently intent on making good on his threats to psychologically victimize her as a prelude to coming after her directly.

Quincy drank more beer. "Buckner's menace goes much further than stalking you," he pointed out. "Not only is he the prime suspect in Jacinta Cruz's disappearance as Jesse, the last person she was seen with, but Buckner has to be considered a suspect in the murder of Sadie Pisano…and maybe others in your circle of friends—"

"What are you talking about?" Giselle demanded, taking a sip of the wine.

Quincy jutted his chin thoughtfully. "According to the coordinator for the search and rescue, a person who led them to Neve Chenoweth's body also matched the description of Jesse—suggesting that he may have known in advance where to find her."

Giselle peered at him. "Are you saying that Neve's death was no accident?"

He hedged, tasting the beer. "I'm saying it may need to be looked into further, along with Yuki Kotake's alleged suicide and, as I said, Sadie Pisano's death. Given that Buckner's been accused of murdering a woman in Virginia, among his other suspected offenses, it's really not too much of a stretch at this point to believe that as part of his warped fixation on you, Buckner may have killed more women..."

Giselle's shoulders slumped at the thought that she could have unknowingly, but still true nonetheless, been responsible for others losing their lives. How was she supposed to live with that? "I'm not sure what to say," she stammered sullenly. "Or what not to..."

"There's nothing for you to say that you haven't already said," Quincy told her. "None of what Buckner has done or may have done is your fault in any way, shape or form, to be clear. Bad things happen to good people all the time—no matter the dynamics that may have come into play—and it can't be prevented by trying to micromanage each and every aspect of our lives. It's not your job to read the mind of an unhinged, spiteful person you once knew. Whatever crimes Buckner has committed, it's all on him. Not you."

Giselle sipped the wine, acquiescing to this reality, no matter how much she wanted to take responsibility, after being on the run from Justin for three years and counting. "So, what now?" she wondered.

"We wait it out till Buckner's in custody. Now that the cat's out of the bag as to his likely whereabouts, law enforcement personnel from multiple jurisdictions are coming after him, hot and heavy," Quincy voiced sharply. "That old adage *He can run, but he can't hide* will bear out. Buckner will have to answer for any crimes he has committed."

"I sure hope so." Giselle sighed. "Not sure how much more of this—him—I can take, honestly."

Quincy touched her shoulder. "You won't have to take anything else he cares to dish out. But in the meantime, I'd like to stay at your place tonight—in case Buckner is stupid enough to show his face and come after you before we haul him off to jail."

Giselle nodded, placing her hand on his. "Yes, I'd like that," she told him. The thought of being alone and possibly forced to confront the man who had made her life so miserable three years ago was enough to make her nauseous. Having Quincy there to protect her and be the man she had come to depend on as a romantic partner and friend was more than she could hope for at this stage of her journey through life.

"Good." Quincy finished off his drink and rose. "Let's go."

"All right."

Sipping a bit more of the wine, Giselle gave him a brief smile, trying her best to block out for now what she'd just learned about her ex, and then stood to accompany Quincy to her apartment.

AFTER FOLLOWING HER HOME, still worried about Justin Buckner being on the loose, Quincy took some solace in the knowledge that they had the murder and kidnapping suspect at a disadvantage. Buckner had no idea that they had pinned down his likely whereabouts and were in full pursuit, no matter what his warped mind had planned for Giselle. As for Jacinta Cruz, Quincy could only hope that it wasn't too late to rescue her from wherever Buckner probably had her stashed away. That was assuming she hadn't already been disposed of by the creep and buried somewhere in the vast Alaska wilderness.

So long as no body has materialized, I can't assume Jacinta is dead, Quincy told himself as he pulled into the parking lot behind Giselle's Honda. But they needed to find her, one way or the other. That notwithstanding, his current focus was on making sure that Giselle—the woman he was planning a future with—wasn't the next person to disappear. If this was truly Buckner's end game, it was incumbent upon Quincy, the ABI, FBI, Taller's Creek PD and other law enforcement with a vested interest to make sure the wanted man failed to achieve his objectives and answered for everything he had done.

After exiting his vehicle, Quincy walked over to Giselle and held her hand supportively, both remaining silent. Welcoming the opportunity to spend the night with her any chance he got, his primary reason this time around was to act as a shield between her and Justin Buckner—now that it appeared that, as Jesse Teague, the stalker and murder suspect was intent on waging a vindictive campaign against Giselle that likely would end in her death.

When they got to the door of her apartment, Quincy could tell right away that something was off. There were clear signs of forced entry. Meaning that whoever broke in could very well still be inside. And dangerous.

"Wait here!" Quincy ordered as he released Giselle's hand and removed his duty weapon from inside a hip holster.

Her eyes widened with consternation. "Do you think it's Justin…?"

"There's only one way to find out." Quincy met her gaze. "If anything goes wrong in there, get the hell away from here!"

Giselle nodded reluctantly and uttered, "Please be careful—"

"I will," he promised and slowly pushed open the door, and stepped inside with his Glock 22 leading the way.

Ready to shoot anyone who caught his eye and was threatening, Quincy cautiously made his way through the apartment, checking every nook and cranny. He half expected to find the place ransacked, perhaps out of frustration that Giselle wasn't there for Buckner to abduct. Or finish off, once and for all.

Instead, there seemed little indication, beyond the front door being forced open, that anything was out of the ordinary in the neat way Giselle kept her residence. But where was Muffin? Had the intruder taken the kitten as a souvenir? Or as a warning to Giselle for what was to come?

When Quincy got to the bedroom, he saw the kitten in a corner. It was lying there unmoving, as if asleep. But the unnatural positioning concerned him. As did the half-filled bowl of water nearby that she had obviously drunk from. What was in it?

As he approached, Quincy heard a shuffling noise behind him and whipped around to find Giselle standing there.

She batted her eyes and explained, "When you didn't come out, I had to know that you were okay."

Even if he wished she had stayed outside and potentially out of harm's way, Quincy could hardly fault Giselle for considering his own safety. "I am," he said tonelessly, knowing that the intruder had come and gone and thereby was no longer a threat. "But I fear that isn't the case for—"

Before he could finish, Giselle had pushed past Quincy and raced toward her kitten, while screaming her name in panic mode, "Muffin!"

At that point, Quincy could only assume the worst. Her beloved little kitten was dead.

Chapter Fifteen

Giselle stood on pins and needles in the reception area at Soldotna Animal Hospital on Sterling Highway, where they had rushed Muffin as soon as they'd established that the kitten was still alive, though unconscious.

"She has to be okay," Giselle cried, believing that whatever had happened to the kitten—who had vomited and had diarrhea before passing out—was likely the result of something in the water she had drunk. It coincided with the intruder breaking into her apartment. She was all but certain that it had been her deranged ex, Justin, sending her a clear message: *First your acquaintances, then your kitten and finally I'm coming to get you*, Giselle envisioned Justin saying menacingly inside her head. "Muffin looked so fragile," she moaned.

Quincy pulled Giselle into his muscular arms comfortingly and said, "Let's just wait and see what the vet has to say, and hope for the best." He breathed warmly onto her cheek. "The fact that Muffin's alive and we were able to get her here has to be a good sign," he asserted.

"I hope you're right." Giselle sniffled and dried her tears on his shirt. "I just can't imagine my life without that adorable little one." At the same time, she did find herself imagining a life with Quincy, whom Giselle found herself growing closer to with each passing day. Even in the face of the danger that Justin posed to both of them as long as he remained on the loose in and around Taller's Creek.

"Then don't," Quincy told her insistently, "until it's been determined otherwise."

Just then, they saw the veterinarian enter the room, getting their attention. Giselle pulled away from Quincy and, with her heart pounding, asked the thirtysomething vet nervously, "What happened to my kitten?"

Doctor Lynette Suzuki—who was slender and wearing a white lab coat, with brunette hair in a midi flick cut—touched her square eyeglasses and responded reticently, "I hate to say this, but I'm afraid she was poisoned."

Giselle tried to come to terms with what she had strongly suspected already as Quincy asked, "What type of poison?"

"She ingested phorate, which is a pesticide that's usually found in organophosphorus insecticides," Lynette explained. "I'm guessing that this wasn't accidental—"

"Very unlikely," Quincy said flatly. "Pretty sure this was a deliberate act!"

"Sorry to hear that." The vet frowned. "Hope you figure out who's behind it…"

"I think we already have," he muttered with an edge to his inflection, glancing at Giselle and back before asking, "So, what's the prognosis?"

"Will Muffin live?" Giselle followed anxiously, eyeing the vet.

Lynette took a breath and then smiled. "Yes, your kitten will live. Fortunately it doesn't appear as though she ingested too much of it—as cats and kittens are sensitive to unusual tastes and are quick to reject them—but enough to cause her to vomit, have diarrhea and likely struggle to walk before eventually losing consciousness. This was potentially life threatening," she admitted, "had you not acted quickly in bringing her here…"

Giselle breathed in a huge sigh of relief. "So, Muffin will make a full recovery?"

"I don't see why not." Lynette flashed her teeth. "The anti-seizure medication we gave her, along with supplemental oxygen and IV fluids, have done their job in overcoming the poisoning. We'd like to keep Muffin for a day or two to monitor her recovery. After that, you should be able to take her home and give her all the loving attention she needs to be back to herself in no time."

"Thank you so much, Dr. Suzuki," Giselle gushed gratefully.

Lynette smiled. "Happy to do my part to get your cute little kitten up on her feet again."

"We'll be sure to do our part to make that happen," Quincy assured her, which warmed Giselle's heart in telling her that he was starting to truly see them as united in their relationship. Which included Muffin and Quincy's family.

On the way back to her apartment, Giselle looked at him from the passenger seat of his car as she considered the near miss with Muffin and Justin, the most likely perpetrator of the poisoning and still at large, and asked, ill at ease, "What now?"

Quincy turned her way and responded, "We grab some of your things and you stay at my house—where you'll be safe, and so will Muffin when she's released—till we can get Buckner in custody."

"All right." Giselle was not about to be defiant in any way in resisting Quincy's take-charge offer to provide her with the security of his home while Justin was gunning for her. "Is it possible that someone other than Justin broke into my apartment?" she had to ask, knowing that there had been some occasional burglaries in the area. Usually with local teens, looking for cash for drugs, as the culprits. Even in pondering this, Giselle wasn't about to give her vengeful ex-fiancé stalker the benefit of the doubt, knowing he was apparently in Alaska, operating as Jesse.

"Possible, yes—probable, no," Quincy told her, gazing over the steering wheel. "Buckner, fixated on you and still thinking he's kept you in the dark as to his presence, had the most to gain by poisoning Muffin and leaving you guess-ing…"

"Figured as much," Giselle admitted perceptively.

"With any luck, the Crime Scene Unit will find his prints or DNA inside your apartment." Quincy pulled into the lot. "Short of that, we still know that he's after you. Buckner isn't likely to stop his harassment—including possibly using Jacinta as bait, if she's still alive—in order to do what he's set out to do."

"Which is to punish me for daring to leave him," she ut-tered painfully.

"Yes, but I'm not about to allow that to happen," Quincy promised. "Whatever damage Buckner's already put into play, he won't hurt you directly, Giselle. Beyond what you've already experienced in your past involvement with the fu-gitive. Now, let's go get your things…"

She nodded and contemplated the lengths to which Jus-tin had apparently already gone in following through on his promises, as Giselle wondered if she would still be able to win the battle against a determined foe before he could be arrested and put away for the rest of his miserable life.

GISELLE AGAIN RAN *for her life, sure that to do anything less would result in her demise. Justin was intent upon making sure she didn't have one more second to cherish, much less hours, days, weeks or years. So determined was he to have her at all costs as his to control like his personal sex slave and trophy wife. Or see to it that she paid a heavy price that there was simply no walking back from.*

But it was a place that she was unwilling to go. Not by a long shot. He couldn't have her. No matter his wishes to the contrary. She deserved so much better in a man. In a husband. In a solid and sustainable relationship. In the great love of her life and times, and father of her children. Much more than a person so distasteful and obsessed with molding her into someone and something she wasn't. She would rather die a thousand times than succumb to his irrational demands. No matter the personal sacrifices she would have to make.

Sucking in a deep, ragged breath, Giselle ran up the quarter-turn staircase in the waterfront mansion to the second story, the determined attacker in hot pursuit like a man possessed. If she could just get to the primary suite and lock the door behind her, maybe she could survive the ordeal by phoning Quincy to come to her rescue. Only then could she ever hope to have a normal life, with a normal and loving man to give her love to in return.

Racing in her bare feet across the hardwood flooring in the long hallway, Giselle nearly tripped but corrected herself from falling. But even losing half a step shortened the distance between her and the man who wanted her dead, whatever it took. Still, she forged ahead, reaching the room she'd once shared with her stalker, but seeing it now as nothing more than a prison for which there was no escape.

Once inside, Giselle barely had a chance to take in the expensive Italian furniture, some of which she had chosen herself, while simultaneously attempting to slam the door shut before he could stop her—when Justin was able to do just that.

Using his superior strength, he forced the door open, knocking her to the floor in the process. Scrambling to her feet, she ran toward the king-size bed, hoping to somehow get to the other side and maybe step onto the balcony for some kind of escape. Instead, he caught up to her, grabbed her by the hair and threw her down hard onto the dark blue comforter.

Before Giselle could even breathe, Justin had climbed on top of her, where he pulled the phorate poison out of his pocket and forced it down her throat; then as she was choking, he placed his large hands around her neck, his face contorted with fury like a demon. She tried to fight him off, to no avail, as she felt her strength fading fast—along with whatever life she had left.

He was strangling and poisoning her to death. And there was nothing she could do about it. Other than accept her fate. And pray that the end came quickly.

Giselle looked into the evil eyes of death. Glaring back at her was Justin.

She tried to scratch his face, wipe the wicked grin of pleasure off it—but he kept just out of reach of her flailing hands and fingernails. Before she could breathe her last breath, Giselle managed to squeeze from her mouth that she detested him with a passion—to which he seemed to draw upon in his contorted face and sick satisfaction in achieving his ultimate objective of taking her life.

GISELLE SHRIEKED AS she sought to fight off her attacker. He seemed relentless in his determination to make her pay for depriving him of his desire to possess her.

A deep and familiar voice began to cut through the dense

fog of sleep as she heard the gentle tone say, "Wake up, Giselle. It's only a dream—" Her eyelids flew open, and adjusting to the low light, she stared into the face of Quincy.

"Quincy..." Giselle's mouth was dry, but she had broken out into a cold sweat.

"I've got you," he said softly, cradling her protectively in his arms.

"Dream...?"

"Actually, a nightmare." He kissed the top of her head. "It's over. You're safe now," he promised.

"I feel safe—with you," Giselle told him as she wept. "Justin was trying to kill me with poison and his large hands," she said, taking a deep breath. "It seemed so real."

"It wasn't." Quincy held her closer. "Just some bad memories manifesting themselves in your head. I won't let him hurt you anymore," he promised, making Giselle believe every word as she clung to Quincy for the rest of the night.

QUINCY WAS UP bright and early the next morning, allowing Giselle to get some extra sleep after a restless night, while he made breakfast. He hated that Justin Buckner had succeeded on some level in getting under her skin through both dreams and his mere presence in Alaska. The sooner they could find the murder suspect and white-collar offender, the sooner Quincy could give Giselle back her sense of security, health and well-being.

He was standing over the electric griddle when Giselle walked into the kitchen. She looked sleepy eyed and was wearing one of his shirts while barefoot.

She said softly, "Good morning."

"Good morning." Quincy saw that her hair was a bit tangled from the pillow, but it was a turn-on nonetheless, like the rest of the package she presented.

"Just grabbed the first piece of clothing I could find," she claimed in explaining the shirt.

"No problem." He grinned. "The shirt looks much better on you than me," he assured her.

She colored self-consciously. "If you say so."

"Hungry?"

"I'm starving," she answered.

"Good." Quincy turned to the griddle and back. "I'm making omelets with shredded cheese, diced ham and sautéed bell peppers."

Giselle smiled. "Sounds delicious."

"Wait till you taste it," he bragged. "Made coffee. Help yourself."

"I will—thanks." She moved closer and met his eyes thoughtfully. "Look, about last night…"

Quincy held her gaze, cutting in to say, "No explanation necessary. After what you were slammed with yesterday… it was a lot to absorb for anyone given the same dynamics—it's quite understandable that it would seep into your dreams as a nightmare."

"Thanks for helping me get through it," she murmured tenderly.

"I was happy to come to your aid—and will gladly do so anytime I'm around." If he had a serious say in the matter, Quincy wanted that to be often. "Time to eat," he told her and flipped her omelet onto a plate.

A few minutes later, they were sitting on a sofa bench at the midcentury-modern wooden table in the eating nook having breakfast when Giselle grimaced and said thoughtfully, "Do you think that Justin has Jacinta? Or is she…?"

"We'll keep hope alive—and Jacinta too," Quincy responded calmly, "until there's solid proof that she's a victim of foul play. In the meantime, we're doing everything we can to find her."

"Okay." Giselle lifted her coffee mug and took a sip contemplatively.

Quincy waited a beat and then threw out casually, but in all seriousness, after tasting his own coffee, "I was thinking that maybe you should take off work for a day or two—till we can locate and bring in Buckner. If he did break into your apartment, besides knowing where you live—he likely also knows you work at Taller's Creek Books and could come after you there…"

"I was thinking the same thing," Giselle responded without hesitation while eating. "Since chances are that it was Justin who sent the orange roses after all, there's no reason to tempt fate. Or put the lives of my colleagues at the bookstore in any further jeopardy."

Quincy nodded, in complete agreement. "Exactly." He sliced a fork into his omelet. "Beyond that, although I have a good security system, to be on the safe side, I'll arrange with the Taller's Creek Police Department to have patrols in this area to keep an eye out for Buckner and any signs of trouble…"

"Good idea." She offered him a tepid smile. "I appreciate everything you've done for me."

"Haven't really done much," he argued, downplaying it. "But I hope to have the opportunity to give you everything you deserve in life."

Her eyes grew. "Seriously?"

"Yeah, seriously." Quincy saw no reason to pull back from the way he felt about her and wanting this to become more of a permanent thing. "We have something really good here, and I want to keep it going."

Giselle gazed at him. "Me too," she uttered in earnest and

paused. "Once Justin is finally out of the picture for good, we can definitely work on that."

Quincy nodded in full agreement and started to imagine just what their lives could be like together—once the bogeyman had been removed from the equation once and for all.

Chapter Sixteen

On Monday, Quincy huddled with the ABI's Major Crimes Unit in Soldotna, along with FBI officials and law enforcement from Taller's Creek and Chesapeake, as they assessed the situation in the search for wanted fugitive and murder suspect Justin Buckner and as yet still missing and presumed to have been abducted Jacinta Cruz.

In Quincy's mind, Justin—masquerading as his late client Jesse Teague—almost certainly was still holding Jacinta somewhere in the Kenai Peninsula Borough, as a thorough search for the documentary-film producer had come up empty. There was no evidence to indicate whether she was dead or alive, much less being held against her will, though this was in all likelihood probably the case.

But this doesn't mean Buckner hasn't killed and buried her—or left her to die, Quincy thought realistically as he stood in front of the conference room and considered the case against Justin Buckner that was growing stronger as the evidence started to come in.

That included DNA that had been collected from Giselle's apartment. When entered into the FBI's CODIS database, the DNA profile matched that of Justin Buckner's on file, indicating that, at the very least, he had been inside her place (putting him in Taller's Creek in and of itself) and almost certainly was responsible for poisoning Muffin.

Just as damning was a fingerprint found by the Crime Scene Unit at the residence of Yuki Kotake. The Bureau's Integrated Automated Fingerprint Identification System got a hit on it, identifying the print as belonging to Buckner— leaving no doubt that he had been at her cabin at some point and could have made it appear as though Yuki had taken her own life with a firearm. Moreover, the toxicology test on Yuki surprisingly had found no drugs or alcohol in her system, which was inconsistent to Quincy, given her history of depression and using antidepressants as a means to control it—both of which were common correlates in cases of suicide. This called into question whether or not her death had been self-inflicted or cold-blooded murder by someone with an axe to grind.

Likewise, Sadie Pisano's drugging and murder, as someone who'd worked at the same bookstore as Giselle, with the orange roses sent there by an anonymous person, might have been a tip-off or forerunner to Sadie's death when the events were broken down. Quincy felt this had Buckner's fingerprints written all over it with what he now knew about the fixated and atrocious ex of Giselle.

Then there'd been someone fitting the suspect's description seen at both the Pippen Trail, where Neve Chenoweth had supposedly died accidentally, and at her candlelight vigil. Quincy would bet a month's salary that they were one and the same person: Justin Buckner. And that, all things considered, Neve's death might not have been an accident as they'd first thought.

Quincy told the group bluntly, "There's every reason to believe that Justin Buckner, using the alias Jesse Teague, is not only in Alaska right now but has very likely perpetrated a number of serious offenses in the state while evading authorities elsewhere—including at least one murder, if not more, and the kidnapping of Jacinta Cruz. Along with poisoning a precious little kitten that belongs to Giselle Kinard, the object of Buckner's misguided and unhinged affections," Quincy had to say, knowing just how beloved Muffin was by Giselle, whom she was back with now, nursing the kitten to full health. His brows drew together as he said pointedly, "I think it's safe to say that Buckner has to be considered armed and extremely dangerous—and needs to be located fast and taken into custody, as he's clearly a loose and somewhat unpredictable cannon."

Lieutenant Ron Valdez chimed in, standing beside him and stating, "I've directed Alaska State Troopers to work hand in hand with other law enforcement to track down the fugitive. Buckner has a lot of places he can hide in our vast and circuitous wilderness, but we have a much better grip on our neck of the woods than he does. That gives us an advantage that he can't hope to match as he tries to evade the law while committing other crimes in Alaska." Valdez wrinkled his brow. "Trying to get to the missing Jacinta Cruz before it's too late is of the utmost importance if we're to find her still alive. We know what Buckner is capable of as a murder suspect in both Alaska and Virginia. As Quincy Lankard has pointed out, time is of the essence in Buckner's capture."

To add to the arrows pointing at the suspect, Sergeant Miriam Fontaine revealed that surveillance video obtained from a neighbor of Sadie Pisano's at Creeklin Apartments showed someone who fit Justin Buckner's current description running away from the building the day the Kenai Peninsula College student had been killed.

When Quincy put this together with other Buckner sightings relative to Giselle's environment, along with more than enough other direct and circumstantial evidence, it seemed to all but clinch that they had the right suspect in their crosshairs in the bathtub murder of Sadie. Which then tied in with other criminal behavior alleged by the suspect in and around Taller's Creek. That included the stalking of Giselle, with the targeting of Muffin a clear reflection of that.

FBI Anchorage Special Agent Leigh McCormick weighed in on the investigation. The thirtysomething, slender African American woman with a raven midlength Afro parted in the middle said authoritatively, "Based on what we have to work with, Justin Buckner, aka Jesse Teague, is not only a wanted white-collar offender—he has morphed into a serial killer. He's suspected in the cold-case homicide of Jenna Sweeney and the much more recent murder of Sadie Pisano, at the very least." Leigh gave a sigh. "Apparently Buckner's homicidal and predatory tendencies are fueled, in part, by a pathological desire to control those he's obsessed with. Such as the case of Ms. Sweeney and, apparently, his long-term obsession with Giselle Kinard—and the retaliatory violence to follow. Some of those targeted by the suspect are most likely incidental victims, as a calculated means to an end. Such as the apparent abduction of Jacinta Cruz. Unless she's found soon, we can only assume that Buckner will want to dispose of her as a hindrance so that he can refocus on the one he's really after—"

Giselle, Quincy told himself before the pretty special agent could finish her insightful and ominous thoughts. It caused the hairs to rise on the back of his neck, aware that with each passing moment that Buckner remained on the loose, he posed a greater danger to Giselle. Though knowing she was safe at his house—with police keeping an eye on the property and otherwise patrolling the greater area—

gave Quincy some comfort, it was hardly enough to want to take his foot off the gas. Not until the threat the murder suspect presented was completely eliminated.

GISELLE SAT ON a cushioned barnwood sectional in the great room playing with Muffin, who was pretty much back to herself, thankfully. The fact that Quincy had welcomed them into his house made things even better. She loved being there and felt right at home, imagining that was the case. Apparently Muffin did as well, as she flew out of Giselle's arms and scurried across the floor and out of sight.

Now, if only Jacinta can be found unharmed and Justin apprehended, it will put my mind at ease on that major front, Giselle told herself as she grabbed her mug of black coffee from the end table and took a sip. She figured that with the authorities hot on his trail, it wouldn't be long before his days of hurting others were over. Then she could breathe again and see just what her life might be like without the specter of her ex looming in the shadows.

When her cell phone rang, Giselle saw that the caller was Ellen Ebsen. She wondered if there was a problem at the bookstore. Or maybe another delivery of orange roses.

"Hey," Giselle answered hesitantly.

"Hey," Ellen said. "I was trying to find a book that appears to be misplaced and hoped you could help."

"I can try…"

After a moment or two, Ellen uttered, "Actually, I just wanted to check on you."

"Really?" Giselle pushed the phone closer to her ear.

"Yeah. With all this business about a killer at large—someone from your past—we all wanted to know that you're okay, along with your kitten…"

"We're both fine," Giselle promised, still feeling guilty

that she had inadvertently brought Justin and his unwanted drama into all of their lives. "Wish I could be there, but with everything that's happened—"

"No one's blaming you for being stalked by a crazy ex-boyfriend," Ellen insisted. "Many of us have been down that road in one form or another—sometimes with tragic results. Thank goodness your situation is currently being dealt with appropriately by the authorities."

"I agree," Giselle told her, "and I appreciate the support."

"Hope to see you back at work soon," she said.

"You will."

Even as she said this, Giselle could only wonder if this was a sign that she needed to get back to what she loved most as a dancer. She hung up and took another sip of the coffee, pondering her life up to this point and where she needed to go from here—and who with.

AFTER PINGS FROM Jacinta's cell phone showed that her last call had been made by a cell tower in the Kenai Peninsula Borough, around Angler Drive, near Kenai Spur Highway, the ABI and other law enforcement agencies put their focus on the wooded area that had a number of farmhouses spread out amid the western hemlock and white spruce trees.

Quincy drove his Ford Police Interceptor Utility SUV into the borough with fellow ABI investigator Alan Edmonston in the passenger seat, hoping to catch a break in trying to locate the missing documentary-film producer.

Beyond that, Quincy needed to put an end to Justin Buckner's reign of terror in Alaska—much of which appeared to be driven by a personal vendetta against Giselle—and elsewhere. But first they had to pinpoint exactly where the fugitive's base of operation was in a region that, even when narrowed in scope, still left Buckner with breathing room to lay low.

"Sorry that Giselle Kinard has been swept up in the entanglement with Buckner," Alan remarked, breaking the silence between them.

"Me too," Quincy said regretfully. He had mentioned earlier that they were involved. "She wanted nothing to do with him—but evidently he didn't seem to get the message. Or actually, Buckner got it loud and clear but chose to reject it like others unnaturally fixated on someone they couldn't possess."

"She did the right thing to get away from Buckner," Alan said supportively. "The fact that he wouldn't leave well enough alone and has come after her doesn't change that."

"True." Quincy stared through the windshield. "We just need to get to him first."

"Yeah." Alan took a breath. "So, is it serious between you two?"

Not needing to even think about the question, Quincy was able to answer straightforwardly, "Yes, it's serious." That was certainly the case from his perspective. He was sure that Giselle felt the same way.

"Glad to hear that. I know I talked about not rushing things, but when you know, you know," he argued, "and you just have to jump in with both feet like I did so many years ago and am better for it."

"That you are." Quincy grinned at him and felt the pressure of hoping to measure up to a lifetime of wedded bliss. He felt more than up to the challenge should he and Giselle manage to get there. "We'll see how it goes." Once they no longer had the albatross of Justin Buckner weighing them down like an anchor.

The conversation was cut short when a call came in from

Lieutenant Valdez, informing them that a small DPS drone had managed to cut through the trees and spot an orange Toyota 4Runner behind a farmhouse on Angler Drive. A run on the license plate showed that it was registered to Jacinta Cruz.

"We discovered that the farmhouse itself is owned by a Harold Tanoue," Valdez said over the speakerphone. "He's been renting out the place to—you guessed it—Jesse Teague, Justin Buckner's stolen moniker. There's no outward sign on the property of Buckner or his presumed abductee, Ms. Cruz, but we can't get a good fix on the interior of the residence," the lieutenant said. "We've got a SWAT team, Special Emergency Reaction Team, K-9 unit and personnel from the Alaska Fugitive Task Force en route."

Believing that Buckner and Jacinta could well be holed up inside the farmhouse, with her life hanging in the balance, Quincy got the address, then told him, "We'll meet them there." He headed that way, putting on the speed, knowing there were no seconds to spare.

After arriving at the location, Quincy parked just out of view from the farmhouse while surveying the place through binoculars. There were blinds on the windows, effectively keeping anyone from seeing inside.

"What do you think?" Alan asked. "They in there?"

"Maybe." Quincy eyed the property and saw, as the drone's aerial surveillance had indicated, no other vehicle besides Jacinta's 4Runner. It led him to believe that, given the location, Buckner would most likely need his own vehicle to get around in. "Or maybe not," he told the trooper. "Let's check it out."

"Shouldn't we wait for backup?"

"Probably," Quincy reasoned but rejected this. "If Buckner is inside, catching him off guard might be the better way to go. Especially if we can rescue his captive at the same time."

Alan contemplated this for a long moment before relenting. "Okay, let's do it."

They left the SUV wearing ballistic vests, removed their Glock 22s from holsters and slowly made their way into the woods and approached the farmhouse. Hearing only the sounds of red-flanked bluetail birds chirping overhead, Quincy signaled to Alan to go around the back, while he would charge in the front door.

Nodding, Alan separated from him, and Quincy gave him time to get in place before moving quickly himself toward the house. Feeling it was now or never, he chose *now* and quietly turned the doorknob of the wooden door, and it opened.

As he was moving inside, ready to confront the suspect, instead Quincy saw Alan rush in from the rear. At first glance, they saw nothing unusual in the sparsely furnished open-concept interior space with worn hardwood flooring.

It was only after he'd made his way to the primary bedroom that Quincy homed in on the female lying on the floor next to an unmade wooden farmhouse bed. He recognized the slender, blond-haired Hispanic woman as Jacinta Cruz. She was naked and surrounded by her own blood. Several puncture marks on her body told him that she had been stabbed. As did the defensive wounds on the victim's arms.

Rushing to her as he called out to Alan, Quincy felt for a pulse in Jacinta's neck and realized that, though seriously injured and unconscious, the documentary filmmaker and Giselle's friend was still alive.

"Call 911!" he ordered as Alan stepped into the room.

As they hoped to save Jacinta's life—while other law enforcement personnel arrived at the house in full force—

her presumed attacker, Justin Buckner, was nowhere to be found, giving Quincy more reason for concern.

JUSTIN WATCHED FURTIVELY from the woods as a patrol car drove by the trooper's house where Giselle was hiding out. He had sent her a message when poisoning her kitten, knowing it would freak her out. Also, this made it clear that he could get to her whenever or wherever he wanted. Even though he doubted she was aware that it was her ex-fiancé who was behind the kitten crisis. Or, for that matter, the ordeals he'd put some others in her new life through.

That included Jacinta Cruz, whom he'd stabbed and left to die.

Not to mention what he'd done to Neve Chenoweth.

Yuki Kotake.

Sadie Pisano.

And all right under Giselle's dainty little nose.

It was merely a prelude of what Justin knew he wanted to do to her—his ex-fiancée who had dared to walk out on him and the relationship in marriage that Giselle had promised him.

Soon, very soon, she would experience in real time the same thing that Jenna Sweeney had made him to do her.

Only then would he be free at last of the rage that had built up inside him like volcanic gases, that powered this need—in fact, requirement—for an eruption of revenge against the one who had betrayed him.

Justin sucked in a deep breath and thought briefly about needing to escape Alaska afterward, with the feds and others intent upon taking him down. He hoped to stay a few steps ahead of them at every turn. Something he had done well his entire life, to one extent or another.

But at the moment, it was Giselle whom he was most focused on. He couldn't wait to see the frightened expression on her lovely face when they were eye to eye. And she was, once again, under his control.

Before he made sure her life had been cut much shorter than she ever envisioned, once upon a time.

Justin regarded the house once more, imagining what Giselle might be doing inside and wishing he were there with her right now, before forcing himself to vacate the scene as another patrol car approached as a deterrence.

Only for the time being.

Chapter Seventeen

Giselle rushed in her car to Central Peninsula Hospital after learning from Quincy that Jacinta had been airlifted there, in serious condition after being stabbed—and was in the emergency department, fighting for her life. The fact that they had found her friend alive at all was, to Giselle, a true miracle, given Jacinta's apparent abduction by Justin posing as Jesse—and his established penchant for harming women who came into his crosshairs.

But that didn't quell her feeling of being ill at ease for what Jacinta had been put through by him as she tried to come out on the other end in surviving. Or the knowledge that Justin had managed to evade capture and was, as such, still on the loose.

He couldn't have gotten very far, Giselle told herself as she reached the hospital. Surely the authorities had to be closing in on him to take him into custody before Justin was able to inflict more damage on those he chose to.

She parked and raced inside the hospital.

Quincy greeted Giselle in the lobby of the emergency department. "Hey," he muttered lowly, giving her a quick hug.

She gazed up at him and asked diffidently, "Any word on Jacinta's condition?"

"Not yet." He frowned beneath his campaign hat. "She's still in surgery."

Giselle's eyes watered. "I can't believe Justin did this to her…" In reality, she knew exactly what he was capable of—forcing her to run away from him as far as she could get. Only for him to track her down and go after people she knew. She wiped her eyes. "He can't get away with this."

"He won't," promised Quincy in a stern tone of voice. "We're scouring the borough for the black Kia Telluride we believe Buckner is driving, as well as any sign of the fugitive. It's only a matter of time before this ends—one way or another."

"I'll believe it when I see it," Giselle muttered with misgivings—fearful that based on his unsettling history of eluding the authorities, Justin would find some way, somehow, to escape the dragnet for his capture. But she also knew how determined Quincy was to bring him in and let the various jurisdictions fight each other for justice in the multiple allegations against Justin. Her tone was softer when Giselle uttered confidently, "I know you'll get him."

Quincy nodded understandingly and looked over her shoulder. "Your friends are here," he said evenly.

Giselle turned to see Seth, Kimberly, Ethan, Pablo and some other friends of Jacinta. All looked terribly distressed, and it made Giselle want to cry again. She embraced them in a group hug, and they all waited with bated breath to learn the fate of the documentary filmmaker.

When the surgeon came into the waiting room, Giselle found herself clutching Quincy's muscular arm in anticipation of the news on Jacinta.

"I'm Doctor Peggy Itamura," she said equably.

Giselle met the large brown eyes of the doctor in her late thirties, who was small boned beneath bloodied scrubs and had black hair in a razor cut, and asked her what everyone wanted to know, "Is Jacinta going to pull through?"

Dr. Itamura sighed and answered evasively, "Ms. Cruz was stabbed multiple times and sustained some serious injuries, including a collapsed lung, along with losing a lot of blood. The surgery went well—better than expected—but it's still touch and go at this point." She took a breath. "The next twenty-four hours will be crucial for her survival. If all goes well, she stands a good chance to make a full recovery. Let's keep our fingers crossed…"

"Definitely," Giselle assured her, feeling this was the best any of them could have hoped for, given the grave manner in which Justin left Jacinta to die. Knowing her friend was a fighter, Giselle had to trust she could overcome this serious brush with death—refusing to believe otherwise. Giselle gazed at the doctor and asked, "When can we see her?"

"It'll be a while," she replied. "Ms. Cruz is still in the recovery room and will later be moved to the ICU, where visitation is mostly limited to family members, as she begins the recovery process, so I suggest you all go home for now. You can come back tomorrow—or call—to check on her."

"Okay," Kimberly said acceptingly, and others were quick to agree.

That included Giselle, who certainly didn't want to impede upon Jacinta getting through this crucial period in her survival. "Will do," she concurred.

As the doctor walked away, Pablo said somberly, "I could use a drink. I'm headed over to the Owl's Den. Anyone care to join me…?"

Everyone was in agreement, except for Giselle and Quincy, who was still on duty. For her part, she had little interest in getting drunk. Or socializing right now. Not till Jacinta was totally out of the woods.

"I'm just going to head home," Giselle told the group politely. She raised her eyes to meet Quincy's, knowing that her temporary residence was his house and had proven to be a good fit. "See you when I see you," she said.

As they began to disperse, Quincy held her elbow and asked, "Are you going to be okay?"

"Yeah." Giselle gave a nod, feeling she needed to be as strong as Jacinta surely had been when she'd undoubtedly gotten roped in by Justin as Jesse—only to live and possibly die to regret it.

"All right." He lowered his chin. "This will be over soon," he asserted.

"I sure hope so" was all she could say to that.

When his cell phone rang, Quincy said, "I need to get this."

Giselle waited and listened to his vague acknowledgments and responses before disconnecting. She watched his face harden while asking him, "What's happening?"

"Buckner was spotted lurking outside the hospital," Quincy told her. "We may have him cornered."

"That's great to hear." Though she wasn't getting her hopes up just yet, Giselle was guardedly optimistic that the nightmare could soon be coming to an end. "Go get him," she uttered, knowing that Quincy was eager to be there to slap the cuffs on Justin for his misdeeds under Quincy's jurisdiction.

"All right." He rested a hand on her shoulder. "I'll let you know how it turns out as soon as I have anything. In the meantime, I suggest you head straight to the house—and stay there till we have Buckner in custody."

"I'll do that," Giselle promised, then lifted her chin and gave him a quick kiss on the mouth. Both for good luck and because it felt good to express how strongly she felt about him and how she interpreted he felt about her.

Quincy smiled at her, touching his mouth in appreciation before running off. She headed in the opposite direction to hit the road herself.

TURNING ONTO NORTH BINKLEY STREET, where the suspect had been seen running toward, Quincy sped in his Ford Police Interceptor vehicle in that direction. Though he hated to leave Giselle at a time when her friend's life was still hanging in the balance, he was sure she understood, considering the sense of urgency he felt to nail Justin Buckner. In this instance, Quincy knew that he and Giselle were on the same page in wanting to end her misery once and for all, with Buckner being taken off the streets. There would be plenty of time afterward to chart a course for their own future. One which he was growing increasingly comfortable with insofar as wanting it to be a lasting one, with all the bells and whistles.

But right now, there was suspected killer and financial crimes offender Justin Buckner to deal with. His prints were all over the farmhouse where Jacinta Cruz had been discovered near death, leaving no doubt that Buckner was indeed his alter ego Jesse Teague and the culprit in Jacinta's kidnapping and violent victimization. To say nothing of his other suspected killings and white-collar crimes. The knife used against Jacinta had yet to be found but would inevitably tie the wanted fugitive to the crime.

Quincy couldn't help but wonder if, in showing up near the hospital, Buckner had actually been hoping to somehow reach Jacinta and finish the job of killing her. If that had been his intention, before apparently aborting the idea, it would have failed miserably. A guard had been posted at

Jacinta's door as the victim of an attempted murder, to protect her from that point on.

When Quincy reached the destination—a small family-owned restaurant called Tulip's Dining and Desserts—where Buckner had last been spotted, police officers, state troopers, AST and FBI SWAT members and a Special Emergency Reaction Team had surrounded the North Binkley Street restaurant after safely evacuating employees and customers.

"Where is he?" Quincy asked Alan Edmonston regarding Buckner.

"The suspect ran through the restaurant and out the back door, where we have him trapped," Alan answered. "Just waiting for the word to flush him out."

Quincy spoke with Trooper Dave Norcross, who headed the SERT. "We need to get this done," he urged him, not wanting to risk the safety of the greater community by allowing the suspect to remain at large a moment longer.

Norcross, in his forties and brawny with gray hair in a buzz cut, agreed. "Let's go get him…"

Assuming that Buckner was armed and, obviously, dangerous, the teams went in wearing body armor and body cameras and were able to apprehend the suspect without incident, as he cowered behind a dumpster.

It was only when he'd been escorted outside to the front of the restaurant while cuffed with zip ties that Quincy took a good look at the suspect. He was in his midtwenties, lean, short and bald-headed with brown eyes, wearing a dirty T-shirt, jeans and tennis shoes.

After identifying himself as being with the ABI, Quincy frowned as he asked the man straight on, "What's your name?"

"Larry Purnell," he muttered out of the corner of his mouth, while wreaking of alcohol mixed with cigarette stench.

Whether he was being straight or not, Quincy had no doubt that the man wasn't Justin Buckner, who was older, taller and had blue eyes. It was a case of mistaken identity. So where the hell was Justin Buckner?

Before digging deeper into that, Quincy got word that Buckner's black Kia Telluride, which they had issued a BOLO alert for, had been spotted on Unkeley Street, headed south.

Feeling his heart skip a beat, Quincy muttered an expletive under his breath as he realized that Giselle's longtime tormentor and multiple-murder suspect was headed right in the direction of his own house, where Giselle currently was—putting her in grave danger.

GISELLE JOGGED THROUGH the woods that consisted of balsam poplar and paper birch trees on Quincy's property. She welcomed the respite of her favorite pastime to both relieve the stress of recent happenings as well as the not-so-recent ones. She would continue maintaining fitness to keep up with Quincy and to hold her good looks well into the future, if she had her way.

She gazed through the trees and saw some harlequin ducks on the river. Giselle thought with a smile about how attached she had become to Alaska and all it had to offer, including a very good-looking and sexy state trooper. Now Justin was trying to ruin all that by pulling her back into his deranged past and a nonexistent future, were he to have his way.

At that moment, Giselle heard a slight rustling of the trees behind her. Instinctively she dug into the pocket of her blue fleece joggers, worn with a black crewneck tank and running shoes, and felt the pepper spray inside. Looking over her shoulder, she saw a couple of wood frogs chasing each other across the dirt—but no other human beings or, for that matter, wildlife to have to contend with.

Relaxing with a measured breath, Giselle realized that there was no reason, per se, to fear being attacked by her ex-fiancé in particular, whom she assumed had probably been captured by now—or was on the verge of it—on the other side of town after being cornered by the authorities. Other than that, she felt relatively safe on her runs in this part of Soldotna.

Hopefully by the time I get back to the house, Quincy will call to share the good news that Justin has been taken into custody, Giselle told herself as she headed back through the woods.

Just as she reached the house, Giselle received a text message from Quincy. She stepped inside, sure he was about to put her mind at ease, once and for all. But then she read the text.

Buckner still on loose. His SUV was seen near my place. May be coming after you. Lock the doors. On my way.

For an instant, Giselle froze as she read the terrifying words again and had to come to terms with the reality that Justin had not been captured. And worse, he could know where she was hiding from him.

She managed to regain her equilibrium and texted him back with simply Okay. Then she quickly locked the doors before pressing the stay button and entering the user code for the security system. Gazing out the picture windows in the great room, she saw no movement of anyone outside the house, suggesting he might not be out there planning to break in and attack her.

I have to stay strong, Giselle mused and believed that

this was a battle Justin would not win in either his revenge against her or remaining at large to go after whomever he pleased.

Only then did Giselle think about Muffin, realizing that the kitten hadn't run up to her the moment she'd stepped inside the house—seemingly desperate for even more attention since being released from the vet.

"Where are you, Muffin?" Giselle asked, getting no kitten response, as she began to walk through the downstairs.

Seeing no sign of her, Giselle headed up the stairs. On the second floor, approaching one of the bedrooms, a muted meow sound came from one of the bedrooms other than the primary bedroom.

When she went inside, Giselle's heart thumped and her eyes sharpened as she saw Justin standing there in the flesh, holding Muffin in his arms.

"Guess cats—and kittens, too—really do have nine lives," Justin said with a snide laugh. Muffin belligerently scratched his hand, and he tossed the kitten to the floor and peered menacingly at Giselle. "Took me long enough, but I finally caught up to you—and fully intend to carry out exactly what I promised were you to ever leave me…"

Chapter Eighteen

Sergeant Miriam Fontaine was well aware that the hunt was on for the wanted fugitive Justin Buckner, whose identity theft had him operating as Jesse Teague. The suspected serial killer who had fled Virginia and a host of financial crimes to wreak havoc in Southcentral Alaska—or, more specifically, her own jurisdiction of Taller's Creek and adjacent Soldotna—angered Miriam to no end. As it would for any crimes of violence against local women and their alleged perpetrator.

That anger, though, did not extend to Giselle Kinard. Last Miriam knew, it was not a crime to relocate to the Last Frontier, as Alaska was known by people everywhere. Even if to escape an obsessed predator—who had apparently pulled out all the stops to pursue her, at risk to his capture. Or death. In Miriam's mind, this made Buckner all the more perilously uncontrollable, and he needed to be stopped at all costs.

When she spotted the black Kia Telluride SUV parked on the side of the road on Pamaner Street, Miriam pulled up behind it in her Ford Explorer Police Interceptor. She checked the license plate to verify her suspicions.

As expected from the BOLO alert, the SUV was the vehicle Buckner was renting as Jesse Teague. After calling for backup, Miriam exited her police car. She immediately whipped out her Glock 22 duty pistol and approached the Kia Telluride.

A cursory glance inside showed that there were a couple of empty beer cans on the back seat, along with a pair of jeans and a dark hooded rain-resistant jacket.

But no Justin Buckner.

Miriam cast her eyes at the heavily wooded area nearby, believing that the suspect had fled into the trees. Or was there a method to his madness?

It occurred to her that Giselle Kinard, as the object of Buckner's fixation, had been given refuge at Quincy Lankard's private residence on Keystone Lane. Which was within reach from where Miriam stood.

She raced back to her vehicle and phoned this in before heading that way, while being informed that Quincy and other law enforcement were already en route and as eager as she was to prevent any further tragedy.

As Muffin scurried nervously out of the room in Giselle's periphery, she found herself just staring squeamishly at her tormentor. He had shaven his full head of hair and added a five o'clock shadow to his face, which had become a little more weathered over the years. But the deep blue eyes were just as hardened, glaring back at her. Justin seemed every bit the physical specimen Giselle remembered, wearing an open gray soft-shell jacket over a rust-colored twill camp shirt, black jeans and dark gym shoes. She noted the knife tucked inside his waistband and blood on his hand from Muffin scratching it.

Stilling her nerves, Giselle asked him straightforwardly, as she considered the security system on the premises that should have been activated with a break-in, "How did you get in here?"

Sporting a crooked grin on his lips, Justin answered, pleased with himself, "Oh, I have my ways. I've learned a trick or two about deactivating security systems, long enough to get in and out, when I need to."

I can't believe he outsmarted the security mechanisms, Giselle griped to herself. She was certain that Quincy had been notified of any break in the surveillance and was very likely en route to his house. But would he be too late to save her? Or could she find a way out of this herself—perhaps making a run for it—short of dying from trying?

Justin broke through her thoughts as he said with a laugh, "Have to admit, Giselle, you were a hard person to track down. Had me going from one state to the next, wondering where the hell you were hiding and how you managed to go underground without a trace. Frankly, I nearly gave up trying—believing you had successfully outmaneuvered me with your disappearing act. But I couldn't do that. Not when I had a score to settle with you—and wasn't about to let you off the hook. Never expected this to come to a head in Alaska of all places." He stopped abruptly as her cell phone rang, locking eyes with Giselle. "I wouldn't answer that if I were you," he threatened her.

She resisted the urge to ignore him and warn Quincy, whom Giselle was certain was the caller, letting the phone ring before it finally stopped. Ticking off Justin right now, she reasoned, while he had a knife, probably wasn't a smart idea. She had to trust that Quincy and his colleagues were privy to her current predicament and that help was on the way.

If only she could stay alive till then.

Giselle cast her eyes at Justin acrimoniously. "Why

couldn't you just let me go, Justin—or should I say Jesse—and move on with your life?"

He chuckled in hearing the moniker. "Guess you would've figured it out sooner or later. I needed a new name to stay under the radar for as long as possible." His brows joined hostilely. "As for the other part—it's because we were meant to be together, Giselle," he insisted pointedly. "You agreed to marry me, and I wasn't going to allow you to renege on a promise. No way! Not when I gave you my heart—before you stomped on it…" He took his angry eyes off her for an instant and reached down on the side of the rustic guest bed and lifted up a dozen orange roses. "These are for you," he said coldly, handing them to her. "Like old times. Somehow it seemed fitting."

Giselle pretended to welcome the roses, putting the flowers to her nose but despising them and the man himself under the circumstances. "You sent the orange roses to the bookstore," she stated knowingly rather than asked.

"Yeah, it was me," Justin admitted. "It was meant to play with your head for a bit—to make things interesting—till the time came to meet up face-to-face."

Narrowing her eyes contemptuously, Giselle threw the roses onto the floor and blared with all but certainty, "Why did you have to go after Sadie? As well as Neve, Yuki and Jacinta, who's now clinging to her life…?"

"Because they were a means to an end," Justin replied heartlessly while confessing to his role. "I warned you what would happen if you ever left me. And I'm a man of my word, if nothing else. I wanted you to feel the pain through these other women you were connected with. Slowly but surely. Till it was your turn. Anything less, and it wouldn't have hit home what a huge disappointment you turned out to be—and just what it would cost you. Staging the deaths as accidental, suicide, random or whatever was easy and only to throw off the authorities—and you... Other than that, they meant nothing to me. Not really. Not even close to the pleasure I'll get when I make sure you—just like Jenna, the last woman I foolishly chose to love, who betrayed me too and had to die as a result—breathe your last breath!"

Justin whipped out the knife, which had a serrated blade that was at least eight inches long, and Giselle found herself backing up to the picture window with the vertical blinds closed. Her pulse racing as he moved toward her and put the knife up to her throat, she risked instant death by stating the obvious, "You won't get away with this, Justin!"

"Watch me." He laughed overconfidently, while effectively cutting off any means for escape. "You see, I've got a plan. I'll take off in your Honda CR-V. I took the liberty of swiping the key fob from your handbag while you were out jogging. Having ditched my own SUV, yours will be the perfect way to make my escape—before the cops piece it together—eventually making my way out of the country, where I'll never be found."

Giselle wrinkled her nose. "You're insane," she hissed at him unapologetically. "Killing someone who detests you won't change that!" *I can't believe I ever saw any redemptive qualities in him*, she told herself with major regrets.

Justin chuckled. "Believe me, I've been called worse," he snorted and ran the knife down her top without penetrating the skin just yet. "And I've been called more favorable names too—by you, Jenna...even Jacinta," he argued satisfyingly.

Giselle sneered and said sarcastically, while trying to buy time that she feared she didn't have much more of, "Maybe we all saw something in you, Justin, that's still there somewhere. It's not too late to stop this and give yourself up with no more killing or stealing money from your clients…"

"You do what you need to do to survive," he muttered as a lame excuse for perpetrating white-collar crimes in betraying those who trusted him the most. "My clients, pompous and sickening at times, got what they deserved." His mouth tightened. "So will you. But first, just out of curiosity, are you sleeping with the trooper you're staying with…?"

Giselle saw the pathological jealousy in his bloodshot eyes at the thought that she had actually found someone in Quincy, who was far more alluring, sensitive, strong and earning of her love and affections than Justin had even been or would be. She found herself answering him brazenly, even at risk of spurring on his resentment, "That's none of your business!"

"That's where you're wrong," Justin countered. "Everything about you is my business. If I can't have you, I sure as hell will make sure he can't either. Or anyone else! Say goodbye, Giselle…"

She braced herself for what was to come but was determined to keep Quincy in her thoughts to the very end of her life, if it came to that—not wanting Justin to win his desperate bid to even control her thinking in these waning moments. Or who she wished to have spent the rest of her life with.

QUINCY FEARED THAT he might have underestimated Justin Buckner's fixation on Giselle and the man's uncanny ability to carry out his acts of criminality almost with impunity—including managing to dodge the authorities and the hunt for the fugitive. That included Buckner being damned lucky enough to buy time when his ultimate capture was delayed by a case of mistaken identity.

Turned out that his lookalike, Larry Purnell, had fled from authorities because of an outstanding warrant for his arrest on drug trafficking and bootlegging charges. This had the effect of having the investigators take their eye off the real ball temporarily. Or long enough for Buckner to remain free and ever dangerous.

Now, after Miriam reported spotting the killer suspect's SUV just practically a stone's throw from Quincy's front door, it was apparent to him what he had already ascertained in Justin Buckner's warped mindset—that Buckner was going for broke in targeting Giselle to kill, having been able to successfully track her whereabouts.

I can't let that happen and won't, Quincy told himself, determined to prevent Buckner from taking away the life of the woman Quincy had fallen head over heels for. The fact that Giselle had not responded to his repeated attempts to reach her by phone was troubling, to say the least. He sped down the road in his SUV and through spotty traffic, barreling toward his house to divert disaster. Hot on his heels were members of law enforcement from various agencies, nearly as determined to put an end to Justin Buckner's thumbing his nose at anyone who took issue with his criminality.

As far as Quincy was concerned, he had much more to lose than anyone else, should Buckner succeed in adding another person to his list of homicide victims. The thought of Giselle dying before he had the opportunity to express how he felt about her was unimaginable to Quincy. This had to end today. But not in the way Buckner intended.

Quincy reached his property and exited the vehicle without ado before dashing toward the house to confront his nemesis. Inside, he spotted Muffin wandering across the floor, looking hapless and helpless but still alive.

Then Quincy heard voices coming from a room on the

second floor—Giselle was being confrontational with Buckner, no doubt trying to buy time in pushing the unstable suspect's buttons—and drew his gun as he headed up the stairs.

"WAIT!" GISELLE SHOUTED, as Buckner seemed more than ready to plunge the knife into her. Likely the same weapon he'd used to stab Jacinta repeatedly, fully intending to kill. It made Giselle nauseous just thinking about it. Right now, though, her very survival hung in the balance. The pepper spray was still in her pocket, but she wasn't in the best position to remove it and use it before he could knife her. "Can't we talk about this?" she threw out desperately.

Justin peered at her and replied frostily, "I think we've said all that needs to be said, Giselle, don't you?" He never allowed a response, when adding, "Say hello to Jenna for me, if you run into her on the other side."

As the level of his depravity sank in, Giselle heard the commanding voice of Quincy utter, "I wouldn't do that if I were you, Buckner. Drop the knife! Now!"

Giselle gazed at Quincy, who was inside the room and aiming his firearm at Justin. If she'd anticipated that he would simply give up, she was sorely mistaken, as she was quickly grabbed by Justin and placed between himself and Quincy.

Before she knew it, Justin had put the knife up to her throat. "I think it's the other way around, Trooper Lankard," he hissed. "You drop the weapon, or I'll just slice her throat right now and take Giselle's pretty head off while I'm at it—before you can even get off a clean shot. So, what's it going to be?"

"Don't do it, Quincy," Giselle pleaded, fearing that losing any leverage they had would be disastrous for both of them.

But Quincy saw it differently, clearly unwilling to sacrifice her life for his own as he lowered the gun while holding firmly onto it.

That gave Justin just enough time to surprise Giselle in using his free hand to remove a handgun from his jacket pocket. Without warning or time for Quincy to react, Justin shot him squarely in the chest.

Giselle screamed as Quincy went down, grimacing with discomfort. The gun slipped from his hand.

Justin told her testily, "Shut up! I want the ABI trooper to watch me slice your throat—" he tucked the firearm back inside his pocket while brandishing the knife "—and then I'm going to shoot him in the head so it's the last thing he ever sees…"

While Justin was preoccupied with his wicked and deadly plan of action, Giselle used the moment she'd been afforded to slip the pepper spray from her pocket. Before he knew what hit him, she sprayed it liberally into Justin's eyes and up his nose and inside his open mouth as he cried out with fury and yelled an expletive at her. He dropped the knife and rubbed his eyes vigorously.

Giselle seized another opportunity and smashed her fist into Justin's nose as hard as she possibly could—hearing the cracking of bones inside while he howled in even more pain like a wounded animal. She tried to reach for his gun, but he grabbed her wrist hard, threw her up against the wall and tried to strangle her, wrapping strong hands around her neck.

As she gasped for air, lungs burning, Giselle watched as Quincy somehow managed to get to his feet and pulled Justin away from her. Then he hit the killer with two solid blows to his shattered and bloody nose and added a stiff uppercut to his chin.

Justin went down like a sack of potatoes yet was able to

maintain consciousness and dug inside his pocket for the gun, aiming it blindly in Quincy's direction.

A shot rang out.

It hit Justin in the forehead, and he went down instantly.

Giselle turned toward the entrance and saw ABI Trooper Alan Edmonston standing there, still pointing his Glock 22 service pistol at the downed fugitive. "Sorry I was a little late getting to the party," he spoke humorlessly.

"In this instance, much better late than never," Quincy quipped and then winced in pain.

Giselle put her arms on his shoulders worriedly. "Justin shot you…"

"Yeah, he did." Quincy unbuttoned his shirt and said, "Fortunately I was wearing a ballistic vest. The shot was enough to knock me off my feet and bruise some ribs, but I'll live."

"Thank goodness for that," she voiced cheerfully. "If anything had happened—"

"I know." He kept a straight face. "I wouldn't give him that satisfaction." Regarding her keenly, Quincy held Giselle's shoulders and asked measuredly, "Are you all right? Did he hurt you?"

"Aside from planning to stab me to death with that knife over there—" Giselle slanted her eyes to where the weapon had landed on the floor "—and attempting to strangle me, not really," she said sarcastically. She angled her eyes at the orange roses scattered across the floor. "He even handed me those roses as part of his dark sense of humor. He wanted me dead. Thanks to you and Alan, Justin never got to do what he'd fully intended."

"His loss," Quincy said mockingly, "and the orange roses are emblematic of that."

"True," she concurred. They both eyed Alan as he moved

swiftly over to Justin and did a cursory examination. Giselle asked him, ill at ease, "Is he…?"

"Yeah," Alan responded equably. "The suspect has been put down and won't hurt you or others anymore."

She breathed a sigh of relief that her long nightmare had come to an end and told them, "Justin admitted to killing Neve, Yuki Sadie and attempting to murder Jacinta—as well as bilking his clients…and didn't seem to have any misgivings for his actions."

"Not surprising for a psychopath—and a greedy, selfish one at that," Quincy stated flatly. "But at least it stops here."

"Yes," she concurred and gazed at her dead ex-fiancé, feeling no sympathy.

"I'll call this in," Alan said and stepped out of the room, giving them a moment alone.

After he left, Quincy moved closer to Giselle, held her hands and locked eyes with her as he said, "With all that's happened, my timing may be off here, but you should know that I'm in love with you, Giselle."

Her eyes lit up in that instant, holding his gaze, and she responded in kind, "As far as I'm concerned, your timing is perfect, Quincy—since I'm very much in love with you too."

He smiled. "Is that so?"

"It's absolutely so," she promised.

"Well, in that case, guess I'm permitted to do this, without any hesitation as to how we feel about one another…"

Quincy took her cheeks and planted a sensual kiss on Giselle's mouth, which she was only too happy to reciprocate.

The spell was broken, though, when the house was suddenly swarming with law enforcement, crime scene technicians and personnel from the State Medical Examiner's Office as reality set in that a wanted fugitive had been brought down on the premises and the follow-up investigation began.

A MONTH LATER, Quincy sat at his desk going over the file on Justin Buckner now that the case had been closed insofar as the various crimes attributed to the man in Alaska over several harrowing weeks.

Stalking Giselle in and out of Taller's Creek and eventually trying to murder her was certainly first and foremost in Quincy's mind. The mere thought of Buckner having succeeded in his master plan at revenge made him want to puke, given the deep love Quincy had for Giselle.

As it was, the eight-inch serrated knife Buckner had wanted to stab her to death with was the same weapon used to attack Jacinta Cruz—with her DNA found on the blade—who was now all but fully recovered.

Then there was the gun Buckner had shot Quincy with as a prelude to the killer's plan to murder him. Being protected by ballistic body armor had saved his life but had been no less traumatic and had averted disaster for any future plans. The firearm itself was a Colt Cobra .38 Special revolver that, as it turned out, the Bureau of Alcohol, Tobacco, Firearms and Explosives National Tracing Center and National Integrated Ballistic Information Network had been able to link the illegal firearm to a murder in Fairbanks, Alaska, last year. The convicted killer, Aurelio McDermott, had apparently sold the murder weapon, which had eventually been purchased by Buckner on the black market in Anchorage.

Luckily he failed to make me another homicide victim, along with Giselle, Quincy told himself, feeling grateful to that effect as he stared at the laptop. Still, Buckner had, unfortunately, taken the lives of locals Neve Chenoweth, Yuki Kotake and Sadie Pisano, while Jacinta Cruz had barely survived her assault. Though the physical evidence was not as rock-solid for the murders as Quincy would have liked, there was enough of it, in addition to forensic and corroborating evidence, along with Buckner's confession to the crimes to both Giselle and Jacinta, to make Quincy comfortable with the belief that Buckner was guilty as sin on all counts.

Same was true for the Virginia murder of Jenna Sweeney, whose one mistake had been becoming the first object of Buckner's unnatural attention. The authorities in Chesapeake had essentially closed the books on the case, believing that there was enough forensic and circumstantial evidence to pin her death on Buckner.

Lastly, the feds' case against Justin Buckner as a crooked certified financial planner had also been put to rest in that the evidence overwhelmingly supported his guilt for embezzlement, wire fraud and related crimes. Attempts were still ongoing to try and recover some of the stolen funds for swindled clients.

Quincy sat back and turned his thoughts to Giselle. Things could not be going any better for them ever since they'd declared their love for one another. She was everything he could ever have hoped for in a woman and partner in a romantic relationship.

But now came the hard part. Was she truly ready to settle down into a life of marital happiness with him? He had deliberately delayed popping the question to give Giselle the needed time to get past the headache of Justin Buckner and decide if she wanted to remain in Alaska to become an ABI investigator's wife and mother of his future children.

Or if—now that Buckner was no longer an impediment—Giselle wanted to return to Chesapeake and the life she fled from, picking up where she left off as a dance instructor.

Though the thought of losing her scared Quincy as much as he was freely willing to admit, worse would be to keep Giselle in Alaska, while constantly second-guessing her decision at the expense of their happiness.

To that end, Quincy had come to a decision on whether

or not he was willing to give up working for the Alaska Department of Public Safety's Division of Alaska State Troopers in order to be with the woman he loved.

It was an easy choice. Being with Giselle in Virginia or anywhere else was worth relocating and taking his career in law enforcement with him.

Now it was time that he put his money where his heart and soul already were etched in stone.

GISELLE JOGGED down the street near her apartment, after having just paid Jacinta a visit. Her recovery from the knife attack by Justin had been nothing short of miraculous. The documentary filmmaker was back at doing what she loved best—and ever grateful for the show of support amongst her friends and colleagues. Jacinta refused to allow Giselle to blame herself in any way for lowering her own guard in being attracted to Justin's alter ego, Jesse—knowing full well that Justin had been charming enough to lure most any woman into his web of deceit and murder, whether Giselle had been his own unhealthy fixation or not.

Accepting this truth for what it was, Giselle was happy to try and return to a normal life, as much as possible. Without the anvil of Justin to weigh her down, as had been the case for too long, now that he was dead and buried. That normality included getting back to running and enjoying the incredible landscape Alaska had to offer during her runs, along with friendly wildlife she encountered periodically.

Most of all, though, Giselle loved spending time with Quincy, the man of her dreams who had come to life in one magnificent and well-built package of masculinity and heroism. She had returned to living at her own place, so as not to make him feel pressure to move to the next level in their relationship—marriage and all it entailed, including starting a family. Yes, she wanted it all, but only when the time was right for both of them and not just on her own time schedule.

Whenever Quincy is ready to ask me to marry him, I'll be his for the taking, Giselle told herself, as she jogged home, where she was making dinner for Quincy tonight, while leaving the choice for dessert up to him.

Epilogue

When he arrived at Giselle's apartment that evening, Quincy was, by his own admission, a bit nervous about what he had planned. Though confident about the results, it didn't take away the butterflies in his stomach one bit.

He knocked on the door, still wearing his work clothes. While he had considered going over to his place to change, Quincy knew that Giselle thought he was *hot* in his uniform, so he stuck with it. But would gladly wear whatever suited her fancy when they were together in their private lives.

She opened the door and greeted him with a gorgeous smile and kiss, then said, "Right on time."

"I couldn't agree more," he replied, grinning, gazing at her in a nice floral sundress and clog sandals. Just then, Muffin came up to them and rubbed against his leg, telling Quincy that she almost certainly wanted him to pick her up, which he did. "Hey there, friend," he said with a laugh, cuddling the kitten.

"Guess you've got her totally hooked," Giselle said, chuckling. She added sweetly, "Just like someone else I know."

"Works both ways." Quincy colored, feeling the love as thick as molasses. "And with you, too, Muffin." He left no doubt.

Minutes later, they were having dinner, consisting of tuna-noodle casserole, lima beans and apple muffins with red wine.

After listening to Giselle talk about her day, Quincy spooned some lima beans and said coolly, "So, the ABI has closed the investigation on Justin Buckner."

She lifted a brow. "Really?"

"Yeah. We were able to tie enough of the pieces together to make the case for holding Buckner fully accountable for the crimes he perpetrated in this state." Quincy sipped wine. "If anything else comes up, we'll certainly be happy to look into it. But for now, the case has been wrapped up. That ghost won't be haunting you anymore."

Giselle ate some casserole and said with an exaggerated sigh, "Well, I'm really glad to hear that it's finally finished. Honestly, I'm so over Justin and all the bad things he did in this world."

"Good. Me too." Quincy took a breath and nibbled on a muffin, while eyeing her musingly. "There's something else I want to talk to you about," he put forth tentatively.

She held his gaze as she tasted wine tensely. "Okay..."

It's all come down to this moment—better not blow it, Quincy told himself, steeling his nerves as he dabbed his mouth with a paper napkin. He waited a beat, then said straightforwardly, "You know how I feel about you, Giselle, and I'm pretty sure I know how you feel about me. So, now that the dust has been settled and swept away, I don't want to wait any longer to take the next crucial step in our lives..."

He got off his chair and dropped to one knee, where he removed a yellow-diamond engagement ring with an eighteen-karat yellow-gold band from his shirt pocket, took her hand and slipped the ring onto her finger for a perfect fit. "I'm madly in love with you, Giselle Kinard, and I'm ask-

ing you to become my wife and a person I can build a terrific future with—including the most wonderful children
we can bring into this world—sharing our cultures and
life's lessons. Whether you want to live in Alaska, Virginia
or elsewhere, I'll happily go where you go. If you say yes,
you'll make me the happiest state trooper in Alaska, if not
the entire country!"

Giselle's eyes watered as she said without hesitation,
"Yes, I will definitely marry you, Quincy Lankard, and
gladly become your wife and mother of any children we
are so very blessed to have together."

"Seriously?" He flashed his teeth and wanted to make
certain he heard her correctly.

"Yes, yes and yes again—a million times yes!" Giselle
voiced delightedly. She looked at her engagement ring, marveling at it. "And just for the record, Trooper Lankard, I'm
quite happy making our home in Alaska, thank you, and
will be even happier to do so as Mrs. Lankard. I love the
idea of integrating our cultures, upbringing and views on
life into our children's lives as we cultivate their futures."

"Wonderful!" Getting to his feet, Quincy was all smiles
as he pulled Giselle up and into his arms. "Thank you for
being you and finding your way into my life."

"Back at you," she gushed, angling her mouth to wait for
his lips to meet hers.

He didn't disappoint as Quincy kissed her passionately,
knowing that what they had could not be duplicated and he
wouldn't want to. Giselle was everything he wanted and
needed in a soulmate, and he would make sure the same
was true in reverse.

When they later spilled the beans with his parents and
sister, they were over the moon with enthusiasm about adding an important new member to the family in Giselle, who

was clearly just as eager to become part of his family as Quincy had known she would be, in giving her a sense of belonging that had been missing in her life.

A YEAR LATER, Giselle Lankard was at Taller's Creek Dance Studio on Windeer Drive, with her popular class for ballroom dancing in full swing. Six months ago, she had seen a dream come true in opening up the eight-thousand-square-foot facility in Southcentral Alaska, which had become her permanent home, with occasional visits to Chesapeake, Virginia, and elsewhere with her husband, Quincy.

Now she was truly living the dream and able to bring what she knew and loved to the local community—offering dance classes for the young, old and everyone in between. Including a variety of dance instruction and programs for beginners, experienced dancers, dance competitions, summer camps and even private lessons.

Wearing a maroon tank leotard, gray leg warmers and black character dance shoes, Giselle had her long black hair—happy to have it back to its natural color—in a topknot bun as she moved graciously between the dance couples, giving instructions along the way.

"Wonderful," she spoke cheerfully to an attractive, white-haired older couple who were celebrating their forty-fifth anniversary by learning how to ballroom dance. Then Giselle told a younger, well-groomed handsome couple that looked like they belonged on the covers of magazines, "You're nailing it!"

All the pairs—and even a few singles—seemed just as eager to master the steps and dance fluidly to the beat of Latin American music.

It was only when she saw the handsome gentleman enter the studio that Giselle's heart did a little leap and check. A big smile spread across her face as she broke away from the dancers and met him halfway.

"Hey," Quincy said, flashing his own toothy grin while dressed in casual attire and comfortable shoes.

"You made it." Giselle tilted her face upward and gave him a kiss on the lips.

"Of course. Just had to ditch the work clothes and get over here."

"Good." She smiled, grateful to have the love of her life on her turf. "Ready to do some ballroom dancing?"

"Yeah, definitely." He glanced about at the couples on the floor. "Looks like you have your hands full today."

"What can I say? Everyone loves to dance," she quipped.

"Hmm…" Quincy gave her the benefit of a level and curious gaze. "Any chance a guy could get a private lesson here?"

Giselle beamed. "Thought you'd never ask." She tiptoed and whispered into his ear, "It'll be cleared out in fifteen minutes. Then I'm all yours."

He grinned sideways, taking her hands. "Wouldn't have it any other way."

"And most definitely, neither would I," she assured him gleefully.

* * * * *

COLTON AT RISK

KACY CROSS

To Charlene Parris—
so happy to have you along on this ride.
PS: Thanks for letting me borrow Matthew and Dani!

Chapter One

Josh Colton's day started at the ungodly hour of 6:00 a.m. most of the time. Today, he'd hit the path to the stables by quarter till. No alarm necessary when living on the bustling grounds of Mariposa. Too much to do and too little time to do it in.

But first, he would ride.

He loved Mariposa. Every inch of the resort bore the mark of a Colton, whether it was a tribute to his mother or a feature selected by one of her children. As the activities director, the stable was all his though.

One of the hands would be happy to exercise Maverick for him if he asked, but he enjoyed the dawn ritual of taking his horse on a gallop across the hard-packed earth of the secret trail, where he never took guests. They got their money's worth on the more sedate but scenic route down through the canyons where he could control the tempo and keep an eye out for local wildlife.

His morning ride wasn't about the sights or packing another activity into an already full day the way he encouraged guests to do. Josh needed this to clear his head, to prepare for another day of pouring his blood, sweat and tears into his mother's dream.

His dream too. And it was all crashing down around him.

As Josh guided Maverick, the strawberry roan he'd hand selected four years ago from the quarter horse breeder in Flagstaff, onto the lesser-known trail, the desert beyond the resort unfolded around him, a tapestry of shadow and emerging light. Dawn painted pastel hues, pinks and soft oranges across the sky, mingling with the retreating night. The crisp air stung his lungs, filling them with the kind of freshness that only existed in these early hours, carrying the earthy scent of dew-dampened soil and the subtle fragrance of desert blooms.

The trail snaked its way through clusters of saguaro, their arms reaching toward the awakening sky; jackrabbits and roadrunners darted away from Maverick's hooves into the brush. To his left, the rugged outline of the canyon walls loomed, textured layers of rock and sediment revealing ancient secrets about this area.

Josh could ride this route a hundred times and never get tired of it. Most days, the steady rhythm of Maverick's hooves against the ground centered him, the horse's muscles working beneath him with a powerful, controlled energy that resonated with his soul because he felt like that too. As if he had so much more to give than what his reins allowed.

But something always pulled on the bit. Holding him back.

This place was his sanctuary, where the weight of responsibility and the complexities of managing Mariposa could be set aside, allowing him to breathe and settle his spirit.

Today, it wasn't working. Because everything was slipping through his fingers, and he couldn't figure out how to close his hand fast enough to stop it.

The resort was in trouble. The knowledge that his father knew how much Mariposa meant to him—to Laura and Adam—and was still trying to take it away from them infuriated him. And Josh didn't bow to the whims of his emotions. He hated being provoked, would rather live and let live, sprinting through his day from activity to activity until he fell into bed bone weary from the effort of living life to the fullest.

He closed his eyes and tried to let the sway of the horse recenter him. No easy feat after his sister, Laura, had been threatened. After Allison's death and Alexis being kidnapped. These were his people, his employees, and coupled with everything else, he had to get back to a good place or he'd fumble the rest of the day, failing at his responsibilities.

He hated letting down Mariposa most of all.

Obviously, he wasn't trying hard enough to cleanse the toxins of negative emotion out of his system. He kicked Maverick into a full gallop and repeated his personal mantra in his head over and over again.

I am part of this land and it is part of me. Together we flourish.

By the time he got back to the resort, everything finally felt manageable again.

He passed off Maverick's reins to Clark, a new addition to his stable staff, who was studying veterinary medicine at Sedona College. "Hey, kid. How's Sheila?"

Clark made a face at him as he deftly got to work on unbuckling Maverick's saddle. "I'm legally old enough to go to war. That means you can't call me kid. And Sheila dumped me."

"Oh, man." Josh took a minute to squeeze the kid's shoulder—and nineteen was definitely still a kid in his book. When had he started feeling so old? "That's rough, dude. You need some time off?"

Shaking his head, Clark hung up the bridle in the tack

area. "Nah, thanks though. Work keeps me from moping, you know?"

Yeah. He did know, at least about keeping work as a top priority and ensuring that all his energy went into the job instead of dwelling on things that couldn't be changed. He'd certainly spent a lot of time doing *that* after his mother's memorial service last month. She'd been gone seventeen years now. And the raw rake of grief could still sneak up on him at times.

"Plenty of other women around, mate," he advised Clark with a sage nod. "Make me a deal. Ask out the next five eligible women you meet, no prejudice. If you don't hit it off with at least one, I'll give you a hundred dollars."

Clark goggled at him. "What? Why?"

"Because women are fantastically beautiful distractions but they're all basically the same." He shrugged. "It's not difficult to find another one you like just as well as the last one. Bet me and see."

"Sure, boss," Clark said with a chuckle and jerked a chin in Josh's direction. "When you're sporting a Thor vibe, women are a little easier to come by. I'm not exactly beating them off with a stick."

Josh raised a brow at the Thor comment, not because he hadn't heard it before even though he'd stopped tying up his shoulder-length blond hair in a top knot, but geez. Chris Hemsworth was like ten years older than him. "I'll give you some tips later. Come find me after your shift."

It was getting late, and Josh had at least twenty things on his to-do list this morning, which his renewed spirit itched to dive into. The resort bustled with activity, maintenance workers mostly, interspersed with delivery people and a few early risers headed for the gym.

"You beat me to work again, boss?" called Luis, the head

groundskeeper, his hands buried in a bed of blooming azaleas. "That's every day this week."

"Can't let you guys outwork me," Joshua replied with a grin. "The mariposas are looking great, by the way."

They'd been his mother's favorite flower, reflected in the name of the resort for that reason.

Luis nodded, pride evident in his eyes. "We're trying something new with the fertilizer. Supposed to be better for this climate."

Josh waved and headed for L Bar. Not his normal haunt, considering that drinking wasn't his sport of choice. But he'd talked Adam into restructuring, so the bar reported to Josh. It was definitely not Hotel Management 101 to align beverage services with the activities director, but he had ideas.

Walking into L Bar, Joshua inhaled the scent of freshly brewed coffee. An excellent surprise, since no one was supposed to be here yet. He hadn't stopped for coffee yet this morning, and he blessed whoever had the foresight to make a pot. Guests had access to Keurig machines all around the property, but he preferred drip style, and the fact that someone had gone to the trouble put a smile on his face.

A second later, a svelte woman with long brown curls and what looked like a painted-on Mariposa T-shirt appeared from the back. Regina Sterling, one of the cocktail waitresses. She returned his smile.

"Morning, Joshua. Black?" she asked, and lifted the carafe without waiting on his answer, then poured coffee into an earthenware cup with the resort's logo on the side. "I remember you saying sugar ruins the taste."

"Thanks." He accepted the cup from her, curious where she'd picked up that specific bit of information since he hadn't ever spoken to her directly about his coffee preferences. "Good coffee will earn you brownie points every time."

Her smile widened. "Never hurts to butter up the new boss."

There was a vibe here he couldn't put his finger on, but he'd been Mariposa's activities director long enough to guess she might be gunning for a promotion. "What are you doing here so early? I thought I'd have the place to myself."

Had been counting on it. All part of his master plan to absorb the energy of this space so he could properly run the bar. While he thrived on challenges, he didn't want acclimation to be one of them.

Her laugh bordered on silvery. "I heard there was going to be some excellent scenery worth getting out of bed early for."

Oh. *That* was the vibe. Smoothly, he shifted his smile to professional mode and crossed his arms to create a physical barrier. "As nice of a compliment as that is, I'm your boss now. You know that means no fraternization."

One of his strictest rules—and he'd personally authored the policy himself. Business and pleasure should never mix, and Mariposa was too important to him to risk upsetting the status quo in any way, shape or form over a woman. Plenty of other fish in the sea, no matter how attractive Regina was. And she was definitely that.

She pouted for a beat. "Too bad. Maybe I'll quit."

"Please don't do that. We need you. I hear you're the best waitress we have."

That hit her in the feels, judging by the pleased look that stole over her face. Deflection level, unlocked. Sometimes it didn't go so well for him when he tried to let a woman down easy with no hurt feelings. But he certainly had enough practice that it came second nature.

"What are *you* doing here this early?" she asked.

"Scoping things out," he returned easily. "Give me a tour?"

Regina nearly fell over herself to comply. As she moved

through the place, pointing out various aspects, he let the space engage his senses, trying to see it through fresh eyes. The bar exuded an air of understated elegance, harmoniously blending modern design with high-end fabrics.

The bar itself was a long, sleek counter crafted from polished dark wood that contrasted beautifully with the lighter, natural stone backdrop. Ambient lighting cast a warm, inviting glow over the area, highlighting an array of gleaming glassware and an impressive selection of spirits arranged on tiered shelves.

Regina fit into this atmosphere, her poise echoing the sophistication of the bar as she gestured toward the seating area. Plush leather stools lined the bar, while a mix of cozy booths and intimate tables offered a variety of seating options. Each booth was semiprivate, with high backs and soft, cushioned seats, encouraging guests to linger over their drinks.

The walls were adorned with tasteful artwork that added character without overwhelming the space. Subtle touches, like the delicate patterns in the fabric and the soft, unobtrusive music playing in the background, contributed to the bar's upscale yet welcoming ambience.

Large, floor-to-ceiling windows framed one side of the bar, offering breathtaking views of the resort's lush gardens and the distant mountains. During the day, natural light would flood the space; while in the evening, the mood would shift to a more intimate, subdued setting.

"This place is great," he commented. "Do you think it would ruin the atmosphere if I added a TV?"

Regina glanced at him. "I thought that was a no-go here. But you're the boss. It matters whether *you* think it would work or not."

More to the point, the CEO of one of the big tech companies had stayed at Mariposa a few weeks ago and had made a pointed comment to Adam about the lack of ability to watch March Madness.

"People come here for the privacy and service, not to get away from seeing their favorite teams." Josh sipped his coffee, the richness flowing over his tongue. Regina had brewed it perfectly, which he planned to enjoy regardless of her motives. "I'm just looking for ways to make the experience here better."

And if he did it right, his father would have no leverage to take it from them.

She leaned in, lowering her voice. "You know, I've got a few ideas myself. Maybe after my shift, we could discuss them?"

He had to give her points for persistence. Joshua met her gaze, not the slightest bit disappointed he couldn't take her up on it. The curse of being the youngest Colton and the one who took his off-hours seriously. Work hard, play hard. But not everyone appreciated his personal philosophy, so he had to maintain strict boundaries with the staff. He had to be stellar at his job, no distractions.

How else could he honor his mother's legacy but to excel at running Mariposa?

"Drop your ideas in the suggestion box, and I'll definitely take a look. We value everyone's input here."

Something flickered across her face, but she nodded. "Can't blame a girl for trying to make a name for herself when there's an open bartender position."

When there was a *what*? First he'd heard about this. "Someone left?"

"Valerie. Extended leave." Regina shrugged. "No one said how long."

Looked like his first official act as the new manager of

the bar would be to hire a replacement, who might or might not be Regina. At least he hadn't been totally off about the promotion vibe. "Good to know."

He chatted with Regina for a few more minutes in an attempt to learn more about her style in case she could be a good replacement for Valerie, and then shoved off to swing by the management office to get cracking on this staffing shortage he'd just learned about.

Adam wasn't in his office at the back of L Building, but Laura was in hers. He poked his head in. "Just the person I was looking for."

Laura glanced up from her computer, an indulgent smile replacing the slight frown. "Hey. What's up?"

"Valerie is on extended leave? Is she okay?"

Wheeling her chair back, Laura laced her fingers together, giving Josh all her attention. "I think so. She didn't give a reason but left her return open-ended. I already hired her replacement."

Well, that solved that problem. "You're a godsend, Ace. And a mind reader. When does the new bartender start?"

"Today." His sister glanced at her phone. "In a few minutes as a matter of fact. HR paperwork manages to take more time with each new employee."

Thankfully, he had no frame of reference. He was more than happy to let Adam and Laura deal with back office nightmares while he spent his day on a horse. Well, part of the day. The downside of taking on new responsibilities—he actually had to manage his new bar staff.

After running down a couple of other topics with Laura while he had her attention, Josh jetted down the hall, intent on heading back to his bungalow for some brainstorming since he had a few hours before his first trail ride of the day.

His phone buzzed in his back pocket. When he pulled it free, he saw a text message from Ava: Free tonight?

Yeah, he was, but lately things with Ava had been feeling…off. Quickly, he texted her back with an excuse, the third time he'd come up with one instead of meeting her for drinks and likely more. Probably it was time to cut her loose, though she'd lasted even less time than the woman he'd dated before her. Candy. No. Cindy? Geez, he couldn't even recall her face.

Now that he'd made the decision that Ava would be joining esteemed company in his rearview mirror, it was time to make a move on the hot bartender he'd met at The Cloisters in Sedona.

Kelli. There'd been something about her from the first, but Ava had still been in the picture. Now she wasn't. Maybe he'd ask Kelli out this Thursday, his one night to live it up since he took Fridays off.

After pocketing his phone, he glanced up to meet the gaze of the woman who had just entered the door to the management offices. He blinked. It was Kelli. The same woman he'd just decided to pursue. The bartender. Had he conjured her up out of thin air merely by thinking about her?

If so, he could get used to that skill. A grin split his face. "Fancy meeting *you* here."

Then it hit him. *Bartender.* Valerie was on leave. Laura mentioned she'd hired someone.

Kelli returned his smile, punching him straight in the gut as her gaze twinkled. "Thursday Guy! Do you work here too?"

Chapter Two

Five seconds into her first day on the job and the first person Kelli ran into was the delicious guy who always sat on the barstool on the far left end, away from the well where the servers picked up drinks.

This was her lucky day.

"I do," he said, his shocked expression replacing the easy smile she'd grown to like quite well. "Work here."

Regular Josh, which was what she called him in her head, wore a pair of cowboy boots and jeans that had obviously been created with his body in mind. She'd only thought he was sexy before. The few times he'd come into The Cloisters to sit at her bar, he'd dressed in mouthwatering long-sleeved Henleys with the sleeves pushed up and joggers.

Cowboy Josh blew away Regular Josh.

"Well, that's a nice surprise," she said and tipped her head toward the offices. "You can show me to Human Resources so I can get started on my paperwork. Maybe later we can meet up for lunch?"

Assuming her new boss didn't have a million things for her to do. Most bar managers slapped a couple of forms in front of new hires and then dumped them in the cooler to get familiar with the layout. Fortunately, she'd moved up in the world to higher end places and she wouldn't be surprised if Mariposa had a lengthy onboarding process.

Before he could answer, a sophisticated blonde woman emerged from one of the offices, and as she caught sight of Kelli, a welcoming smile appeared on her face. "You must be Kelli. I'm Laura Colton. Nice to meet you."

Kelli extended her hand to the woman who had hired her over the phone. "In person, anyway. I felt like we really connected when we spoke. I'm grateful for the job and looking forward to working with you."

"Well, there's been a slight change since I hired you," Laura said and glanced at Cowboy Josh.

Oh, he must do something with horses. When she'd researched Mariposa after being approached about this gig, she'd read that the resort prided itself on its extensive trails and scenery best viewed on horseback. Josh no doubt looked amazing on the back of a horse.

"As long as the change isn't that you don't need me anymore," Kelli joked. "I'm totally flexible."

Laura shook her head. "That's definitely not the change. But since we spoke, management of the bar staff has changed hands, so I won't be working with you. Instead, you get this guy."

She pointed at Cowboy Josh and Kelli met his gaze, still looking for the punchline. "You're shuffling me off to work with the horses?"

Josh's expression had smoothed out. Gone was the shock, but neither did he remotely resemble the open, approachable guy she'd hoped was working his way up to asking her out. Though why it had taken this long, she wasn't quite sure. Had she been too subtle in her *I'm totally available* vibes?

"Not quite," he said. "I'm actually your new boss."

Oh. Well, that was *lovely*. She could envision a few late-night scenarios involving the beer cooler and a thorough rundown of all the ways she wouldn't mind being bossed by Boss Josh.

"You'll be in good hands," Laura promised her and vanished with an efficiency that Kelli would like to learn.

"Since I guess we have to officially meet in a whole different capacity, I'm Kelli Iona," she said and stuck her hand out.

Boss Josh shook her hand. "Joshua Colton. The staff calls me Joshua."

The staff. Which included her? She blinked. "Joshua. Colton."

That's when the second half of his introduction hit her. He was a *Colton*? Not just her boss then, but one of the owners of Mariposa. The vast land she'd covered on her moped to get here belonged to him. All these impressive buildings and the luxurious pool. The offices they stood in. The bar she'd stand behind to do her job. He owned all of it.

"Laura is your sister?" she guessed faintly because she had to say something, and she wasn't used to struggling for words.

He nodded. "And my brother, Adam, rounds out the trio of Coltons who operate this place. The bar staff moved under me yesterday. Apologies for dropping this on you with no warning. I can completely understand if this is not the job you thought you signed up for. No hard feelings."

Wait. Was he giving her a chance to back out of taking this job? Simply because he'd be her boss? "Are you hard to work for or something?"

She laughed but he didn't. This was so weird. She'd have sworn they had a spark. Or at least an ember. He never met anyone at The Cloisters on Thursdays. He came alone and spoke only to her, nursing drinks like they were on life support.

"I'm told I'm a great boss," he said simply and rubbed the back of his neck. "It's just…boy, am I botching this. My sole intent was to make sure this is still a job you want. Some people take jobs because they jell with the person who hired them. If that's you, okay."

Her mouth might be hanging open a little. Seriously? He thought a little thing like a new manager would throw her enough to walk away from the best thing that had happened to her in recent memory. No thank you. This job represented a step up in the world.

"I'm good," she told him. "I'm a roll-with-the-punches kind of girl."

That got a brief smile from the-staff-calls-me-Joshua. "Apologies, I don't usually leave new employees standing around in the hall. Follow me."

She did, appreciating the view from the backside as much as the front. But the weirdness continued through the relatively short paperwork session that had as much to recommend it as a root canal. Neither did the sexy guy from The Cloisters make an appearance. He'd vanished into whoever this guy became when his last name swallowed him.

That was fine. She could give him a break. He'd been caught off guard by his sister hiring someone he already knew for the open bartender position. Once they both got over the first day hump, he'd started treating her to his slow, easy smile, the one she'd started seeing when she closed her eyes at night.

It wasn't like he could possibly have reservations about her skill set. He'd taken a first-row seat for the last three weeks to watch her make drinks.

"Let's head over to the bar," Josh suggested when she'd

signed the last form—a nondisclosure agreement that told her the guests here must be of the highest caliber.

And yes, she could think of him as *Josh* in her head as much as she wanted to, and he couldn't stop her.

That was probably most of the problem. He'd changed their dynamic by slapping his full name down in front of her, creating this strange, artificial distance. It would fade eventually.

"This place is gorgeous," she murmured as she walked with him out of the office area.

They crossed the spacious lobby, where guests could lounge near the floor-to-ceiling panoramic windows or head into what looked like a very elegant restaurant. She'd searched for pictures online but there weren't any, even ones posted by guests, which was a bit of an oddity. Most people liked to talk about their vacations, and she'd often been asked to take a ton of pictures for her customers to post on social media. Sometimes they even asked her to be in the pictures or filmed her making drinks.

"This is L Bar," Josh said and held open the door for her, then ushered her inside the place that she would call home for eight hours a day.

The sophistication of the bar nearly took her breath. This was exactly what she'd hoped for when she took the job. The bar itself, a sleek masterpiece of polished wood, gleamed in the low light, and when she ran her hand over it, the richness of it sang through her fingertips. Ambient lighting was more than just warm and inviting; it was strategically placed to highlight the bar's best features. The array of glassware gleamed, meticulously arranged for both aesthetic appeal and efficiency.

An impressive collection of high-end liquors reached nearly to the ceiling. Macallan, 25 Year Old, of course, sat near a bottle of Hennessy Paradis and beyond that, a Don Julio 1942 Añejo. On one of the higher shelves, she spied a bottle of Appleton, but not the merely expensive twenty-one-year-old rum. No. This was a bottle of sixty-year-old that the Jamaican Minister of Tourism gave as gifts. It was the only way you could get a bottle and she wanted to ask who had been the recipient.

"This is exquisite," she murmured and lifted the pass-through to examine the well, then turned to check out the dishwasher, only to see there wasn't one. "Is there a back area?"

Josh pointed. "Through here."

She headed in the direction he'd indicated, but realized it was a bit presumptuous to go first, so she slowed down at the door, then turned to step out of the way. He didn't react fast enough and stepped into her instead of away. They bumped torsos and well... Josh had a lot going on there.

His hands came up under her elbows to steady her and his gorgeous blue eyes peered down at her with concern. "Sorry about that. You okay?"

Define okay. Because her heart had kicked up a billion notches and she had an instant where her body connected these dots, arriving at the conclusion she was about to be kissed. By someone who knew how. Her stomach got in on the action, swooping toward the floor.

And then he stepped away, running stiff fingers through his shaggy blond hair, which somehow made him look more appealing instead of rumpled like everyone else on the planet would.

"Sorry. I mean, yes, I'm fine. It was my fault for stopping like that," she mumbled, wondering how it was possible to be jealous of hair.

Except he'd just wrapped those fingers around her bare

skin and she knew what it felt like. That little taste hadn't been nearly enough.

"Why did you stop?" he asked, a totally legit question with a lame answer.

"I don't know. I guess because I didn't know where the dishwasher was."

That got a hint of a smile from him. "That's what you want to see? The dishwasher?"

"It's an important part of every bartender's setup," she shot back. "No clean glasses, no serving guests. Most bars have one in the front."

Without another word, he led her into the back area where twin Miele G 7000s sat waiting for the first round of glassware. The sight of them made her eco-conscious heart gallop back into the danger zone.

"These are top-of-the-line." She touched the Wi-Fi symbol. "Can I download the app and control them with my phone?"

"Of course," Josh offered easily. "You're the one in charge around here. I'm told the app is a necessity, so you don't have to spend time back here away from guests. Let's go to the front and you can fill me in about your experience."

Okay, so no backroom snogfest in her future, at least not today. Clearly Josh had not been struck by all the romantic possibilities that came along with the counters and walk-in coolers in this back area.

Josh slid onto one of the barstools as she rounded the bar to the server side. Finally, something familiar. It eased her somewhat frazzled nerves to be back on even ground.

"What'll it be?" she joked.

He lifted a brow. "What can you make?"

All right, so maybe not too even ground. "You were serious about wanting me to tell you about my experience?"

He shrugged. "I didn't interview you. Laura did. Obviously, I'm aware that you've bartended for at least three weeks at The Cloisters. But beyond that, what makes you qualified for this position?"

Point taken. She'd been dumped on him as a new employee, and he didn't take anything for granted when it came to areas of his responsibility. Noted.

But if this was a job interview, she was sorely underdressed. She'd thrown on a pair of dark pants and a white shirt, as instructed, planning to wear a Mariposa smock over it. She'd have to make an impression with her skill set, then.

"I've honed my craft in high-end resorts, just like Mariposa, first in Hawaii and then the mainland as I worked my way east. My flair for mixology isn't just about mixing drinks—it's about creating experiences. Each cocktail I make is a story in a glass, tailored to delight our guests and elevate their stay here."

"You're from Hawaii?"

She nearly rolled her eyes. He knew that, since she'd told him so just last week. "Yes, Molokai. But I didn't start bartending until I moved to the big island after high school. It's all I've ever wanted to do, and I love it. The people, the regulars. The music. I've been behind a bar for seven years. Is that enough experience for you?"

Josh uncurled his fingers and let them rest on the bar as he contemplated her. "Why this job? Why not stay at The Cloisters?"

It was a legit question, but it put her back up for some reason, as if she'd done something wrong by job-hopping. "I've worked at four different bars that shut down while I was employed there. You haven't lived until you show up for work to find a sign on the door that says Closed Permanently. And rent is due in three days. This is not an industry well known for longevity. So I adapt. I move on."

"That's why you're a roll-with-the-punches-girl," he said, his expression unfathomable.

She shrugged, suddenly aware that he was in Boss Josh mode. He didn't need to know about her *real* reasons for taking the job—how no roots had been what she'd thought she wanted, but it turned out that moving on also meant being pretty lonely.

Mariposa represented something more than a paycheck. A potential for permanence. She could envision buying a house here in Sedona, more so than any other place she'd lived, and it felt like the right time.

Kelli stepped back, her gaze locked on his so there was no question as to her sincerity. "So, there you have it. Passion, experience, creativity, adaptability. That's what I bring to the table, or should I say, the bar. Did I pass?"

"It wasn't a test." Josh stood and held up his hand, traffic cop style. "I just wanted to get a sense of your professional credentials. Laura did a background check, so we're all good here."

The heavy glass door at the entrance to L Bar opened to admit a woman about her age with long brown hair and the kind of body that made men stupid. She was accompanied by a rail thin guy with a thatch of dark hair sweeping down over his forehead. He towered over everyone.

Josh smiled at the newcomers. "Just in time. Kelli, meet your new coworkers. This is Regina Sterling, the cocktail waitress, and Kyle Littlebird, the barback."

Regina eyed her coolly, not bothering to shake hands. "You're the new bartender?"

"Word travels fast," she said, scrabbling to unravel the undertones, which were not friendly.

Usually, bar staff easily welcomed new people, since turnover in the hospitality industry was so high. Everyone had been on the other side of the equation multiple times and besides, you didn't get into serving people if you didn't get along with all personality types, or you didn't last long.

Kyle on the other hand immediately stepped forward, shaking her hand. "I work hard and I'm here for you. Anything you need. I have to leave right at four though, which I know is terrible, because it leaves you to do all the cleanup."

"Kyle is a single dad," Josh explained when she glanced at him. "The night shift bartender comes in at four, so it's not too much for one person to handle once she takes over service."

"I have to pick up Lily from the sitter and start dinner," Kyle said apologetically, as if Kelli might be unhappy with the fact that her barback had a life and responsibilities.

"That's totally fine," she assured him with a smile. "I'm looking forward to trying out those stellar Mieles in the back."

Instantly, she had an ally in Kyle, who might even be younger than her, but it was hard to tell. He had amazing cheekbones passed down from his Native American ancestors and a perpetual smile that he flashed as he flipped razor-cut bangs out of his eyes every other minute, which gave him a skater boy vibe that didn't necessarily go with story time and animal crackers.

"I asked Regina and Kyle to spend a couple of hours showing you where everything is," Josh told her. "I have a trail ride, so I'll check in with you later."

Kelli nodded, eager to learn the setup so she could make drinks without searching for a key ingredient. It usually didn't take her long to memorize the location of every type of alcohol, though this was by far the largest display of top-shelf liquor that she'd seen. The shelves behind the bar went all the way to the ceiling, making the literal top shelf accessible only by ladder.

Josh vanished through the heavy glass doors and Kelli glanced at her new colleagues. "I'm thrilled to be here. This is my first day shift job, so hopefully it's not too different than the night crowd."

That had been one of the main perks in her mind. Day shifts frequently went to tenured staff, typically those with an eye on a management position so they could learn the administrative side of things. She'd never had an interest in that, plus it would have meant staying in one place for longer than her style would dictate.

Used to dictate. Sticking around Sedona meant a departure from her norm and it felt right. Terrifying. But still like a good decision.

Kyle jumped right into his job, opening cabinets to start organizing the bar for the day. He cheerfully asked her what order she preferred the well liquor bottles to be placed in the speed rail, and whether she wanted the margarita salt rimmer on the left or right.

During all of this, Regina made a show of setting up the guest seating area, pulling chairs from the tabletops where they'd been placed last night in anticipation of the cleaning crew. But in reality, she watched Kelli the whole time. If the other woman meant for Kelli to sweat it, that wasn't happening.

It wasn't until Kyle loped to the cooler to tally the day's beer order that Regina sauntered over, a decided gleam in her eye.

"You and Joshua know each other," she said, and Kelli didn't think it was an accident that it came out accusatory instead of conversational.

She lifted her head. "That's right."

Regina tossed hair over her shoulder and shoved her hands in the front pockets of the apron tied around her waist. "In case you missed it, there's a strict no-fraternization policy here at Mariposa. So any designs you have on the boss are out of question. He's totally off-limits to you."

And you, she silently added, since this felt very much like an ambush. She also didn't voice her disappointment. Funny how Josh hadn't mentioned anything of the sort, though the employee handbook HR had emailed her probably spelled it out pretty clearly. Her new boss expected her to read it and figure it out on her own.

"Well, they probably have that policy for a good reason," she told Regina evenly. "This place caters to high-end customers who should take center stage."

A good reminder to her too, since apparently she wouldn't be dating Josh after all. He wasn't going to be a fun walk-in cooler buddy who volunteered to help her stock cases of beer and keep her warm at the same time. It shouldn't be such a downer. But it was.

Regina slunk off and Kelli turned her attention to the thing she did best—mix drinks.

The first day flew by, and it wasn't terrible, despite Regina. She lived up to her mean girl name pretty much always. Kyle however, she liked immensely. The guests adored him and his silly dad jokes, which he told with a straight face as if he had no clue that most twentysomethings didn't even *know* dad jokes.

The nighttime crew arrived on a wave of chatter, including the bartender, a tiny Black woman named Tara. She and her staff had apparently been together awhile as best Kelli could tell from the few minutes of conversation she heard during the shift overlap.

Once she'd cleaned up the bar area from the day's service and turned the till over to Tara, Kelli left via the back entrance, near where she'd parked her moped. It was a bit of a trek back to her apartment in Sedona, but the moped got great gas mileage and she'd made enough at The Cloisters to pay cash for it.

One negative—drivers often didn't respect the fact that she'd be hamburger meat if they followed too close and hit her rear tire. Like this guy in her rearview mirror who wouldn't back off, no matter how many times she tapped the brakes.

Ugh, he was driving really dangerously, his car a mere inches from her bumper. After a long shift, Kelli didn't have the patience for jackholes who thought they owned the road. Carefully, she signaled and steered into the next lane over.

The jackhole changed lanes too, sticking with her. Keeping his car exactly the same distance from her moped.

Okay, this was starting to make her mad. Had she accidentally cut him off or something? But he still had the weight advantage so she couldn't afford to play chicken with her life.

Kelli eyed the upcoming side street, gauging her speed. She could make it if she slowed down, but given the driver's proximity, it would be dicey to try that.

He inched closer. She went for it anyway, swerving at the last second. Her back tire skidded around the corner, slamming her heart into her throat.

Behind her, the car's brakes squealed but she didn't stop. With a crunch, his front bumper hit something. Probably the curb. *Karma, baby.* Kelli resisted a fist pump because her hands were shaking. But she'd escaped unscathed, barely.

Chapter Three

Kelli took a completely different route home, sticking to side streets and backtracking a couple of times, her pulse never quite settling. The cool evening air against her skin helped, since she'd broken out in a sweat.

That guy had been *following* her.

Right? Why else would he have tried to make that turn at the same time she had?

She didn't see him again despite keeping most of her attention on the vehicles around her. Finally, her apartment building came into view, and she sucked in a deep breath for the first time in forever. Once inside her sanctuary, she bolted the door, a habit she'd started on the Big Island and would never stop regardless of where she landed. Today, it felt extra necessary.

That had been too close. And also ridiculous. Why would someone be following her? She'd never done anything interesting in her life except leave home.

Once she hit the living room, her angst started to fade. This was her sanctuary, a place untouched by jackholes on the road. The walls were adorned with souvenirs from the myriad bars she'd worked at over the years—each a testament to her journey, her freedom. Each item held a story, a memory, a piece of her soul. They were reminders that her life was hers alone, dictated by no one else's terms.

Better now, Kelli moved to the kitchen. Tonight, she would cook. Chicken Long Rice, a traditional Hawaiian dish, never failed to center her. As she chopped and stirred, the fragrances of home filled her small apartment, transporting her to a simpler time, before she knew what it was like to be smothered.

Naturally, her thoughts shifted to Josh. Josh Colton. Josh-u-a. Her boss.

Also the horse guy, the owner, and probably a dozen other titles she hadn't been informed of because it wasn't her business to know. Her heart squelched. She'd so been looking forward to getting to know him better once he finally asked her out. He'd been taking his sweet time about it too, and she'd almost flipped it on him and asked *him* out.

Obviously, the no-frat policy of Mariposa had put a big damper on that anyway, but she'd never been much of a rule follower in the first place. People skirted those policies all the time.

She had a feeling Josh wasn't one of those people though.

It was fine. More than fine. Independence was her mantra, and she wasn't about to let anyone disrupt that. Not even the-staff-calls-me-Joshua.

With the meal simmering on the stove, Kelli sat down at her laptop to check off her most dreaded chore of the week—a carefully composed email to her parents. A check-in. More *Hi, I'm not dead* than a rundown of anything remotely personal. Her fingers hovered over the keys as she contemplated how much to share, how to phrase it to keep the judgment to a minimum.

They didn't like her chosen profession. Her mother had told her more than once that bartending was for drifters and people with no college degree. Well, her mother had been right on both counts, actually. She probably wouldn't appreciate hearing that she'd spoken it into existence since Kelli had vowed to go the exact opposite direction of the one her mother had planned for her.

Kelli typed a sentence explaining she'd gotten a job at Mariposa, and immediately deleted it. Too much detail and she had the NDA verbiage fresh in her head from the on-boarding.

She opted to say she'd moved to a new bar in another part of Sedona and threw in a few bones about liking her co-worker. No frills, no emotion. The emails were always the same: formal and detached. A bridge over the vast emotional distance she had put between herself and her overprotective parents, who had nearly killed her spirit.

As she hit Send, a pang of something twinged in her chest. She shook the feeling off, refusing to delve too deep. Instead, she focused on the now—her independence, her career, her choices.

As she ate, she read articles on her laptop curated for her by the app she used to find things of interest. Today's topic: advances in reclaiming plastic from the ocean. The color of the water in the photos reminded her of Josh's eyes though, and twice she lost her place as her attention drifted.

What was with the ridiculous flutter in her chest?

She liked men, sure. They were fun sometimes, but she never let one invade her sanctuary, let alone her thoughts. No one else had a say in what happened in her life besides her. She could decorate the way she wanted. Spend her money how she saw fit. Date who she chose, and best of all, she never had to watch a movie that she hadn't picked. She'd escaped her early twenties without ever having a serious relationship and she saw no reason to change that.

It was just that she hated to miss out on something because of bad timing. She hated to miss out on anything for any reason. That was the whole point of moving away from her jailers. So she could suck the marrow out of life.

And Josh Colton had become somewhat of a challenge by removing himself from the playing board. She hadn't figured out what to do about that yet.

JOSH DESERVED A do-over on this day already and it was barely nine o'clock.

His desperately needed early morning horseback ride had not only *not* cleared his head, a sudden cloudburst had poured rain down on him and Maverick. And the trail.

The horse hadn't seemed overly bothered, and normally, getting caught in the rain ranked high on Josh's list of great experiences. But this time, it just made his ride miserable as the trail grew slick and rain soaked into every fiber of clothing he wore. And it was still chilly this early in April in the mountains.

Plus, the wind blew the rain sideways, funneling it straight into his eyes. The whole point of wearing a Stetson was so that it would keep the rain off your face. Major fail. He turned back to the resort halfway into his planned ride.

Two of the hands had called in sick and Clark already had the day off to take an exam, so Josh opted to clean up the muddy horse and equipment himself. Not that he minded taking care of Maverick, but he was cold and wet and not at all centered. Then it had taken nearly thirty minutes in the shower back at his bungalow to both warm up and feel clean. What was wrong with him today?

The rain had stopped by the time he headed for L Building. The sun tried to break through the clouds, and the wet paths glistened beneath his feet. While unexpected, and definitely not forecast, the rain washed away the dust that perpetually coated everything this close to the desert. The flowers seemed extra perky.

He let go of his bad mood and urged it to slip away in the face of his blessings. Which were plentiful.

I am part of this land and it is part of me. Together we flourish.

Rain included. He paused a moment near the thatch of mariposas that never failed to remind him of his mother, feeling more like himself again.

But when he strode into L Bar, iPad in hand for his notes, Kelli had beaten him there. Already behind the bar, she turned when he pushed open the heavy glass door. The humidity had added a wild wave to her long brown hair, curling it up in chunks around her face and shoulders. She had on the standard Mariposa smock that everyone on staff wore while serving guests, but she'd added a blue scarf at her neckline that feminized it and drew attention to her face. Which was still arresting.

Man, his deliberate avoidance of Kelli had not dulled his raging attraction to the very off-limits bartender. What was he going to do with all the crackle between them?

He cleared his throat. "Good morning."

"Boss Josh," she called with a smile that felt a little more like a smirk than wholly appropriate when addressing the person she'd just identified as her manager. "Do I have to approve expenditures through you or am I allowed to just order things I need?"

Off-kilter again, he opened his mouth and then closed it. This was not the conversation he wanted to be having with her, nor was it the conversation he'd intended to start this morning. "Uh, what do you need that isn't already here?"

She paused her enthusiastic emptying of one of the storage cabinets under the sink. "So, I'll answer that by asking you a question. How good of a bartender was Valerie?"

Obviously, he needed to sit down for this if she was about to tell him that Valerie had been skating by. He slid into one of the barstools and his gut panged over the fact that it wasn't at The Cloisters, and he wasn't supposed to notice that the light in here complimented Kelli's face, making her skin glow. "Competent. We never got any complaints."

She pointed a martini shaker at him. "But she never got any rave reviews either. Did she?"

Actually he didn't know. It had never occurred to him to check on something like that. In his mind, the bar staff did their jobs and served drinks and guests enjoyed themselves. His job was to elevate that experience and somehow, he'd missed that staff could be a huge part of that.

"So Valerie was a competent bartender, but her style doesn't match yours and therefore, you need some equipment that she wouldn't have ever used," he summed up, raising his brows. "Is that the gist?"

The smile she beamed in his direction punched him in the gut. "Exactly."

"Order whatever you need," he muttered, unthrilled with the huskiness of his voice.

"Mahalo," she said sincerely, covering his hand with hers in a light physical addition to the verbal thank-you.

Women touched him all the time. Surely. Although he couldn't actually remember the last time. Maybe that was why the brush of her fingertips rocketed through every nerve ending in his body.

"Well, this is cozy." Regina strolled to the bar and dropped a bag into one of the chairs.

Josh yanked his hand off the bar and sat on it. Kyle followed Regina into the room and leaned over the bar to clasp

Kelli's palm, which quickly morphed into a fist bump followed by a choreographed set of finger movements that shouldn't have come so natural to two people who had just met. Though it was obvious from Kelli's delighted smile that she liked being on the receiving end of Kyle's flamboyant handshake.

Okay, the flare in Josh's chest felt a lot more like jealousy than anything. Because he couldn't greet Kelli however he wanted. He was the boss. He didn't like that designation so much at this particular moment.

But this was his lot. He had a mission: to discuss his plans for introducing mixology classes at the resort with people who had the most knowledge. It was a project close to his heart, one that he believed could elevate the guest experience to new heights. Laura and Adam both had their plans to keep the resort out of their father's hands, and Josh had his.

Kelli leaned a hip on the ice maker, relaxed in her element despite being new to Mariposa. "What brings you to L Bar this fine morning, Joshua?"

The almost insolent roll of her tongue around his name made the back of his neck flush. It was a dig. He got it. Telling her that staff called him that hadn't done jack to put much-needed distance between them. Instead, he'd probably made it worse.

Because hearing her call him Joshua did not make him think about work. At all.

"I wanted to talk to you." He lifted his gaze to include Kyle and Regina. "All of you. About the new mixology class Mariposa is going to start offering to guests. I was thinking it would be fun if the staff participated."

"You want me to sit by the billionaire owner of a professional sports team and act like I'm having fun learning how dirty a martini is supposed to be?" Regina gave him the side-eye. "What should I say when he asks me my hourly rate?"

"No one is going to think you're for hire, Regina," he shot back as Kyle snickered. "This is a high-end resort. Everyone knows we don't cater to that kind of behavior."

"How will they know that when this is a new thing?" she countered and crossed her arms. "Maybe they'll think offering playmates along with their alcohol education is part of the gig."

The beginning of a headache knifed through Josh's temples. "Forget participating. You can stand at the front of the class with a sign that says *not even for a billion dollars* if you prefer."

That got a sly smile out of the cocktail waitress. "Well, a billion dollars is a whole different kettle of fish—"

"Back to the point of this conversation," he cut in and slashed at the air to stop Regina from further derailing his plan.

"I'll help," Kelli offered with a tiny smile that shouldn't feel like such a lifeline. "What did you have in mind?"

"Something fun. Something where they can learn. Maybe they find a new drink they like, and they come back and order it, driving business back to the bar." As he spoke, he started to realize the plan needed a lot more meat than that. Which was why he'd come to the bar staff—so they could work together to create a meaningful agenda.

She nodded. "How long do you want the class to be?"

Rolling his shoulders, Josh consulted his iPad, which had exactly zero notes. "I don't know, an hour?"

"Okay." She braced her hands on the bar and leaned into it. "That means an abbreviated intro session on tools and techniques, probably about fifteen minutes or less on flavor profiles and balancing, twenty to twenty-five on experimentation and creation and maybe ten to critique and wrap up. Does that sound like what you have in your head?"

No. Not even a little bit. What he had in his head was a dawning realization that he'd only been playing around at being attracted to Kelli before. The full-blown deal walloped him as he absorbed that seeing her in her element did things to him that he had yet to fully reconcile.

Not a shock. He'd met her in this exact scenario, as a bar patron while she commanded the space on the other side, competent, friendly, gorgeous. The life of the party.

Hearing her give voice to an idea she'd just proven to be more nebulous than he'd realized put him in a dangerous place. Namely, annoyed that he couldn't fire her so he could take her in the back room and have his wicked way with her.

Bad, *bad* scene to be dwelling on.

"Yeah, that's great," he said with feigned enthusiasm, which also annoyed him because this was his idea, and he should be happy that Kelli had started crystallizing it for him. "Have you done this before?"

"I ran a mixology program at a social club in L.A. The place charged for them, fifty bucks a head. So they had to be good. More than just classes—they were experiences. We focused on exotic ingredients, the stories behind the cocktails. The participants loved it."

Joshua tapped out notes on his iPad, which he'd only just remembered he should be doing, his mind turning over her points, considering what would actually flip a class into an experience. The problem was that he already knew. *Kelli.* Kelli would make it an experience.

But he needed more than a beautiful woman at the front of the room leading the guests through the steps to make a drink. This mixology experience, and he already knew that's what he'd call it, needed to be memorable. Cemented in guests' minds as something "extra" that Mariposa could give them over and above an exclusive resort.

After all, it was still his job to provide activities for guests to do during their stay.

"Cocktails have stories?" This from Kyle, who had been avidly hanging on every word that came out of Kelli's mouth. Looked like someone had a crush on the new bartender.

"Sure," Kelli said with a shrug and a grin for the bar back. "You can talk about the origins of certain drinks, like how the Old Fashioned was supposedly invented in the early 19th century at the Pendennis Club in Louisville, Kentucky, said to be created in honor of Colonel James E. Pepper, a prominent bourbon distiller in the area at the time. Or how the margarita was invented for a dancer who was allergic to everything except tequila but didn't like the taste of it straight."

Kyle's eyes widened. "How do you know all of that?"

"I'm a professional," she said with a wink that put a knot in Josh's throat for reasons he didn't want to examine.

"Okay," Josh said brusquely. "These are all great ideas. But we need to elevate this mixology experience. Make it something truly worthy of the Mariposa name."

Kyle and Regina looked at each other and then back at Josh. But Kelli brightened instantly.

"How about 'Desert Under the Stars'?" she suggested. "We could incorporate local folklore, astronomical facts, desert-inspired cocktails. Do it outside, near the pool. It's classy, educational and distinctively Mariposa."

And he could see her in the middle of it all, the glorious canopy of the sky behind her as she did what she did best— charmed everyone in a hundred-yard radius. His throat tightened again. Which was getting ridiculous.

"That's good," he said gruffly. "I think we can go with that. I'll work more on this on my own later. I'll let you all get back to work. Thanks."

Kyle and Regina melted away, both intent on their morning prep. Kelli didn't move, just stood there leaning on the bar, her gaze intent on his. "I'll lead the class if you want."

"I hadn't really thought that far ahead," he lied.

Of course she was the right choice. It just meant he'd be working with her even more closely as the experience took shape. He'd already had to exercise an extreme amount of will to stay out of the bar when she was behind it. Add in a project that he hoped to stamp his name all over with Kelli at the center of it, what chance did he have of maintaining even a shred of his sanity?

Zero. Worse, he didn't have much of a choice. If he went with the desert stars idea, it would be at night. Kelli worked at L Bar during the day. Not difficult math. She'd be available. Better yet, she'd be available nights until then as they hashed out details, heads together in a quiet, secluded space. Like his bungalow.

Josh shook that off. No bungalow. No seclusion. They could lay out whatever needed to be laid out in…someone's office since he didn't have one. Which had desks. Walls. Doors he could push her up against and—

Shoving away from the bar, he gave Kelli a two-finger salute. "Thanks for the ideas. I'll get back to you."

As he strode out of the bar, his throat still hurt, and the last thing he wanted to do was get back on a horse for a trail ride in what would be ankle-deep mud for hours yet. That was fine. He needed that time to put up a double wide set of construction barriers between him and Kelli.

Before he crossed a line he couldn't uncross.

Chapter Four

Despite never having worked day shift before, Kelli fell into the rhythm easily by the end of the first week. The guests had a whole different dynamic, which she'd anticipated. But what she hadn't considered was how much more time she'd have to chat with them. Learn about *them* instead of just their drink preferences. And long periods of time with just a few customers led to a great deal of free time to experiment.

That worked out on several levels.

A well-tanned gentleman slid onto a barstool, the same one he'd claimed every day at one o'clock. Today's loud tropical-themed shirt had parrots printed all over it, and he wore a Panama hat that looked ridiculous on him, but Kelli grinned as she placed a napkin in front of him.

"I've been waiting not so patiently for you, Mr. Allen," she told him. "After our conversation yesterday, I came up with a new drink just for you."

She reached for the coconut rum, guava juice, passion fruit syrup and a few other key ingredients, threw it all in a shaker with ice, and flipped it over her shoulder to catch it behind her back.

Mr. Allen loved that move and she loved the hundred-dollar tip he left her each time he tabbed out. He made all the appreciative noises as she strained the drink into a highball glass, finished it off with ginger beer, a trade se-cret that gave her drinks a signature taste that guests constantly asked her to reveal but she never would, and stuck a live orchid on the side as a garnish.

When Josh got the bill for her extravagant purchases, he'd probably have a cow. Oh, well.

She placed the highball glass on the napkin in front of Mr. Allen. "There you go. A cocktail inspired by my Hawaiian roots, a sweet blend of exotic fruits with a hint of the islands' untamed spirit."

He took an enthusiastic sip. "Kelli, this is amazing! What do you call it?"

"Aloha Sunset." A naming wizard, she was not. But it would do.

The man took another sip, savoring the flavors. "It's like a vacation in a glass. You've got some serious talent."

Kelli's smile spread. "Thank you, kind sir. I think it's important to bring a little bit of yourself into what you do, don't you agree?"

She already knew he did, based on their conversations. He owned a talent agency in L.A. and had begged her more than once to come see him in a professional capacity. He seemed to think he could get her work in commercials, which he assured her could pay very well. It was almost tempting but she'd left L.A. once already and had no plans to go back, even though the work sounded like it had enough flexibility to fit her lifestyle.

She liked Arizona. And Mariposa. The energy of this place bled through the soles of her feet the moment she stepped off her moped, but then the luxury and the promise of escape surrounded her, creating a dynamic that sucked her in.

She'd never experienced anything like it.

She chatted with Mr. Allen for a bit and when he finally set off for his tee time, she took advantage of the lull, calling out to Kyle that she was taking a break. In just a week, he'd become a great fill-in for her as long as no one asked for anything too complicated.

Ducking into the back room, she took a quick side trip to the restroom. The exit door beckoned, so instead of jetting to her place at the bar, she stepped outside. The chill of the morning had long burned off and a boatload of sunshine warmed the earth, reflecting off the rocky red sandstone formations that felt close enough to touch way out here.

The scenic overlook near the back entrance to L Bar had quickly become one of her favorite places on the property. The view was breathtaking—a vast expanse of desert landscape and mountains in the distance. She inhaled deeply, the air tinged with the scent of wild sage and adventure.

From here, she could see the trail leading off into the canyons beyond the ridge, where a group of guests on horseback had just come into view. Josh rode at the front on a reddish-colored horse, moving with grace and ease in the saddle as if born to it. Talk about your excellent scenery—there was a sight she hadn't expected to see, and she wouldn't apologize for staring.

Josh Colton was a handsome man on the ground, but astride his horse, their muscles moving in sync with powerful confidence, he became magnificent. The fitted shirt he wore didn't hurt and the Stetson he'd tilted down to shade his eyes gave him a rakish flair that made her throat dry up.

What a dang shame all that prime real estate had a big Hands Off sign. If he made even one tiny move in her direction, she'd blow off the no-frat policy in a heartbeat. But he hadn't so far. He seemed to be much more intense about his job than she'd have guessed from what little she'd gotten to know about him on Thursday nights at The Cloisters.

Honestly, she'd have said he had an adventurous streak. It was something they had in common, or at least she'd thought so. They'd talked a bit about their interests, and she'd pegged him as the type who went white water rafting for fun and lived for adrenaline rushes.

As she watched his horse pick its way along the trail so the guests could easily follow, she wondered what would happen if she got him away from the job for an hour or two. Would he morph back into the man she'd met before coming to work at Mariposa? The one who smiled at her frequently and went out of his way to ask her about her day?

She missed that guy.

She let her gaze soak him in for another beat and then turned back to L Bar, aware that she'd left Kyle alone longer than she'd intended. But she couldn't shake the what-if scenario that she'd conjured up out on the overlook.

What if *she* made the move? What if she could lure Josh out from behind the boss shield that he'd thrown up? What if he really was a rule breaker at heart? He might be waiting on her to let him know she would happily chuck the entire Mariposa Employee Handbook out the window if it meant she'd be given a chance to run her fingertips over the well-defined biceps she'd seen peeking out from his sleeves.

Now that was an intoxicating cocktail if she'd ever heard of one.

When she got back to the bar, a fiftysomething ash-blonde woman sat at the bar on the same stool Mr. Allen had vacated. She gave Kelli a smile when she caught sight of her.

"You must be the bartender everyone is raving about,"

she said. "I heard you make a Hawaiian drink that I shouldn't miss."

Kyle loomed over Kelli's right shoulder. "Mrs. Logan wouldn't take a single thing I offered her. Said she'd wait for you as long as it took."

Kelli had always had regulars for as long as she'd been bartending, many of whom had expressed similar sentiments. It was not uncommon to arrive at work to find the bar two deep with patrons insisting only she could make their drinks the right way, but that kind of devotion usually took time to develop. "Well, that's a lovely compliment, Mrs. Logan. Sorry to keep you waiting."

The older lady waved that off. "Mr. Kyle here showed me a million pictures of his adorbs daughter, so it's all good."

Kelli went to work creating a second Aloha Sunset, aware that Kyle watched her every move. She slowed down and showed him exactly what went into the drink. Most barbacks hoped to become bartenders one day and often paid attention to what went on behind the bar as pseudo training, but not every bartender took the time to teach properly. There was a lot of expectation for you to think on your feet and learn fast in the frenetic pace of a busy watering hole, but Mariposa was far more amenable to a calmer pace.

It was nice to think about having the ability to teach Kyle some things without sacrificing quality service to guests.

Mrs. Logan accepted the drink and sipped it, her eyes closing in apparent pleasure. "This is every bit as good as George said it was. I didn't believe him. I was going to razz him at dinner about letting a cute bartender shade his taste buds, but this is something else."

"Thanks." Kelli grinned. "You can still think of me as the cute bartender if you want though."

By the time Mrs. Logan tabbed out, Kelli had learned she

owned a chain of chic clothing boutiques up and down the West Coast, and then became her favorite customer when the woman gave her a five-hundred-dollar gift card to shop at her online store.

The customer base here exceeded anything she'd ever experienced. If this kept up, she could start thinking about meeting some financial goals far sooner than she'd expected. It wasn't out of the realm of possibility that she could have enough money for a down payment on a house inside of a year.

Once that dream unfolded in her head, she couldn't make it dissolve. Sure, she'd been toying with the idea of putting down some roots, but she hadn't dared think about the timing.

A year wasn't that long. She shivered with awe and anticipation. Visualized her bank account growing at this same clip, putting the energy of it out into the universe.

She carried that with her through the end of her shift, marveling at the providence that had brought her here to this place. After stopping in the employee break room to get a bottle of water before she rode her moped home, she started to emerge from the side room where the drinks were kept cold in a refrigerator, but pieces of a conversation happening in the main room brought her up short.

"...glad they caught Allison's murderer."

A second woman spoke then in a hushed tone. "I can't believe she was killed right here on the property. I'm still looking over my shoulder."

Wait. Were these women talking about a *murder* that had happened *here* at the Mariposa Resort? Kelli hastily ducked back into the alcove housing the refrigerator, feeling not one bit of guilt at listening in to the conversation now that she knew they weren't talking about some crime drama the women had been watching on TV, like she'd first assumed.

"I was just starting to feel better about it," the first woman said, her voice lowering. "Until Alexis was kidnapped. I mean, she works here too, same as Allison did. That could have been any one of us!"

Kelli sucked in a breath before she made a noise and gave herself away. She didn't know who the women were and they might not take kindly to someone eavesdropping, nor did she have any guarantee they would talk to a newcomer about these events.

But none of this could really be what it sounded like. Surely they weren't talking about Alexis, Mariposa's concierge? Who else could they be talking about though? There wasn't another person employed at the resort with that name.

Geez. Alexis had been the one to recruit her to come work for Mariposa—and the woman had been *kidnapped*? Was the staff in danger?

"That business with Glenna Colton is still bothering me," the second woman said. "I don't know where she got all her information, but it's her fault the media knows anything at all. We work so hard to keep things here private and she goes and ruins it all."

Who was Glenna Colton? Another sibling she hadn't met yet? And what did the media know? Kelli had searched for information on Mariposa before her interview but had never thought to read any of the news articles. Most of that stuff was clickbait.

"I know, right?" the first woman said, her voice lowering even further, causing Kelli to have to lean in to catch the last part. "Kim at the front desk told me that she walked in on Laura and Adam talking and only heard the last part of the conversation, but it was clear to her that the resort might be in trouble because of Glenna. I think she and their father are trying to take it away from Laura, Adam and Joshua."

The second woman groaned. "What if we all lose our jobs because of these scandals? People aren't going to want to come here if—"

The woman must have exited the break room because the conversation abruptly cut off. Ugh. And now she didn't feel like she knew anything at all other than some terrible things had happened to people employed at Mariposa and someone named Glenna had it in for the current owners.

All this information sank Kelli's good mood. Just as she'd decided this job was a godsend, the universe conspired to steal her joy over things finally working out in her life. This serene and luxurious resort seemed to be bursting at the seams with intrigue and danger, none of which she wanted any part.

Nothing she could do about it now except be the best bartender she could be and ensure guests here had a great time for the scant bit of time she had any influence over their stay. Maybe she could feel out Kyle to see if he knew any further details of what the women had been talking about.

Anxious to get home and decompress after learning all this terrible news, she finally emerged from the side room moving faster than she should be and smacked into something hard and unyielding that knocked her off balance. She glanced up into Josh's blue eyes as he caught her, keeping her off the floor with strong hands at her waist, fingers nipping in to brand her flesh.

"We've got to stop meeting like this," she told him breathlessly, cursing her stupid voice, which had obviously not gotten the memo that it shouldn't be affected by Joshua Colton. Not when he was off-limits.

"You've got to stop running into me," he murmured but

unlike the first time, he didn't immediately drop his delicious grip on her waist. "I didn't hurt you, did I?"

"Is this the part where I should compliment your hours in the gym?" she asked wryly as she rubbed at the place where her sternum had taken the brunt of the meetup with Josh's abs. "Feels like I got smacked with a side of beef."

His grin lit through her, tugging deep at places that hadn't been tugged in a very long time. It was giving her ideas. Very, very bad ideas. The kind that masqueraded as good ideas and would feel amazing when they became a reality.

"No gym for me," he said nonchalantly. "Just a lot of physical activity as part of my job."

That seemed to remind him that he shouldn't be touching her in a way that would look pretty intimate to an outsider. He released her, stepping back and taking all his glorious heat with him.

That's when she realized she hadn't seen him in several days. "Is that why you haven't been by the bar? You've been busy with trail rides?"

"Well, I was off yesterday, but as for the rest of the week…yeah. I have a lot of responsibilities that require hands-on attention."

Like her? There was a glint in his eyes that she'd totally take as flirting if they were at The Cloisters. Heck, she might take it that way now. There were no rules against *that*. "Anytime you want to put some hands-on attention toward the brand-new daytime bartending staff, you come on by."

"I hear you've been settling in fine without my help," he muttered, running his hand through his hair. Flustered. It was cute. Especially since she'd been the one to rattle him.

"Doesn't mean I wouldn't appreciate pointers from my boss. Some guidance on how to work with the staff more seamlessly. Maybe a bit of background about the resort."

More details about whoever Glenna is, and if she and your father really have the power to take away Mariposa from you. Kyle wasn't the only one she could feel out, but Josh would have to darken the door of L Bar to make that happen. She wondered how he felt about the subtext of what she'd heard from the women a few minutes ago—assuming it was true. Did he worry about losing the resort? He seemed to love it.

All at once, she wanted to know everything about him, not just details to satisfy her curiosity.

Josh nodded, his expression contrite. "I'm sorry. You're right. I should spend some time with you making sure you have everything you need to be successful in this job."

With that, he murmured something about needing to get back to the horses and melted away, leaving her to watch him go, unable to squelch a dizzying round of *what if*.

Chapter Five

Josh's strategy to avoid Kelli and burn out his extremely inconvenient attraction to her hadn't worked. Understatement. All it had taken to burst into flames and incinerate instantly was five seconds in the employee break room with Kelli unexpectedly in his arms. Where he'd very much wanted to keep her.

Instead, he'd done the right thing and left her there. Alone. With no one around to see them if he'd wanted to take another five seconds and pull her closer.

No. Bad line of thinking. Anyone could have walked in and seen them. Sure, he could have easily explained it away with the truth, but he had a feeling his face might have telegraphed an entirely different story.

Since distance had failed miserably, the next morning Josh elected to make good on his promise to spend some additional time with Kelli—as her *boss*. Nothing more. He could present the status of his mixology event plans to her, get her thoughts and nail down a date to start, hopefully next week.

Having sanctioned time with his new bartender put an extra bounce in his step that everyone noticed. Clark even teased him about it when he took Maverick's reins after Josh's morning ride. Laura commented twice when she waylaid him on his way to L Bar with some paperwork that "couldn't wait" according to his sister, whom he loved, but didn't like very much at the moment.

The paperwork turned out to be tax related and took over an hour. Even that couldn't dampen his mood. It was silly to be so eager to see Kelli, when in reality he could have dropped by the bar twenty times over the last few days. But hadn't because of a flawed strategy.

He was proud of his restraint though. It seemed he could resist someone he'd previously have described as irresistible. So no reason not to reverse course.

But when he finally disentangled himself from Laura's tax issues, the bar had already opened for the day. Which meant guests had already started to trickle in despite it not yet being noon, his personal threshold for when it was appropriate to start pouring alcohol down his throat. Guests, not so much.

Josh pushed open the glass door, agog at the number of people already bellied up up to the bar. Six, no seven. That was a lot for a resort that only allowed a hundred guests max, many of whom may be at the pool or playing golf, for example.

Was there something going on he hadn't been told about?

Folding his arms, he leaned on one of the cocktail tables, curiosity a living breathing thing. Kelli glided into view, a silver cocktail shaker in each hand, a ready smile on her face. Clearly in her element. The bar was buzzing with excitement, a palpable energy that seemed to pulse with the rhythm of her movements.

He watched, captivated, as she flipped a cocktail shaker over her shoulder, catching it effortlessly with a grace that belied the complexity of the maneuver. She did the same thing with four beer bottles in a row, then cracked the top off each one with a bottle opener in under a second. Each move was a dance, a performance that enthralled the guests crowding the bar, their eyes following her every twirl and twist as they cheered and shouted in support.

Good grief. He'd known she had some skill, had seen her flair for bartending on several occasions at The Cloisters. But this was something else, something beyond talent sliding well into art. She owned the space around her, pouring liquor with precision, her smile never wavering, even as she juggled multiple guests calling out orders.

For a moment, Josh let himself forget he was her boss, forget about lines he shouldn't cross, forget about rules he shouldn't break, and just enjoyed the poetry behind the bar.

One of the guests shoved off a barstool and headed for the door, glancing at his watch. When he caught sight of Josh, he nodded. "Colton, that's some addition to the staff you've got there. Whatever it costs, keep that one around."

"Noted, Mr. Fuentes," Josh said with a smile, recognizing the gentleman who had sent his kids on a trail ride yesterday.

"My golf buddies are going to love her Aloha Sunset as soon as I can get them in here after our tee time."

Josh smiled and nodded like he had a clue what Mr. Fuentes was talking about as the man pushed his way out of the bar and headed in the direction of the links. Since he couldn't get near the bar anyway, Josh opted to watch the show for a little while longer, drifting closer to listen to Kelli interacting with the guests.

He sensed rather than saw Regina sidle up behind him, her heavy perfume a dead giveaway as it permeated his space. He glanced at her sideways as she plunked a round serving tray down on the table in front of him.

"She's gotta go," Regina announced with a pouty mouth. "That woman is a menace."

"What?" Josh laughed. "I literally just got a rave review from a guest. Kelli's not going anywhere."

The look Regina gave him didn't bode well and had a lot of *I see more than you think I do* laced through it. "No one is sitting at the tables. They're all over *her*, fighting for the barstools and ignoring the fact that I have rent due that isn't going to get paid if all the tips flow in Miss Pineapple Princess's direction."

"Maybe learn to flip some beer bottles," he suggested mildly. "There's room for everyone here at L Bar. You'll find your place in this new ecosystem."

Wishful thinking, possibly. But Regina surely didn't expect that Josh would eliminate a successful hire in favor of an existing employee. After all, if no one was sitting at the tables, he didn't need to pay a cocktail waitress, which he probably didn't have to point out. That made her catty comments even more perplexing.

Probably Regina held a grudge about Kelli getting Valerie's spot. Josh felt for her, he really did. But no one got a free ride at Mariposa, himself included. Everyone worked for what they wanted.

Regina stormed off in the direction of the walk-in refrigerator, hopefully to spend a good long while stocking beer and cooling off. Josh glanced back at the bar, noting that one of the guests had moved over to the pass-through, which had been left open—by Regina most likely, who didn't seem too interested in protocol at the moment.

The pass-through swing gate should be closed if no one was sitting at the tables and Regina wasn't even on the floor, since she should be the only one who needed to pass back and forth. But Kelli owned the bar area, and he didn't want to interfere with her setup if she'd left it open for some reason.

As he watched, one of the guests actually stepped across the threshold into the bar area. Josh narrowed his gaze at the man, trying to place him. Generally, he tried to learn the names of all the guests on the property for a number of reasons, mainly to ensure everyone felt welcome and properly elevated, since everyone who came here had some level of note.

This one, he hadn't met, an unusual occurrence in and of itself. It was a rare guest who didn't end up partaking of at least one of the activities on the property. Josh oversaw all of them with a personal hand, often driving guests to the hot-air balloon launch site or standing in as a fourth for golf if one of the players got called into a last-minute work fiasco at the companies they owned.

The guest said something to Kelli, who smiled, but didn't break the routine of mixing the next drink, a professionalism that Josh appreciated. But that guy shouldn't be on the other side of the bar. It was against the rules.

In a move too quick to be believed, the guest reached out and pulled Kelli toward him, as if he meant to yank her into an embrace, his arm snaking around her waist.

Instantly, Josh strode toward the bar, his blood on simmer. No one touched his employees, especially not that one.

Before he'd taken two steps, Kelli set down the bottle of liquor she had in her right hand and firmly removed the guest's arm, folding it against the guy's chest. Then she spun him and marched him back toward the pass-through.

To her credit, he went along with it like a meek little lamb despite the fact that he probably had seventy pounds on the bartender.

Just as Josh reached the area, she pushed the guest back to the right side of the threshold and shut the swing gate, leaning on it. Her gaze had never left the guest, and from this vantage point, Josh could hear what she was saying to him.

"I appreciate that, Mr. Weinberg, but your wife wouldn't." She treated him to a genuine smile that had not one bit of malice in it, despite having just been subjected to unwanted advances. "I'm taking your last drink off your bill to show there are no hard feelings, but I'm afraid it's time for us to part ways. You don't want to miss your tennis game later."

She picked up a leather receipt holder and pulled out the tab, then trashed it and printed a new one, handing it to the guy.

The guest, Mr. Weinberg—whose name was now emblazoned on Josh's brain—nodded, seemingly contrite and took the receipt holder. "Okay, Miss Kelli. You're the boss."

A bit sheepish, the man leaned over the bill and signed it to charge against his room number.

"Let me escort you out," Josh told him in a tone that brooked no argument and put a firm hand on the guest's elbow to make the point that Kelli wasn't alone in this decision to cut him off.

Leaving Mr. Weinberg on the other side of the heavy glass door, Josh darted back to the pass-through, his gaze on Kelli, who had opted to watch him throw out the handsy guest instead of returning to her other patrons.

"Thanks," she murmured, her brown eyes liquid as she peered up at him. "I didn't tell him I was the boss, by the way. I know that's your job."

Ha. She had nothing on him. "That was totally a boss move, Kelli. Amazing. I couldn't have coached an employee to handle that situation any better than you did, let alone expect someone to remember anything about de-escalating in the moment when someone is putting their hands all over you."

Kacy Cross   57

Actually, he was still a little bit in awe that he'd had to do nothing more than take out the trash. If he didn't already have a raging attraction to his new bartender, that would have done it.

She shrugged, a tiny smile playing with her lips as she acknowledged the compliment. "Not my first rodeo. I helmed the main bar at a multilevel club in L.A. There were eight bouncers on the floor at any given time and I was lucky to see one twice in a night. You learn to handle drunk frat boys as well as the ones who never grow up."

"Still. You shouldn't have had to do that here." He ran a hand through his hair, a myriad of paperwork dancing before his eyes. "Are you okay? Do you need to take some time away?"

She glanced back at the number of occupied barstools. "I'm fine. Taking a break would mean letting Regina close the tabs. No thank you."

Almost smiling at that, he nodded. "I'm going to write up the incident for HR and speak with Adam. If you want to press charges, you have Mariposa's full support. I'll act as your eyewitness."

Plus, he'd be tasking Adam with having a private word with Mr. Weinberg so it was clear that the resort did not tolerate behavior of this sort, nor would they give him a second chance. One more infraction, and he'd be asked to leave, as well as likely banned from returning. But that was up to Adam.

"I'm fine," she repeated. "It's over. My customers need me to get back to work."

Kyle strolled out of the back, hefting a case of vodka in both hands, his gaze shifting back and forth between Josh and Kelli as if realizing something was up. "Hey, Joshua, what did I miss?"

A lesson in how to handle security, a factor that Josh needed to take into account. Mariposa employed a slew of security staff headed by Roland Hargreaves to sweep the grounds 24/7, and Adam had told him they did rounds through the bar at night when people tended to drink more, but obviously that needed to change to include daytime rounds as well.

In the meantime, he'd have a word with Kyle about filling the gap.

"See me before your shift in the morning," he told the barback, suddenly glad that Kyle at least looked intimidating before he opened his mouth and let on that he was a teddy bear, not the fierce warrior his build would indicate.

Meanwhile, it was late, and Josh had spent far too long enjoying Kelli on the move behind the bar instead of bringing up his mixology class with her. He had to go prepare for his first trail ride of the day and also handle all the details of reporting the incident. He made a mental note to check in with the Reservations Desk to find out how long Mr. Weinberg would be staying at Mariposa, information he would also pass along to Adam.

He reluctantly waved goodbye to Kelli and shoved off to get started on the mountain of tasks that had been added to his day, thanks to entitled jerks. Unfortunately, a lot of people with money seemed to fall into that category, and Josh should pick a different profession if he didn't want to be exposed to them.

The incident stayed with him all day and he couldn't shake off the disgust that one of his employees had been subject to that kind of inappropriate behavior. But at the same time, he could not get over how well Kelli had handled it. Not only handled it, but did so without coming unglued.

She'd stayed on an even keel the whole time, a facet of her personality he'd never experienced before, but liked. A lot.

Despite knowing it was an awful idea, he found himself heading for L Bar at five o'clock. The fact that he was even free was a minor miracle because normally he'd be engaged in something at this time.

Okay, he might have suggested to Knox, one of the riding instructors, that he would benefit from working with the large animal vet who had arrived to do annual vaccinations on all the horses. That left Josh free to check on Kelli. It wasn't a crime.

As Josh arrived at the bar, he spied Kelli on the other side of the heavy glass door heading in his direction, so he pushed it open for her, allowing her to pass. "Just the woman I wanted to see."

His tone probably should have been a little more professional and a lot less warm, but oh, well. Too late now.

She smiled. "I'm fine. You have that *I need to make sure everything is okay* look about you."

That pulled a grin from him. "What's wrong with wanting to make sure you're okay?"

"Nothing, except you already did earlier. Nothing has changed."

That was wrong. Everything had changed, but Josh couldn't quite put his finger on when. All he knew was that they stood in the lobby of L Building, where fifty people might pass by at any moment, and he hated knowing that someone might question why he'd moved so close to her. But he couldn't stop himself from dragging her scent into his body with each breath.

"Have dinner with me, then," he blurted out and nearly bit his tongue off.

What was *wrong* with him?

She arched a brow, her gaze traveling down his length and back up again as if she'd accidentally stumbled over a talking iguana. "Are you asking me to break the rules?"

"Absolutely not," he stated firmly, eyeing her right back so she'd see he meant it. "As friends. There are no rules against a boss having dinner with an employee he has no plans to kiss."

Also known as the second thing he'd blurted out that should have stayed unvoiced, because now that's all he could think about—kissing Kelli. It had an alliterative lilt that made it fun to repeat, even silently in his head.

And now that he'd told her he had no plans to kiss her, he had to make good on that. Joshua Colton was many things but not a liar.

She squeezed her eyes shut and nodded once. "I'd like to have dinner with you then. As friends."

Chapter Six

Dinner as friends.

It was the sign Kelli had been waiting on but not the one she'd hoped for. Josh wanted to be friends. *Okaaaay.* What wasn't to like about that? A man friend had no say over her life, wouldn't try to tell her what to do, no sanctuary invading would happen. They wouldn't be violating the resort's policies, and she could sate her curiosity about him as a person.

Regardless, she could not shake the vague sense of disappointment that lay heavy behind her rib cage.

She followed Josh down one of the stamped concrete paths toward the back of the property, where the private bungalows she'd never seen up close lay nestled in individual thickets of trees, the natural stone outcroppings providing physical barriers between the adobe buildings.

"This place is adorable," she murmured as he unlocked the door on the one furthest away from the others. "I didn't know you lived on the property."

Josh shrugged. "Seemed expedient. I used to live in one of the suites in L Building but that started feeling too much like a dorm room, so I had this bungalow built to spec."

Somehow, when she'd agreed to dinner as friends, she'd envisioned having a burger at Applebee's or some other casual place in Sedona, not being whisked away to the very private residence of Joshua Colton.

Or that he'd casually inform her that he'd cook. A man cooking for you did not scream *friends*. With benefits, maybe.

Oh, goodness. Was that what he'd meant, and she'd been too dense to connect the dots?

Her belly fluttered as she weighed out how stupid it would be to take him up on any offers of that sort. And how much she'd regret it if she declined.

Getting ahead of yourself, dingdong.

No one had offered her anything except dinner. With a deep, cleansing breath, she stepped across the threshold of Josh's bungalow. And gasped.

"Oh, my goodness, your view!"

Transfixed, she floated to the floor-to-ceiling glass that made up two whole walls, meeting at a ninety-degree angle that created a panoramic frame for the mountains beyond the trees. The sun had just dipped below the horizon, throwing a kaleidoscope of colors across the sky. Out here, it felt like you could grab a handful of inky blue and pull it around you like a blanket.

"It's pretty spectacular," he murmured. "I confess I might have hoped to impress you with it. Anyone can take you to a restaurant, but what kind of friend would I be to not share this with you?"

Oddly touched by the sentiment, she glanced at him over her shoulder as he came up behind her, standing so close she could feel his heat, but somehow not nearly close enough.

"Well, as your new friend, I highly appreciate the, erm..." *Don't say benefits.* "Advantages. What are you cooking for me?"

"I have no idea," he admitted and ran a hand through his

hair, a move she'd noted he did a lot. "This was a somewhat spontaneous invitation, born out of an intense desire to get out from under the microscope of L Building."

That, she understood. "Your siblings would give you a hard time if they knew we were...friendly?"

"Among other things, yeah," he mumbled darkly. "Plus, it's really no one's business if we want to spend a few hours talking without an audience."

That sounded an awful lot like code for getting to know each other better because he was interested in being more than friends. Otherwise, why would it matter if anyone knew or saw them?

Oh, my. They were on the brink of a *forbidden* romance, and she couldn't suppress the shiver. Never had she thought she'd find such a prospect so thrilling, but here they were.

"This secret is totally safe with me." She mimed locking her lips. "I'd rather no one else know about my private life anyway. I'm not a big blabber to my coworkers about things they'd just be jealous about."

That's when Josh moved just a tiny bit closer to her in what might have been somewhat of a sway. She felt her own body respond in kind.

"You think the bar staff would be jealous to find out you're having dinner with the boss?" he murmured.

"Well, there's no dinner in the mix yet," she reminded him, and it was supposed to come out as a joke, but her voice ended up being too breathy to be called anything other than stimulated. "But anyone would be green with envy over missing out on this view."

"Agree with that."

But she could feel his gaze burning her cheek and she knew if she turned her head, she'd see him staring at her, not the sunset behind the mountains. Okay, this was officially the best date she'd ever been on that she probably shouldn't classify as a date.

She had the distinct sense they were both being careful not to officially cross the line. Yet.

That's when Josh stepped away in a disappointing rush, taking all his deliciousness with him. Proving the point. This was a delicate balance between genuine desire to follow policy and genuine desire for the exact opposite. On both sides, as best she could tell.

"I'm going to see what I have to eat," he announced and edged into the small kitchen on the other end of the room.

His open-air bungalow didn't have a lot of places to hide, so she enjoyed the Josh Show instead of the sunset. He moved with such fluid grace, more dancer than athlete, though she knew from the last time she'd watched him in his element, he was no slouch in that department either. Not bulky, like a meathead who lifted weights two hours a day, but lithe and capable in the saddle, which told her he probably did a lot of activities well that required stamina and strength.

Oh, well, that was not a good thing to realize while trying to cool herself down from his earlier skin-scorching episode by the window.

"Tell me what it's like to live at a resort," she called and crossed the room to the island separating the two rooms, leaning on it unconsciously until she realized that was her go-to position when a bar separated them.

"See—microscope," he said with a laugh and held up a bag of wheat-colored grain. "I'm making quinoa and chicken salad, if that's okay. Are you allergic to anything? Have an aversion to weird stuff in your food?"

Charmed that he would bother to ask, she shook her head. "I'm from Hawaii. We eat poi."

"Point taken."

She watched him pull out chicken breast and a bag of spinach, entranced that a man would have such things readily available in his refrigerator. "You spontaneously cook for friends often?"

"First time."

He drizzled olive oil in a heavy grill pan that nearly made her swoon with envy—her own had come from a big box store, but his sported the logo of a pricey brand that mere mortals could only dream of owning. Though the swooning may have been already in motion after learning that he didn't bring women back to his bungalow twice a week.

Well, to be fair, he hadn't said that. She'd filled in a lot of her own blanks, especially when he'd been so adorably unsure what to cook.

Josh took a clamshell of cherry tomatoes and sprayed them with an organic vegetable wash that he clearly used often since he kept it by the sink, then rinsed them and turned to dump the grape-sized tomatoes on the cutting board he'd placed on the island in front of her.

"I see now why you don't have an ounce of fat on your body if this is the way you eat regularly."

He glanced up, meeting her gaze, chef's knife forgotten in his hand as a delighted smile spread across his face. "How can you tell that?"

"Please," she scoffed. "We women have our ways."

Such as shamelessly checking him out on the sly when he turned up at the bar. Or openly gawking, like she was doing now. It wasn't hard to tell he was built like a marble statue carved by a master when he wore formfitting clothes as a matter of course, his Mariposa T-shirt clinging to what had to be washboard abs or she'd be very disappointed.

She didn't think she'd be disappointed if Josh whipped

off his shirt to prove her right. Judging by the sudden and intense heat between them, she suspected he might be thinking about that too.

"We need a new subject if I hope to keep all of my fingers intact while slicing small objects," he informed her wryly. "So I'll go back to your question. I've lived at Mariposa for almost ten years, so all my adult life, and I love it. I have horses and a big sky, a continual influx of guests who look to me for guidance on how to have fun, and I'm partners with my family. Probably not the best example of work-life balance, but I make sure to have plenty of downtime. Which is why I don't cook for people. I can be very much an introvert after hours."

"Am I intruding, then?" she asked sincerely, suddenly struck that she'd taken him up on an invitation he'd possibly only offered to be polite.

Josh made a face. "I wouldn't have brought you here if I considered it an intrusion."

"Then let's get back to how you're the master of fun," she suggested lightly. "I have yet to experience that side of you. What would you advise me to do if I came to you looking for fun?"

Yes, sir, she was flirting. No, she wasn't ashamed of herself, and she'd probably keep doing it if he kept giving her such excellent bait.

His gaze swept her with decided assessment and a chaser of appreciation that she didn't mind a bit. "You look like a hot-air balloon girl."

"I do?" She laughed, totally caught off guard that he'd actually answered the question as an activities director, not a man interested in getting a woman under him later. "What about me says hot-air balloon?"

"The wild curl of your hair. The way you immediately gravitated toward the sunset instead of my bookcase full of books and knickknacks. The fact that you jump from job to job effortlessly, always open to something new. I could go on."

Well, that would be fine with her if he did. The flutter in her belly spread, taking wing in her heart as she internalized that Josh had been paying such close attention to her. That he seemed to have pegged some deep-seated aspects of her personality that she'd never quite realized would reveal so much to the right person.

"I've never been in a hot-air balloon," she told him. "But it's now very high on my list of must-have experiences."

Their gazes locked, neither of them looking away.

"I'll take you sometime. Though, to be honest, it's not really something I consider fun. It's spiritual. Which I have a feeling you might appreciate more than fun."

He pivoted back to the stove to flip the chicken and begin wilting the spinach, breaking the spell he'd put her under.

Her tiny little crush on her boss exploded into something she had no clue what to do with. "I have a feeling you might be right."

Though she'd never considered her favorite experiences in life spiritual, she recognized instantly what he meant. The sunset called to her because the colors made her chest ache. The panorama of the mountains reminded her that the world was so big and so open, and she could explore every last centimeter of it if she wanted to.

Josh held up a finger, presumably to stop her from continuing the conversation, and concentrated on throwing the rest of dinner together. In no time at all, he dumped everything into two earthenware bowls, one cobalt blue, the other emerald green, and set them on the table for two in his tiny nook.

"Sorry for cutting you off," he said as he held out a chair for her, allowing her to slide past him, then pouring her a glass of ice water from a pitcher he'd pulled from the refrigerator. "You're very distracting and I didn't want to starve you."

Oh, she was starving all right. For more of Joshua Colton.

"Yeah, I'm glad I wasn't the one having to wield that chef's knife. But it's only fair that I return the favor because this is amazing." She pointed at her forkful of his quinoa chicken. "I have a sudden urge to make kalua pork, lomi lomi salmon and poi and trust me when I say I wouldn't make that for anyone but you."

"Because no one else cooks for you that you'd need to reciprocate?" he asked, his own fork forgotten.

"Correct. But also because it's an enormous pain to make, and you're the only man I would consider worth it."

Probably too much information and too on the nose, but she didn't care. Josh interested her and she'd rather be honest about it.

"You don't have a line of dudes waiting in the wings to romance you with chicken and wilted vegetables?"

This was the part where she should play it close to the vest, make him sweat. But why? She'd never understood it when women went out of their way to play games. What if the guy you were interested in took your caginess as lack of interest and shoved off? Ridiculous to let a great man slip through your fingers because of some dumb made-up ploy to snare him.

"No line. I don't date much," she admitted. "Hard when

I always work nights and honestly, so few men I meet justify the effort."

"Dating isn't supposed to be an effort. You're hanging out with the wrong men."

Oh, that wasn't in question. Especially in comparison to the man sitting across from her. All it took was the *right* one to see the difference. It made her bold enough to want to open up a little. To take a chance on something wonderful happening. Continuing to happen. It had been wonderful since she walked in the door.

"I actually never dated much," she murmured. "I had really overprotective parents growing up. By the time I managed to get out from underneath them, I'd already missed out on all the firsts most teenage girls got to experience."

"That's a shame."

It was all he said. His gaze never left hers as he ate, content to let her continue without throwing out a practiced line about all the things he could show her or to offer to be her guide into the more carnal pleasures. Other guys had been quick with both, which in her naiveness, she hadn't realized were lines.

It had only taken a broken heart and a second trip in that direction to stop dating and stop telling anyone about her lack of experience.

She'd known Josh would handle it differently.

"I appreciate that. I'm spending my twenties making up for lost time. You'd think that would make me less picky about who I date, but I find the opposite to be true. I built it up in my head for so long that no real men measure up."

Until tonight.

It was scaring her. If she'd learned nothing else from her parents, it was that she never wanted to give someone else the power to hurt her. Control her. And men in positions of power—like Joshua Colton—were often anxious to do both. She'd never appreciated the no-fraternization policy more than she did in that moment.

Chapter Seven

Who knew that throwing down the friendship card would be the key to unlimited access to Kelli? Not Josh.

But he was nothing if not a man who could capitalize on an opportunity presenting itself. After they finished eating dinner, which took almost an hour, he dumped the plates in the sink, flicked the water on for half a second and called it good.

He couldn't wait to spend more time with her on this pseudo date that could never go anywhere. The brilliance of this shift in dynamics nearly left him breathless with anticipation.

Kelli stood in the center of his living room, her hands clasped and her body tensed as if about to make an escape. "Thank you for dinner. It was lovely, but I've taken enough of your time."

Mayday. She was bailing. Josh's chest squeezed even as he recognized the wisdom. Friends had dinner and then they left to go back to their own lives. They didn't hang around and tempt fate.

"What's your hurry?" he said instead of *good night* like he should have. "It's early. Stay for a few more minutes and check out the patio on this place. You won't be disappointed, I promise."

For some reason, that seemed to sway her, and she nodded. "I can stay for a few more minutes. I do have to get
up early."

Yeah, he had an early morning in store as well. What did
that have to do with anything? He grinned. "You've never
stayed up so late that it made no sense to go to bed, so you
just…didn't?"

She actually laughed at that. "Of course I have. Deliberately though. You don't seem to understand what it was
like growing up with Malia and Kimo Iona, two of the most
traditional Hawaiian people ever born."

"Tell me," he said as he guided her to the sliding doors,
opening them on the tracks that allowed him to fold back
both glass walls.

Kelli's eyes widened as she watched the whole of the
south and west walls vanish, leaving the living area open to
the covered patio. "I didn't realize these were doors! That's
a neat trick. Must be very handy for entertaining."

"Since you're it for my guest list lately," he commented
dryly, "let me know how entertained you are in a bit."

She glided onto the patio, heading straight for the railing, resting her hand on it as she tipped her head up to the
sky. That section of the patio wasn't covered and the river
of black stretched overhead, stars layered through it in no
discernible pattern. It felt very much like staring into the
heart of the universe. Which he knew because he stood in
that exact spot frequently.

"It's like nothing I've ever seen," she murmured. "How
do you sleep with this for company?"

"Sometimes I don't," he said with a shrug. "Those are
the times it doesn't make sense to go to bed. You only have
one life and sleeping it away has never appealed to me."

She glanced at him as he joined her at the railing, studying him for a beat before she turned her attention back to the stars. "You've really never had a party in this space? That seems like a waste of a great design."

Sure he had, right after he'd had the house built. And a number of parties for two. But his interest in that had waned over time as the breadth of people he surrounded himself with got narrower. Most women appreciated his money and his name far more than they appreciated him. Ava had hinted more than once that she'd love to see the resort, but he'd never brought her here, or the handful of women who had come before her. It was far preferable to judiciously protect his space and keep it drama free.

"Parties are overrated," he told her. "And I'm outside too often for most people's taste. It's hard to bond."

The hush of the mountains made an excellent backdrop for Kelli as she stood there soaking in the view. He felt it in his throat, her beauty melding with the land, the absolutely rightness of her energy entwined with his.

A big chunk of his will cracked off and floated away to be absorbed by the night. He was in so much trouble with this woman. It was too late to reel back what had already happened, how he felt drawn to her as if cosmic forces had separated them a million years ago and they'd been fighting to return to each other ever since.

In short, he could keep pretending to everyone else, but not to himself. And he couldn't walk away from her right now.

"Sit with me for a while," he said and jerked his head toward the loungers tucked into the corner. "I have blankets."

"You're speaking my language," she said with a laugh, chafing at her arms. "I wasn't expecting to be out after dark and didn't bring my jacket."

"You should have said something earlier," he admonished

her lightly and dragged both loungers closer to the edge of the patio, then tugged on her hand to guide her to the one on the left, helping her get settled.

As he draped a thermal blanket over her legs, he glanced up to find her watching him instead of the stars.

"You're nothing like I expected," she told him, pursing her lips. "Which is a strange thing to say when I had plenty of expectations."

This, he had to hear. He settled into his own lounger, forgoing the blanket for the moment since he liked the chill. "Oh?"

She shot him a look. "Come on. You sat at my bar three Thursdays in a row. You came there to see me—don't deny it."

"I would never." He held up his hands, palms out. "I did come to see you. You're amazing behind the bar, a force of nature. I'm not at all shocked Alexis recommended you to Laura."

"You didn't come for my ability to flip a shaker over my shoulder. Wait, did you?" Her expression screwed up in dawning shock. "You weren't the advance scout all this time, were you?"

"No," he admitted, though he should have taken the easy out.

It would have gone a long way toward cooling things off between them if he told her he'd been working with Alexis to find a replacement bartender, but it would be a lie, and besides, the bar staff hadn't reported to him at the time.

He'd prefer it if everything between him and Kelli stayed pure and honest.

"Okay, so that's why I had expectations," she said with renewed color in her voice. "I thought you were going to ask me out. Of course, I then got a few things in my head about what that would look like. Where you might take me. How you would act on a date. You're none of those things."

She'd thought about him? What had she gotten into her head? It nearly killed him to bite back the questions because he definitely wanted to know if she'd visualized him kissing her under this river of stars—he certainly had. Probably more in the last ten minutes than before she'd been hired on at Mariposa though.

Instead, he crossed his arms before he forgot he wasn't supposed to reach for her hand. "That doesn't sound like a positive."

"Oh, you're scoring much higher right now than you had been in my head," she said with a tiny laugh. "Let's just say my imagination has been broadened considerably, along with my standards. I would have said yes by the way."

To the kissing? Because he was having a hard time thinking about anything else.

"If you'd asked me out," she clarified, obviously having gained mind reading skills in the last two minutes.

But not the type that allowed her to discern how much he wished he could bridge the gap between them, apparently, because she pulled the blanket up over her chest, burying her arms beneath it to form a physical barrier between them. Probably not on purpose. But he should take it as a warning anyway.

Sinking down in his lounger, he tried to push himself back into the boss realm, but it was so distasteful, he couldn't do it. He was well and truly screwed at this point.

"I'm not asking you out," he muttered. "It's against the rules."

That he'd personally authored. He, of all people, knew the pitfalls and had been trying to help everyone else avoid them.

"Oh, yeah, right. I know," she said brightly. "I read the

manual. You should probably know that I'm not much of a rule follower though. Courtesy of my parents."

That was literally the last thing he wanted to learn about her. Because he *was* a rule follower, and he was having a hard time hanging on to his reasons why. One of them needed to be strong. "You conveniently skipped out on telling me about them. Did they lock you in your room and starve you as punishment?"

"Yeah. They did actually."

Her expression broke his heart as he sputtered to reel back what should have been a joke. "Kelli, I... You— I mean, first and foremost, I'm so sorry. I had no idea, which doesn't excuse such a comment, but—well, please know that I am not prying into your life. Unless you want to talk about this, and then I'm all ears.

She smiled and reached out a hand to touch his knee, just for a brief moment, which normally he'd be all over. Yes, it did produce a zing or two, but he was too busy being horrified at both the reality she'd just presented and how far he'd stuck his foot in his mouth.

"It's okay, Josh," she murmured, and he should absolutely not be reveling in her calling him that. He should be correcting her, insisting that she call him Joshua like the rest of the staff.

But he kept his mouth shut.

"I wouldn't have mentioned it if I didn't want to talk about it. Though you'll have to forgive me because I'm pretty rusty at being transparent about my childhood. Usually I keep every last detail to myself."

But she'd told him. He felt strangely honored. And at the same time, like he should be hunting down these horrible people and demanding they make restitution.

"I'm listening, then," he said simply.

"There's not much more to it." Her gaze had returned to the stars, and he fully understood why it would be easier to talk to the universe than directly to him. "My parents are very traditional. Very set in their ways, and they wanted me to become the wife of an important businessman, like my mother did. I was to look a certain way and act a certain way and if I thought it was more fun to sneak out to the beach with my friends than to attend a boring social graces class, they made sure my punishment would make me think twice the second time."

By locking her in her room, apparently.

"Did it?" he murmured.

"Almost never," she returned with a tiny smile.

The punishment definitely did not fit the crime in his mind. Or the mind of anyone with a conscience or a sense of how wrong it would be to try to crush the spirit of this incredible woman.

He couldn't help but reach out then, lacing his fingers through hers and squeezing, suddenly aware of how easily she could slip away. And what a travesty that would be.

He didn't like losing things.

"Sounds like your parents made you resilient," he offered bluntly. "Instead of contrite. Good."

"Their brand of punishment just made me a lot more careful about where I hid the money I was saving up. I feared my mother would find it and take it away, along with my hope of getting out from under their iron rule. Eventually I had enough to jet and I did, to the Big Island. Bartending was something I fell into because everything is expensive in Hawaii, but there is no shortage of tourists who think nothing of tipping big with their vacation money."

Eventually finding her way to the mainland. He could fill in those blanks. She was putting distance between herself and Hawaii for preservation. The bravery required—it took his breath for a moment.

"Thank you for trusting me with your story," he murmured, and she glanced at him for a second, then down at their laced fingers, but she didn't try to pull free, thankfully. He wasn't done touching her, not by half.

"It's not very interesting so far," she said with a wrinkled nose. "I survived and moved on. Every day is the first day of the rest of my life."

"I can totally get on board with that philosophy."

Not just because he appreciated why she'd adopted it, but he lived by similar mantras: *Don't waste time brooding when you could be living. Live each day to the fullest. Honor the land and it will replenish you.*

These were all things he'd repeated to himself while riding Maverick. Things that centered him. How fitting that Kelli would likewise be a twin soul who understood the importance of not poisoning yourself with negative messages.

She was amazing. He could easily see himself falling into the woman and never surfacing.

The thought should scare him a lot more than it did.

"Then you understand," she said with a thread through her tone that sounded a lot like relief. "How important something like freedom is to me. How I build my life to suit *me*, no one else."

"As you should." That also resonated. He appreciated his own freedom a whole lot more in that moment, and vowed to continue remembering how blessed he was to have Mariposa's lands to roam to his heart's content.

For as long as that lasted. The reminder about his father's plans soured his throat.

"Being independent is really important to me," she continued. "That's why landing this job at Mariposa has been such a godsend. I'm saving to buy a house, which maybe feels a little strange, considering I just told you how important freedom is to me. But I'm starting to feel like I need a home base. A place to land, where I can always come back to."

That, he definitely understood, and his heart hurt for her that she'd been robbed of a home thus far. "That's what this resort is to me. I get it. Probably more than you could ever know."

"Tell me," she said with a small smile, reminding him that he'd said the exact same thing to her earlier.

So he did.

"A place to land is what enables you to soar," he murmured. "Because you know you'll always be supported. Always be able to rest when you need it. But still call the shots as to when you fly away the next time. My mother did that for me. I'm sorry you never got to experience that."

"I have it now." She squeezed his fingers, still laced with hers. "My apartment is mine, even though I don't own it. But one day, I'll have my house. You're playing a big part in helping me achieve that. This mixology class you came up with will bring a lot of attention to the bar, which will be huge. Resort guests probably don't think about a bar as a destination, or an activity and I appreciate that you're trying to change that."

It was a sobering reminder that he was her boss—first and foremost. She was not a twin soul who had suddenly made him feel like he'd found someone who could really get him and who he was at the core.

Besides, a woman who spent a lot of time protecting her freedom and telling a man how important independence was to her definitely didn't fit the profile of someone looking for a soulmate. Quite the opposite. In fact, that was likely her whole point in bringing it up. *Hands off my life, Josh.* She couldn't have spelled out any more clearly how much she was *not* the relationship type.

That was great. Perfect, in fact. Neither was he. It meant he could really relax with her, that they were on the same page. Nothing was going to happen between them. Nothing could have anyway, not with the no-fraternization policy, unless she quit. That obviously wasn't anywhere in her plans.

It was better this way. That's how he'd come into this dinner not-a-date initially, and he had no call to be thinking about Kelli any other way than as a friend. He could keep doing what he did best—co-own and run Mariposa according to his skills and strengths—and she could be his rock star bartender. They could work together without fear.

And he would get to spend as much time with her as he felt like without any worries of falling for her.

Chapter Eight

If Josh was feeling even half of what Kelli was, she wished she knew the secret of how he kept himself from floating away on a sea of bliss.

Though, in retrospect, she kind of appreciated that she'd stayed firmly in this lounger under the stars. It would have been a shame to miss even a moment of...whatever this was.

When was the last time anyone had just *listened* to her talk? And he had, for hours. Prior to tonight, Kelli had never thought about a list of perfect dates, or what qualities she'd be looking for in a man. Apparently, the universe just dropped it in your lap, no list needed.

"You told me about your mother passing," she murmured during a longer lull in conversation. "But you've never mentioned your dad. Is he not in the picture?"

He stiffened. She'd become so fine-tuned to every iota of Josh after sitting here in the dark with him for hours that she felt his distress instantly, even though they weren't touching skin. They were touching something all right, but it was far more affecting and deep-seated than the mere meeting of fingers between lounge chairs.

They were touching souls.

"You don't have to talk about your dad if you don't want

to," she said. "You should know that by now. I'm here for whatever you want to talk about."

"Sore subject." Josh blew out a breath. "My dad is what you call a piece of work."

"Tell me," she said, letting her lips curve up.

It was their catch phrase now. Something they said to encourage the other one, and both of them had used it liberally in the last few hours. She'd never shared anything like this with a man before, let alone a secret expression with meaning to only the two of them. It was sexy and affecting and wholly exhilarating.

He returned her smile, but it didn't reach his eyes, which she shouldn't be able to discern out here in the dark with only the stars for light. This was another instance of being able to read him like a book and she liked it. A lot.

"My father is the CEO of Colton Textiles in Los Angeles and lives in Beverly Hills. That should pretty much be the story right there."

But it wasn't, not even close. She heard the frustration in his tone and knew there was more. "So he doesn't live near here or have anything to do with the resort? Is he part owner?"

"No," Josh bit out curtly. "Much to his dismay. But recently it came to light that he owns the land, apparently. Also known as the sore subject."

"Oh. That sounds…complicated." Her parents had some money and prestige, but she sensed it was nothing like what the Coltons must have. The more money, the more problems, in her experience.

"It's a lot of things. Primarily, it means he can sell the land unless we can find a way to stop him."

"And that's something he wants to do? How does that

even work if he sells the land that the resort you own sits on? That's what you're saying. Right?"

Josh ran a hand through his hair, a habit that had become way too endearing, because it always happened when he seemed to have big feelings about something. She liked discovering these fascinating revelations about this man. It was the ultimate *tell me* and she couldn't stop drinking it up.

"Well, that's the thing," he said. "He's trying to sell it to us. Me, Laura and Adam. He needs the cash. But we don't have that kind of money, not in liquid form. The resort itself is worth far more than that, but it's tricky to raise capital against the buildings because of the odd ownership logistics. Not to mention the bad press."

Bad press? She'd never heard about anything of the sort. "What does that mean?"

"You didn't hear about Allison? Our yoga instructor was murdered, right here on the property. It was horrific. So sad and such a waste of a lovely person. She was one of my best employees."

Oh, *that* bad press. All at once, she wondered what the media had said about Mariposa for it to have ranked notice with the Coltons. Clearly it couldn't have been good for business, or he wouldn't have brought it up.

Now she wondered if she should have done more to educate herself on the stories after overhearing the women in the break room talking. "I did hear something about that, but that's not the fault of the resort."

"Your opinion is in the minority," he countered dejectedly.

How dare anyone think the Coltons had sanctioned a killer to come onto their property and allowed a madman to do something unconscionable? Despite the fact that she had worried about her own safety after overhearing the two employees, she realized how silly it was in this moment.

And how much she wanted to deck someone for putting that misery in Josh's voice. "So your dad is causing you financial problems in an attempt to rectify his own, and meanwhile, you're battling a media scandal that shouldn't be a thing because you had nothing to do with it. That's ridiculous."

His smile gained a bit more warmth. "I didn't realize how much I would enjoy the sound of righteous indignation in your voice."

"Well, you can have a lot more of it if you want," she said, her mad gathering steam. "I'm extremely angry at your father right now."

"Don't be. He's not worth it. Hasn't been for a long time."

That sounded like another offshoot to the story that he hadn't gotten to yet, but he had enough fire in his own voice that it might be prudent to tread lightly in case a bombshell like a murdered employee waited in the wings. "Is this another time when I should encourage you to tell me or let it go?"

They'd already graduated to a place where she could sense nuances of his moods, interpret the placement of his hands on his thighs, instantly read the fine lines around his eyes. He didn't want to talk about his father, but she yearned to know everything about him. Even the parts he might think she'd judge him over. She wouldn't.

Whatever his father had done, she wished only to support Josh in his healing. If he needed that from her. It frustrated her that despite the fact that it felt like she'd known Josh her whole life, their budding relationship was still very new.

Josh stared up at the sky, his head tilted back so far that it didn't seem as if he saw the stars at all, but instead might be fighting to get his emotions under control. Without hesitation, she reached out and slipped her hand around his wrist. Silently encouraging him.

"My father had a long-standing affair with one of Mariposa's employees," he murmured so quietly she had to lean forward to understand the words, which had the double benefit of being closer to him and allowing her to fully slide their fingers together. "It was difficult for my mother, very in your face, especially when Dani came along. My half sister."

This came with a facial expression she couldn't interpret. "Did you ever meet her?"

"Yeah, of course. My father got custody of her a while back and she's a part of the family now."

But still quite *in your face*, as he'd said. And he loved his mother, unquestionably. Likely these were the big feelings he'd been battling. The fact that he'd call his half sister *family* despite her very existence being painful to his mother spoke volumes to Kelli about Josh's character. His unexpected depths. She craved more of this extraordinary man.

"Thank you for telling me," she said sincerely.

"Most of it I probably shouldn't have told you," he said with a half laugh. "Maybe you can have a sudden bout of amnesia?"

She held up her hand as if swearing an oath. "I would never repeat a word of what I've heard tonight. Or any other day either. I want you to feel like you can trust me with anything."

The pause lengthened as he swallowed. "I do trust you. It's just not something I talk about with anyone. Ever."

But he'd told her. The deliciousness of that winnowed down into her blood, warming it along with everything else.

Who needed blankets when you had Joshua Colton making you feel like he'd wrapped you in something special?

She squeezed his hand, loath to break the spell.

Josh had no such reluctance and glanced over at her. "I hope you see why I'm so adamant about following the no-fraternization policy. My father thought nothing of flaunting his relationship with Mariposa's head housekeeper. It created this imbalance of power and hurt my mother, as well as Dani's mother, who had to work together. Actions and decisions have consequences, and I've never had the slightest desire to push mine onto someone else."

She nodded. "I get that. But it doesn't have to be like that between us."

"No, and it's not. It won't ever be." He flashed her a smile. "That's what makes being here with you so great. That's part of trusting you. Of knowing that you understand and get why it's so important to me. Mariposa is everything. It was my mother's and now it's mine."

"You don't want to jeopardize what you've built here," she finished for him, her heart soaring as she internalized what he wasn't saying—that he'd told her because she was different. Because he knew things between them would unfold in the opposite vein of what had happened with his father. "I would never be a party to that. I do get it. I have zero intention of ever hurting you or Mariposa."

"You have no idea how much that means to me." He sat up then, still holding her hand and bringing it closer to him, almost as if he intended to kiss her knuckles and the heat of his breath nearly made her swoon. "I don't mind confessing that I've never even been tempted to trash that no-fraternization rule before."

Until now.

The warm honey of his words spread through her whole

body as her eyelids fluttered closed. Light from within brightened everything. Then she opened her eyes and realized the sun had started to throw morning rays into the sky above them, splitting the stars.

"Oh, my goodness, we talked all night," she exclaimed breathlessly. "I had no idea that you planned to actually test me on whether we could stay up late enough that it made no sense to go to bed. Did I pass?"

Josh laughed and stood, pulling her to her feet. She had the sense that he meant to step away, to lead her toward the door, but their gazes tangled and neither of them moved. Until he slipped a hand behind her waist and drew her close. Into his embrace.

It was just a hug. But so much more than that at the same time. A seal on their conversation, binding them together irrevocably.

She loved being the exception to the rule. The whole of her childhood, she'd been forced to follow other people's rules, to toe lines she'd never drawn. She refused to do that as an adult, which Josh seemed to get fully. And the fact that he was willing to chuck away something that had so much meaning to him for *her*...*giddy* didn't even begin to describe her mood.

Of course, that might be the lack of sleep playing a factor too.

"I should go," she mumbled into his shirt. "I have to go home for a bit and get ready for a long bar shift. I'm sure you have things to do too."

"Yep," he agreed without releasing her, his lips buried in her hair. "Coffee for one. Not my favorite word at the moment."

Not hers either. She much preferred the sound of coffee for two. Maybe soon that would be a thing.

Reluctantly, she slipped from Josh's arms, already feeling like she might start weeping at the loss of his heat. For more reasons that one. It was *cold* out here without her jacket. The ride home on her moped would be bracing to say the least.

The sun had climbed a little higher by the time she'd said her final goodbye. She made her way home, *euphoria* the only word she could pick to describe what a night of being with Josh felt like. Imagine if they had done more than talk. She might not survive such an experience.

But that didn't stop her from imagining it. From letting herself get caught in the sweet pull of hope as she passed the red rock formations that had stood sentry over their mind-altering conversation.

After parking her moped in her designated spot, she practically broke into a skip as she rounded the corner to her apartment. The door stood ajar. She froze.

Her joy shattered all over the sidewalk.

Had someone broken into her apartment while she'd been away? Had her sanctuary been *invaded*?

The early morning chill seeped into her bones as she stood there, unable to force her legs to work. Or her brain. Someone had tried to follow her the other day, and now this. The murder of the yoga instructor at Mariposa flashed through her mind all at once. Was this how it had started for Allison?

Well, it wasn't how things would end for Kelli Iona. Anger flared within her, hot and fierce. This was her home, her refuge from the world, and someone had dared to cross her threshold without permission. Swallowing her fear, Kelli stepped forward, one hand clutching her cell phone as she dialed 911.

"I'd like to report a break-in," she told the dispatcher with more calm than she'd have believed she could muster as she scouted around the parking lot for the car that had nearly hit her on her way home from Mariposa.

"Is the intruder still in your home?" the lady on the other end of the line asked.

"I don't know." A problem that Kelli intended to rectify immediately. "The door was open when I got here."

The dispatcher promised to send a unit immediately and strongly advised her to wait for the officers before entering the apartment. After a long night of no sleep, all Kelli wanted to do was take a shower and drink some coffee. If the police would be here soon, that meant Kelli would have backup in no time if she chose to check things out herself in advance. Right? Or was that how the too-stupid-to-live heroines always acted in horror movies, and she'd be walking right into the masked serial killer's trap?

Waffling, Kelli stood at the threshold, phone held high like the world's most ineffective club, but it was all she had.

"Hello?" Her voice echoed in the stillness of the apartment. There was no response, only the soft creak of the door as it swung wider at her touch.

Kelli's pulse thrummed as if a ukelele string had been plucked in her throat as she stepped inside, her eyes scanning the darkness for any sign of movement. The familiar contours of her living room greeted her, everything seemingly in its place, yet the air felt different, heavier, as if the intruder had left some of his dirty essence behind.

She'd have to burn essential oil to rid the place of its greasy, gritty feel. A lavender and eucalyptus mix for cleansing and calming would do the trick, or she'd never be able to sleep here later, regardless of whether she'd missed one night of sleep or twenty.

Nobody jumped out at her, thankfully. Fingers trembling, she reached for the light switch, flooding the room with light. The shadows fled, but the light did nothing to rid her stomach of the rock lodged in it.

She stood stock-still until a uniformed police officer knocked on the frame of the open door. Her name tag read Officer Brooks. Kelli answered all the woman's questions as her partner did a thorough sweep of the small apartment. Officer Hernandez declared the place intruder free, then crossed his arms as Officer Brooks took notes.

Then came the hard part. Cataloging her things to see what was missing.

Methodically, Kelli moved through her apartment, checking everything, careful not to touch anything per the officers' instructions so they could sweep for fingerprints. But it soon became evident that nothing had been taken. Not her jewelry, which wasn't worth much in the first place, but she did have a set of diamond earrings that any thief worth his salt would at least snag in hopes they might net a few hundred dollars. Her TV still sat on its stand and her iPad hadn't been shifted even a millimeter from where she'd left it on her bedside table.

"I don't understand," she said to Officer Brooks. "Why would someone break in and not take anything?"

Officer Brooks' expression flattened. "Are you sure you didn't leave the door open yourself?"

What, like she was making this up? Something told her these by the book officers wouldn't appreciate that she could tell her sanctuary had been invaded because the air had changed. "I never leave the door open. I always lock it."

The police officer nodded. "Uh-huh."

"Also, there was this guy. He followed me home from work."

That got the officer's attention. "Did you get a license plate? A description?"

"Not exactly. I was trying too hard to get away." Which totally counted in the grand scheme of things.

"Uh-huh," Officer Brooks repeated. "Well, seems as if everything is as it should be. If you find anything missing, you can call to update the report. Have a nice day, ma'am."

They were leaving.

Why wouldn't they though? The intruder hadn't stuck around and until she could identify any stolen property or come up with a license plate number, there was nothing for the officers to do here. It wouldn't surprise her to find out they didn't believe her about not leaving the door ajar, and this cheap apartment building didn't merit security cameras. She watched them drive away, hesitant to shut the door and be alone in the apartment that felt wrong.

But this was her life. Not the hazy watercolor picture in her head of the evening with Josh. The way he'd made her feel had faded from her mind far too fast in the aftermath of fear and adrenaline that had awaited her at home. Kelli sank onto her couch, the buzz slowly ebbing from her veins. The intrusion had left an indelible mark on the place she had considered her escape. She wrapped her arms around herself, seeking comfort.

She had a fleeting thought that it might be nice to call someone to come hang out with her for a while, but she didn't know who that would be. Josh? He had a job to do and besides, how needy would that come across? She didn't have any good friends in this area. The downside of being so transient. She liked everyone, so it wasn't that she didn't meet people, but they were shallow relationships because she knew she would be moving on at some point.

Until recently. The job at Mariposa had solidified her un-recognized desire for something permanent. The break-in today had sped up that timeline. She'd buy her own house, one that didn't feel violated.

Besides, she didn't need anyone. Least of all Josh.

Chapter Nine

Josh normally had a lot of energy, but today, even he had to admit the spring in his step might be a little overkill. He couldn't help it. Kelli had infused his blood to the point where he thought his veins might burst—though they were just great friends, of course.

At the stable, Clark didn't even bother to temper the smirk as he took Maverick's reins. "Someone got lucky last night."

Which was both true and not even close to true in the colloquial sense. "It's not like that."

"Sure. Wipe that smile off your face." Clark glanced at Josh over his shoulder as he pulled the saddle from Maverick. "I dare you to try."

That wasn't happening so the kid might have a point. The wrong point, but perception was everything—it was the whole reason the no-fraternization policy mattered. If people thought Kelli was getting special treatment, that would be as much of a problem as an imbalance of power, even if their relationship wasn't physical.

"I'm just happy to be alive today, you know?" Josh said with feigned casualness, hoping to veer away from the idea that he'd spent last night with a woman.

"Yeah, I do know."

The smirk was back, so Josh gave up. "I have to swing by the office, so I'll see you later."

Clearly he'd underestimated how unusual it was for him to be in this type of mood because the moment he crossed the threshold of L Building, Laura stopped him as she crossed the lobby with a paper cup full of coffee.

"Well, well," she said and sipped, sweeping him with her gaze over the top of her cup. "Who is she?"

"Who is *who*?" he shot back with more heat than he should have if he hoped to get out of this unscathed, but come on. "There's no she."

"Adam said he saw someone leaving your bungalow this morning, but he didn't get a good look at her." Laura sipped her coffee pointedly. "Care to revise your statement?"

Great. That was the downside of living near your siblings—your extremely nosy and far too observant siblings. No privacy whatsoever in a place that prided itself on privacy.

"Adam should get a life."

"That's not an answer."

On purpose. Josh had zero desire to explain anything to anyone named Colton, especially his lovesick sister, who rarely opened her mouth without breathing out the name Noah on a sigh. Besides, he couldn't afford to accidentally slip and mention Kelli's name or expect anyone to believe that they were just friends who spent all night together fully clothed. Even though that's exactly what had happened.

"Not everything that happens in my life is up for discussion," he muttered, hating that he'd ended up in this position in the first place. He liked his sister, and his brother for that matter, but not when they were poking their noses into something that could have very difficult consequences.

And he'd cut off his own arm before causing Kelli problems at Mariposa after she'd spilled her heart out about how much this job meant to her.

Laura ignored her coffee as she eyed him. "I seem to recall you were singing a different tune when I first got involved with Noah. Is that how it is? You can be concerned, but I can't?"

That took him back a step. Of course he'd been concerned about Laura jumping into a relationship with Noah after she'd gotten her heart broken by that creep Quentin. No one wanted to see her go through that kind of misery again. Granted, Noah made Laura happier than Josh had ever seen her, so he'd given the dude a pass. For now.

"That's different," he told her with a lofty wave. "This is me we're talking about. I don't do serious. When was the last time you saw a woman leave my place twice?"

Unimpressed with his stellar diversionary tactics, Laura just flicked a nail over the corrugated holder around her cup. "I haven't seen a woman at your place at all. Yet here's one who showed up and no one knows anything about you dating someone who might be the real deal. That's the whole crux of this conversation. You never seem to be starved for female companionship, but it's always felt like you keep them away from home on purpose."

Josh crossed his arms and stared down his nose at his sister. "And why is that, one wonders? Is it possibly so that I can avoid this exact third degree from my family?"

"Fine. Keep your secret lover locked away in your basement so no one can learn a thing about her." Laura threw up an arm theatrically and he would have laughed at both the gesture and the comment under normal circumstances.

But he had a feeling he'd just painted a huge target on the path that led to his bungalow. Everyone would be watching to see if Mystery Woman darkened his door again, which of course meant she couldn't. Ever.

Good grief. What if Adam had approached Kelli, found out who she was and started in on the third degree with her?

His buoyant mood evaporated. "I'm being totally straight with you when I say it would be shocking if I ever saw her again."

If by *saw*, everyone could agree he meant romantically. Of course he would physically lay eyes on Kelli. Many times, in fact. But he wouldn't again make the mistake of putting her under this microscope, not when he'd completely failed to realize anyone could have seen Kelli leaving. The fact that it had been Adam probably worked in their favor because his brother might not actually know what Kelli looked like, unless he'd strolled by the bar for no reason Josh could think of.

Dangerous, all the way around. And now his chest hurt from holding all of this together.

Laura rolled her eyes. "You're acting like I'm going to tar and feather her. I just want to know that my baby brother is as happy as I am."

Here we go. His sister thought happiness could only be achieved by becoming *falling all over yourself in love.* "I am happy. Let it go, Ace."

Finally, his sister let him escape from her clutches. That had been close. And he wasn't out of the crosshairs yet.

Disappointed that he couldn't invite Kelli back to his place for another just-friends date—a repeat he'd actually been one thousand percent sure would be forthcoming—he shelved his plans to stroll by L Bar and manufacture an excuse to hang around.

This was better, he told himself as he purposely spent an hour inspecting the tennis courts on his hands and knees, much to the amusement of the landscape guy who was hand watering the potted plants surrounding the court.

Not his normal gig, no. But he needed to be outside in the sunshine with a task that allowed him to unwind and think.

The way Josh had felt after that epic hug he'd shared with Kelli this morning had been less than friendly. He'd known it at the time but brushed it off as unimportant as long as he didn't let *her* know that. But now that he'd had a minute to cool off, it was totally not legit to have immediately started thinking about ways to skirt the rules.

They existed for a reason. Not the least of which was to protect Kelli from gossip and from feeling like her employment with Mariposa had invisible strings tying her to Josh.

Plus, now that he knew her better, he absolutely should consider that she wouldn't appreciate feeling pressured. How many times had she made the point that she liked her freedom? The woman had made a huge trek east to ensure she could carve her own path, for crying out loud, and the first thing Josh had done was jeopardize that.

He'd never thought of himself as noble but that's what this tightness in his chest was. A realization that he couldn't be selfish here and make things difficult for Kelli by pushing a friendship on her that would ultimately end up not being enough for him.

Then he'd start looking for ways to make it more. Which would have to be on the sly, and he didn't operate like that. Not ever.

Resolute in the knowledge that he had to find his boss mode around her sooner rather than later, Josh headed for L Bar after all, despite his earlier vow to stay away. It was way past time to put his mixology class idea in motion, which he'd been forced to put on the backburner yesterday after the Weinberg incident. And then work had been the last thing on his mind for the entirety of the twelve hours or so that Kelli had been under his roof.

Probably he should change his middle name to Waffle.

The bar wouldn't open for another half hour, so he used the employee entrance around the back, which had a digital keypad for easy access. As Josh shut the door behind him, Kyle muscled his way out of the cooler, hefting a plastic crate full of individual beer bottles, presumably on his way to the mini fridge in the bar area.

"Hey, Joshua, I came by the office this morning, but you weren't around. Laura mentioned you were out on the property somewhere." Kyle flipped hair out of his face. "You said you wanted to see me."

As indictments of his mental headspace went, this one might be the worst. He'd totally forgotten that he'd told Kyle to find him before his shift so they could talk security. Fortunately, he had the world's easiest out. "Yeah, my fault. I had a tennis court emergency. But that's why I came by, so we could chat about what happened yesterday."

"With the handsy guest? Yeah, I figured I was due a cussing out for not being on the floor to help Kelli."

Josh shook his head at the worry lines creasing Kyle's face. "No, no cussing. You're not in trouble. But we clearly have a very popular bartender on our hands now, and I need to know that I can depend on you to keep your eyes open and your arms crossed threateningly. Let's walk through a new schedule for restocking so that you're not off the floor during peak hours."

"That sounds like a good plan," Kyle said, his tone gushing with relief. One thing about Kyle Littlebird—you never had to guess what he was thinking.

"If you need another mini fridge or a second glass rack, you tell me," Josh instructed. "You shouldn't ever struggle to do your job if it's in my power to help you."

This part of his job came easy. He and Kyle talked through logistics until they were both happy with the changes they'd made, which would ensure that neither Kelli nor Regina would be left alone at any point during their shift.

It was a stopgap that would work until Josh got word from Roland Hargreaves about the additional security staff requested for L Bar. Feeling a lot better about his role as the boss, Josh popped into the front to have a word with Kelli because it would be weird if he didn't. Besides, he really did need to talk to her about the mixology class if he ever hoped to get it going.

Kelli stood near the pass-through restocking the garnish tray with cherries, orange wedges and olives, her hair cascading down her back in long brown waves. She hadn't seen him yet, and he had the overwhelming urge to step into her space and wrap his arms around her from behind so he could feel her against him as he breathed in the scent that hadn't left his head since earlier this morning.

His throat caught and his knees went so weak he had to halt for second.

Then she turned around, maybe because she'd heard his quick intake of breath. Suddenly, the fact that he didn't have the latitude to fold her into his embrace became far less important.

Something was wrong. Her eyes weren't as bright as they normally were and there was a slight slump to her shoulders.

"What? What is it?" he asked as he forgot every last protocol he'd scrolled through his head for the last hour and crossed to her in two steps. Before he could check the notion, he took her hand in his, swallowing her fingers.

He couldn't not touch her.

"It's...nothing. It's fine." She shook her head, not meeting his gaze, which of course meant it was something.

"Did someone bother you again? A guest?" A *Colton*? If either Adam or Laura had said a *word* to her—

"No, no, nothing work related."

He blinked. Considering the fact that she'd been out of his presence for less than four hours, something had to have happened at home. "Did you get bad news? A past due bill in the mail?"

Her lips lifted slightly. "That would have me on the floor in hysterics. I pride myself on paying bills before they're due."

"Then what? Tell me," he murmured, well aware that he shouldn't have invoked the intimacy of last night with their signature phrase and yet, wholly unable to stop himself.

That's when her gaze flicked to his, and finally, finally, he could breathe again as he filled his senses with her.

"The door was open when I got home," she admitted on a hushed whisper. "I thought it was an intruder."

Fierceness he didn't recognize forked through his gut. "Are you okay? Were they still there? You didn't go in, did you? You should have called me. Next time, call me."

The half laugh she gasped out did not do a thing to calm him down. "Josh, you're not responsible for me. I called the police. They came. It was fine."

He dropped her hand as Regina strolled into his peripheral vision. What was wrong with him? He should never have crowded Kelli like this in the first place, and she'd shown him exhibit A for why she hadn't called him. She didn't need him. She could handle herself, just like she had with Weinberg.

It didn't stop him from wanting to gather her close and take care of all her monsters, big and small. That was literally the last thing she'd asked for and he had to reel it back. Right now.

"I um…have to go do a—a thing," he muttered and stabbed his finger through his hair, which was annoying him all at once. She didn't protest as he turned and stalked away.

At some point he was going to have to put on his big boy pants and figure out how to be around her without wanting to throw all the rules out the window, but today wasn't that day. How was he going to get his mixology class started if he couldn't even have a professional conversation with Kelli?

By the time he saddled up for his first trail ride of the day, the sleepless night started to weigh down his shoulders. He mainlined an energy drink and threw a second one in his saddlebag along with a protein bar and some other pick-me-ups of choice like dried fruit. That way, he didn't have to go back to the main building at all.

This certainly wasn't the first time he'd worked a full day after forgoing sleep in favor of an activity that had far more to recommend it than being asleep for six hours. It was, however, the first time he'd tried to do it while sorting through the thorny morass of emotional angst that was Kelli Iona. The harder he rode, the less energy his brain would have to torture him.

That plan worked until sometime after four o'clock, when he led the incredibly slow-moving group of guests around the final bend of the easy trail. The western sky had a strange color to it that he didn't like. The wind had picked up when he hadn't been paying attention and Maverick sidestepped off the path in clear agitation.

Not good. He squinted at the horizon, zeroing in on the strange light quality until he realized the reason everything felt dim. A sandstorm was coming.

Instantly, he picked up his horse's pace, calling to everyone that they needed to get back to the stable quickly. He maintained his calm so that the horses would too. Panic would not help anything.

They had maybe forty-five minutes, if they were lucky, before the first sting of projectile force sand would hit.

The group made it back to the stable without any thrown shoes or twisted ankles. Josh advised all the guests to go back to their bungalows or L Building and stay inside until the resort notification system gave the all clear.

With every stable hand on high alert, they got all the horses into their stalls in record time. The ticking clock in his head sped up when he glanced at his phone and realized it was a little after five. Kelli would be off work soon, if she wasn't already, and would probably jump right on her moped with no clue a sandstorm was about to hit. She hadn't lived here long enough to have experienced one or to know what the brown smoky cloud on the horizon meant.

That was enough to cue the panic. He sprinted in the direction of L Bar and just managed to catch her as she strapped on her helmet.

Kelli glanced up in surprise as he grasped her arm. "You can't ride your moped home."

"What? Why not?"

"Because we're about to get hit with the equivalent of a mile-wide tornado mixed with enough sand to bury an elephant," he told her tersely. "There's no time to explain. We have to get indoors. Follow me."

And miraculously, she did.

Chapter Ten

Heart lodged in her throat, Kelli clutched Josh's hand, almost tripping in her haste to keep up as he dashed down the path to the back of the resort, taking the left fork away from the guest bungalows like he'd done the night before.

They were heading toward his house. She recognized the plot of mariposa flowers with their white heads and particular concentration that made the entire bed look like a carpet of white.

"Are we trying to break the land speed record?" she huffed, thinking now was not the right time to be second-guessing her workout routine of walking back and forth behind the bar and becoming a couch potato during her off-hours.

Josh definitely had some legs on him. And while she had no idea what he meant to do with her once he got her to his house, she highly approved of this plan. Obviously he'd thought about her all day the same way she'd thought about him, but in stark contrast, he didn't seem to think things had gotten a little strained right there at the end of their conversation this morning before the bar had opened.

Apparently, he hadn't been offended after all by her staunch claim that she didn't need him. What a relief. He'd readily dismissed the prickly parts of her personality far more quickly than anyone ever had in her life. It was kind of swoony.

The wind had picked up and brushed across her skin with a fine grit, as if she'd just brushed by a wall of sandpaper.

"We have to hurry," Josh instructed over his shoulder. "The storm is coming in a lot quicker than I hoped."

Storm? It wasn't raining. More grit hit her and the air around them grew hazy with an odd quality as if smoke had starting billowing up from the ground.

As Josh halted in front of a bungalow that didn't have the enormous patio that marked it as his place, she glanced in the direction they'd come to see a cloud of brown bearing down on them like an enormous hundred-foot wave. Her eyes widened, which let in a lot more of the dust than she'd expected and that's when her beleaguered brain connected the dots.

This was a sandstorm.

Her first. Only. Hopefully the last. Because suddenly, she got Josh's urgency.

"You can stay here," he shouted over the sound of the coming apocalypse or whatever was making that shrieking sound from the inside of the dust cloud. "It's next door to me. Text me if you need anything, but Kelli? Get inside and don't open the door or windows until I tell you it's all clear."

With that, he practically shoved her inside and slammed the door. With him on the other side. The sandstorm side. Goodness, was he going to try to make it to his place in this mess?

She almost flung the door open to demand that he come inside with her and stay. But his instructions not to open the door took on new meaning when the whole bungalow shook from the force of the wind.

Probably with Josh's athletic body, he made it to his bungalow in record time. Sure enough, her phone vibrated in her pocket and when she took it out, his name flashed on the screen.

She hit the answer button, amused that he'd opted to call instead of waiting for her to text him that she needed something.

"You better be at your place," she said with mock severity as she put the phone on speaker and wiped her eyes, which still stung from the grit. "And not calling me from the road."

"Ha, ha," he said, and she could hear the amusement in his voice. "My house is literally right next door. If there wasn't all of this dust in the air, you could look out the window and wave."

Even though he'd just told her it would be useless, she moved to the window to peer outside anyway. Oh, my, it was the color and consistency of beige smoke outside, thick and blinding. She couldn't see more than about a foot. No wonder he'd rushed her along as he pulled her away from L Building. She would have been caught in all of this halfway home and stuck on the side of the road with her moped, likely breathing all of that dust and sand into her lungs too, with no way to filter it.

"This bungalow doesn't belong to anyone?" she asked and glanced around, taking in the pristine interior, which now had a layer of dust on it that thinned out the farther from the door the eye went.

The honey-colored hardwood floors extended into the tiny kitchenette and beyond to the bedroom, where she could see a fireplace through the open door. Native American–style rugs stretched across the floor in the living area and bedroom, with classic furniture pieces placed over them in both rooms. The place felt elegant and spacious—and expensive.

"It's one of a few empty bungalows reserved for Colton family members and friends," Josh said.

He meant his father, most likely, judging by the tightness in his voice, whom he'd mentioned almost never visited. That made her feel slightly better about being here, as long as she wasn't putting anyone out.

"I appreciate the gesture then," she murmured, wondering where in the world she could stand to shake off her clothes and opted for the area near the door that had already been messed up from her entrance. "I confess, I wasn't sure where you were taking me, but this never crossed my mind. I thought we were going to hole up at your house again."

The pause on the other end lengthened until Josh cleared his throat. "I'm trying to respect your space while making sure you're safe."

"That's some hardcore overkill, Josh," she teased. "How long does a sandstorm usually last? An hour? Surely we could have hung out for an hour at your place without harm."

"Maybe an hour, yeah. A sandstorm is usually followed by a doozy of a thunderstorm though," he said. "You should plan on staying overnight."

All at once, she wished they were in the same place or that he'd initiated a video call so she could better pick up on the nuances of this conversation because she'd swear there was an unspoken vibe here she wasn't sure she liked. "Is this about the intruder in my house last night? I told you it was fine. I might have left the door open myself."

"It's about a lot of things, Kelli." He blew out a breath. "If I wanted to be sure you weren't left alone at your house, is that so bad?"

Now somewhat dust free, she sank onto the couch, noting it was extremely comfortable. Far more so than her cheap one at home, not that she'd tell Mr. Colton that. "Josh, I like my apartment. I like that it's mine. I pay for it with no one's help and that means I call all the shots. If I stay here, I'll feel like I owe you, and I'm not comfortable with that."

"Fine. Pay me back for it," he said far too fast.

"I can't afford a night at this resort!" she shot back. "It costs more than two months of my apartment's rent, for crying out loud."

"Good thing you're staying in a bungalow that isn't for guests," he returned so smoothly, silk might as well have flowed out of the line. "The cost of a night in a Colton bungalow is zero dollars. The only payment we require is that you have breakfast with one of the family members in the morning."

She bit her lip to keep from laughing because she was still miffed that he'd set this up so that it would be hard for her to say no. And frankly, she didn't want to say no. It wasn't like she could leave right this minute anyway, and if he was right about the imminent thunderstorm, it might be hours before her primary transportation method became viable. A moped worked in Arizona most days, but not today apparently.

"You're the family member I'm assuming?" she asked though she already knew his probable answer.

"Of course. Though I can call Laura to swing by if you prefer?"

"I half think you're serious."

"I am. This is entirely aboveboard. I texted Laura and Adam from the stable as soon as I realized the storm was coming. I would never allow an employee to stay at the resort, whether it was in a family bungalow or one for paying guests, without alerting management."

She let that sink in. He'd arranged this before he'd even known if she had already set off from Mariposa on her moped. His brother and sister knew she was here and were apparently fine with it. Did that also mean he'd told his family that they were more than friends?

Goodness. Did that mean they *were* more than friends? She'd had no time to think about whether she wanted it to become a known fact that she and Josh were feeling their way around something different and special.

"I don't know if that makes it better or worse," she said faintly.

Joshua Colton had her spinning in circles.

"Better," he assured her. "This is nothing more than your boss being concerned about your safety. It's nice that I'm killing two birds with one stone by ensuring you don't have to go back to your house if you don't want to."

"But I don't have any of my stuff here," she protested lightly, totally unsure how to interpret his decidedly pointed reminder that he was her boss. Probably that he'd presented it that way to his siblings. Which was a relief. "What am I going to change into after I take a shower?"

Honestly, was that even the biggest concern? She also had no food and no shampoo. Impromptu stays at luxury resorts were for rich people who had that kind of stuff figured out ahead of time. And for people who weren't employees.

"You haven't explored the place yet, have you?" Josh asked and she could hear the smile in his voice. "This is Mariposa. We take strides to ensure we've thought of your every need before you do."

What in the world was that supposed to mean? She slid off the couch and wandered into the kitchenette, phone flat on her palm as she pulled open the minifridge with the other hand.

It was full of food. Prepackaged meals in clear glass trays with airtight lids, an instruction label affixed to the top that she could tell from here would explain how to heat up the dish in the microwave. Bottles of water, wine, beer, energy drinks, charcuterie trays wrapped in plastic, fruit cut up into bite-sized pieces.

Dazed and a bit starstruck, she made her way into the bedroom, already pretty sure she knew what she would find. She opened the closet, which was bigger than the one at her apartment by at least twice. Yep. Full of clothes with the tags still attached, but not price tags because that would be gauche, she had a feeling. These were designer tags, ranging from Ralph Lauren to Balenciaga. An array of sizes, of course, and she predicted she'd have no trouble finding something that fit.

The bathroom, which rivaled something from a movie set, didn't disappoint in the way of supplies. The bottles of body wash, shampoo and conditioner arranged attractively in the tiled niche sported the intricate label of a brand she'd never heard of, probably because it was of the "if you have to ask the price, you can't afford it" variety.

"See anything you need that's missing?" Josh's voice floated from the phone in her hand.

"My willpower," she muttered. "You realize this is way above and beyond anything I'm used to. How will I go back to being poor after this?"

Josh laughed. "Easy. Don't. Stay forever."

She took it as the joke he'd surely meant it to be. Staying forever would never work, for a million reasons, first and foremost because a man taking care of her long term, like she was some kind of kept woman, sat like ash in her mouth. That wasn't what he was offering her though. Josh understood her need for independence. She had no call to get testy about all of this.

This bungalow wasn't real life. It was a gift, a temporary

solution to a problem given to her by her employer. If she wanted to be charmed into having very warm feelings for Josh as a result, that was her business.

She started to tell him the Mariposa fairy godmother had forgotten some crucial items until she opened the middle drawer of the vanity. Personal products lay in neat rows, including a toothbrush, toothpaste, hairbrush and other individually wrapped items that would have been embarrassing to have to ask for.

"One night," she told him, sticking that stake in the ground and stomping on it. "You're already spoiling me."

"Not me," he protested. "This is how all bungalows are stocked."

Logically, that made sense, given the price of staying at Mariposa, but she was having a hard time accepting that there were people who expected this level of luxury when they traveled. Did rich people even pack suitcases? Why would you go to the trouble if *this* waited for you on the other end of a plane ride?

"But you're the one letting me stay here," she insisted. "So it's you who is responsible for my future disillusionment when I go back to being regular Ella after getting the Cinderella treatment."

"You're welcome," he deadpanned, and she rolled her eyes.

"Thank you, Joshua. You're the best, Joshua. Whatever can I do to repay you for this unexpectedly wonderful night of pampering, Joshua?"

"Stop calling me that," he muttered. "It's weird."

"Oh? I thought the staff was meant to call you Joshua. I'm staff, remember?"

"Yeah, every minute of every day."

She let that roll through her for a moment. "What does

that mean? You're treating me like an employee with all of this luxury?"

"One hundred percent yes," he answered, and she could almost see him crossing his heart. "I would have done the same for anyone else who needed a place to stay. It just so happens that no other Mariposa employees ride a moped and had their apartment recently broken into."

She got it then. This was a master class on skirting the rules without actually breaking them. His finesse impressed her, made her feel extra special.

There were no other Mariposa employees being carted to exclusive bungalows during the sandstorm. No other employees being explicitly told not to call him Joshua. In fact, she'd never heard anyone call him Josh. She'd only done it the first few times to give him grief because she'd met him as Josh first, before he'd become her boss. It was how he'd introduced himself at The Cloisters. She hadn't come up with that on her own.

Now it did feel weird to call him Joshua, and it was interesting that he thought so too. Yet another rule—this one unwritten—that he'd made her the exception to.

How delicious was that? She hated rules in the first place, especially if they kept her from having exactly what she wanted. In this case, Josh.

She glanced at her phone's battery level. "Oh, no," she said aloud without thinking.

"What? What's wrong?" Josh demanded and she rather liked him springing to attention on her behalf, especially with a sandstorm between them. He couldn't actually *do* anything, leaving her completely free to handle her own problems.

"I wasn't prepared for a night away from home and I don't have a charger for my phone."

"There's one for each type of phone in the drawer in the kitchen."

Dutifully, she walked back to the kitchen and pulled open the drawer he'd directed her to, which did indeed have charger cables for everything imaginable, neatly labeled. She selected the one for her phone model and plugged it into the wall.

"Now we can talk all night again," Josh said with a note in his voice that could only be called gleeful. "Want to switch to video?"

No, actually. She kind of liked the voice-only option. There was something to be said for getting to know someone this way, without benefit of seeing them. There hadn't been much light last night either, only the stars. It felt more intimate this way, not less, and she chalked that one up to Josh being so outside the lines.

If she wasn't careful, she'd fall for him, and she really had no idea how to handle that at this point.

"I don't think I can actually go two nights in a row without sleeping," she confessed. "As lovely as it sounds to talk all night again. Besides, I'm going to take a bath in this amazing tub you've gifted me."

The long silence on the other end stretched until Josh cleared his throat. "You're taking a bath right now?"

Yes, no video option was way better than clueing in Josh that he'd put a wicked smile on her face. She took him into the bathroom with her, then donned the fluffy white robe from the back of the door after the water grew cold. They ate dinner together without a break in the conversation despite not being in the same place. The promised thunderstorm rolled in, lightning crackling outside her window and buckets of rain pouring down on the roof.

They ended up talking until after midnight, when she

couldn't keep her eyes open any longer and had to beg him to let her sleep. The man was a machine, and it was no chore to imagine that his stamina applied in many situations.

Dreaming of him all night should have prepared her for the knock on the door in the morning. But opening it to find Josh leaning on the doorframe, a hibiscus bloom in one hand that he held out to her with a smile, kicked her hard in the heart.

He was hotter than lava normally, but Josh fresh from the shower with his damp hair shaggy around his face defied her vocabulary.

Kelli held the flower to her nose and inhaled, glancing up at him over the petals. "What are you doing here so early?"

"Came to get my payment." He laughed when she raised her brows. "Breakfast. You promised."

"I have to get home," she protested, thinking it was better to return to reality sooner rather than later. And maybe put some distance between her and the very charming, very dangerous to her mental state Josh Colton.

"Sure," he said with a lopsided smile and jerked his head at the golf cart behind him. "Let me drive you to your moped. There are some downed trees, and the path is a little sketchy."

"Okay," she said mostly because she couldn't think of a reason to say no. She didn't want to say no. There was a lot of that going around, and it was starting to scare her how much she wanted to spend every waking moment with this man.

Josh shut the door behind her as she followed him to the passenger seat and didn't protest when he held out a hand to help her up into the cart. But he didn't immediately let go of her hand and when she glanced at him, he pierced her with his gorgeous blue eyes.

"Rain check," he said firmly. "On breakfast. No arguments."

Oh, my. It seemed he might be of the same mind in wanting to spend more time with her, and she *really* didn't know what to do with that besides nodding her head. Easy since that's what she wanted too. She'd deal with the consequences later.

Chapter Eleven

Josh dropped Kelli off at her moped and watched her steer down the road employees used to travel back and forth to the resort. Guests arrived via helicopter, so he wasn't too worried about any of the arrivals and departures today, but the road hadn't been fully cleared yet.

He'd have driven her home in his Range Rover if she'd have let him, but he got the vibe loud and clear. *Back off.*

It was killing him to give her space, but he'd done it. For a brief, shining moment, he'd been patting himself on the back for coming up with the idea of breakfast as repayment for the bungalow, but she'd brushed that off quicker than water rolled off a duck's back.

Fine. It was fine. He shouldn't have been jumping through hoops to rescue her from the sandstorm in the first place, but he couldn't let her drive off into a situation that could have easily been deadly for her or someone else.

If it made him happy to take care of her, she didn't have to know. He'd let her think he'd treated her the same as any regular Mariposa employee, as if allowing staff to use the family bungalow happened every day and twice on Sunday. This was the first time to his knowledge, largely because he didn't make it a habit to get involved in his employee's personal lives.

Kelli had been special even before she'd become his bartender. Now he didn't even have the power to describe what she'd become to him. Or how difficult a position he found himself in.

Josh swung by the stable after stowing the golf cart back at his house, already anticipating a huge cleanup job in store for him. Secretly, he was thrilled to have something to take his mind off the woman he shouldn't even be thinking about, let alone rescuing.

As he stood outside surveying the damage from the storm, Knox Burnett strolled around from the back, his Stetson pushed way back on his head. He'd tied his long hair back in a ponytail with a length of intricately braided colorful string, which meant the guys had already started on repairs while Josh had been off flirting with Kelli.

"'Sup, dude," Knox called and stuck out his hand for a ritual fist bump. They'd been friends a long time, often taking larger groups on trail rides together and hanging out on off days.

"What's it look like?" Josh asked and jerked his head toward the back side of the stables.

Knox took off his hat and wiped his forehead with the sleeve of his plaid shirt. "A mess. Couple of crossbeams came loose and took out part of the roof. None of the horses were hurt, so that's a relief. Just spooked 'em plenty so we might want to think about skipping any trail rides this morning until we can have some of the hands work out their jitters."

The wind had been fierce last night, probably gusting up to sixty or eighty miles an hour. It wasn't surprising the building had taken a hit.

"Good thinking." Josh nodded. Though he hated to cancel anything, it was a smart suggestion. "We don't want any guests bucked off. Have you checked out the trail this morning?"

Knox shot him a look. "That's your deal, man. Why would I have done that when you're always out there first thing making the rest of us look bad because we don't get up at the crack of dawn-thirty?"

"I...overslept this morning," he muttered, which was a huge lie. He'd been lying awake waiting until a reasonable hour to dash over to the bungalow next door. "I'll send one of the hands to see what we're dealing with on the trails while we work on the loose crossbeams."

He followed Knox to the back of the stable and threw himself into a backbreaking morning of clearing a solid six feet of roof where the storm had trashed the joints. His hands took the brunt of it, earning him two splinters and a cut finger where a nail had pierced his gloves. Good thing his scheduled trip to El Capitan wasn't until May—his hands might have enough time to heal by then. Couldn't rock climb with banged up hands.

But that reminded him that he'd be gone for four days and wouldn't get to see Kelli. Maybe she could go with him on the down low. Wouldn't that be something...

The idea of taking Kelli with him on his trip to Yosemite planted itself in his chest and he couldn't shake it loose. What would it be like to have that kind of easy latitude? To plan a special vacation with a woman and actually be able to talk about it in the open with someone like Knox?

Hey, dude, I met someone.

That was a pipe dream at the moment. Maybe in the future. He could bide his time. Besides, he'd never taken a woman on a trip before. What if she hated the idea of camping in a national park? Or thought it would be boring to watch him scale a giant rock?

Of course, he'd have to figure out how to navigate breaking the rules in such a spectacular fashion. And tiptoe through the minefield of Kelli's boundaries. She might be unwilling to let him pay for everything and then tell him she couldn't afford to go on a trip for four days. They were barely friends at this point. He had a long way to go before he could think about approaching a subject like a road trip together.

The fresh air after the storm should have put him in a great mood, but Kelli had him so twisted up, he ended up brooding his way through the morning. Most of the work crew stayed away from him. He worked well past lunch and then grabbed a sandwich from the employee break room before finding Knox so they could make a judgment call on afternoon trail rides.

"The trail is garbage," Knox told him grimly. "Needs a solid crew to clear it, but the guys have all been working on other stuff. Downed trees on the resort proper mostly."

"I'll have Adam call in a third-party company," Josh said, well aware that if Mariposa had issues, lots of others would too, and it might be days before they could get someone out here. But he'd deal with that when he had to.

Knox nodded and shoved off to cancel his private riding lessons for the afternoon. Josh headed for L Building so he could have an in-person conversation with his brother about how critical it was to get on this problem. Because if Josh couldn't lead trail rides, what would he do to stop himself from dropping by the bar to see Kelli?

"Just who I was looking for," Laura called as he walked by her open office door.

"Would have been more successful finding me if you'd gone to the stables," he advised her with a glance designed to point out the fact that she was still seated behind her desk. "It wouldn't kill you to get out of that chair occasionally."

She wrinkled her nose. "I'll leave all the outdoor stuff to you, thanks. Valerie sent me an update and she's not going to be back from leave as quickly as she thought. Probably at least another three weeks she thinks."

"Wait. What?" His brain had just melted and reformed. "What do you mean three weeks?"

"I told you that Valerie was on extended leave."

"Yeah, but I would have called extended leave six months." As the boss, he should have asked, not assumed. The back of his neck prickled as he took in the implications of what Laura was telling him. "Now you're saying she might be back in three *weeks*?"

This possibly changed everything. In three weeks, Kelli would be out of a job, and he'd be one hundred percent free to pursue her. Which he would. In very specific ways. A fierce wave of sensation sliced through his gut as he thought about how an evening with Kelli would unfold if she was no longer his employee.

Then it hit him that Kelli would be out of a job. This was terrible. She needed this job and loved it. And he'd banked on his rockstar bartender being behind the bar, serving up Aloha Sunsets to guests who started thronging the bar at 10:00 a.m. on the dot. Plus, Valerie wasn't the right person for his mixology class.

"You look like you swallowed a bug," Laura said, eyeing him. "You okay?"

"Fine," he rasped, because what was he supposed to say to all of this? *I'm a selfish jerk who wants a woman to be let go from a job so I can spend the night with her the way I want to* didn't have quite the ring he was looking for. "I had no idea Valerie would be back that soon."

"Well, she's not yet," his sister pointed out pragmatically. "She could very well let me know it'll be another three weeks after that. She doesn't seem to have a handle on it."

"And that's just...okay with Mariposa management?" he managed to get out. "To let Kelli hang with the promise that she has a job until our real employee makes up her mind about when she's coming back?"

Laura had resumed typing on her keyboard but paused to glance at him. "Kelli knew her employment here was contingent. She agreed to take the job fully aware that Valerie would be coming back at some point. You act like I'm pulling the carpet out from under her, when this was all part of the recruitment process."

Only no one had shared this with him, least of all Kelli. She couldn't have mentioned that all of their conflict would be gone soon? No. Because she didn't really see him being her boss as the issue between them. Not even a little bit. *Her* problem was with relationships in general, apparently.

He had no call to be so disappointed. None. She'd been clear from the beginning that she valued her independence and he'd been the one to manufacture a connection out of thin air. That's why she'd gone out of her way to mention that she didn't date much. Not because she hadn't met anyone she gelled with as well as she did with Josh—which he'd taken to mean he was special—but because she wasn't looking for someone to gel with.

Well, that was great. He didn't do relationships either. He had a long-standing affair with the ground beneath his feet and Mariposa would always be more important to him than any flesh and blood woman who came along.

"Okay, cool," he muttered. "I'll mention to Kelli that her employment contract has been extended. I'm sure she'll roll with it."

Because that's what she did. He should take a lesson.

He stalked from the office and ran into Adam in the lobby. Fortuitous since he'd come to L Building to find his brother in the first place.

"Hey," he called, and that's when he noticed Noah Steele standing next to Adam, the tension between the two evident in the stiff lines of their carriages.

His sister's boyfriend was welcome at Mariposa anytime, but given that his presence usually meant trouble, Josh got why Adam wasn't the slightest bit relaxed. Noah gave off a vibe like he meant business 24/7, and having seen the homicide detective in action, Josh believed his intensity was warranted.

"Noah wants to talk to us," Adam said and pointed back the way Josh had just come. "In my office."

It was a day for disruptions, apparently. Josh sighed and followed the two men. There'd been a time when both he and Adam would have ganged up on Noah, standing firm between him and Laura, but they seemed to have panned out in the relationship department.

Laura silently watched them pass by her office through her open door, a pen in her mouth. If she knew the reason for the detective's visit, she didn't let on, her face a mask.

As soon as they entered the office, Adam took the chair behind the desk, leaving Josh and Noah to claim the two seats in front of it. Noah sat on the edge, curiously keyed up, even for him. He clasped and unclasped his hands, bunching up the muscles beneath his tattoos that normally made him look like a guy not to be messed with. Today he just looked like he wanted to bolt from the room.

"Thanks for seeing me," Noah said like this was a job interview or something. "The thing is that I wanted to talk to you both about my relationship with Laura. You know I love her very much, right?"

Adam lifted his hands palms up. "Yeah, of course. If we couldn't see that for ourselves, she'd certainly remind us of it often enough."

Narrowing his gaze, Josh eyed his sister's boyfriend. "You're not about to tell us you got some other girl pregnant or something, are you? Because if so, I greatly appreciate you telling us behind closed doors where there are no witnesses."

"What? No!" Noah sliced the air curtly. "That's not even possible since I've fallen in love with Laura. I don't even see other women. How could I? She eclipses everyone else."

"Good answer," he mumbled.

Josh sank down in his chair, crossing his arms over his chest because whatever was going on inside felt a lot like jealousy that Noah could speak about the woman on his mind with such clarity. As he should. Laura was an amazing person and Noah was incredibly lucky that she'd given him the time of day.

"In fact," Noah continued, rubbing his hands together. "I'd like to ask her to marry me, but I felt like it was important to ask the both of you first."

"Say what?" Josh blurted out and sat up as Adam steepled his fingers, sweeping Noah with a very Colton-like once-over.

"You're serious," his brother said, and it wasn't a question.

Noah nodded. "I am. Very. I know we haven't been together that long, but I didn't need more than about thirty seconds to figure out that I want to be with Laura the rest of my life. No question. Why would I want to wait to have everything I've ever dreamed of?"

Why indeed? "Are you asking for permission? Or telling us that you're going to anyway regardless and this is just a courtesy notice?"

Noah met his gaze and held it, not flinching, which Josh gave him points for. Grudgingly.

"I'm asking for her hand in marriage. The old-fashioned way," Noah added, his hands finally still as if he'd found his center. "From the family that counts."

Adam glanced at Josh and a wealth of unverbalized pain passed between them as it sank in that Noah got the fact that Laura would care nothing about their father's opinion of who she married, but her brothers were a different story. Noah had been paying attention. He'd earned a slew of points for that alone.

Adam nodded. "I respect the sentiment and the courage it took to come here. I'm one hundred percent on board."

"I'm not," Josh threw in, gratified when Noah's face fell because it told him that marrying his sister meant something to this man. As it should. "I want to talk to Laura first. I can appreciate the same things Adam does about your intent, but this is not the Middle Ages. Laura's say is far more important than mine."

Noah nodded a bunch of times, his expression stoic. "I get that too. I'm happy to wait."

"What, you mean you'll wait while I talk to her now?"

"Exactly." Crossing his arms, Noah leaned back in his chair, apparently content to stay put as long as it took.

Points for that too. Josh shoved out of his chair and opened the door to see Laura pacing outside her office, pen still in her mouth. She turned on her heel when she heard sounds from the direction of Adam's office, her expression so heartbreakingly expectant that he could immediately tell what answer she hoped her brothers had given.

"Is this what you want, Ace?" he asked her, keeping his voice low because this was a conversation for just the two of them, no outside participants needed.

Her eyes grew shiny and huge as she nodded, folding her arms around her waist. "More than anything. What did you say?"

He flashed her a brief smile as his heart constricted. Things were changing. She'd already started spending more time at Noah's place than Mariposa, and once they got married, the disconnect between the siblings would only get worse. She'd probably have a couple of kids who would annoy her cat, Sebastian, or they would get more cats. It wouldn't be just the three Coltons any longer and the passage of what would never be again made him misty.

"That your answer is more important than mine," he told her gently. "And I have it. I give you my blessing, as long as you're okay with the fact that I still don't trust that guy. But I trust you, and if this is the real deal, okay."

His sister pulled him into a long hug, and he let his emotions off the leash for the length of it.

"Thank you for caring," she murmured sincerely. "Not many brothers would."

"I'm happy for you," he said just as sincerely. "I truly am. Live every minute to the fullest and don't look back."

It was far past time to let Noah off his self-imposed hot seat. With Josh's approval secured, Noah shook his hand, then moved easily into Laura's space, slinging one tattooed arm around her waist and pulling her close.

Yeah, yeah, he got it. Noah was the one who would worry about his sister now. Noah was the one who got to have everything he wanted out of his life. But as his soon-to-be brother-in-law pressed a tender kiss to his future bride's temple, Josh had to amend the broody thoughts squeezing his chest—he was getting what he wanted out of life too.

He wanted the resort. He loved Mariposa. It was just that he'd started wishing for something more and didn't know how to turn it off.

Chapter Twelve

After two nights of intense conversation with Kelli, on his first night of being Kelli free, Josh should have slept like a log. He didn't. He rolled around, convinced he'd turned into the dude version of "The Princess and the Pea."

Only it was more like a potato someone had clearly stuffed under his mattress. Sometimes it felt like forks underneath his back, poking at him. The Swedish manufacturing company would not get away with this subpar wear on his mattress and he composed an entire email complaining about it in his head before he finally had to concede that the bed wasn't the problem.

Kelli was. He had it bad for her and it turned out not spending the night talking to her could in fact be less restful.

Finally he gave up at 4:00 a.m., which used to be the time he'd crawled *to* bed not so long ago.

Okay, it had been a while. Years actually. It was just that he'd always thought he'd eventually get back into that party groove, devil may care about the consequences.

Instead, he'd become an adult while he hadn't been looking. Laura getting engaged put a big, huge highlight on the point that none of them were getting younger. The fact that Josh voluntarily threw himself on the back of a horse before dawn some days should have been a much bigger clue that he'd become a better version of himself. One that enjoyed being responsible and practicing his set routine.

Was it any wonder that he'd started thinking about how other aspects of his life had changed? How he didn't like his empty bed so much anymore? But how to solve that problem when there was only one woman he wanted to see staring back at him from the other pillow—that was the million-dollar question he had no answer for.

This was the first time he could ever recall not having a woman fall into his arms the moment he'd decided that's what should happen. It was messing with his vibe.

Maverick navigated the trail like a champ and Josh used the time to do some much-needed recon on the conditions. The storm had dumped a lot of branches and debris across the path he normally guided guests down, but it wouldn't take long for a crew to get things back in shape. For now, he didn't mind being a crew of one while he battled the stuff going on in his head. The physical labor would do him good.

He jumped down and went to work, elusive peace finally settling into his chest as he communed with his land.

He'd just cantered into the wide clearing near the stable when he heard the chime of his phone indicating a text message had come in. Since he'd cast Ava off, he hadn't given his number to any other women, so it could only be Adam or Laura.

Adam. His brother's name flashed on the screen with the preview, but a few words was all he needed to know what Adam wanted. It was a summons.

Wary after the last time he'd been called to Adam's office to hear Noah's surprise announcement, Josh washed his hands and thought about taking a shower in case the Pope had come to visit.

But Josh strolling through the management office after

just dismounting from a horse was pretty commonplace and this was who he was. Take it or leave it. He opted to jet straight to L Building and see what Adam wanted. Laura was already there, seated across from their brother, her expression serious.

"Josh, sit down. We need to talk about Mariposa," Adam began, his tone more somber than usual. "This thing with Clive is not going away."

Josh tensed, sensing the weight of the conversation about to unfold. And that it was not going to end happily like the engagement conversation. "What's going on? Did he come back with another loopy idea like asking us to pony up millions of dollars we don't have?"

"No. And that's the point. He's definitely still planning something, but we can't wait around for that and then scramble to find a defense." Adam locked gazes with Josh. "You know what I mean. It's time to go on the offensive."

"You did something already." It wasn't a question. Adam always got that look when he'd blazed ahead, always one to beg forgiveness rather than ask permission.

Most of the time, he didn't even bother asking for forgiveness, because in his head, he hadn't done anything wrong.

"I've been working on a deal." Adam steepled his hands. "An unconventional one, but it will work. You're familiar with Sharpe Enterprises?"

Josh lifted his hands. "Because I'm such a mover and a shaker in the business world? Not even in passing. I know what kind of tequila we have behind the bar and the manufacturer of every piece of equipment in the stable. Do you?"

"This is not an inquest, Josh," Laura murmured. "It's a conversation. Between three people, all of whom have an equal voice."

Her point and her tone gave him much-needed space

to take a deep breath. "Sorry, it's just that this feels like a heavy subject and Adam is playing Lord of the Numbers over there—"

"It was just a question," Adam broke in, his fingers still in the shape of an A in front of him because being a suit came so naturally to him that he didn't have an off mode. "You answered it. Sharpe Enterprises owns luxury resorts all over the world. Dubai, Cairo, Buenos Aires, you get the picture," Adam revealed, his gaze never leaving Josh's. "They're interested in buying half of Mariposa."

Disbelief, adrenaline, fury and a million other emotions shot through Josh as he bolted from his seat. "Half? Are you serious?"

"Yes, it's a solid offer." Laura nodded, her voice steady. "This partnership could give us the capital to buy out Clive's shares and keep control of the resort."

Et tu, Brute? He eyed Laura. "You knew about this?"

"I was aware that Adam was working on it, yes." She wouldn't meet his gaze, her palm smoothing the fabric of her skirt over and over. "Just like I was aware that you'd react like this, which is why we kept it to ourselves until we had something to talk about."

Images of Mariposa—each corner, each memory of their mother—flashed through his head. The land beneath his feet wouldn't belong to him any longer. Sure, Adam had carefully explained this hotel chain would only own half, but a soulless corporation would slowly leech away the core of Mariposa until there was nothing left.

They'd have a say in every aspect of how the Coltons ran the resort. Maybe not majority but a say.

"Mariposa is ours. Mom's legacy. You want to hand it over to some corporation?" He practically spat the word.

Adam exchanged glances with Laura, probably because

they'd already talked about how to handle Josh and it was his turn to do the mollifying. "This deal is not about handing over control, Josh. It's about securing Mariposa's future by funding Clive's money grab. We keep operational control, and Sharpe ensures we own the land from now on."

A knot of frustration formed in Josh's throat and no amount of swallowing eased it. Everything was slipping away faster than he'd expected. This deal could be done tomorrow or the next day.

He whumped into the chair, his body weighing a million pounds all at once.

Desperate now, he tried to reason with his siblings, wondering when they'd landed on opposite sides of this. "And what if they decide to change everything? Our vision, our values?"

Laura reached out, her voice softer. "We've thought about that. The agreement includes protective clauses. Our core values, the essence of Mariposa, stays intact. *We* stay intact. They can't make a power move to oust any of the three of us. They can't sell any of their shares to Clive."

"Ace, geez. You're missing the whole point." He pressed a thumb into his temple, right where it felt like Laura was driving an ice pick engraved with Sharpe Enterprises through his brain. "This is Mom's place. Even with a bunch of lawyer speak in the contract, can you honestly say handing over half of it won't change that?"

Adam sighed, a rare vulnerability bleeding into his expression as he rubbed at his head in kind, as if Josh was the one giving him a headache. Good. If Adam didn't watch out, Josh would be happy to keep going until they all had migraines.

"I don't like it any more than you do," Adam said, his voice growing weary. "But the reality is, we're at a crossroads. Clive's underhanded tricks have left us in a precarious position. This could be our best shot at keeping Mariposa in the family."

Yeah, their father was the real villain here. He tried to keep that fact front and center as he wrestled with the idea of actually signing a document giving 50 percent of Mariposa to a corporation full of people he'd never met. He could see the logic—as ice-cold as it may be—even as it scraped against everything he knew to be true about what it meant to him to be a Colton. To own Mariposa.

Rock, meet hard place.

"And what about the staff? The people who've made their lives here? Do they just become numbers to Sharpe?" Josh asked, though there was only one on his mind at the moment.

What would the new owners want to change that might affect Kelli? Who would protect her job?

"We'll ensure that doesn't happen. Our people are what make Mariposa special. That won't change," Laura said, conviction in her voice.

"You can't promise that," he bit back fiercely, though even he could tell this was a lost cause. Laura and Adam presented a united front, an impenetrable one. After all, in a vote, it would be two to one.

"Josh, we love Mariposa too," Adam murmured and shut his eyes for a beat. "I've poured my soul into this place, the same as you and Laura have. At great personal expense, I might add, which you're no stranger to. Though also like you, I count the cost as completely worth it. I would not make this decision lightly. And I certainly wouldn't make it if we had any other choice."

"What if I say no?" he asked, aware that his crossed

arms made him look belligerent, but he'd stopped caring ten minutes ago.

Adam stood then, shoving his hands in his pocket to signify the end of the meeting, a trick he employed when he was done with a conversation. "We wanted to discuss it with you. We're a team. If you don't want to do this, we're willing to listen to other ideas. But make no mistake, Josh. You have to devise a workable plan to come up with the money to buy the land from Clive. We don't have much time. You've got twenty-four hours before I have to give Sharpe the go-ahead."

The room felt suddenly claustrophobic, the walls closing in as if he'd stumbled into a fun house at a carnival. Josh followed his brother to his feet, unable to breathe. How could he possibly come up with an alternate plan in one day?

He had a feeling Adam knew it would be impossible. "That's ridiculous. I need more time."

Adam rubbed at his forehead with the palm of his hand. "I wish I could give it to you, but Sharpe is already wary because of Allison's murder and the other high-profile stuff that's happened with Alexis. If we'd closed the deal a few weeks ago, they might be singing a different tune. Unfortunately, I was taking it slow to be sure Sharpe would accept all the safeguards we asked for. This was not an overnight process, Josh, and we have to accept fast before they back out."

As if Josh needed another layer of complexity stacked on top of this already high-stakes deal. And Adam had caused this tight deadline himself by trying to do the exact thing Josh had been arguing for. It should have mollified him, but he still had enough mad to go around that his brother and his sister had dropped this deal on him with no warning and no options.

"Fine. I'll take every minute of that twenty-four hours," he practically snarled and stormed from the room, stopping just short of slamming the door, but only because there were other employees about. Not because he had an overly strong sense of propriety at the moment.

As he strode through L Building, the sense of the walls closing in intensified. Then they started crumbling.

Visible through the floor-to-ceiling windows, the sand shimmered under the bright sun, sending a spike through his heart. Anyone who loved this land as much as he did would never have come up with this horrific plan—but at the same time, he already knew what his answer was going to have to be. *Yes.*

If an alternative existed, they would have already thought of it. They'd have to sign the deal and start praying that they could do it on their terms. Protect the staff, protect their values, fight for Mariposa's soul.

Maybe he could start saving money and eventually buy the shares back. It was a thought.

Despair settled over him, warring with reluctant acceptance. Both weighed almost more than he could manage. Worse, the only thing he wanted to do was crawl to L Bar and bury his head in the crook of Kelli's neck. Breathe her in. Center himself in her the way he usually could only replicate with a long ride into the desert.

A desire to do exactly that weakened his knees. He wished his life could be that simple.

The way to L Bar lay to the left. He veered right and pushed out of the building into the bright sun. It should be cloudy. Sunshine and the blackness in his heart didn't go together.

What was wrong with him? He was never like this. The resort's future had been on his mind for weeks, but the addition of Kelli to his psyche had really started doing a number on him. In the not-so-distant past, he'd have burned a woman out of his blood with some very pointed tried-and-true techniques involving a trip back to her place and the latitude to do whatever he wanted with her.

Then he'd move on to the next thing that struck his fancy. Always with Mariposa waiting for him at home. That was the issue. The potential loss of even half of his mom's legacy coupled with the thorny problem of Kelli had unseated him to the point where he didn't even know which way was up.

Especially when she didn't seem into things like forever and diamond rings. Things he'd never in a million years believed he'd care about either, but here they were. And honestly, he couldn't envision any version of himself that could finally overcome all the obstacles between them, only to let her go after a couple of dates.

He could not deal with any more loss.

Chapter Thirteen

Kelli didn't see Josh for two very long days. She tried not to read into it, but honestly, she'd been the one to push back about breakfast the morning after the sandstorm. A mistake, obviously. He'd taken it as a brush-off, when in reality, it had been anything but.

This was why she didn't date. Men never understood her weird signals. But that stemmed from the fact that she'd never really figured out how to maintain her independence and keep a man around. Mostly because she'd never met one she wanted to keep around.

At the very least, he should have come by to talk about the mixology class. Maybe she should prod him along and that would allow her system a very much needed hit of Josh Colton.

Near the end of her shift, she texted him before she lost her nerve.

Come by the bar. Had some ideas for the mixology thing.

His response came almost immediately:

Great timing. I had something to talk to you about too

That sounded ominous. She fretted through the last thirty minutes of her shift, glancing toward the door to the bar every fourteen seconds until she finally spied Josh's shaggy blond head through the glass. Her heart jolted as he sauntered across the room with his easy, rolling gait that told a story of a man comfortable in his own body.

Then he caught sight of her and smiled. Oh, my. Her throat went a little dry as she popped the top off a beer bottle and handed it to a customer without fully focusing on the guest. She crossed to the pass-through where Josh had taken up residence.

"Fancy meeting you here," she croaked and cleared her throat. "I was starting to think my boss was a ghost."

"Sorry." He shoved a hand through his hair, sweeping it from his cheeks. "Lots of cleanup and stuff going on from the storm."

Betsy, one of the servers at the restaurant, had told her that Josh personally helped clean up the stables, which had taken a pretty heavy hit. The reason Betsy knew was that he'd done it shirtless for a good portion of the day, drawing quite the audience, which Kelli found out after the fact. That would have been a sight to see. She was sorry she'd missed it.

"I would have helped if I'd known," she told him, feeling a bit better about not seeing him if he had a legit excuse. "I thought you were avoiding me."

Oh, good job, girl. Come out of the gate swinging.

He didn't seem to mind, waving off that possibility. "Not on purpose. It's just…some stuff I'm dealing with."

That's when she noticed his smile hadn't fully reached his eyes and he wasn't his usual vibrant self. "What's wrong? Tell me."

Yeah, she was shamelessly invoking their previous intimacy, like he'd done to her to get her to tell him about the incident at her apartment. For a long moment, he shut his eyes and sucked in a breath, his expression morphing into one full of such angst and indecision and hurt that her heart exploded.

"I'm taking five," she called to Kyle and pulled Josh into the back room, near the cooler, where no one could see them.

Then she pulled him into her arms and held him tight. He stiffened for a millisecond and then melted into her so absolutely that she felt him clear to her bones. His palms slid into grooves on her body that seemed to be made for him, his fingers nipping in at her waist as he gathered her against his solid torso. They were buried in each other, and she'd never felt more like she'd just come home in her life.

"There you are," she murmured. "I was starting to think I'd imagined the connection from the other night. Nights," she corrected. "The shorter, phone-only one still counts."

"They all count," he growled into her hair, his lips fanning heat across her skin. "This is not what I intended to do when I came here."

"I'm not going to apologize. Unless it's international apology day. And then I'd just be doing it for sentiment."

He huffed out a laugh, as she'd intended, his embrace growing the tiniest bit tighter, which she didn't mind at all. But then he pulled back, leaving her cold and empty as he stepped away, sweeping his hair back in his habitual gesture that she'd missed. Along with rest of him.

"What is it?" she murmured and wrapped her arms around her own chilled body since she'd lost Josh's heat. "What's got you looking like your dog died?"

"We have to sell half of Mariposa," he blurted out with a grimace. "It's not common knowledge. I shouldn't be telling you. But I feel like I'm about to explode."

Her heart lurched as she registered how very upset he was about this and possibly how much he didn't want to be talking about it. Because she was an employee or because he didn't know how to open up to someone who cared about him?

This was all her fault. He had no idea that she wanted to be the person he came to with heavy burdens. How scared she was that she was already in too deep with him and holding him at arms' length had done nothing but damage their relationship.

"What can I do to make it better?" she murmured and ran a hand up his arm to squeeze his shoulder, physically unable to keep herself from touching him while he processed his pain. "You can trust me."

In more ways than one. With his secrets, definitely, but she wanted to feel out how it worked to let someone in other ways too. What it might be like to know she was the person Josh turned to whenever he hurt or wanted to celebrate.

That's what they'd started that night at his place, but this was the other side of the coin. The not so fun parts of a relationship, where you dealt with bad stuff together.

They weren't in that place. Not yet. But she could easily see the path toward that kind of intimacy laid out before them, and she wanted to be on that road.

Josh leaned into her space as she trailed her hand down his arms to his fingers, tangling them with hers.

"Nothing to be done," he said with a shrug, his mouth a straight line. "The deal is legit. I spent a lot of time in a lawyer's office hashing out the details. They're trying to make me sign it with a bunch of BS deadlines, but I got them to extend the offer for another month. It's probably not going to make a difference though."

So that's why she hadn't seen him around. He hadn't even been on the property.

"I'm sorry," she murmured. "This must be devastating."

The briefest touches of amusement flitted through his expression. "You're the only person in the world who seems to get that. The buyer is going to deposit millions of dollars in Mariposa's bank account and all I can think is that we made a deal with one of Satan's archangels in hopes of keeping Satan himself away."

"This is about your father," she said with dawning certainty, recalling what he'd told her that night under the stars. "You did this to beat him at his own game."

"Yeah."

He didn't elaborate and she didn't ask him to. She got it. What a difficult position to be in—sell parts of your business off to keep someone else from taking all of it.

"Don't worry," he said and ran a thumb across her knuckles as he laced their fingers together more tightly. "Your job is safe."

"That was literally the last thing I was thinking about," she told him wryly. "Bartending jobs are a dime a dozen. Resorts that are your birthright are not."

His gaze found hers, searching and full of misty emotions that turned his irises a heartbreaking blue. "How are you even real? My own brother and sister don't even get how this whole thing is affecting me, but here you are, in perfect sync."

Ridiculously pleased that she'd properly conveyed that she did in fact care about him, she smiled up at him. "I'm paying attention, Josh. Always."

"I am too." Somehow they were a breath apart. Within kissing distance. "I know your job is safe because Valerie's not coming back to work for a few more weeks. That's what I needed to tell you. I thought you would be pretty happy to hear that."

Because they could keep seeing each other at random times during the day? Yes. That did make her happy. "I am."

He nodded. "I know how important it is for you to buy your house. Your home base. I'll fight for you to stay here as long as humanly possible so you can get it."

Her heart stuttered as she breathed him in. Wishing he would close the gap between them. "You have been listening."

At least to the things she'd said out loud. The part where the definition of home base had started to change—that he didn't know. Because she hadn't told him that *he'd* very quickly stepped into that role, even as she'd pushed back on their blossoming relationship so that very thing wouldn't happen.

Too late.

"I like listening to you," Josh said, tilting his head so that it rested on hers. Also known as not kissing her. But to be fair, they were in the back room of L Bar where anyone could walk in and find them. Skirting the rules was one thing, but outright flaunting their relationship in front of the staff might be a little bit much.

She slipped from his grasp, nearly weeping with the effort it took to physically separate her body from his. "Come over tonight. I'll cook dinner for you. You can make breakfast."

His eyes didn't look heartbroken any longer. They were a stormy blue with waves crashing on the beach, hurricane strength winds blasting through everything in their path.

"Time to cash in that rain che—" He broke off as the swinging door to the front opened, admitting Adam Colton. Josh's brother, the manager of the entire resort. Laura, their sister and comanager followed him into the back room.

Holy crap, speaking of people walking in and finding them!

Kelli automatically backed up a step, thanking their lucky stars she wasn't still standing in Josh's embrace, like she had been literally a minute prior. Her heart pounded like they'd been caught though, and there was enough tension in the air to choke a horse.

"What are you guys doing here?" Josh demanded, but hopefully she was the only one who realized his defensive tone likely had more to do with what they'd almost been caught doing rather than the intrusion itself.

Adam glanced at Kelli and back at Laura, then locked eyes on his brother. "We have a situation."

JOSH PUSHED INTO Adam's office, thoroughly sick of being called into it. "What is it this time?"

He didn't bother to sit down. Or temper his glare. He was still angry about being forced to come up with an alternative to selling to Sharpe, despite successfully arguing for an extension on signing the deal. Sharpe had been the ones to agree to the new deadline, not Adam, and there was still tension between them because Josh had gone around him to ask for it.

Adam didn't sit behind his desk either, just crossed his arms and lifted his brows in Laura's direction. His sister was the one who approached him, her eyes wide and full of something he couldn't place.

"What's your relationship with Kelli Iona?" she asked him point-blank. "Before you answer, you should know I'm asking in an official capacity, not as your sister."

What? This was about *Kelli* somehow? It was only because of his fond feelings for Laura that he didn't blast her for asking him something so wholly inappropriate. Technically she had a right to ask, since she generally handled employee issues. But still. "She's my bartender. Only. What were you expecting me to say?"

Laura stared at him, her blond hair falling against her cheeks to frame her blank expression. "Whatever the truth is. I'm not going to lie, you looked pretty cozy with her in that back room. How often does a scene like that occur on a daily basis?"

"Never," he bit back even as the memory of embracing her the day she'd returned home to find her door ajar flooded in. "I haven't even been to the bar in a few days. At all. Do I need to pull in Kyle and Regina to have them vouch for that fact?"

What in the world was going on? This wasn't a random drive-by conversation. Something had happened, but he felt precarious all at once, as if every interaction with Kelli might be called into question, despite being perfectly innocent.

As far as everyone else knew, anyway.

The real problem was that he knew he had feelings for her. That his integrity was so compromised that he couldn't even see above the hole he'd dug for himself. But he'd dare anyone to come up with proof that even the slightest hint of impropriety had happened. That counted.

"You tell me," Laura countered. "What will Kyle and Regina say if we do ask them to make statements about your relationship?"

"That I'm her boss. Nothing more," he insisted, praying that would be true in case Laura was of a mind to call his bluff. "I've answered your questions. Now answer mine. What is this all about?"

"We've heard some rumors filtering through the ranks," Adam told him, his expression maddeningly blank. "Some employees are whispering that Kelli is getting special treatment because she's sleeping with you."

"What?" A red haze crept through Josh's vision as he clamped down on the seething mass of emotion roiling in his chest. "That's... I don't even have words for what that that is. It's ridiculous. Lies. All of it."

Not because he hadn't thought about it a million times or more. Not because he didn't want it to be true. But ironically because Josh had been doing his level best to follow the no-fraternization policy.

Maybe failing at intent, but not the letter of the law.

"There's not even the slightest basis for it?" Laura asked, her gaze probing him as if she could see that there might be more to this than he was letting on. "Why would they manufacture something like that out of thin air?"

Josh's harsh laugh scraped at his throat as he blinked at the picture above Adam's desk of the red rock formations just outside the walls of the resort, trying to center himself with a less than stellar facsimile of the land he loved. "I'd like to know the answer to that myself. Get one or two of them in here and let them accuse me of that to my face."

Adam shook his head. "It doesn't work like that. No one has filed a formal complaint. At this point, we're just trying to get to the bottom of what's going on. It's a bad look and employees are friends with people who work at other hotels and resorts. Rumors travel fast and they're saying that Kelli got the job solely because of her relationship with you."

Oh, dear Lord. "I didn't even hire Kelli!" he bellowed. "Alexis found her, and Laura hired her. How in the blazes would I have had anything to do with that?"

"That's part of what we're trying to get in front of, Josh." Laura rubbed at her temples. "If we don't squash this, they'll implicate me and Alexis in this too. Make us complicit in bending the rules."

Now the tightness in her shoulders made sense. That more than anything else pulled his plug. Weary all at once, he sank into one of the chairs ringing Adam's desk, his own head beginning to throb. "I'm baffled by this. Not just that the employees would manufacture a relationship between me and Kelli that doesn't exist, but that the two of you believed these lies."

That was what hurt maybe more than anything. Granted, he'd crossed a few lines that he probably shouldn't have, but he'd obeyed the policy in the ways that counted. Good grief, he'd never even kissed the woman. Not yet anyway.

Now he wished he had. At least then he'd be guilty of the crime they were trying him for.

Adam and Laura exchanged glances, but it was Adam who finally spoke. "You're officially denying that there's anything between you and Kelli?"

"Yes," he barked. "Officially. Unofficially. Upside down and inside out. There is nothing going on and nothing to see. Kelli got this job because she's a great bartender. She doesn't get any special benefits for any reason, least of all because she's sleeping with me. Can I go now?"

"Not until you can explain this." Laura pulled her phone out of her pocket and tapped twice, then held the phone out.

Warily, he took it and glanced at the screen. It was a picture of him at The Cloisters, his head bent toward Kelli's as she laughed at something he said.

Chapter Fourteen

This time, Josh's vision went gray instead of red.

Someone had followed him to The Cloisters. And taken pictures. Of him and Kelli. Then waited for an opportune time to leak it online. The implications exploded in his head, sending fragmented pieces of shrapnel everywhere, into his throat, his lungs, his heart.

"This is not what it looks like," he ground out hoarsely. "Sure, I hung out at a bar a few times, which no one who knows me would find the least bit surprising. She worked there. End of story. This was weeks ago."

Weeks. Why would someone post this photo today?

"Well, yes, of course," Laura murmured. "It's obviously at another bar and employment records easily prove that Kelli is working here at Mariposa now. But the damage factor is very much current. This photo is everywhere online, especially on gossip sites, where they're linking the two of you."

"I can't stop the lies people spread on the internet," he protested as panic started swirling in his stomach. He couldn't stop them, but he also couldn't stop whatever fallout happened as a result.

Kelli.

If this was his inquest, what was happening to her? He'd left her behind at the bar to finish out her shift with a prom-

ise to catch up with her later about her ideas for the mixology class, never dreaming what he'd been about to walk
into. Had someone from HR come in behind them and fired
her? Without even a chance for either of them to explain?

Oh, no. Kelli would be so crushed. Not just to lose her
job, but she'd see it as the Coltons stripping away her independence. Ruining her chances for getting that house she
wanted. Not just the Coltons, but him.

This was a *disaster*.

"The issue is not what people are saying on the internet."
This from Adam who had for some reason taken on the bad
cop role. "It's what employees at Mariposa are saying."

"And you're taking their side in this," he concluded
bleakly, his early fight all but drained away.

Correction. This wasn't an inquest. It was an ambush.
They'd both known about the photo before they'd brought
it up. This whole setup had been designed to get him to
confess before telling him they had proof he'd known Kelli
before she'd been hired.

Adam shook his head, his eyes blinking closed for a beat.
"I'm not taking sides. I'm firmly wearing my general manager hat here. Every employee on this property has seen
this. The comments have not been kind."

Sucking in a breath that did not help clear his lungs or his
head, Josh met his brother's gaze. "What are they saying?"

"That being the boss means you get to skirt policy. That
it must be nice to do whatever you want without fear of ter-
mination."

His brother's expression resembled granite as he delivered this latest crushing blow. Because everything came
together at once as the ghosts of former employees, whom
he'd personally fired for violating the no-fraternization policy, came back to haunt him. "This is different."

The protest was lame. Even he knew that and didn't need Laura's pitying looks to solidify it.

She pressed her mouth together twice and then opened it. "It doesn't matter what it *is*. It matters what it looks like. Kelli stayed in the Colton family bungalow during the sandstorm. One of the things they're saying is that Kelli is getting perks because of her relationship with you."

"That's ridiculous."

Said with far less fervor than what he felt in his chest because Laura's point wasn't lost on him. She *had* gotten that perk because of her relationship with him. He would never have thought of putting another employee in the bungalow next to his. Not that he would force anyone out into the storm. But his focus had been solely on the one employee because of his personal feelings for her.

And here he'd thought he'd been so clever in ensuring she'd stayed in a totally separate building. The irony. It was almost laughable.

"Funny, but last time I checked, it's really hard to sleep with someone when they're not even in your house," he pointed out caustically. "Which is it? Am I sleeping with her or giving her perks? Because it can't be both. Not when we're talking about her staying on property during the sandstorm."

"That piece is easily fixed," Adam said, his tone flat. "We can pass the expense through her paycheck, as we should to be aboveboard. Then it's no longer worth gossiping about because she's paying for it."

A sick wave sloshed through Josh's stomach. "You can't charge her for the full night's rate. She'd end up owing *us* money. Besides, it's not a normal bungalow that we allow guests to stay in."

"Let me handle that." His brother waved that off. "Her

pay statement falls into the category of protected data, so I have no intention of sharing it outside of a subpoena. I'll make it a nominal amount and that problem goes away."

"The rest of them don't," Laura interjected quickly, lest Josh think all of this was over. "I need to handle the employees. We'll make a joint statement that we've found no evidence of wrongdoing and that you've denied the relationship."

"Why do we have to make a statement?"

The entire concept horrified him. Trotting out his private affairs to everyone was the exact opposite of the kind of reputation he'd been cultivating at Mariposa for *years*. People should know already that he followed policies to the nth degree. It was literally the reason he hadn't made a move on Kelli.

"Because Sharpe got wind of this and demanded a formal inquiry into why Kelli hasn't been fired," Adam said. "Discord among employees is a huge red flag. So is an owner violating company policy and not being disciplined."

And there it was. All of this rolled into a neat little ball— the merger was at stake over this issue. "That's why you're questioning me."

Laura nodded. "We have to handle this officially. Even though you're our brother, which makes it hard, but also it makes us related. We can't be accused of preferential treatment either."

"Are you firing Kelli?" he asked, his indignation factor multiplying all at once. "She's my employee. Technically you can't."

"Technically, you report to me," Adam corrected. "So I can fire her. But if you say there's nothing going on, then I have no reason to."

Josh froze for an eternity, blinking as he processed

that. "That's it? I say there's nothing going on and you believe me?"

Laura let a tiny smile slip. "I believed you the entire time. I just had to be sure."

His brother bopped him on the shoulder with his own version of a smile. "Not our first rodeo."

They'd had his back the entire time. Adam had already known coming into this room that he'd be handling the bungalow deal with Kelli's taxes, not that Josh could pretend to have a clue what that resolved. But he trusted his siblings fully and had never appreciated them more than he did in this moment. Sharpe Enterprises aside.

In fact, this show of solidarity went a long way toward smoothing over the rough spot in Josh's soul that had the merger written all over it.

"You sure know how to make a guy sweat," he allowed, his heart beating somewhat normally for the first time. "The statement is a good idea. I can't even imagine what Kelli is thinking about all of this, but I'm pretty sure she'll appreciate something official that makes it clear she's done nothing wrong."

Even though he still balked at the idea, he would do it for her. She deserved to have her employment experience untainted. Though now both of them were going to have to work alongside employees who had already been whispering about them, which sounded like as much fun as walking across broken glass barefoot.

"The statement serves many purposes," Laura told him, her management face firmly back in place. "We're saying in no uncertain terms that you and Kelli didn't violate the no-fraternization policy and she didn't receive special treatment during the hiring process or thereafter. I need the employees settled on the matter."

"And I need it to settle Sharpe's nerves," Adam threw in, because of course that was at the top of his mind.

It should be at the top of Josh's too. The implication was clear. No more hints of impropriety. He got it. Not only was he putting Kelli's job at stake, he would be sowing discord among employees *and* ruffling the feathers of the corporation who was supposed to be saving them all.

Plus, he wanted Kelli to know and internalize that he hadn't crowded her. He understood how much she valued her independence and this job equaled that. It was time to demonstrate that in big, flashing letters.

He couldn't touch her again.

KELLI SAT IN the HR lady's office for what seemed like a million years. Alone. Patsy had told her there was an issue that management needed to talk to her about, and then vanished, but no one with the title of "manager" had showed up yet.

She'd chewed three of her nails down to the quick before the door opened and Adam Colton blew in. He had this imposing manner about him as if he knew his place in the world and expected you to honor that. Josh had it too, but it came out as confidence that he didn't mind you noticing. It was the difference between unapproachable and approachable and she had her preference.

Boy, did she.

"Thank you for waiting, Ms. Iona." Adam didn't sit, but leaned on Patsy's desk as the HR lady herself came in behind him and stood at the fringes of the office as if she couldn't quite figure out where to stand now that the big boss was in the house.

Obviously, this wasn't a standard type meeting at Mariposa.

"Am I allowed to ask what this is in reference to?" Kelli

asked politely, knowing full well she hadn't done anything wrong so this could only be some paperwork mix-up or maybe she'd forgotten to take a required training class for new hires.

And even if she had done something wrong, she'd become a master of owning her choices. Never again would she allow someone to make her feel like she should be ashamed for wanting to live her life on her terms, the way her parents had constantly treated her.

"Sure," Adam acknowledged with a nod. "There was never any intent to be cryptic here. We just needed to get some information first before we spoke with you. Patsy is here in case you have any questions."

"Great," Kelli said with a smile. "Questions about what?"

Adam cleared his throat. "It has come to our attention that you and Joshua knew each other prior to your employment here at Mariposa. A photograph of the two of you showed up online today and has circulated quite widely among the staff members. As our primary goal here is to maintain a respectful and equitable workplace for everyone, we are informing you about it."

That was not what she'd expected. At all. Flabbergasted didn't begin to describe the emotion winging through her chest. She could barely breathe and now they wanted her to *defend* herself? "A photograph? Of me and Josh? I don't—I can't imagine what...it can't be of anything *illicit*. A photo of that nature couldn't possibly exist. It must be fake."

The whole concept nearly made her throw up. If it was an illicit photo, it was doctored and who would do that to her? Or Josh?

"Oh, no." Adam threw up his hands, his expression clearly shocked. "It's not that kind of photo. It's just one of you working at The Cloisters with Joshua sitting at the bar. Very aboveboard."

"Then—" There was something she was missing here. "I'm sorry, but I'm not following what the issue is. I don't even work there any longer."

"No, and that's the problem." Adam said with a small smile. "You work here now, and Joshua is your direct supervisor. Some of the employees are a bit disgruntled about perceived favoritism and potential policy violations between you and Joshua."

Adam paused for a moment, presumably to gauge her reaction but she didn't give him one. She couldn't, at least not until she understood what she was being accused of.

Though she could read between the lines well enough by the fact that Josh wasn't present. And that his brother had called him by his full name.

It was a subtle and powerful way of separating them in everyone's mind. That must mean someone thought there was something going on between them. Something more than the friendship they'd been cultivating.

Her head came up. Nothing *had* happened. No matter how much she wished for the opposite. No matter how many times she'd *almost* broken the rules, she hadn't. Josh hadn't.

"What favoritism?" she asked with far more calm than she actually felt. "What violations? Am I permitted to have these accusations in writing?"

Adam shook his head. "The matter is settled. The investigation has been completed. I want you to hear that it's important to us to maintain a fair and transparent work environment, so we take these concerns seriously and act immediately. We're committed to ensuring everyone understands all employment decisions, including job assignments and recognition, are based solely on professional criteria and individual performance. I feel confident that we can say we've done that in this situation."

"Wait, wait, wait." Kelli scrubbed at her cheek as she stumbled over the words trying to form in her mind. "You've already investigated? I'm sorry, I feel like I'm ten steps behind."

That's when Adam sat in the second chair in Patsy's office, bringing him down to her eye level, a smile with a lot more warmth on his face. "I'm not reassuring you, I can see. Apologies. Let me start over. My concern here is to make sure you feel like you're being taken care of by Mariposa management and not made to feel uncomfortable by the baseless rumors being circulated through the staff here. Patsy will be your main contact if you feel you are being harassed or bullied."

That's what he was doing here? Reassuring her they weren't going to put up with people gossiping about her and Josh?

Knock her over with a feather. Her mouth opened but nothing came out.

Adam filled the gap. "Joshua has officially denied any relationship and Mariposa is making a public statement to the effect that the rumors are completely fabricated. I hope that will be the end of this."

Her heart rolled over as she heard the words but it took a minute for them to fully penetrate. Josh had *officially denied* any relationship.

Well of course he had. What would she have expected, that he'd name her and claim her in the face of what had the potential to become a huge scandal?

The rules were clear. Boss-employee relationships were forbidden. It was one thing to stand a little too close to each other near the beer cooler. To hang out on Josh's porch after hours on a property with no security cameras in an area where employees didn't normally go.

To fantasize about how supremely good it would feel to give in to what they'd been flitting around the edges of.

It was another thing entirely to admit to your co-owners and siblings that you were well on your way to violating the policy, and would, given time.

"Oh. Okay," she managed to say faintly as she scrabbled to gather up the loose ends of all this so she could process what was happening. "I appreciate that."

"Joshua said you would," Adam allowed with a tiny bit more cheer. "He insisted you be told that he's taking care of dispelling all rumors. I believe he's as horrified by the idea that someone would think you were involved as you are."

"Right, yes. Thank you."

Wait, what? *Horrified* by the idea? She wasn't horrified. She was…confused. Especially after being told that Josh was horrified. Was he? Had she completely misread him all the times they'd been together?

"One more thing. Since you stayed in one of our bungalows, we've decided to charge you for it so there's no appearance of favoritism or perks." He waited a beat, as if she might possibly have the capacity to form a question, then continued. "We'll deduct it from your paycheck."

"Sure, that's fine." What else would she say? Then she tried to do the math, but her brain didn't even have the right information to calculate whatever he was talking about. "How much will the rate be?"

A million dollars with her luck. Obviously, this had come up in the conversation with Josh, and he'd agreed to this, even though it had been his idea to lend her the bungalow.

But Adam just smiled. "Manageable. The rate I'm using

is fifty dollars. And Laura approved a hiring bonus that we neglected to give you, so consider it even."

She blinked. That was...unexpected.

"If you have any more questions, please sit here with Patsy as long as you like." Adam stood up and glanced at his watch. "I'm expected for another meeting, but don't hesitate to ask Patsy to reach out to me if you need anything."

A clue how to react would be nice. In a daze, Kelli blinked as Adam left, then assured Patsy she didn't have any desire to stay in this chair a second longer.

When she stepped out into the lobby area of L Building, she caught sight of Regina leaving the bar, her apron in her hands as if she'd just gotten off work. Kelli started to wave but the scowl on the cocktail waitress's face answered her unasked question—Regina must be one of the employees whispering about Kelli and Josh's relationship. And not in a good way.

Regina spun on one foot and hurried in the other direction. Away from Kelli.

Chapter Fifteen

It was only when it was too late to make different friends
that Josh realized his current ones had no clout of any kind.
So he was managing this issue on his own.

"Are you sure the managing director of—" Josh wedged
his phone between his shoulder and chin so he could check
his notes "—Hotel Honeys still isn't taking calls? It's important that I speak to him about the photo posted in your
gossip column."

The bored-sounding receptionist on the other end of the
line repeated the same thing she'd been saying for three
hours. "He's busy. Do you want me to take another message, Mr. Colton?"

Josh gritted his teeth together before he told her—again—
that calling him Mr. Colton made him feel ninety years old,
which really didn't matter at all if he couldn't get anyone to
help him get that blasted photograph taken down.

"Fine. Yes, give him another message. I'll be here waiting."

So far, he'd gotten through to two of the eight sites featuring the completely harmless and yet somehow explosive picture of him and Kelli at The Cloisters. They'd both
promised to remove the post within twenty-four hours, but
even if they did, he had to concede the damage might be

done. Especially if he couldn't even speak to someone at the other six online 'zines. And plenty of people had cross posted the pictures on social media. That, he couldn't do anything about but hope.

He still had to try though. He'd promised Adam and Laura he would do everything in his power to get the scandal under wraps before it blew up even further. They didn't have to know that at least 50 percent of his motivation lay with Kelli. This must be killing her.

All this over a picture of him at a bar. Of all things. And for his trouble, he'd been forced to let Knox take the lead on two trail rides, which would cost Josh something dearly as soon as his buddy figured out what he wanted in exchange for the favor.

Two days later, he'd finally managed to get all the sites to comply with his takedown request, except one, who wasn't impressed with his argument that neither he nor Kelli had given consent to be photographed. Apparently he was welcome to sue.

Given Josh's mood, he almost called Mariposa's lawyer to do exactly that, but in a more rational moment, realized that a court case would take months and cost north of 50k. He could live with one site.

Surfacing after the worst two days of his life, he took his first morning ride since the incident, as he'd started calling it, and came back the most centered he'd been in a long time. Everything was manageable from here on out.

Finally, he could get back to his day job. Which meant he could casually stroll by L Bar and spend a few precious minutes in Kelli's company if he felt like it, and he did.

Josh took a shower for no sane reason other than he didn't want to see Kelli for the first time since the incident smelling like horse. Then Adam waylaid him before he could head to the bar, asking for an update about the photos, so Josh spent an hour assuring his brother that he'd done as asked.

It was the least he could do for someone who'd always had his back. The incident had gone a long way toward repairing the damage between them after the Sharpe merger debacle, ironically. The whole thing was ironic. Josh didn't appreciate the universe's sense of humor.

No one stopped him when he beelined to L Bar. Finally. It was already opened for business, which annoyed him because he'd hoped to see Kelli before she got busy. He probably should give it a few more days, let his insides settle, but he wanted to see her and there were no rules about that.

He *was* still her boss.

But when he got inside the bar, there were already five people belly up to the Kelli Show, and Regina even had a couple of tabletops going. Great. *Thanks Adam, for ruining a carefully planned day.* When had Josh started being frustrated that guests were enjoying the amenities Mariposa offered? Irony again.

One of the patrons at the bar turned his head, the light catching his features. Matthew Bennett. Josh scowled and picked up the pace, drawing up alongside his stepmother's flunky.

"What are you doing here?" he demanded, letting his gaze slide over the least welcome addition to the guest list at Mariposa since Allison's killer.

Matthew glanced up from his morning cocktail, an Aloha Sunset if Josh didn't miss his guess. "Look what the cat dragged in. Don't stand there and hulk. Take a seat."

"I have nothing to say to you," Josh countered, wishing he could slap the smirk off Matthew's face. But odds were

high he'd come as a paying guest and a lot of people probably considered them distantly related.

Josh didn't. His stepmother might be Matthew's aunt, but
he didn't claim either one of them. The fact that Matthew
also managed Glenna's business affairs meant something
too—and none of it was good.

"How long have you been here?" Josh asked, wondering
what else he'd missed in his two days of downtime while
he struggled to manage this latest crisis. His stepmother's
manager's presence here could not be a coincidence. One
or both of them wanted something.

"Not long," Matthew responded pleasantly, which instantly raised Josh's suspicions. "Long enough to figure out
this is the best ticket in the place."

Matthew lifted his glass and tilted it toward the other
side of the bar where Kelli had just emerged from the back
room. Her gaze instantly snapped to Josh, and he forgot all
about everything, including how to breathe.

Good grief the woman hit his system like a sunrise—
bright, beautiful, full of promise and warmth. He smiled
and meant it for the first time in days.

Kelli did not smile back. In fact, she cut her gaze to Matthew and strolled right up to the guy to speak to him directly. "Ready for round two?"

Gone was the smirk on Matthew's face, replaced by an
engaging grin that had much too much familiarity in it for
Josh's taste. "You know it, Ms. Kelli."

Blinking, Josh watched as Kelli completely ignored him
in favor of refilling Matthew's drink. Then she chatted with
his stepmother's business manager for a solid three minutes.
Which Josh knew because he counted.

"May I speak with you?" he growled to Kelli, cutting
off something Matthew had said, which was rude, yes. He

didn't care. Besides, what could Matthew possibly say that would be of any interest to a thinking woman?

"I'm working," Kelli responded sweetly without turning her head or acknowledging Josh's presence in any way other than her short response.

What in the world was this? Was she *mad* at him? His timetable for clearing the air sped up. "It can't wait."

Finally, Kelli glanced at him, her expression blank. "Talk, then."

Matthew was watching the whole thing, his amused gaze flitting back and forth between them while he sipped his drink through a straw without a care in the world. This was not the scene Josh had expected to walk into and it was throwing him for a loop.

He stared Kelli down. "In the back. It's not a conversation for public consumption."

Without a word, she turned and glided to the back, calling for Kyle to watch the bar for a minute. When Josh followed her through the swinging door, she'd moved well away from the threshold, her arms wrapped around herself as if he'd chilled the place simply by walking into it.

"Are you okay?" he asked, wishing he could pull her into his arms. But knew better. Didn't make it any easier to deny himself.

"Fine," she responded shortly, refusing to look at him again.

"Something is wrong," he countered as the frost in her tone sliced across his skin like a thousand knives.

"Nothing is wrong, Joshua," she emphasized, and that's when his stomach fell out, plunging to the floor. "What do you want?"

Frustrated at the direction of the conversation, at the fact that she was clearly upset with him, at the *Joshua*, he raked

a hand through his freshly washed hair. Fat lot of good it
had done him to take a shower between riding and here.

"I'm your boss. I don't have to want anything to speak
to one of my employees, do I?" Which was so not what he
wanted to say, but really that's what he *should* say.

"No, sir," she said so agreeably that he wanted to punch
something. "You are still the boss, and you are welcome here
at L Bar anytime you like. What can I do for you today?"

"Stop being like this," he growled. Was it not awful
enough to have spent the last two days arguing with everyone on the planet about consent to publish and misappropri-
ation of likeness, legal terms he could now claim expertise
on? Was this distance from Kelli part of his row to hoe with
all of this too? "All I could think about was breaking free so
I could come see you. Find out how you are. What you've
been dealing with as a result of the photo."

"I'm fine." Said so woodenly that he didn't believe her.
"There's nothing wrong. I have customers."

Kelli shifted, clearly about to flee, and he couldn't help
himself. He grabbed her hand before she could move out
of range. Even that small bit of contact sang through him,
raising sparks along his skin.

"Wait, Kelli. Please." She halted and he sucked in a
breath. "I'm sorry. For whatever I did. I tried to make sure
you would experience the least amount of fallout from the
photo as I could. If it wasn't enough, tell me what I can do."

She studied him for a brief moment. "I appreciate everything the Coltons have done for me. Thank you. It's more
than I would have expected, given my station here."

Her station? Mystified, he stared back. "Now I know
something is wrong. Did Adam tell you to call me Joshua or
something? It really doesn't bother me if you call me Josh."

He preferred it actually, but to say that felt like the exact wrong direction to take this conversation, no matter how much he wished that wasn't the case.

"I don't know how to answer that," she said in that same infuriating monotone. "There's nothing between us, as I've been so carefully told on multiple occasions, so I don't owe you any explanations."

Was she *upset* that he'd made a statement correcting the lies being spread? "Kelli, that's the only thing that's true in this whole debacle. I'm not sleeping with you. Therefore, it was important to be clear on that to everyone. We're completely aboveboard on this. We have been. We will be from here on out."

"Exactly," she said with raised brows. "We're nothing to each other except boss and employee. So that means there's not much to talk about."

With that, she left him standing there, fist clenched and barely enough will to keep from driving one—or both—through the Sheetrock next to the door. But what would he have her say? That she couldn't bear this distance between them? That she wanted to break all the rules and throw caution to the wind?

He couldn't respond to either the way he wanted to, even if she had said that. Good thing she seemed to be on the exact right wavelength. The ill-fitting vibe between them wasn't fixed, not by a long shot, but they were exactly where they should be—nothing to each other. How ironic that *Kelli* was the one enforcing the guardrails on their relationship when he should have never let it get to this point in the first place.

Reminding himself that this was why the rules existed in the first place didn't help.

His day did not improve when he stalked out of the stable leading Maverick for the first trail ride of the day—first one of the week, since he'd been playing Damage Control Director for two days—to find Matthew Bennett standing in the middle of the group.

Great. The universe had it in for him today. And it wasn't like he could shirk his job—he didn't *want* to skip out on yet another trail ride. Besides, this was his role at Mariposa, not moping around over a woman he couldn't have.

"Small world after all," Matthew commented cheerfully.

As if Matthew didn't know Josh was the activities director and therefore most likely to be leading a trail ride. "Save it, Bennett. Let's get through this without bloodshed."

Matthew flinched with a good deal of dramatic effect and held up his hands. "I'm just here to ride horses. Any blood drawn will be on you."

"Then I guess we're square."

Warily, Josh mounted Maverick and launched into the opening spiel of basic horse etiquette and technique, the same one he gave at the start of every trail ride. It was an easy speech, rote by now, so he kept an eye on Matthew as he talked. The guy seemed to be listening and didn't do anything egregiously wrong when it was the guests' turn to mount.

As the ride wore on, Matthew seemed genuinely interested in the scenery, asking questions that weren't too annoying and generally behaving himself. Josh grew suspicious. What was that guy even doing here? Spying for Glenna no doubt.

When Josh got back to the resort, he handed Maverick off to Clark and strolled from the stables toward L Building, which could be a legit destination for him at any given part of the day. The fact that Matthew was headed in that direction might have something to do with it too, though Josh would call it a coincidence if anyone asked.

Matthew headed for L Bar because of course he wanted to slurp up another Aloha Sunset served up by the rock star bartender, whose skill set should have been the subject of any Mariposa gossip being circulated. It was possibly the worst idea on the planet for Josh to get within a stone's throw of Kelli. But did he stop striding toward disaster? No.

Adam saved him from himself, drawing up next to him like his brother had learned how to materialize out of thin air.

"Did I just see Matthew Bennett on the premises?" Adam muttered, pulling Josh over to one of the alcoves designed for guests to hang out in comfort as they waited for their companions or took a call.

"Yeah, he showed up earlier today. I got the impression he'd just arrived, but a quick check with reservations would tell us for sure."

"Did he say what he was doing here?" Adam craned his neck to watch Matthew disappear into L Bar without commenting what they were both likely thinking—that anything the guy said was suspect.

"Enjoying the lovely Mariposa amenities, apparently," Josh said with a layer of sarcasm. "He took a relaxing horse-back ride and is now on his second trip to the bar. I was tailing him because reasons."

"Yeah, I don't disagree with keeping that guy in our sights."

Josh spied Laura's bright blond hair as she jetted across the lobby, carefully avoiding guests, to join them in the alcove, her gaze on the heavy glass door of L Bar. "What is Matthew Bennett doing here?" she hissed.

"Feel free to speculate," Adam told her. "That's what we're doing."

Laura scowled. "I don't trust that guy. He stopped me

earlier to congratulate me on my engagement. What is that all about?"

"Clive probably told him," Josh said.

"Well, sure. I'm not questioning how he found out, but why he'd go out of his way to comment on it. He's up to something." She eyed the door to the bar, which unfortunately sat at the wrong angle for them to see into it.

In all fairness, the guy hadn't specifically done anything wrong, but anyone who would work for Glenna had to have a couple of screws loose, never mind the fact that they shared blood. Plus, they all knew Glenna had been the one to leak Allison's cause of death to the press.

Josh cocked his head. The timing of all of this felt awfully *not* coincidental. What were the odds that someone linked to Glenna would be in this area of the country at the same time photos showed up online that could cause problems for Mariposa?

Chapter Sixteen

Josh had a lot of nerve showing up at the bar and asking if Kelli was okay.

No, she was not *okay*. She'd endured two days of long looks and whispers. Employees talking to each other who broke off when she came into view. Josh had made a public announcement denying their relationship and thus none of the scandalous elements stuck to him—but that same sentiment didn't seem to apply to the help.

Supposedly, if she felt harassed, she could have gone back to Patsy, but Kelli had never run crying to someone else to fix her problems. She threw her shoulders back and did the work.

Except she'd never had to deal with something like this, where she missed Josh with every fiber of her being, but still had enough mad left over to fuel her whole day.

Even being mad frustrated her. Mad about what? Josh had been so clear from the beginning that a Colton couldn't date an employee. She'd been the one to manufacture something out of it. Something other than the friendship he'd been careful to mention on more than one occasion was the only thing on offer.

Besides, what had she expected? That he'd trash his legacy and his entire future over her? That he'd tell everyone he'd renounced his birthright so he could date her in some kind of modern King Edward-Wallis Simpson abdication?

That calmed her down for a little while as she worked through her shift, and then she'd remember that Adam had been the one to talk to her, to tell her Josh had denied their relationship. The man himself had washed his hands of her, apparently. Never to be seen again.

Then he'd shown up with concern and confusion stamped all over his face. His still gorgeous face, the one she saw when she closed her eyes. Her careful control and balance slid away. All she'd wanted was to bury herself in his arms. *Her*—the independent one, who didn't need anyone. Every warning, every message she'd told herself had flown out the window simply by Josh walking into the bar.

Ugh. She had to get over him. Riding home on her moped from the resort normally worked to clear her head, allowing her to be fully relaxed when she got home. It didn't work this time.

After parking her moped in her designated spot, she trudged around the corner to her apartment, her soul in shambles. It took her until she reached the door to realize that it was open again.

Her heart slammed into her throat. Not this, not now.

Had she left it open this time in her stupor? Because she wasn't sleeping well, that was for sure. She couldn't even remember getting dressed this morning, let alone whether she'd pulled the door shut or not. But surely she'd locked it. That required a key, and she wouldn't have just walked off.

Well. Anything was possible given her current mental state.

But if she had closed it, that meant someone had broken in and the first time wasn't her fault either. The first time *wasn't* her fault. The police had tried to make it seem like she went around being irresponsible with her home, when that just didn't ring true.

Done with this noise, she flung the door open and called out, "Whoever you are, you better be gone, because I'm armed and dangerous."

Ha. That was a lie and if the intruder was still here, he should be laughing right about now. Except none of this was funny. She was so tired and heartsick and had no mental energy for whatever was going on here.

No one answered. That was something at least. She didn't hear any scrabbling in the apartment either, like someone was in there diving for cover or grabbing one of her kitchen knives from the butcher block.

Though she probably should head straight for her own weapon.

Gingerly she stepped into the apartment. And gasped. The entire place had been upended. Ransacked. *Destroyed.*

The living room, where she'd personally selected each piece of furniture, the rug, the art on the walls, lay in ruins. The intruder had slashed the couch cushions, their fluffy white insides spilling out like open wounds. The coffee table lay on its side, and what had formerly sat on top of it—a few magazines, the TV remote and a small ceramic bowl full of Kahelelani shells from the beach near where she'd grown up in Molokai—lay scattered across the floor. Framed photographs of the places she'd worked over the years had been swept from the bar separating the kitchen from the living room, all face down on the tile.

She picked one up. The frame and glass had both cracked across the middle in a diagonal. In such shock she could scarcely work up a keening sound, she set the broken frame down on the bar, her gaze flitting across the destruction in the kitchen. Her spice rack had been knocked over, tops removed to allow grounds to fling in a multitude of colors across the floor. Drawers hung open, their contents strewn haphazardly wherever they'd happened to land.

The bedroom and bathroom held more of the same, her bed stripped and the mattress slashed, along with all of her pillows. Her toiletries, once neatly lined on the shelf, lay in the sink and on the floor, some still leaking their contents, forming small, colorful pools on the white quartz. The mirror was smeared, smudges ghosting its surface.

Well, at least the intruder had been nice enough to leave prints in his quest to ensure that he'd touched—ruined—everything she owned.

Both hands to her mouth, she stood there and surveyed the mess, her brain unable to grasp at coherent thought. What was she supposed to do? There was nothing left. She had renter's insurance, but that would take some time to process and meanwhile, she couldn't cook dinner or take a shower, or even get dressed since all her clothes had been ripped from their hangers and lay in tatters on the floor of her closet.

Including the beautiful things she'd purchased from Mrs. Logan's boutique with the gift card she'd been given. The damage to the fashion pieces was possibly the biggest crime.

And now, she couldn't even go to work in the morning. She shut her eyes as that indignity settled into her stomach. Who did you have to call when you couldn't make it in to your job? Your *boss*.

That wasn't happening. She couldn't even fathom dialing up Josh and telling him her apartment had been destroyed. But she had to call someone, and Laura Colton's contact information was right under Josh's.

She hit dial before she could change her mind. Laura answered on the second ring.

"Hi, Kelli, is everything okay?" Laura asked.

Of course Laura would clue in immediately that Kelli wasn't calling to ask if she wanted to go out for brunch. "Oh, actually...no. I'm coming down with s-something," she stammered. "So I'm not going to make it to work in the morning."

The pause on the other end of the line grew deafening before Laura finally spoke. "I understand. I'll let my brother know. May I tell him how long you think you might be out?"

Oh, man. She'd really screwed this up. There were undertones here that she hadn't intended to convey, but Laura had picked up on them anyway. Kelli might as well have opened with *I don't want to talk to Josh so I'm going to ask you to do it for me.* "Oh, I'm not sure. Maybe just one day."

Another pause. "Okay, so you have a one-day illness?"

Kelli shut her eyes and prayed for help in getting through this conversation. She wasn't a liar by nature—growing up, she'd always been extremely honest about where she'd been and who she'd been with, even when it resulted in disciplinary measures. Then she'd started being smarter about not getting caught so she didn't have to lie.

A male voice asked who was on the phone. Oh, man, she'd totally spaced that Laura wouldn't be alone. "I didn't mean to interrupt. I'm terribly sorry."

"You didn't interrupt," Laura insisted. "Noah is extra cautious because of the things that have been going on at the resort."

Since the events Laura was referring to happened prior to Kelli's employment period, they hadn't been forefront in her mind. They were now. She glanced around her apartment, snapping a new lens in place over the one she'd used before to survey the place.

What if all of this was related to Allison's murder? Or Alexis's kidnapping? Was she in danger too?

"Laura, are you with Noah?" she blurted out. "He's a detective, right?"

She knew he was. Laura had told her that on more than one occasion; she talked about him all the time with little hearts in her eyes.

"Yes and yes. Why? Do you need one?"

"Hypothetically speaking, if someone came home and found the contents of their apartment had been destroyed, but this person had already called the police once before and they didn't listen when you said someone had been in your apartment, what would he advise that person to do?"

Kelli rolled her eyes at how awful that had sounded. *Way to cover the real story.* Only an idiot wouldn't have figured out she'd really meant herself.

But Laura didn't call her on it. She calmly repeated exactly what Kelli had said to Noah and then told her to call the police. "He says it's always better to have something of that nature on record regardless of whether the local police do anything about it."

"That makes sense." Maybe this time, they would at least believe her. No one would wreak this kind of destruction on their own property. No one sane anyway.

"Kelli, he also says it would be really dangerous for that person to stay at their apartment overnight after someone had broken in. They might return."

Oh, goodness. She jerked her head around to where she'd left the front door wide open. Why hadn't she considered that? "I…see the point he's making."

"Did this happen to *you*, Kelli?" Laura asked gently. "Is that why you called to tell me you won't be into work in the morning?"

"Yeah," she admitted with a guilty flush, figuring it was well past time to come clean. "I'm sorry to bother you with it. I just didn't know what else to do."

"Please tell me you're going to take Noah's advice and stay somewhere else tonight."

She hadn't gotten that far yet, and the urgency in Laura's voice started to bleed over into her own stomach, panic flipping through it like a live fish. But where would she go? She didn't have friends here yet, not ones she could call at the drop of a hat and show up unexpectedly to stay for a few days. "I…will. I'll figure something out."

"Do you not have anywhere to go?" Laura asked and didn't wait for answer. "Never mind. You can stay at the resort. I insist. Call the police, and for goodness sake, go wait in your car for them with the doors locked."

"I, um…don't have a car. I drive a moped," she filled in weakly. Didn't everyone know that? Laura wasn't staying at the resort every night so maybe she'd never seen Kelli coming and going to work.

"Then I'm sending someone to pick you up," Laura told her firmly. "No arguments. This is not a negotiation."

"Oh. Okay." She'd never seen this side of Laura before, but obviously the woman ran Mariposa with that steel undercarriage. It reminded her a lot of Josh all at once. "I'm hanging up now to call the police."

After promising Laura that she'd wait inside the house with the door locked and a cast-iron skillet in her hand, Kelli did as requested—ordered—and called the police.

A different set of officers came, possibly because she'd reported a different crime, and these two didn't waste any time asking her if she'd left the door open. They asked her endless questions and moved outside when another team came in to start bagging evidence and taking fingerprints or whatever happened in this type of scenario. She hoped never to become an expert on it.

Exhausted all at once, she watched as one police officer reentered her apartment while the other one stood near her as some type of sentinel, she was pretty sure. The firearm at his side gave her a great deal of comfort that she wouldn't normally associate with guns, but if the intruder returned, she'd rather the nice policeman be on her side.

Someone called her name and she turned to see the last person she could possibly deal with at this moment striding toward her from the parking lot.

Laura had sent Josh to pick her up.

Chapter Seventeen

Kelli barely had time to squeak before Josh swept her up in his arms and crushed her to his chest. He was babbling a long string of words that she could barely decipher in her stupor, but one thing she did know for sure—her body didn't get the message that she was mad at him and had gotten busy melting against all the hard planes of his.

How could a man feel like a wall of granite and be so welcoming at the same time?

"You were supposed to call me," he muttered as his lips found a spot near her ear, finally allowing her to understand him. "Why didn't you call me?"

"I'm nothing to you," she reminded him, her voice muffled against his shirt since he still hadn't released her. "Remember?"

Of course, present circumstances made her statement a little laughable, if she'd felt like laughing over the fact that a man had publicly denied their relationship and then ridden to her rescue almost in the same breath.

"Stop saying that," he demanded and pulled back far enough to catch her gaze with his, but still didn't let go of her waist. "It makes me insane. We're something. Friends."

A wave of emotion nearly took out her knees. *Friends.* That's what they were?

Somehow, she managed to loosen his grip so she could step out of the circle of madness that was Josh's embrace. "Friends don't hold each other like that."

Finally, he backed off, sweeping hair from his forehead repeatedly, clearly agitated. "I'm sorry, you're right. It was over the line. I was just out of my mind with worry when Laura called me."

"I'm okay," she told him, wrapping her arms around herself, which was a poor substitute for the paradise she'd just willingly wrenched free from. "You didn't have to come. Laura could have sent one of the maintenance guys or something."

Should have sent one of them. Anyone else but Josh, who clearly thought there was still something between them, which made zero sense.

"Are you kidding? It was always going to be me," he told her flatly. "Get whatever stuff you're bringing so I can drive you back."

"I don't have any stuff."

Maybe some of what she owned had survived but all at once she didn't have the energy to sort through anything. That would come soon enough when she called the insurance people and had to make a claim.

"You're not coming back here," he countered, as if she might have been telling him that to argue. "You'll need clothes and pajamas and whatever else."

"The intruder ripped all my clothes apart," she told him, weary all at once as she thought about having to sit in Josh's vehicle with him in the driver's seat and very much within touching distance for the entire length of time it would take to get to Mariposa. Even one minute would be difficult, given her current state of mind. "Everything is ruined."

Josh's mouth compressed, his expression unreadable.

"Then ask the officers if you need to stay for anything else, or if you can go."

It turned out they didn't need her any longer and she had no excuses to stay out of the passenger seat of Josh's blacked-out Range Rover. He helped her into the SUV like this was a date, and she sank into the buttery soft leather. This was the nicest vehicle she'd ever been inside in her life, and her father had driven a Lexus.

Then the man slid into his seat and, oh, boy, had she been right that it would be torturous to sit here with his woodsy-manly scent taking up all the space. Acute awareness hovered against her skin, raising goose bumps. She'd blame that on the blast of air-conditioning that swept over her as he started the engine. He didn't have to know how bothered he was making her. Still.

"Thank you," she murmured, dredging up her manners from somewhere. "For coming all this way just to pick me up."

"You're welcome," he said, his voice tense. "Laura cleared it with Adam for you to stay in the same bungalow as last time. You're welcome to all the clothes and toiletries since yours were destroyed. We'll work something out on the cost. Laura's treat. She insisted."

Kelli frowned. "I didn't tell Laura about my clothes."

Josh stared straight out of the windshield at the road as he drove toward Mariposa. "I did. I texted her while I was waiting on you to check with the police to see if you could leave."

She sank down in the seat, feeling overwhelmed and raw and vulnerable. "Everyone doesn't have to know every detail about what happened. I can take care of myself."

"No one said you couldn't." Josh blew out a frustrated sigh and tapped his index finger on the wheel. "Can you do me a huge favor and just...forget about all the tension between us? Let me get you settled in a safe place. Indulge me in this so I can sleep tonight. Please."

Josh's tone bordered on wheedling, and she did a double take. His expression resembled a brick wall, his only tell that incessantly tapping finger as the Range Rover ate up the concrete.

"Why is it so important to you that you be allowed to take care of this for me?" *I'm nothing to you, after all. Right?*

"This is all wrong, Kelli," he growled. "What's going on between us sucks. I hate that you've thrown up all these guardrails and I hate that I can't knock them down and I hate it's the right thing to do to walk away from you. Especially when I can't."

She let the rough texture of his voice wash over her as she stared at him. "Why can't you walk away?"

"Because I care about you," he practically shouted, pressing the palm of his hand against one eye as if his brain had squished out and needed to be pushed back in.

Or probably that was her own brain needing to be attended to because it certainly wasn't processing any of this very well. He *cared* about her—as a friend. She should jump on that with both feet and be happy for what was possible, not mourn what wasn't possible.

Except happy felt more like a long phone call while she languished in a bath or a sweet, tender man on her doorstep holding a hibiscus flower.

"What am I supposed to do with that?" she asked, hoping he had an answer, because she surely didn't.

"Tell me how you really feel," he said with a heavy sigh. "And I guess you just did. It's fine. You don't have to do anything with it. I shouldn't have said anything, but honestly, I would have thought it would be fairly obvious that I didn't drive all the way into Sedona to pick up a mere employee."

"Josh."

Before she could fully articulate her abject confusion, he held up a hand. "I know what you're about to say. 'It's not me, it's you.' That you're just here for the paycheck and not all this heavy emotional BS. Nothing has changed. I get it. I'm still your boss and I need to shut my mouth before I say something else that makes it worse."

"I don't really see how this could get any worse."

He was trying to say that he had *feelings* for her. Apparently. In some roundabout way. But he didn't intend to act on them and better yet, could read her mind and knew what she was going to say about it before she did.

"I know," he said with so much misery that she almost reached out to snag his hand in hers, before she realized that had been her first inclination—and that she couldn't. "I've botched everything. And you're not interested in being tied down in the first place. Even if we could be together."

She squeezed her eyes shut before the sting turned into actual tears—and not for the reasons she would have said at the beginning of this conversation. "Here's a tip for you, Josh. Next time you want to have a conversation about something, maybe don't start by telling me what I'm going to say and how I feel about it. I can speak for myself."

He fell silent, heightening the tension between them instead of allowing her to forget about it as asked. How could she forget that everything was so weird between them when nothing had changed?

Well, that wasn't true. Now she firmly believed that everything she'd felt between them hadn't been a figment of her imagination. He'd been drawn to her, the same as she'd been to him. But what did that matter if he wasn't going to do anything about it?

Mariposa came into view as Josh drove up the back road to C Building, keyed in the code to open the gate and parked his SUV in the employee lot. She'd seen it there before, so this was probably where he kept it since guests arrived at Mariposa via helicopter. It wasn't a subtle dig at her status, though it would be easy to read into it if she'd still hung on to some of her mad from earlier in the week.

It had all fizzled though. Every last bit of anger she'd clung to after he'd thrown their budding relationship into the shredder had faded. None of this was his fault. Circumstances sometimes didn't allow for things to work out. She knew that. Had mastered the art of moving on. She would this time too.

Huffing out a breath, she turned to him before he could exit the car. "I'm sorry. I was hurt that you publicly denied our relationship. I shouldn't have been. I know why you did it. It was just...hard to hear. That's all."

The employee parking lot was well lit, for security reasons most likely, but his expression wasn't any easier to read for it. She wished all at once that they were back at his place on the patio, staring up at the stars as they talked about everything and nothing, perfectly in sync.

But that ship had sailed. It was a good thing they weren't in that place, mentally or physically, or she'd have an even harder time remembering they weren't meant to be.

"I'm sorry too," he said simply, and she had the impression he would have said more but thought better of it. "I wish everything had happened differently."

"But it didn't," she finished for him and that seemed to be that. They were on the same page.

"Let me walk you to your bungalow," he murmured. "I should have brought my golf cart but I was in a hurry."

"It's okay. I like to walk," she said and meant it. Especially when walking included a beautiful sunset-soaked path and an equally beautiful companion.

When they reached the bungalow she'd stayed in before, Josh turned to her before she could slip through the door, his eyes back to that heartbreaking shade of blue that she sometimes daydreamed about. Not lately. But she had a feeling the particular scenario she'd played over and over in her head might be making a resurgence. Probably she shouldn't let it. But no one else had to know if she spent 24/7 imagining what it would be like to kiss Josh, especially not him.

"Are you sure you're okay?" he asked huskily, his fingers repeatedly sweeping hair from his forehead.

"You know this place is bigger and more luxurious than my apartment, right?" She gave him a look that made him smile and that was almost worse than being in the SUV with him. "I'm fine. I'm letting you rescue me. You should be thrilled."

There was not one smidgen of thrilled in his expression. "This is nothing. Courtesy of Laura. Officially, anyway, and it was smart of you to call her, by the way. Despite what I said earlier. I wish I was the one you called, but that's not how things are."

This was killing him. It was there in his expression, the one he'd carefully kept schooled thus far. But for some reason, he'd elected to let her in on his high level of angst. That more than anything put her in a precarious frame of mind.

"Seems like you still ended up on my doorstep regardless of who I called."

"Yeah. Also courtesy of Laura."

Why she'd done that remained a mystery. She could have

Colton at Risk

just as easily asked Adam to fetch Kelli, all things being equal. But she hadn't. Almost as if she might know a little something about Josh's feelings for Kelli. Did that mean Laura was okay with her brother bending the rules?

Well, that didn't matter. The person who needed to be okay with it was Josh. "I sense very strongly that I need to shut the door now. With you on that side of it."

He nodded, his gaze holding fast to hers, unvoiced things swirling in the space between them. "You know I'm right next door if you need anything."

"I'll take that under advisement."

And with that, she shut the door before she told him that she'd likely have nightmares about someone in her apartment. Relive seeing all of her precious things smashed to pieces on the floor. Imagine what might have happened if she'd returned home while the intruder had still been there.

At least she wasn't being forced to stay in her apartment after it had been so thoroughly violated. She still wished Josh had insisted on closing the door with him on *this* side of it.

She cooked dinner from the plethora of freshly stocked staples, her thoughts on the man in the next bungalow, who was likely eating his own solitary dinner. It seemed like such a waste to be spending the evening alone when it seemed as if they both wished it could be different.

But it wasn't. She deserved to have someone in her life who could act on his interest. And vice versa. If she wanted to cook dinner for a man, she should be able to without fear of repercussions. Without fear of being fired. Without fear that she'd never be more important to him than this resort— or worse, fear that she'd been the one to take it from him.

It was decided. She and Josh were nothing to each other and this time, it was her choice.

Sometime after dinner, her cell phone rang. Her heart did a funny little dance, even though she'd just told herself that she wouldn't be getting stomped flat by Joshua Colton ever again. Obviously nothing south of her head had gotten the memo.

Maybe she could have one tiny little all-night-long call with him. Just for old times' sake.

Except it wasn't Josh's name on the screen. It was an unknown number, so she declined it. Robocalls. They were so annoying, but she'd had her cell phone number for over ten years, and supposedly that made them worse.

The phone rang again almost immediately, which she declined again, but then it rang again while it was still in her hand.

Uneasiness flitted through her stomach. This was nothing. Right? Happened all the time.

Only not on a night directly after her apartment had been broken into.

Silly. She was letting paranoia take over and kick up her nerves for no reason. Maybe she could find a distracting show to watch on the enormous TV in the living area.

The phone rang *again*.

She switched the phone off and stared at it for a solid five minutes. She couldn't just leave her phone off indefinitely. She used it for all sorts of things like banking and to pay her rent. To text friends and get work-related emails.

Besides, it didn't matter whether she used it to solve quadratic equations for underprivileged hedgehogs or played *Candy Crush* for five hours straight. It was *her* phone. She refused to be bullied into turning off her phone simply because a stupid company had decided to put her on the "keep calling" list.

As soon as she switched the phone on, a slew of missed

calls and voice mails lit up the home screen. This was ridiculous. The next time the ringer chimed, she stabbed the
phone icon to answer it.

Impulse was not her friend and yes, conventional wisdom
said not to answer because then the scammers knew it was a
good number. She wasn't conventional and never had been.

She raised the phone to her ear. "I don't know who this
is, but stop calling me."

"You know who this is," a low voice growled. Not a ro-
bocall.

The second flutter of unease skittered down her spine.
"I don't. You have the wrong number. Stop calling me."

"You got the wrong number when you took the money.
We want it back. You have one day to get it."

"What? What money?"

"Don't play dumb, sweetheart. We know it's not in your
apartment. You must have stashed it somewhere after your
piece-of-work ex dumped the money at your place."

Was *that* what the intruder had been looking for? This
guy on the phone was responsible for trashing her things
over some misunderstanding. He'd destroyed not only her
belongings but her peace of mind. *And* left the door ajar the
first time he'd come by—a hill she'd die on every time because she had not been the one who'd done that.

Anger burned through her. "I don't know what you're
talking about and another thing—"

"Money. One day," he repeated succinctly. "I'll be by to
pick it up."

Chapter Eighteen

The guy hung up leaving Kelli staring at the phone in disbelief.

What on earth? How was she supposed to come up with money that she didn't have and had never been given? And who was this ex she was supposed to tap for delivery services?

This was obviously a mistake of some sort, but the call history still showed an unknown number. It wasn't like she could call the growly voiced man back and argue with him that she had no clue what he was talking about. Likewise, he wouldn't be terribly impressed with her logic that she hadn't dated anyone since she'd settled in Sedona either.

Actually, she hadn't even gone out with a guy since L.A. and that had been over two years ago. There was no dictionary on the planet that could describe that guy as her ex, since they'd gone on half a date, which she'd bailed on midway through after realizing he assumed buying her a watered-down drink meant she'd willingly go back to his place for a round of horizontal tango.

Honestly, the poor quality of her caipirinha had been the bigger insult. Who took a bartender to a place with subpar drinks but a huge loser?

Restless for more reasons than one, Kelli roamed the bungalow. The very last thing she should do was call Josh, but she didn't set her phone down like a good girl.

What could Josh do? Nothing. He'd already done the one thing that could have made a difference—brought her to the resort and concealed her in one of the most secure places in the area. Security guards regularly circled the property, their gazes alert and their weapons within easy reach. The main compound was gated.

Which made the phone call more perplexing. Did the caller know she'd moved locations? Oh, goodness. Had he been watching her apartment for her return and then followed Josh's SUV to the resort?

Kelli skirted the coffee table and pressed herself up against the wall in the living room near the window, but out of view. Landscape lighting illuminated the exterior of the bungalow in a ring around the building, but they were solar powered and not very bright. Mood lighting more than security lighting.

The vast desert stretched beyond the perimeter, the sky reaching even farther and full of stars. The intruder could be anywhere out there. *Uneasy* didn't begin to describe her mental state, but she didn't need Josh to protect her. She'd been taking care of herself for a long time and would for the next forever.

Whoever the guy was, he couldn't touch her here. Probably. She did her level best to push the entire night out of her mind and slept fitfully without once resorting to dialing up her neighbor.

But she did keep her phone clutched in her hand and might have pulled up his contact record a couple times just to reassure herself that she could call him if something changed. Not because she needed him! But it was kind of soothing to think about hitting the call button and hearing his voice rumble through the speaker.

What was not soothing was thinking about texting him to come over and then slipping from the bed to let him in the side door. It would be the opposite of soothing to hear his voice in her ear via his actual lips with the rest of the man attached and close enough to touch.

Somehow that ended up being the thing she fixated on as dawn finally eked its way over the horizon. Her vow to stay firmly in the friendzone or whatever this weird place was that she and Josh had fallen into felt dangerously at risk, which was not helped by the man himself showing up at the bungalow's front door just after she finished breakfast.

Not that she was surprised or anything. But as she opened the door, his lazy smile hit her square in the solar plexus, and she had to remind herself why she wasn't going to pull him into the bungalow and shut the door—because he still clung to the rules, and the rules said they weren't supposed to date. As long as he held the employee code of conduct up between them as a barrier, there wasn't much she could do to toss it.

No hibiscus this time, which she understood even as she kind of mourned the fact.

"Good morning," he murmured. "Sleep well?"

"Not even a little bit," she muttered, regretting it instantly because of course he jumped right on that.

"Thinking about things you shouldn't have been?" His gaze never left hers. "Sounds like we're *both* going to be zombies today."

Oh, boy. Yeah, she totally wanted to take the bait and ask him what he'd been thinking about. But she didn't. *Go, me.*

"You shouldn't say stuff like that," she grumbled, well aware that it wasn't a denial and that he would pick up on it. "Just because I forgave you for the relationship denial statement doesn't mean that flirting is a good idea. We're friends, or something, I guess. Let's leave it at that."

He nodded, losing not one iota of his sexy, coiled energy that made it feel like he was seconds from doing something spontaneous and visceral involving his hands on her body. She'd become attuned to it from the first moment she'd met him at The Cloisters, and it had only gotten more affecting once she knew what it felt like to be swallowed by his embrace.

Good thing she didn't have any other Josh experiences fresh on her mind. Not real ones anyway.

She cleared her throat and shifted her gaze to the golf cart on the path behind him. "Here to drive me to work?"

"Whenever you're ready."

In the end, she let him because arguing that she could walk to L Bar would have only been for show. Probably they could both use a reminder that she could take care of herself, but honestly, she didn't have the energy for it today. Yes, largely because of a sleepless night thanks to the man next to her, whom she couldn't seem to eject from her head, but also because of the phone call. Which she elected not to share with Josh. Her burden to bear.

It was interesting—and telling—that he didn't seem to mind one bit tooling around Mariposa in a golf cart with her as his passenger. What it told her, she didn't know. That he felt safe, given he'd issued a statement that there was nothing going on between them?

She spent her shift at L Bar turning over the phone call and how to handle it, but in reality, there was nothing to do. It wasn't traceable, she didn't think, which was probably what the guy had intended. An oddity considering how big of a mistake the caller had made in confusing her with someone else. You take the time to be sure your number doesn't show up on caller ID but not that you've contacted the right person?

Probably he'd figure it out when he realized she didn't have the money. It would be over, and she'd have worried Josh unnecessarily.

A part of her had to concede that she didn't tell him for deeper reasons. Maybe a bit of holding on to her own problems instead of sharing them because he wasn't volunteering to be that person in her life. She didn't owe Josh anything.

Predictably, he showed up right at the end of her shift with his golf cart, leaning on the front bumper in an effortless slouch, arms crossed in a pose that announced how comfortable he was in his own body and could likely use it in ways her imagination hadn't begun to explore.

"You didn't have to come by," she told him as she shut the back door to the bar behind her.

The look he gave her spoke volumes, but he accompanied it with the words too. "Yes, I did. I like being the one who gets to make sure you're taken care of."

"That's very…friendly." Her voice was breathless enough to betray every stray flutter going on beneath her skin.

What was wrong with her? She'd gone a long time without anyone in her corner. It wasn't like she'd been looking for a white knight to swoop in and solve all her problems. She should be telling him to shove off.

She didn't. She'd blame it on fatigue.

This time, he deposited her at the door of the bungalow and left without fanfare, only shooting her one soulful glance laden with a thousand extra layers that weren't difficult to interpret in the slightest.

He wanted to stay. But couldn't. And understood that

she wasn't going to ask him to, even though he wished she would.

The man was driving her bonkers.

She picked up her phone to text him a few choice commands along the lines of *slow your roll*, but the second she touched it, it started ringing.

Unknown number. Fingers frozen all at once, she stared at the screen, an internal debate raging through her chest. Answer it. Don't answer it. Answer it.

It was pretty close to the time the creepy guy had called her yesterday. Was her one day up?

Of course she had to answer it, if for no other reason than to tell him once again he had the wrong person.

"Stop calling me," she demanded as soon as she hit the phone icon.

"I will," the same guy growled. "As soon as I have my money. I'm standing in your apartment but you're not in it. That's not going to go well for you."

Her blood chilled in her veins. "The police are watching my place. You'll be arrested very soon."

The guy laughed. "They left earlier this morning. You think I'm that dumb?"

"Well, you're harassing the wrong woman, so I'd say that's in question, yes."

"You're already overdue for a roughing up, sweetheart. For that, I'll add in some extra pain."

His voice had turned almost silky smooth, as if he regularly threatened women and had a particular tone he liked to use to terrify them. It was very effective. Her fingers went numb and she couldn't swallow all at once.

Thankfully, she wasn't still at her apartment. Noah's advice might have saved her life, and it gave her a bit of courage. "You don't know where I am or you'd be here already. So I'd say I have all the cards."

"You can say that all you want, but this is not a negotiation. The money doesn't belong to you and I'm going to get it back, one way or another."

"I don't see how that's possible when I don't have your money and have no idea what you are talking about."

Be firm. Be direct. That was the key to getting this guy off her trail.

He laughed again. "That's exactly what I thought you'd say. So we'll play this another way. Get my money. Bring it to the address I'm going to text you. You're not going to call the police and you're not going to screw me over. Got it?"

"Or what? You can't threaten me. You don't even know who I am, or you'd know you had the wrong person." Where her bravado came from, she had no idea, but it felt good just the same.

The guy paused long enough to put a catch in her throat. "I know where you work, sweetheart. Mariposa. Hanging out in a gated resort is only going to protect you for so long. Eventually, you'll have to leave."

She swallowed a curse. He knew where she *worked*?

Did he know she was here on the property at this moment? Or was he just referring to the fact that she'd be at Mariposa during her regular shift?

It didn't matter. He didn't know she'd been given a place to stay for a while. He *couldn't* know that. She'd be safe here—after all, the resort catered to celebrities and very wealthy individuals. Adam had already doubled security after Allison's murder, according to what everyone said, and it wouldn't be so easy to get to her. She hoped.

"You can wait around for me to put myself in your clutches. It's never going to happen." Just as soon as she figured out how to get a permanent invitation to live on the grounds. And someone agreed to let her have this family bungalow forever. She could make this work.

The slight wave of hysteria rising in her chest buckled her legs and she sank to the couch. Which turned out to be a good thing since creepy guy wasn't done with his threats.

"Then we'll move on to what we call Plan B," he growled, back to his menacing voice. "You get me that money. Or me and my buddies will be taking a trip to Kaunakakai to have a little chat with Mom and Dad."

Chapter Nineteen

After two nights of resisting his sexy neighbor, Josh deserved a medal. And maybe some new skin on his palms. He'd had to do something to keep himself from reaching for his phone, and clenching his fists until he drew blood seemed to be the winning combination.

This whole scenario with Kelli right next door sucked.

Not the part where he knew she was safe. That he liked. The part where he'd been the one to personally remove her from whatever danger lurked at her apartment—also good.

Everything else, not good. Especially not being able to touch her. And not being able to text her whenever he thought of something he wanted to share with her, like the particular way the blanket of stars wheeled above his patio. Not being able to open his eyes in the morning and see her silky brown hair spread over his pillow might rank the highest on his list of not good things.

But when he arrived to drive her to work on the third morning, he forgot about his running tally of things about Kelli being next door that made him fruity in the loops.

"What's wrong?" he demanded as his gaze flitted over her ashen face.

"Nothing." Her gaze cut away from his. "I'm fine."

She was so clearly not fine that he almost laughed like

she'd told him a joke, but there was nothing funny about the worry lines etched into Kelli's temple. Her pretty lips sagged and there was something missing in her overall aura, a sparkle he'd come to associate with her.

He'd never seen her quite this deflated, not even the other night when Laura had sent him to fetch her after she'd returned home to find her apartment ransacked. She'd been righteously furious at the intruder and managed to blast a little bit of it in his direction once she'd opened up about the tension between them.

But this was totally different.

"Kelli, come on."

Slick. What did he expect to follow that with? An indictment of her caginess, as if she should know better than to withhold her burdens from him?

That would only be a thing if they were involved. And frankly, he had a feeling that if they were involved at the level he dreamed about, he'd already know what was wrong because he'd have been wedged at her side when it had happened.

Frustrated—again—he raked a hand through his hair, shocked he had any left, given the number of times he'd resorted to that move to remind himself not to reach for her.

He tried again. "It's not over the line for one friend to ask another friend if something is bothering her. Or for the other friend to actually tell him. Right?"

Her lips lifted in the faintest of smiles. "It's not over the line to ask. The other friend is just tired."

Josh didn't bother making a flirty joke about what had caused her lack of sleep because it clearly was not the same thing that had kept him up. "I'll have a word with the head of housekeeping. How dare they leave you an uncomfortable room."

That had been meant to be a joke because there was no way she'd found the bungalow's hospitality lacking in any way. But she didn't smile as she climbed into the golf cart without another word.

He followed her lead and slid into the driver's seat but turned to her instead of taking off. This was an area where employees didn't typically go unless they had a specific purpose, so they could maintain a little anonymity here before motoring off toward L Building.

"Is this about what's going on between us?" he murmured, not at all sure he should be bringing it up in light of the tenuous truce they seemed to have reached, but nothing he'd done or told himself had squelched his desire to be the one she told everything to. "Because everything I've said thus far has been true."

I care about you.

It hadn't been a random comment, or something designed to get her talking—the sentiment had been wrenched loose from someplace deep inside.

"Josh, you have to realize all of this is confusing for me," she told him, the tiniest bit of emotion filtering into her voice, a vast improvement to the last few minutes. "You're off-limits and yet, you keep crossing over into dangerous territory where I start to think you're in limits, only to be pushed back again. I don't know how to navigate this."

That made two of them.

She'd pressed her palms into the leather seat of the golf cart as if bracing herself to keep from toppling over. He risked covering the one closest to him with his own hand and that first sweet hit of her zinged through his fingertips.

It wasn't enough. He picked up her hand and folded it into his, hanging on for the brief period of time he was allowed to be close enough to do so.

"I don't know how to do this either," he confessed. "But being at odds is far worse. I missed you. I don't know what it looks like for us to be friends, but I mean it sincerely when I say I'd like to figure it out."

She nodded, squeezing her eyes closed. "I missed you too. This is one of the hardest things I've ever had to do."

Which humbled him, considering some of the nightmares she'd endured growing up. "Then let's act like friends. I'll start over. Good morning, Kelli. I spend a lot of time paying attention to you and I can tell something is wrong. I would very much like to have a conversation about it so I can fix it, because whatever is going on inside you is painted all over your aura, and it's killing me."

She glanced at him. "Really?"

Was she kidding him right now? "Um, yeah?"

Beyond the perimeter of the land where he'd built his house and the family bungalow, the sounds of Mariposa drifted through the juniper and cypress trees dotting the divide between resort property and private property. They didn't have a lot of time before they both needed to be other places, but right now, he could only focus on her and the delicate distress signals beaming from her beautiful brown eyes.

"I don't think this is something you can fix, Josh." She blew out a breath. "I've been getting phone calls."

His senses tingled. "What kind of phone calls?"

"I don't know. I wasn't going to tell you, but it's kind of veered over into the realm of terrifying and I'm…scared."

His senses went straight into full tilt protect and destroy mode in a millisecond flat as he pulled her hand into his lap so the rest of her wasn't so far away. And then did what he'd been aching to do for an eternity, sliding an arm around her and nestling her into his embrace.

Well. As best he could with the steering wheel in the way.

It was more than good enough though when she relaxed into him, burying her face in his shoulder. The sweet scent of her hair crossed his eyes, but he wouldn't break this embrace for a million dollars.

"Nothing is going to happen to you," he promised, and he might as well have signed it in blood as the vow settled into his very bones. "I won't let it. Tell me."

Everything clicked into place in his heart as she heaved a sigh that felt like relief, like sliding into a place where they could say *tell me* to each other.

"Someone called me the night of the break in," she mumbled against his shirt. "He said he'd been looking for his money and since he didn't find it in my apartment, I should get it and give it to him."

"What? What money?"

"Keep saying that and you might get to the same number of times I asked him that by this time tomorrow. I don't know what money. It's clearly a case of mistaken identity. Or so I thought."

There was more and he wasn't going to like it. He could tell. His spine tensed in anticipation, but he didn't interrupt now that she'd finally elected to spill her guts.

At least he'd figured out how to get her to talk to him. Though he still wasn't sure what had broken the dam. Neither did he think it would be helpful to blast her for not telling him right away. The night of the break-in had been *two days* ago.

"He called again last night," she admitted. "But this time he threatened my parents in Hawaii. He knew the name of the village I'm from, which is not something he could have guessed. This guy also knows I work here at Mariposa."

A fierceness he didn't recognize welled up inside him, spilling out of his pores. "He's not going to get to you here."

She nodded. "It's the bright spot in all of this. You brought me to the one place with more guards than you can shake a stick at."

"He's not going to get to you because *I'm* standing in his way," Josh corrected her and lifted her chin with his thumb so she could properly witness the rage inside him snapping to get out. "I'm not going to let him touch you, whether he thinks you're Kim Kardashian or Mother Teresa risen from the dead."

This was not a simple matter of Kelli being scared. This was a *threat* against a woman Josh cared about. A threat this guy led her to believe he could carry out on Josh's land. It didn't matter that he hadn't heard the caller directly threaten Mariposa—it was enough to know that the creep had uttered its name.

"You can't follow me around 24/7," she protested with a half laugh.

He lifted a brow. "Challenge accepted."

He'd deal with the consequences of that reality later. All bets were off. Nothing mattered except her.

"Meanwhile, I have to get to work," she told him, the corners of her mouth drifting upward, so he'd take that as a win. "My boss doesn't like it when I'm late."

"He sounds like a real killjoy. Want me to beat him up for you?"

She actually laughed at that, and the sound trilled through his gut with so much warmth that he clamped down on it, trying desperately to cling to it even as it faded far too quickly.

"If you would just tell him that we still don't have the

mixology class ironed out, that would be swell. We need to get it up and running ASAP."

Yeah, that was the last thing on his mind, but it did give him an excuse to hang out at L Bar all day long, so there was that. "I'll send him by after I give him a proper cussing out for letting it languish this long."

It was not lost on him that he should be the one pushing it, not her, but he appreciated the fact that she was trying to segue them back into business. *Appreciated* was the wrong word. He hated it. But recognized that it was necessary.

"Josh?"

Man, he could get used to the sound of her voice calling him like that. Especially since he still had her wrapped up in his arms and she'd made zero move to pull free. "Yeah?"

"Thanks. You letting me stay on your property might have saved my life."

A fact not lost on him either. "You staying here wasn't really optional, so no thanks needed."

He tightened his arms around her, savoring this one last hit, and reluctantly released her. They did both have work whether he liked it or not. And he really shouldn't be touching her like that, but oh, well.

He dropped Kelli at the back entrance to L Bar with a wave and a promise that he'd be back once he took care of a few things, then watched her walk all the way inside and shut the door. Immediately, he pulled out his cell phone and scrolled his contacts to Noah.

His sister's fiancé picked up almost immediately. "Josh. Is everything okay? Is something wrong with Laura?"

"Relax, it's not about Laura." Though it did warm Josh's heart that his sister had picked a man so clearly invested in her health and well-being. "I need you to look into something for me."

THE REALITY OF promising Kelli he'd be her shadow smacked him in the face when he strolled into the bar an hour later, after checking in with Knox to be sure his buddy could take Josh's morning trail rides and individual instruction sessions.

The place was packed. Again.

Regina cruised by, her pretty face relaxed but calculating. "Hey, boss. Find you a table?"

"Yeah, actually. That would be great."

She led him to one on the fringes, where he could still watch the Kelli Show behind the bar but stay out of the heavier traffic areas. Apparently, he wouldn't be indulging in the fantasy where he and Kelli spent hours together behind the bar mixing drinks and talking while they pretended to be working out the logistics of the mixology class he wanted her to helm.

Instead, he pulled out his phone and made notes. Number one: schedule classes after Kelli's shift ends for the day.

There was no way he could pull her from this crowd or he'd have a mutiny on his hands.

It was no chore to sit and watch Kelli work, even when his butt went numb from sitting on a wooden cocktail chair for hours. She was worth it. Not just because it gave his system a hit every time her gaze sought his across the room, locking on for a second or two before flitting off again. Not just because it was a sheer joy to watch her charm his guests.

Both of those were great. But he mostly enjoyed the fact that she was safe. And he could ensure that without raising eyebrows.

How he was going to accomplish that overnight, he hadn't worked out yet.

That was a problem for Later Josh.

At one o'clock Kelli finally got a bit of a lull in the crowd, likely due to guests drifting toward lunch, a concept he could get behind as well. Josh texted Kelli to take a minute and join him at his table, amused when she glanced at her phone and then up at him with her eyebrows askew.

She ducked under the pass-through and he got to watch her walk across the room, so it was a win all the way around.

"You rang?" she said with heavy sarcasm, but her eyes held a bit of sparkle that told him she didn't mind. "I have customers."

"Kyle can watch the bar for a while." When she was this close, he could see the little green flecks in her brown eyes, and he enjoyed the contrast. "Eat lunch with me and let's talk mixology."

Since she'd been the one to bring it up earlier, she couldn't really say no, but he couldn't quite figure out why it felt like she wanted to. There was still some tension between them that hummed just below the surface, and he'd like to chuck it all in the abyss, but in reality, it was probably a good thing. A reminder that he should be keeping his distance.

She slid into the adjacent seat, engulfing him in her scent, and he forgot all about distance, swaying toward her. Just as he started to reach out to lace his fingers through hers, a runner bearing two plates fresh from the kitchen pushed open the glass entrance door with his back and deposited Josh and Kelli's lunch in front of them, seared ahi tuna nicoise with haricots verts and new potatoes.

A welcome distraction. He couldn't touch her like he wanted to. Shouldn't. Especially not in public. What was wrong with him? He cleared his throat. This was not a date.

"Is this okay?" He nodded at the dish in front of her as he quickly responded to the text he'd received from the Mariposa system that allowed for tips to be added to the bill.

She eyed the dish. "Better than the protein bar I usually stuff in my face around this time."

"But?" He drew out the *u* in hopes of lightening the mood.

"What is all of this about, Josh?" She held his gaze, her expression the opposite of light. "This is like a thirty-five-dollar-a-head lunch and I'm probably way off on that, even factoring in that you likely get an owner's discount or something. And if you say this is us being friends again, I'm going to punch you."

"No violence needed," he said with a laugh and held up his hands to hide the fact that he was scrambling. "We're going to talk about work. This is a work expense. We're right here in view of everyone, all aboveboard."

As far as everyone else was concerned anyway. What was going through his head had not one iota of innocence threaded through it, but last time he checked, the rules said they couldn't date, not that he couldn't fantasize about it.

It felt like she might be picking up on that. And wasn't okay with it. Had he not properly addressed her confusion earlier? He was acting like a *friend*. Only.

"Besides," he continued. "Even if I didn't plan to expense this, I would totally buy lunch for a friend. Next time, you can pay. Would that make you feel better?"

"Probably not, but let's go with that for now." She still looked skeptical, but she picked up her fork. Progress. "I had this idea about the mixology class."

Then she spent the next thirty minutes regaling him with her knowledge of what went on behind a bar, as if he needed another clue that she was stellar at her job. They wrapped up lunch with a solid plan for the class, which was the only thing he could mark down as job related that he did that day.

Noah needed to come up with something on Kelli's caller

fast, if for no other reason than so Josh could step back for a hot minute and get his head on straight. Being Kelli's shadow worked for him in so many ways, but he needed to reel it back. Or something. This wasn't the first time she'd questioned whether he'd crossed the friendship line, and he couldn't afford to mess up now, not with the Sharpe Enterprises merger still in the works.

Only friends. Kelli and I are just friends. Kelli is my friend. Only.

Maybe if he kept that mantra on repeat in his head, he could get through the next few days.

Chapter Twenty

By day three, Josh had things mostly under control. Kelli let him ferry her around the property with mostly good humor, and he didn't buy her any more extravagant lunches. She cooked dinner for two, which balanced the scales in her head apparently, and sent him back to his bungalow with a plate. They didn't eat together unless they could do it in public, always with work as the subject on record.

Precarious didn't begin to describe the hold he had on his willpower, but he'd clamped on with both hands and hadn't let go yet. It counted.

Noah still hadn't turned up anything on Kelli's caller-slash-intruder, but he had some promising leads after he'd discreetly questioned a few of Kelli's neighbors at her apartment complex, as well as some of the staff at Mariposa. Josh's urging to get on with it fell on deaf ears. Detective work couldn't be rushed, as Noah informed him, and required a lot of meticulous combing through of details.

Boring stuff, and Josh had never appreciated his job as the activities director more, especially because it meant he didn't have to sit around on his hands while waiting on an invisible axe to fall. And he had more than one looming around up there: the Sharpe merger go-ahead, whether

Glenna would poke her nose into something again and cause more trouble, the dangerous criminal after Kelli.

It was maddening. And he needed to get away from it all for a few hours.

"We have a dilemma," Josh announced as soon as she opened the door to her bungalow, bagel in her hand telling him he'd interrupted her breakfast, but he scarcely noticed.

Kelli wore a bright pink sundress that hugged her body, and her hair waved across her shoulders, looking soft enough to touch. He tried not to react, but geez, had a woman ever looked more beautiful in the morning than this one? The sunrise did amazing things to her complexion.

"A bigger dilemma than when to hold the mixology class?" she returned and crossed her arms, leaning on the doorframe in a way that seemed casual but blocked access so that he couldn't sweep past her into the bungalow.

This was not the first time she'd done it. But whether she'd adopted the stance to keep him on this side of the threshold or stop herself from stepping aside, he hadn't figured out yet.

Maybe some of both. They didn't talk about the subtle precautions they took, but they both did it. Neither of them had opened that can of worms by unspoken agreement, but it felt like he'd stepped into a pressure cooker every time he got near her.

"I told you yesterday that we can hold the class at four o'clock. Kyle can handle the bar for an hour, especially when everyone will be in your class," he told her—again.

And then she'd argue that it wasn't Kyle's job and that he had to leave right at five, and then he'd argue that Tara came in at four and they'd go round and round about it. So instead of a rehash, he held up his hand.

"That's not the dilemma. It's Friday," he said and when

she lifted a brow, he made a face at her. "It's your day off. And mine. I'm not sure what it means that you forgot."

"That Noah still hasn't locked up the creepy caller, I'm basically freeloading off of Colton generosity in the meantime, and the insurance guy still hasn't told me when I can expect to get the money to replace my things." She ticked off each point on a finger as she spoke. "Did I miss anything?"

"Yes. That you need a distraction." They both did. "It's our day off. You're spending it with me. Don't bother arguing."

"When have I ever?" she tossed back with a scrunched-up face she probably didn't mean for him to find adorable, but here they were.

"At least three times an hour," he reminded her and clapped his hands twice. "Chop, chop, you need a jacket and possibly you might want to do something with your hair."

"What's wrong with my hair?" She lifted a self-conscious hand to her brown waves, and he almost snagged her hand to drag it away but caught himself at the last second.

Friends didn't touch each other casually.

"Nothing. It's perfect. What I meant was, you might want to braid it or put it up in a ponytail. Or leave it down. Up to you, but I recommend at least having the option later if you change your mind, so stick an elastic in your bag."

She didn't move from her stance at the door, eyeing him. "You're taking me somewhere. Where?"

"It's a surprise." He mimed locking his lips as her gaze flickered with interest and not a little delight, and if he enjoyed putting that sparkle there, no one had to know. "I figured you might want to get away from everything as much as I do."

"I'll get a jacket."

She vanished from the doorway, leaving it wide open, so

he stepped inside and shut it like the neighborly sort of guy he was. Who knew how long she'd be?

But she didn't spend an eternity getting ready, which might be one of her best qualities. When she reappeared a few minutes later, she'd opted for the braid, allowing a few wisps to curl around her face, highlighting her cheekbones. Instantly, it became his new favorite hairstyle on her.

He swallowed, his throat suddenly dry. "Ready?"

Practically bouncing in anticipation, she nodded and followed him out of the door, hopping right into the golf cart with zero hesitation.

"I hope this little jaunt lives up to your expectations," he muttered, second-guessing everything he'd planned today.

"How could it not?" she returned brightly. "No one has ever taken me on a surprise day-off activity."

That shifted things in his gut with unexpected ferocity. What was wrong with the other people in her life? Josh Colton would gladly be the one to step up.

"You don't want to grill me about what it is?"

She gave him a look. "That would ruin the surprise."

True to her word, she didn't ask a single question, even as he held open the door of his Range Rover for her, then drove away from Sedona toward a private airstrip not far from the resort. The sun had risen enough to be fully above the horizon, but the day hadn't heated up yet, a plus.

When he pulled off the highway and approached the airstrip, they'd arrived late enough that their impending activity could no longer be a secret unless Kelli had turned blind in the last few minutes.

Her gasp of surprise and wonder eliminated that possibility. "You're taking me on a hot-air balloon ride?"

"I told you I would," he reminded her, pleased that he could claim responsibility for the sheer joy radiating from her face. "I'd like to add a second company to Mariposa's roster and figured you could help me evaluate this one. But it's a secret shopper kind of situation. Mum's the word. I don't want them to know I'm a potential business partner."

"We'll be tourists for the day," she said with a nod, her glee undisguised.

If he'd known this would be the thing to put a smile on her face, he'd have done it a long time ago. If she didn't spend the day thinking about the threats the intruder had made, that would be even better.

Their plan in place, he parked and helped her down out of the Range Rover, which was a completely legit reason to grasp her hand and lay his other palm at the small of her back. The snap, crackle and pop inside his gut wasn't the kind of reaction a guy should have to a friend, but at least he managed to let go of her before he did something that clued her in.

The balloon, orange and brown with whimsical green cactuses all over it, had already been inflated to its operational level, towering over the airstrip and the squat hanger in the back. A wide, woven gondola sat on the ground, attached to the envelope, the burner sending propane up into the cavity. Standard stuff, nothing to put him off this company yet.

Another couple stood near the gondola, clearly fellow travelers. That was fine. Josh hadn't expected to have the ride all to themselves, since he was intending to evaluate the outfit's operations on the down-low. This was their chance to blend as they played tourists.

The couple smiled as he and Kelli took their places in line behind them.

"Hi!" The female half of the couple called as her hair blew in her face twice in a row from the strong breeze. She swiped it back, her gaze on Kelli. "You were so smart to braid your hair. This is my first time in a balloon. I'm so excited. And nervous. I'm Theresa, by the way."

Kelli, who had never met a stranger to the best of Josh's recollection, immediately reached into her bag and produced an elastic hairband. "Want me to braid yours really quick? I got advanced warning to be prepared, so I brought an extra."

Despite the fact that she hadn't been talking to Josh and he benefited from the gesture in no way, his heart shimmied a little as he absorbed the depths of Kelli's kindness. It was rare in his world to see people go out of their way to do something meaningful for someone else with no expectation of getting anything in return, which was an indictment of the resort microcosm in and of itself.

This woman rocked him on a regular basis, and he could scarcely keep up. He had to peel his gaze from her with more than one admonishment to keep his eyes in his head where they belonged.

"Oh, my goodness, you're a lifesaver," Theresa gushed, then turned and stood stock-still while Kelli made short work of plaiting the woman's dark hair into a fat braid with deft fingers while Josh and the male half of the couple glanced at each other and nodded in the universal dude code required of them when their companions bonded.

"I'm Phillip," he said and stretched out his hand. "You guys on your honeymoon too?"

Josh nearly choked on his tongue as images of him and Kelli honeymooning filled his head instantly. "Not us, no. We're um…that is—"

"Feeling things out still," Kelli supplied with a laugh, apparently on track to save everyone in a mile-wide radius today. "No labels needed."

Of course that was the right response, the one that should

have reeled off his tongue way before it did hers. He offered a weak laugh. "Exactly. I'm Josh, and this is Kelli. We're just enjoying the day."

"Oh, sorry," Phillip said, ducking his head as he glanced between the two of them. "I just assumed…never mind. I'll shut up now."

Theresa and Kelli started chattering, leaving Josh to replay that whole thing in his head to arrive at the conclusion that he must be telegraphing more of his non-friendly feelings onto his face than he thought. Great. His only saving grace—they weren't at Mariposa.

He needed to get himself together ASAP.

They boarded the balloon after a brief safety spiel from the operator, who played the part of tour guide, pointing out the major areas of the landscape as the balloon ascended. Kelli stood beside Josh, her hands gripping the edge of the basket maybe a little harder than necessary.

"You okay?" he murmured as they lifted straight up into the vast blue.

"It's just really high. I wasn't expecting it to be so disconcerting." Color drained from her cheeks, and she shut her eyes, her knees wobbling.

Without hesitation, he stepped into her space, wedging her back solidly against his torso, his arms settling around hers as he held on to her. "Hey, now. You're okay. Breathe with me here. This is not scary. Spiritual, remember? You're one with the clouds."

She melted against him, her fingers sliding into his to lace tight, her rib cage expanding and contracting against his as she did what he requested, breathing in and out. Letting him hold her together.

Just for a minute, he let her essence knit him back together in kind. He'd have to release her soon. But right now, she needed him, and he'd move a thousand pounds of sand with a teaspoon before giving up this opportunity to be her steadying force.

"That's it," he murmured in her ear, his gaze on the sprawling beauty below. "There's Red Rock State Park. You've seen it from the ground lots of times. This is not like that. You're seeing it from the viewpoint of the Almighty. A tapestry of His finest work. Open your eyes and look at it."

He could tell the exact second her eyelids blinked open. It was like light flooded her body. And his.

"It's breathtaking." Kelli's voice filled with wonder as she nestled deeper into his embrace.

"I agree." But it wasn't the view stealing his breath; it was the woman.

He'd crossed the line into dangerous territory, chucking everything he'd told himself into the breeze, letting it all blow away the moment he had the chance. The gulf between where he should be and where he'd ended up widened the longer he stood here and didn't let her go.

There was a moment, at the peak of their ascent, where the world seemed to pause. Rules didn't matter, all the angst and tension bled away. Kelli's thumb brushed over his, a spark of connection that seemed to electrify the places where their bodies touched. The door to what could be cracked open.

The shift was unexpectedly validated by Theresa, who glanced between them, a knowing smile on her face. "Looks like you've figured it out."

If only that were true.

The pilot announced their descent, effectively dimming whatever spigot had been opened between them. A blip in time and reality where Josh had let himself live in a space where he and Kelli could be whatever they wanted to each other.

Definitely not friends.

But there were so many barriers to something more, he couldn't even see over the pile of reasons he couldn't turn her in his arms and kiss her against the backdrop of never-ending sky.

Plus, he should have been evaluating the balloon operator. The safety precautions. The route, the cost factor, the propane equipment. None of which he'd actually paid attention to, not that he could dredge up an ounce of remorse. The balloon ride had been worth every penny he'd shelled out for it.

"That was amazing, Josh," Kelli breathed when they'd climbed back into his SUV. "I would have missed the entire thing if you hadn't stepped in. I was convinced I'd never be able to open my eyes. Thank you."

"You're welcome," he muttered and started the car, his mood disintegrating as he realized she hadn't experienced anything earthshaking about their relationship during their balloon ride. She'd even said she wasn't into labels.

Just friends worked fine for her.

The problem was, it didn't work for him any longer, if it ever had. And he didn't know how much longer he could keep lying about it to himself. Or her.

Chapter Twenty-One

When Kelli got back to the bungalow after having her entire center shifted by Josh Colton, she thought about crawling into bed and sleeping for a million years, but his touch still lingered on her skin. She couldn't shake the tingles, and they got worse whenever she thought about how he'd felt against her back, his arms around her, fingers tangled, as he held her tight.

Best first hot-air balloon ride ever, hands down.

And the worst, because standing with him in the balloon's basket like that, as well as riding in the car with him, sleeping a literal stone's throw away, was slowly driving her around the bend. He did these things that made her think he might be finally shedding his Just Friends era, but then dropped her at the door of her borrowed bungalow as if it had never occurred to him that if he came inside and shut the door, no one else ever had to know except her.

At the end of the day, he really *shouldn't* do that. Honestly, she didn't want to sneak around like a criminal. It was a good thing he had such strong character that wouldn't let him buck the system.

Ironically, his ethics made him enormously attractive. But at the same time, come on!

The fantasy she'd started having, the one where he picked

her and threw the rest of his life in the garbage, haunted her. For more reasons than one. She couldn't let him do that. She would never be able to live with herself. It made zero sense for her to imagine him doing that in the first place when he'd so firmly held to his friends-first mantra.

Funny thing, his hard body against hers hadn't felt the least bit friendly. And blending that breathless anticipation with the endless stretch of blue surrounding them as they soared through the sky had marked her inside in a way she didn't know how to undo.

When her phone rang, she nearly jumped out of her skin, and she didn't know what label she hoped to see on her screen less—Unknown or Josh.

It was neither. Tara's name flashed across the screen, Mariposa's nighttime bartender, who apparently had an extremely hot date Saturday night and wanted to know if Kelli would switch shifts with her the following day. The perils of trying to date while working the night shift every weekend was not lost on Kelli, so of course she agreed. And maybe the possibility of having some Josh-free time appealed to her a little too.

She texted Josh about the schedule change, expecting a short *okay* or something in response. Instead, she got a pounding on her door that had Josh's signature all over it.

"Something wrong with your texting fingers?" she asked as she levered open the door six inches to peer at him through the crack.

A bigger crack would just let more of him inside, and she didn't need another reminder that she could look and apparently touch, but everything else was off-limits.

"You can't sit here all day tomorrow by yourself," he said, shoving a hand through his hair, which still looked windblown from the balloon.

She raised her brows and clamped down on the wholly inappropriate response to his hair, his utterly devastating masculine confidence and his presence as a whole. "Is that in the employee handbook too? I'm looking forward to it actually. I never get time to myself."

"It's not safe, Kelli. I have a trail ride that I can't pass off and I can't be in two places."

"I sleep here overnight by myself," she pointed out, proud of herself for not infusing even an ounce of invitation to change that into the statement.

"That's different. I'm still thirty seconds away if something happens. Tomorrow I won't be."

She crossed her arms. "What do you suggest then?"

That's how she ended up wearing a pair of expensive jeans and boots from the closet of the bungalow and accompanying Josh on his trail ride the next morning. Her argument that she'd never been on a horse in her life fell on deaf ears, along with her point that he wasn't responsible for her 24/7 and that he'd already taken care of her well beyond what could reasonably be expected from an employer.

A boyfriend—that was a different story, one he seemed completely unwilling to examine.

It had started to bother her that he'd essentially swooped in and manhandled his way into her life while still holding her at arm's length. Maybe at the beginning of all of this, she'd had half a thought that his protective streak might segue into something else, which she'd be more than okay with.

But it hadn't. Josh was still giving her these maddeningly infuriating mixed signals.

That was fine. Despite the magic of yesterday, today already felt different—more grounded, literally and figuratively. Josh had to work, not play tourist with her, and since this was the first time she'd had the opportunity to closely observe him in his world, she did so shamelessly.

The man had either been born on a horse or got on one as quickly as possible after exiting the womb. He moved in sync with the animal as if they could read each other's minds. It wasn't too far-fetched as a theory when she'd already noted how deeply in tune he seemed with everything in his environment.

Including her. Or at least he had been at one time.

Kelli was so busy worshipping the horse god with her eyes that she hadn't mounted her beast yet. One of the other trail guys noticed and walked over to her, leading his own horse by the string thingys. Josh had mentioned what all the equipment was called earlier but she'd lost all of it in favor of swooning over him.

"Having trouble?" the other trail guy asked with a charming smile. "It's Kelli from L Bar, right? I recognize you."

"You do?" She zeroed in on trail guy, searching his features to see if she could place him.

Nada. But she'd met his type a million times. Knockout cheekbones. Stetson pulled down over his brow at a cocky angle. Hair falling past his shoulders, silky with expensive conditioner. Probably never left a bar without a woman on each arm.

"I'm Knox," he returned easily. "We've never met, but Josh mentioned you a couple of times. I can see why."

"Because I can sling vodka into a shaker most likely," she told him with a laugh, well aware that he was flirting with her and equally well-versed in deflecting it.

Why though? Was there any reason she couldn't flirt back?

The employee handbook just said no fraternizing between

direct lines of report. No boss-employee relationships. Peons could date each other all they wanted.

She let her smile broaden and infused a lot more warmth. "Knox is an unusual name. Is it spelled with a *K*?"

"Yes, ma'am." He winked, though why that comment seemed to naturally go along with the gesture, she had no idea. "Confess, now. You're not a secret ringer on a horse, are you?"

She laughed, shocked that it was genuine. Guys like this picked up a lot of women for a reason—because they were usually a pretty fun time. She liked fun. Maybe she could like Knox with a *K* too. "I've never been on a horse ever, so there's your true confession."

"Good thing I'm here, darlin'," he drawled and jerked his chin at the others, all of whom were mounted and waiting on her. "Give me a sec to let the boss know to take them on ahead while I work with you."

Kelli glanced up to find Josh's gaze burning a hole through her, his aura visibly disturbed compared to a few minutes ago. So he'd noticed that she hadn't climbed up on her ride but elected not to come to her rescue. Noted. Even though she knew exactly why he hadn't; it sat across her shoulders like she'd shrugged on a heavy sweater in June.

Trail Guy Knox sauntered over to "the boss," a moniker she should adopt immediately to keep it front and center. They exchanged words, which should have been fairly innocuous, but judging by the looks on both of their faces, whatever they were saying to each other had a touch of heat to it.

Josh glanced up and met her gaze, his expression stormy and his carriage stiff, but then he wheeled his horse in a tight pivot and set off toward the larger group. She was too far away to hear what he was saying to them, but she had the impression it was a "let's go" kind of roundup.

Trail Guy Knox returned to her side with what she'd started to think of as his trademark smile back in place. "Sorry 'bout that. Boss wanted to make sure I knew to take extra good care of you."

Oh. Josh had been warning Knox to be sure to stick to her side like glue for security purposes. Maybe Knox had balked at the idea or something, but the way he aimed his megawatt personality in her direction didn't feel like a man opposed to the idea of individual attention.

Great. She had no issues with her own personal cowboy for the duration, especially not one who had no qualms about laying on the charm.

Knox dived into a spiel of instructions, both patient and kind when she fumbled even the simplest of his commands. She shook her head as her foot refused to stay in the wedge-shaped place he'd pointed to. He took the opportunity to lean in quite close as he physically helped her figure out how to manage the action, one hand covering her boot and the other at her back.

Despite the fact that the man could be described as hot on a bad day, his touch did nothing for her. Shame. But not shocking in the slightest since her stupid brain couldn't even focus on him. Instead, it had gotten busy wishing Josh had stayed behind for this one-on-one instruction near the Mariposa stables.

Finally, she managed to swing up on the horse, which obviously had more patience than Knox and Josh combined. Wow, it was really high up here and the ground was very far away.

Knox practically vaulted onto his own horse with scarcely any effort. "Doing okay, Ms. Kelli?"

"I'm not on the ground yet," she said with a laugh. "So I'd call that a win."

"I won't let you hit the deck," he promised, matching her grin. "Let's catch up with the others. Follow me."

As they set off on the trail, the resort fell away behind them and the desert opened up, as majestic on the ground as it had been from the air yesterday. This part of the landscape lay close enough to Red Rock Canyon to have clay-colored soil.

Knox rode beside Kelli, offering tips and anecdotes that made her laugh. The larger group came into view ahead, not moving very fast. Her horse guided her right to the back flank, as if he'd done this a thousand times, and probably had. The guests who'd elected the morning trail ride had twenty plus years on her and many more zeros in their bank accounts, so she appreciated her personal cowboy, whose attention hadn't wavered from her once.

"Did Joshua invite you to check out the trail ride, or did you come on your own?" Knox asked, a hint of curiosity in his tone.

"Uh," she responded brilliantly, scrambling as she weighed out why he'd ask that if Josh had indeed told him that she needed a babysitter at all times. "Maybe a little of both? I haven't worked here that long, and I've never seen this part of the resort. It's beautiful. I only ever see it from my window."

Knox nodded. "And the bar faces the other way, so you don't even get a view of this part."

Considering she'd meant the bungalow window, it was lucky he'd covered her slip. Heat rose in her cheeks as she envisioned correcting him. *Oh, I'm staying in the Colton family bungalow, like they adopted me. Josh—he lets me call him Josh—acts as my chauffeur, driving me all over creation at the drop of a hat.*

"All of Mariposa is great," she commented lamely.

"I heard all the rumors about you and Joshua," he said with a lift of his chin toward the man at the head of the group. "Not that I believed them. He's never even looked at an employee crossways, so I knew it was pure made up BS."

She should have figured that's why he'd asked the question about how she'd ended up on the trail ride. "Thanks, that makes one of you."

Some of the staff still avoided her, but most of them had returned to normal, waving at her in the break room, conversations no longer cutting off abruptly when she came into view.

Her companion grinned. "Me, on the other hand, I know how to treat a lady. You wanna see some of what Sedona has to offer, you come find me."

Her gaze automatically sought Josh. He'd rounded one of the switchbacks, doubling back toward the tail end of the group at a higher elevation, so she could see his face this time, but wild junipers threw shadows across it, so she couldn't tell what he was thinking. The distance between them felt like miles.

"I might take you up on that at some point in the future," she told him vaguely, not that she actually would unless she could perform a Josh exorcism on herself. It wouldn't be fair to any man, let alone one as nice as Knox, to feign interest when someone else occupied her thoughts.

The ride was beautiful, the landscape a vibrant palette of colors and textures. Kelli tried to concentrate on the scenery, commenting to Knox when she saw a group of buzzards circling in a tight vortex. Since the sight was on her side, he leaned in to see it better, maybe a little too close and not accidentally. When she glanced at Josh, he was watching them with a hooded expression.

When they paused for a break, she slid to the ground and her knees nearly buckled. Man, stiff didn't begin to describe her poor legs. Walking it off, she circled the group in a wide arc, as a lot of the guests were doing the same.

When she turned at the edge of a canyon, she smacked right into something hard and unyielding. Her heart catapulted into her throat as she looked up into Josh's thundery blue eyes.

"Enjoying yourself?" he rasped, setting his Stetson back on his head.

"Why does that sound like an accusation?" she asked, her tone oodles more even than what was going on inside her. "You didn't give me a choice about coming along, so here I am. Was I not supposed to have fun doing it too?"

He huffed out a long-suffering breath. "I meant with Knox. He's got a way with the ladies, so you should probably steer clear of him."

"Maybe that's what I'm after," she countered, a little stung at the implication that she couldn't handle a player if it came down to it. "Someone who can plainly state his interest in me and then act on it."

Josh's jaw worked as he clenched it and unclenched it several times. "Did he hit on you?"

"That would imply that his attention is unwanted." She crossed her arms and stared at him. "Besides, it's not like I'm in a relationship with someone else and therefore unavailable. Right?"

The tension coiling between them, far different than the normal kind, couldn't have been cut with a machete. This had power and teeth, both with the ability to rip her to shreds. But she couldn't walk away before pushing a few more buttons, mostly because she hadn't done anything wrong and didn't appreciate being made to feel like she had.

"Right," he bit out and she had the impression he'd debated with himself about his response. "But you're not going to find what you're looking for with him."

"And how would you know what I'm looking for, Boss?" she flung back at him as his expression hardened.

It was such an unusual reaction from him that she nearly did step back then. She took in his rigid stance, his clenched fists and the way his muscles bunched under his plaid shirt, as if he could barely contain himself. Honestly, he looked like he was about to punch someone, and his stance leaned toward Knox, marking her own personal cowboy as the likely target.

That's when she realized. "Oh, for crying out loud, Josh. You're *jealous*."

Chapter Twenty-Two

"What? I am not." He was. *Completely* jealous. Utterly. Irrevocably.

It was inexcusable too. Not only was Knox Josh's friend, so was Kelli. Allegedly. There was absolutely no reason Knox and Kelli couldn't date each other, and he should be encouraging them to do so.

In fact, Knox could move right into Kelli's apartment and probably do a pretty good job of scaring off the intruder, at least as good as anyone else who cared about her. Later on, they could get married and have all the non-Colton babies they wanted.

Or as best they could after Josh murdered Knox.

Kelli's perusal of his person gave him a huge clue that she could probably tell he wasn't in his right mind. But to be fair, he hadn't been since forever. And he was likely fooling himself if he thought he'd been doing a good job covering how hard and fast he was falling for this woman.

"Beg to differ, but you've been glowering at Knox since minute one when you elected not to come help me figure out how my horse works," she told him, like he might not be aware that he'd been flinging mental daggers at his buddy for no good reason.

"I had other guests," he muttered. Lame excuse and her

expression said she agreed. "Besides, I can't openly show favoritism after all the rumors."

"No one is talking about that any longer."

She waved that off, leaving him with almost nothing to hold in front of him to keep him from stepping into her space, to relive the feel of her in his arms when he had the latitude and lack of audience to allow it.

The tension in his spine started to hurt his back.

"Fine," he growled, wishing he could canter off alone to find a spot where he could lie down in the sand and let the sun bake the stupid out of him. "I didn't help you because I'm the boss and it's the underlings' job to assist the riders. Happy?"

"Not even a little bit," she told him. "I'm over this trail ride and over your attitude. In fact, why don't you take the night off? I'll drop myself off at work."

"Don't be ridiculous," he snapped. "I promised you I would make sure you'll be safe and that includes taking you to and from work."

Plus, it was one of the highlights of his day and the thought of losing it—no, of her taking it away—nearly knocked his knees out from under him.

For some reason, reminding her of his vow amplified the mulish expression on her face. "I can make my own way to the bar and back to the bungalow, Josh. I don't need a bodyguard on the property with all the security already in place."

Clearly his completely logical arguments were falling on deaf ears. "Let's call it an extra precaution then. If someone is with you, the creepy caller guy will think twice about hassling you."

"You might have a point," she said with a smile that he didn't believe for a minute meant she'd come over to his way of thinking. "I'll ask Knox to take me and pick me up, then."

Despite the fact that he'd literally just told himself Knox could fill that bill, the idea put a red haze across his vision. "No. Absolutely not."

"Why not?" She jammed her hands down on her hips. "You just said I needed someone. Knox is someone."

Yeah, someone who needed a few teeth knocked out. When he'd asked Knox to be sure he kept an eye on Kelli, he hadn't expected to have to watch the guy substitute "eye" for "hands." But what had he thought would happen when dropping a woman as beautiful as Kelli in front of Mariposa's most notorious flirt? Best he get used to seeing Kelli with other men.

The thought had him clenching his fists again.

"You have someone. Me," he stressed. "I'm taking you and picking you up. Nonnegotiable."

"What if I say no?" she asked, her tone just this side of taunting.

"I'll...fire you," he announced, which made her laugh for some reason, and the sound took some of the wind out of his sails. "What can I do to cut this argument short, Kelli? I'm not going to give. You're not going to stop pushing my buttons, and I have to get back to the trail ride. How do I get you to let me handle keeping you in one piece without bloodshed?"

Her gaze locked with his, searching for something and he wished he could give her whatever it was she wanted.

"Why is this so important to you?" she asked.

"Because it's the only way I can spend time with you legitimately. Without anyone raising eyebrows," he told her, his voice hoarse with the effort. It was the honest truth. "Be mad at me all you want, but don't make that the reason something happens to you. Let me do the one thing I can."

She nodded, thankfully, without pressing him on his confession. "Just do us both a favor and try to be less of an idiot in the process."

With that, she strolled back to her horse and climbed on by herself, which could possibly be a testament to how good Knox was at riding instruction, but Josh would ride off a cliff before admitting that.

His mood did not improve.

He led the guests back to the stable area, reeling off points of interest in his practiced spiel without missing a beat, but he certainly didn't pay a lot of attention to what he said. A sense of anticipation had started to grow in his gut, and he had to restrain himself from kicking Maverick into a full gallop to settle his nerves.

Something needed to change, but he couldn't for the life of him figure out what that was or how to change it.

He drove Kelli to L Bar in his golf cart for her evening shift, both of them uncharacteristically quiet. The rest of the night stretched before him, long and boring as the clock ticked off the hours until midnight. Kelli texted him at ten after twelve, but he was already standing outside the back entrance of L Bar like a big loser with nothing better to do.

When she slipped from the door and closed it behind her, he flipped that on its head. No, he absolutely did not have a single thing better to do than bask in this woman's presence. She glowed in the security lighting surrounding the building, when most people would look washed out.

"Have a good day at work?" he called as she swept past him to hop into the golf cart.

"Let's don't do this right now, Josh," she told him as he slid into the driver's seat.

"Do what, drive you home? You want to go someplace else?" He took his foot off the accelerator.

"Yes, back to my apartment. This is not my home, a fact

that seems pretty easy for you to dismiss," she countered, her arms crossed. "Along with a lot of other things that are being swept under the carpet."

This felt a lot like a continuation of their earlier disagreement, which was not a vibe he wanted to carry through to this evening. "I'll take you back to your apartment if that's where you want to go. I'll sleep on the couch."

"There is no couch. Or a bed, for that matter. There's nothing there to go home to, which is part of the problem." She slumped in her seat. "It's fine, just drive."

He had enough experience with women saying it was fine to know that it wasn't fine. But what was he supposed to do about that?

Cautiously, he put the golf cart into motion and steered toward the back half of Mariposa, unable to let things lie like he probably should, but this tension between them was killing him. "Are you still mad about earlier?"

"Depends. What do you think I have to be mad about?"

It sounded like a test, one he had no prayer of passing. "I'm not sure. That's why I'm asking."

"So you're not actually aware of when you're acting like a Neanderthal. Good to know."

It wasn't that far to his place, but it felt like it took a million years to reach the concrete slab near the door where he parked the golf cart. Finally, he unclenched his hands from the wheel and glanced over at Kelli. A mistake in capital letters, because moonlight made her look even more amazing than she normally did. Ethereal even.

"I don't want to fight with you," he murmured and sighed as she slid from her seat without a word, heading for her bungalow. Which was dark, but not really out of his line of sight or anything, so he could keep an eye on her from here.

He followed her anyway. It would be silly not to see her safely to the door at this stage of things.

But she whirled halfway down the path, her hair flying out in a silver river to land against her shoulders. She poked a finger in the middle of his chest. "If you don't want to fight with me, then stop being an idiot."

"You'd think that would be easy, wouldn't you." It took all his willpower not to grab that finger, then the whole hand, and pull the rest of her against him. "Just to be clear, what am I being an idiot about this time?"

She squeezed her eyes shut as if trying to muster up strength. "You don't get it, do you? You said you do all this hulking bodyguard nonsense to spend time with me on the up-and-up, but why can't we just spend time together because we want to?"

As gauntlets went, throwing that one down did exactly as intended, challenging him to step right into the fray. He took it literally too, moving into her space, pushing into that finger against his chest. "You know the reasons why."

"Because you're a giant chicken," she informed him with a saccharine smile that he didn't for an instant mistake as amusement. "You seem to find a lot of excuses to put your arms around me during hot-air balloon rides and figure out ways to drive me around all over creation and slap stupid labels like *friends* all over everything. Then you *lie* to me about being jealous of Knox. Why don't you try owning what's going on between us for once?"

Her palm flattened out against his torso, her fingers nipping in. He crushed her hand with his, holding it in place. Holding *her* in place. "What do you think would happen if I did that?"

"Something amazing," she murmured, her gaze locked on his as bright, beautiful heat flared between them.

He should tamp it down, push it away, but this was the first time in hours he felt like himself. Like he could soar if he held out his arms the right way. But then he'd have to let go of her hand and he had zero intention of doing that.

She shifted even closer, within kissing distance, and her lips were right there, moonlight spilling over the scene with silvery promise. *Own it*, she'd said. For once. For just a brief, fleeting moment, he would do exactly that, as requested.

He could regret it later, but the one thing he could not do was stop himself from meeting her halfway, their mouths crashing together in a fiery consummation of everything that had swirled between them for an eternity.

This was A Kiss in every sense of the word. Nowhere to hide, no way to call it anything else.

That's when he let go of her hand in favor of hefting her into his embrace, exactly where he wanted her. Just for a minute, he told himself even as he knew that was a lie.

Because he needed *more*. He needed *her*. Exactly like this, her mouth under his, her hands roaming up his back to tangle in his hair as her sweet touch lit him up inside.

Scarcely aware of where he began and she ended, he let it all wash over him, every ounce of her essence, reveling in the feel of her filling him up, to the brim. *Amazing.* Yes. That's what this was, this culmination of what had started an eon ago when he'd first laid eyes on her and then it had grown into something bigger than he'd ever imagined he could experience at the hands of a woman.

He walked her backward, his mouth working down her gorgeous throat. Her back hit the door of her bungalow as he claimed her lips again, drinking from her fountain as she quenched the thirst he couldn't slake any other way.

Her mouth separated from his and he groaned his disapproval, nipping back in for round two, but she lifted her chin, capturing his gaze in hers as she murmured, "Come inside."

Nothing would please him more, but as soon as he stopped kissing her, sanity rushed back in to cool the heated places inside. "I think that would be a mistake."

One he'd love to make, over and over again. But once he tasted her forbidden fruit, he'd never be able to force himself to give it up. So much rode on him not giving in and rolling around in his weaknesses. Mariposa's very future might be at stake.

Her expression iced over as she shook her head. "Still being an idiot, I see. You can kiss me like that and walk away?"

"Not because I want to," he muttered because yeah, this was not a breeze. But he had to be stronger than this. "Because of the rules. You know we can't date."

And if he came inside, he could guarantee that he wouldn't leave until morning, and the experience would be intense enough to qualify for about seventy dates.

"Really, Josh?" Her gaze burned through him with a million watts of disappointment. "That's the card you're going to play?"

"How about I throw down some other cards too?" he muttered, scraping a hand through his hair, but it just fell back down into his face. "Like the fact that this job is important to your house fund, and you don't want to lose your independence in the first place. If I come inside, it's not a casual onetime hookup, not for me."

Honestly, he'd been a little hesitant to lay it all out there so bluntly, but as long as he was *owning* things about his feelings for her, that was a pretty big deal-breaker. She should hear that truth right up front, so she'd be super clear that was at least half of the reason why he could walk away.

Her mouth fell open. "Is this the part where I get to speak for myself? Because I never said any of that."

"You did," he countered. "That night on my patio. You talked about how much you value your independence, which doesn't sound like a recipe for being serious with a guy. You wanted this job at Mariposa because you knew the tips would get you to the next level financially. Why you'd be so cavalier about potentially losing this gig is a little perplexing, honestly."

"Because bartending jobs are a dime a dozen, Josh!" she shot back, hands on her hips. "You never once asked me what I think about the general concept of relationships or even more to the point, what I think about one with *you*. Stop putting words in my mouth and spit the important ones out of yours."

She cocked a hip and stared at him expectantly while he scrambled to figure out why it felt like he'd just lost every thread of this conversation. Cautiously, he licked his lips and asked, "How do you feel about relationships?"

"I'm in favor of them, especially when you're the other half. Moron." She rolled her eyes and huffed out an annoyed breath. "You know this is a temporary job, right? Tell me you know Laura only offered me a two-week contract. All we had to do was wait. Then I get a job at another bar and we live happily ever after."

Yeah, he had known that. It didn't matter. "Valerie extended her leave."

"That's so not the point," she stressed. "Eventually, we'd be in the clear, which you have to know. So that means I'm saying, no thank you to your wishy-washy invented barriers that you threw down between us because you're scared. You made all of this up in your own head, pushing me away for no reason other than the fact that you don't have a clue what it looks like to own your choices. Guess what? I deserve better, *Joshua.*"

With that, she whirled and flung open the door to her bungalow. Then slammed it in his face.

Chapter Twenty-Three

Righteous anger kept Kelli warm for about four minutes.

Then the reality of what she'd said to Josh dumped over her like ice water and she couldn't breathe. Not that she regretted telling him the truth, but to put such a pin in everything—it was so...final.

That's what she'd needed to do though. Clean break. No chance that he might think it was okay to keep things status quo. Or worse yet, that he should chuck everything he'd worked toward with the resort in favor of a relationship with her, which given the circumstances, looked like an even remoter possibility, but this way, he'd never have the chance to make that choice.

There'd been a moment when she thought he might. Right after he kissed her.

That's why she'd had to point out the transient nature of the no-dating rule, which frankly, he should have cared enough to figure out a way around that didn't involve setting fire to the employee manual. *If* he'd thought she was worth it, a question that he'd answered in spades—he didn't.

That realization came with another bucket of ice water that stayed with her overnight as she tried to sleep off the shocking remnants of what felt like a broken heart. Which seemed silly, given that she and Josh had never taken things to that serious of a level. At least not officially. But unofficially, she'd started falling for him that night on his patio and nothing that had happened since then halted that downward slide.

Not even telling him she deserved an effort on his part.

Kelli moved through her shift the next day like a wooden puppet being jerked by the strings, courtesy of an invisible puppet master called lack of sleep and way too much angst over the fact that Josh never stepped through the door of the bar one time. She pretended like she wasn't watching the entrance, but the third time Kyle followed the line of her gaze and asked who she was expecting, she had to concede that laying it all out for Josh hadn't really solved much of anything.

She still had it bad for him. And he was still choosing not to act on the things swirling between them.

"Sorry," she told Kyle, who was learning to make a Long Island Iced Tea. "I'm distracted."

"You need to go out with some of us tonight," Kyle suggested as he splashed Coke in the glass of liquors and mixed it with the long metal spoon kept near the well for this exact purpose. "Me, Knox and a few of the girls from housekeeping. We're hitting The Cloisters. It'll be fun. My mom is watching Lily overnight and will stuff her so full of grandma time that she'll never want to come home. Might as well live it up."

The Cloisters. She almost laughed at the irony, but it was a reminder that Valerie would be coming back to work soon, and Kelli needed to figure out the rest of her life. She'd managed to amass a good chunk of change from working Mariposa's bar, more than she'd ever imagined thanks to word spreading about her Aloha Sunset.

Her plan to get in and get out at Mariposa had worked

from a financial perspective, but where was she supposed to go? The insurance people were dragging their feet on handing over money so she could replace her things, and tomorrow, her apartment should be cleared for her to return to, not that she had any desire to actually go back there after living in the literal lap of luxury for a few days. Plus, stepping foot in her apartment equated to extending an invitation to the intruder to come by for a chat. No thank you.

Kyle was still looking at her expectantly. She should go out with her coworkers, especially if Knox would be there. She'd liked him, and it gave her a perverse sense of justice to imagine that word would get back to Josh pretty quickly that she and Knox were seen hanging out together.

Which was why she couldn't do it. Not because she wanted to spare Mr. Colton's precious feelings but because it wasn't fair to Knox—or Kyle—to use either of them to perpetuate Josh's jealous streak.

Just as she opened her mouth to decline, the door opened to admit Laura. Not the Colton she'd been expecting. Laura never came into the bar, mostly because she had no reason to.

Today, she strode straight over to where Kelli and Kyle were standing behind the bar, skirting Regina with scarcely a look.

"Kelli, I need to speak with you in my office," she said without preamble and glanced at her watch. "I've been made aware that Kyle could possibly fill in for a few minutes?"

Nodding, Kelli took off her apron and set it under the bar on a shelf, automatically pulling out the cash she'd been handed for tips. Not because she thought for a second that the stack of bills would be at risk, but old habits died hard. Back at the beginning of her career, the loss of her entire night's worth of tips could mean not paying rent that month.

And she didn't know what this was about, therefore, it wasn't unreasonable to assume she might not be coming back to the bar. Her pulse fell out of rhythm as she sorted through the possibility that Josh had asked Laura to fire her.

He wouldn't. Would he?

The moment she followed Laura into her office, the presence of Noah set her nerves off on an entirely different tangent. "Is this about the break-in and the phone calls?"

But before he could answer, she felt Josh's presence at her back a moment before he slipped into the room and brushed past her without a word. But not without the very brief press of his palm to her arm, on the backside where no one else could have possibly seen him do it.

Nothing in her body seemed to be working quite right with the dual punch of whatever Noah was about to tell her and Josh with his stealth presence she suspected might be solely as support for her.

If this was what owning his choices looked like, she might be a fan. Jury was still out.

"Thanks for coming on short notice, Kelli," Noah began, his voice grave.

He'd elected to wear short sleeves today, an armful of tattoos on display that she'd have to spend an hour to fully examine for details. She'd met him once before in person, when he'd been strolling through the lobby with Laura, but he'd been wearing long sleeves then. She kind of liked the idea of Laura with this man, who seemed unapologetically willing to pass for a bad boy while simultaneously adopting his detective persona like a second skin.

"Of course," Kelli said, surreptitiously wiping her hands on her navy pants that made up the bottom half of her Mariposa uniform. "It wasn't a bother to walk across the building. What is this all about?"

It hadn't escaped her notice that he'd never answered her original question about whether he'd come to speak to her about the break-in.

With both hands, Noah leaned on the desk from Laura's side of it, a subtle show that he and the manager of the resort were in sync. "I need you to hear that I'm working closely with the Sedona police department and Roland Hargreaves in Security here at Mariposa. Everyone is on high alert to ensure your safety,"

This was not helping her pulse settle down.

"That's quite the way to start out this meeting." She glanced at Josh, who stood in the corner of the office, his arms crossed and his expression wary and hooded. "Am I in danger here?"

"Absolutely not," Josh growled. "We're doubling security and I have a written request in to Adam to install security cameras around the perimeter of the property."

Even she knew that Mariposa prided itself on privacy and that guests often came to the resort because of the lack of cameras. The fact that he'd even bring up such a thing to his brother meant this was a serious situation indeed.

"Can someone fill me in here?" she asked with a tiny laugh, her gaze shifting between Noah, Laura and Josh. "I appreciate that you're taking precautions, but why?"

"Someone has mistaken you for Valerie," Noah said. "Several someones. And they believe you were given a very large sum of money by Valerie's boyfriend."

Oh, goodness. Everything suddenly made a terrible sort of sense. "I knew that guy who called me had the wrong person. But he trashed my house, not Valerie's."

"As best we understand it, Valerie's boyfriend got mixed up with the wrong people and told them he dumped the money with her," Noah told her. "We're not sure at what point these people uncovered that Valerie worked at Mariposa, only that they did. It's a safe bet they don't realize you're not Valerie. We're not inclined to correct them of that idea just yet."

"*You're* not inclined," Josh countered in his growly voice. "I got outvoted."

They'd come to Josh about this first, she realized as she took in his blank expression and rigid stance. Out of professional courtesy because she worked for him or because Josh would soon be Noah's brother-in-law?

Either way, his reaction did a lot to soothe her rattled nerves. Out of anyone in this room, she'd pick Josh to be in her corner any day, and his Neanderthal approach to playing bodyguard over the last few days bordered on clairvoyant.

Which she suddenly appreciated a whole lot more than she'd let on to him, that was for sure. And she had a feeling he'd sensed that this entire conversation unsettled her deeply.

That's what the palm press against her arm had been about. She exhaled and tried to work through this rationally. "How did you figure all of this out?"

Noah's mouth flattened. "Through a very long session of connect the dots. I'm not at liberty to divulge a lot since it's an active investigation, but I can tell you that the money they want is connected to a bank robbery, so these people we're dealing with are not upstanding citizens."

Laura put a hand on Noah's shoulder as she spoke to Kelli from her spot behind her fiancé. "Valerie didn't say why she needed to take extended leave all of a sudden, but it wasn't too difficult to read between the lines, knowing what we know now."

Nodding, Kelli did a little of her own dot connecting. "You think she and her boyfriend ran off with the money?"

Oh, man, did that mean Valerie's position might become permanently open? The timing couldn't be worse, considering she'd just reminded Josh last night that this job was temporary. What if it ended up not to be? How could she turn down the flood of cash this place had generated for her grateful bank account?

Then there wouldn't ever be a continuation of their conversation where Josh came to his senses and asked her on a proper date after she no longer worked for him.

"Well, *she* might have," Noah said with a small grimace. "But the boyfriend is in jail at the moment."

No one had to tell her the boyfriend likely had been the one to help fill in the blanks. She'd watched enough episodes of *CSI* during incredibly slow periods at bars with TVs that she had a basic understanding of police work, as much of it as they may have portrayed correctly, anyway. "So where does this leave us? You're going to arrest the unsavory people that Valerie's boyfriend associated with and we all move on?"

"It's not that simple," Josh interjected with another glower at Noah. "They don't have a bead on these guys despite an entire apartment full of stuff that should have their prints all over it."

"We've gone through this," Noah said evenly. "Being able to tie the suspects to a crime scene only works if you have their prints in the system already—we don't—or we pick them up for an unrelated charge—we haven't. They're proving to be surprisingly good at staying under the radar. So until they surface, we have to wait for them to make a move."

"What, like call me again?" Kelli asked as her stomach flopped at the news she wasn't even close to in the clear yet. "Can you trace an unknown number if they call my cell phone?"

"It depends," Noah hedged, throwing up a hand to ward off the look Laura shot him, which Kelli appreciated. "I'm not trying to stonewall the question. It's just that burner phones are incredibly hard to trace. Doesn't mean we can't. But it's not guaranteed. Sedona PD isn't a big operation, and we'd probably have to ship out the forensics to a better-funded city."

If the guy even called again. He might not. But if he did, Kelli had an idea that might be even better than trying to do some hocus-pocus with phone records. "What if we set up a sting operation?"

"A what?" Josh barked. "And who is 'we'? Noah is the only person with a badge in this room."

"A sting operation," she repeated calmly, more enthused by this idea the longer she thought about it. If she wanted her life back—and the ability to move on if it came to that— this was a solid plan. "With me as bait."

"No," Josh broke in before she'd scarcely articulated the last word. "I hate every word of that statement and no one with half a brain would agree to that."

Noah cleared his throat. "Actually—"

"Don't finish that sentence," Josh warned him, his expression thunderous. "Or you'll prove my point about the ratio of brains in your head."

"I'm the only one who looks like Valerie," Kelli explained before Josh could cut her off too. Speaking of acting like a Neanderthal, he was going for a gold medal today. "Presumably the bank robbers will agree to meet me if I tell them I have their money. And we can have lots of people with guns surrounding the area. It'll be really safe. Right?"

"Sure," Josh said, his glower back in full force but this

time aimed in her direction. "If you're at home under heavy guard and we put a police officer in a brown-haired wig instead. That would be completely safe and would also be something I would agree to."

"Are you under the impression this is your decision?" she demanded, rising to her feet with the tide of anger surging through her blood. "If Noah agrees, we're doing this, like it or not."

She had to get out of this place where it felt like Josh cared about her, but wouldn't cross any of his lines in the sand. The quickest path to leaving Mariposa and the madness of falling for Joshua Colton was ensuring Noah and the rest of the police caught the bank robbers—with her help.

Chapter Twenty-Four

The carpet had been pulled out from underneath Josh's feet so many times in the last few days that he could barely figure out how to walk without stumbling over yet another example of how he'd screwed up everything.

Kelli was mad at him—for reasons he still had no idea how to fix—then, Noah had actually agreed to her incredibly dangerous sting operation idea, and everyone at Mariposa was giving him a wide berth because he'd possibly snapped at a couple of people who got in his way.

At the end of the day, he retreated to his bungalow after dropping off Kelli, who, it turned out, obviously had a Ph.D. in the silent treatment. He couldn't figure out what to eat for dinner and his refrigerator had nothing interesting in it, which didn't matter because he wasn't looking in it anyway since he could see Kelli's bungalow from the kitchen. It was the perfect angle to keep an eye on the house without having to strain.

If that bank robber creep came anywhere near her, he'd personally dismantle the guy's spinal cord with his bare hands. And Noah wanted to let Kelli parade around in a sting operation like a tasty shrimp on a hook in barracuda-infested waters.

What was Josh supposed to do about all of this *stuff* churning around in his gut?

He had to eat, so he pulled out…something and threw it in the microwave. When his phone rang, and he saw Dani's name in the center of the screen, he nearly pounced on the device. Finally! Someone who had no connection with Mariposa, who could conceivably have an entire conversation without mentioning the resort one single time.

He hit the answer call button. "Hey, you."

"Tell me what in the world is going on at Mariposa," his younger sister demanded.

Weary all of a sudden, he hefted himself up on the counter and leaned against the cabinet behind him, where the view of Kelli's bungalow wouldn't be impeded by the wall next to the window above the sink.

"Which part?" he asked.

"The part that makes you sound like that."

That would be all of it, unfortunately. So he started at the beginning and told Dani about Allison's murder and how Noah had come to the resort to figure out who was responsible for his foster sister's death. The drone footage of Alexis nearly being killed by the faulty guardrail, then being kidnapped. The shady dealings with Valerie and her boyfriend's associates, who had put Kelli in danger.

How he, Laura and Adam suspected Glenna had a hand in at least some of it being leaked to the press.

"Wait, wait, wait," Dani interrupted, and in his head, Josh could visualize her face scrunched up, a look she always got when trying to work something out. "You think *Glenna* had something to do with all of this? Why?"

Man, he'd really fallen down on the job keeping Dani in the loop. He'd just seen her at Christmas, but that felt like a million years ago. "Because Clive is trying to take the resort from us."

He outlined the facts they'd learned, namely that Colton Textiles owned the land under his feet, and how Clive had been pressuring them to give him money to prevent him from selling the property out from under them.

That little gem sent Dani off on an explosive tirade. She'd gone to boarding school in Switzerland for a reason, and it wasn't her love of hot chocolate.

None of them held any affection for their father, nor his wife.

Dani had opted for distance though, despite Josh's attempt to pull her into the fold. He was closer to Laura in age, but he and his younger sister had always gravitated to each other from the first day she'd come to live with them after her mother had given up custody to Clive.

"You're leaving something out, J," Dani accused him lightly. "Spill the tea to me now, please. You know I'll figure out how to yank it out of you either way. It's so much nicer when it's a conversation instead."

"I met someone."

Geez, he hadn't meant to blurt that out right from the get-go.

Or maybe he had. Dani didn't have a vested interest in ensuring a Colton held themselves to the highest standard. She didn't care a thing about Mariposa's rules.

And their father's relationship with Dani's mother had been the catalyst for the no-fraternization policy in the rule book, after all. She might be the one person who would fully understand why he stuck to the letter of the law so adamantly.

"Ooooh," she crooned. "I could feel you holding back.

Tell, tell. What's she like? And don't you dare start with gorgeous because I knew that one already."

"She's not gorgeous," he told her with a laugh. "That would be like saying the Grand Canyon or the Matterhorn is gorgeous. You don't apply such a mundane, boring word to something crafted by a master's hand into a work of art."

Dani snorted. "Now I know you have it bad if you're resorting to poetic devices to explain that you think your girlfriend is hot."

"She's not my girlfriend," he returned, even as he mourned the fact that he couldn't be having a chat with his sister about the completely straightforward, totally fun time he was having with this great woman he'd started seeing. "It's complicated."

"Somehow, I don't doubt that. It's you, after all, J," she said with a laugh. "Now explain to me what's complicated about telling this woman how you feel. You've never shied away from that before."

"She's my employee." The silence on the other end of the phone gave him a perverse sense of satisfaction. Not many men could render Dani speechless. "Now you're starting to get the whole picture, yeah?"

"You could say. I've started about four responses and stopped myself." She sighed. "I want to tell you that it shouldn't matter. That you're not like him. Would that make a difference?"

"No, because rules are rules. The last thing I need to do is make a spectacle of a Colton who doesn't have to follow them. That would play right into Clive's hands. We're convinced Glenna has a spy at the resort. Probably one of the staff she's paying off."

"Simple solution. Fire your own personal Matterhorn and then marry her."

She was kidding. Probably. "Funny you say that. I think I mentioned something to that effect once. The real kicker is that her employment is temporary. I'll be free to do whatever I want with her soon."

Actually, that might not be so true anymore. Now that they knew Valerie had been caught up with the bank robbers, who knew when she might be back in the area. Even so, he had zero interest in giving her back her job until the woman did some explaining about her involvement. He'd give her the benefit of the doubt—after all, she wouldn't be the first woman to learn from the police what her boyfriend had been getting up to in his spare time.

Regardless, Kelli had proven to be a popular bartender with an inventive streak that he appreciated as the owner of the bar she helmed. Was he really going to let her go if/ when Valerie came back? That would be ridiculously stupid of someone who claimed to be the boss.

"Sounds like you've worked yourself into a tangle over this woman," Dani said with a simplicity that did manage to encapsulate the entire horrible situation. "What does she say about all of this?"

"That I'm an idiot," he relayed glumly.

Dani cackled. "I love her already. Why exactly did she decide this?"

"Because she said I made up all the problems between us. Why in the world would I do that?" Humming a bit, Dani waited without comment, which did exactly what she'd intended and made him think about it. Then rush to fill in the blanks. "I refused to be like Clive, Dani. That's not who I am."

"I'm pretty sure we've already covered that. Besides, look what a great sister you got out of that deal. Not all relationships have to end up like his and my mom's, or even his and *your* mom's, which I know you know. Now, say what you're really afraid of."

Kelli's bungalow sat right there in his line of sight, still darkish with the ring of landscape lighting around it. Adam had agreed to install security cameras around the perimeter of the area where Josh's and the private bungalows sat, a good solution to the request without infringing on the guests' area. It didn't make him feel any better about keeping her safe.

And maybe that was part of the problem. He had zero control over anything when it came to her and that's what scared him. He loved her independent streak, even though he knew it would be the reason everything crashed in around him.

"I don't know," he muttered. "That I don't have any guarantees. I could lose her so easily, just like I lost my mom. Poof. Gone. And then what would I do?"

"Remember that you had a lot of good times that you'll 100 percent miss out on if you don't take the shot?" Dani suggested gently. "Why are you talking to me about this and not her?"

Excellent point, one that suddenly filled his heart so fast that he could hardly breathe. "I have to go."

"Bye," Dani said without preamble, laughing as she hung up.

He texted her immediately:

Come visit. If I get this right, there will be an empty bungalow right next to mine

Dani: Text me back when that's a done deal and then we'll talk

JOSH PRACTICED WHAT he'd say to Kelli as he walked the path between their bungalows, which took about four seconds. Not nearly long enough to get it all right in his head, which was why when she opened the door, he blurted out, "I don't know how to stop being an idiot."

She leaned on the doorframe, her gaze focused on his for the first time since he'd kissed her, the barest hint of a smile curling her lips. His heart rolled over. Painfully.

"Showing up on my doorstep is a good first move toward figuring that out," she said.

"You say that like your presence grants me some kind of special insight," he muttered. "When in reality, the sight of you generally makes me stupid."

Kind of like now. The moon hadn't risen yet so he didn't get to see her wearing his favorite silvery color, but it didn't seem to matter what the circumstances were; she stole his breath every time. And his wits.

"Are you here to apologize or…?" She waited.

Yes. And no. All of the above. "I don't have any answers. I don't know how to fix things between us. But I want you to know that I'm working on figuring it out. And then I'll apologize because I'm sure I'll have a few more things tacked onto my tally sheet at that point."

It was the lamest possible thing he could have said.

But she just nodded like it was fine. "I can appreciate a man who takes his time to get it right."

Okay, he seemed to be racking up points on the pro side thus far. Maybe he could get a few more in before he had to retreat to work on whatever this plan ended up being. If it ended up being a plan in the first place. One thing at a time.

"I also withdraw my objection to the sting operation." It would kill him to stand by while she threw herself in the path of a speeding train, but he'd be there to yank her off the tracks if need be. "I do know I needed to say that much."

Her expression softened. "You're doing pretty good for a guy who professes an inability to stop being an idiot. This is all going a long way, just so you know."

Good. Great. If this terribly conceived meeting could be defined as having a conversation with her instead of assuming how she felt, like he had been, he'd take it. Especially since he'd started to embrace how true her point was. He hadn't asked her how she felt about some pretty major things, all of which he regretted after Dani had held up that mirror to his face during their phone call.

Kelli was still speaking to him, a definite improvement over the last little while, so it was a good time to stop being a big chicken. Especially if she intended to go forward with the sting operation. They might not have a lot of time to talk between now and then, and he needed to clarify a few things. "It's come to my attention recently that I may be inventing problems that don't exist."

Her smile kicked up a notch. "I heard that somewhere too."

"So I wanted to ask you how I can best honor your need to be independent while being in a relationship. With me," he threw in hastily. "Just to be clear."

"That's an excellent start to a very important conversation, Josh," she said, her gaze a little misty. "I appreciate the fact that you brought it up, so I can tell you that my biggest issue is with my choices being taken away. By anyone. As long as *I'm* making the choice to be in the relationship with you, that's my definition of independent. Does that help?"

"So much," he assured her as his heart rolled over again.

Her grace in being willing to have this conversation now, after the fact, humbled him. This was stuff he should have gotten right from the very beginning, and he had zero excuse. Man, she'd really called it when she'd said she deserved better.

This was not it. She deserved to know that he could make an effort, that she mattered to him. This time around, the theme of their relationship—and there would most assuredly be one, assuming he got this right—would be *choices*. Josh owning his and also ensuring she had the latitude to make hers.

There was just one tiny little problem. He was still her boss.

But it no longer felt like the huge, impossible hurdle it once had. And he had an excellent idea how to solve it.

Chapter Twenty-Five

The night of the sting operation went nothing like Kelli would have envisioned.

No one gave her a gun. Noah, acting in his role as her liaison to the Sedona police department, did make her wear a bulletproof vest under her shirt, which was heavier than expected and twice as uncomfortable. The earpiece he gave her didn't show at all once she smoothed her hair over it, and she could hear Noah talking to her through it, another surprise because the thing was tiny.

The Sedona police had chosen her apartment as the safest spot for a meeting with the bank robbers because it provided multiple vantage spots for the scary-looking snipers they'd installed on the roof.

Josh showed up wearing a black nondescript hoodie and skulked around in the background, not making a peep. That was the biggest shocker of them all. She'd one hundred percent expected that he'd have plenty to say to Noah and still have some words left over for her.

But he stayed out of the way, respectful and quiet.

It was like he really had turned over a new leaf, which made her heart happy. She'd started out determined to put this bank robber threat behind her so she could move on once Valerie came back to L Bar, even if moving on meant from Josh too. But at the same time, taking a new job also meant she and Josh could make a go of being together.

If they both wanted that. And frankly, she didn't know if she did. He'd said some good things during their conversation the other day, things that made her think some of what she'd said had started to sink in.

But they'd left things up in the air and left her with a vague sense of disappointment that he hadn't made a grand gesture to show her how much she mattered to him. She still worked for him at Mariposa, so that barrier continued to exist, but she'd given him plenty of examples of how that issue could be taken out of the equation.

It was up to him to walk through the door she'd opened.

She'd tried not to miss him. But that wasn't going very well. It was so odd being in this place where she knew there were big feelings between them, but she couldn't run over and throw herself into his arms like she ached to.

For one, he wasn't supposed to be here. And the solid feel of his arms around her wouldn't do anything except confuse matters.

Noah motioned her over to the stairwell where she'd told the creepy caller guy to meet her. She shouldered a backpack supposedly full of the stolen bank funds. It was really copy paper in stacks with a few real bills seeded along the top. The bank robbers were supposed to show up to retrieve the money, she'd hand over the backpack, and step back as Sedona's finest leaped out of hiding to capture the criminals.

Sounded too easy to her, but scenes like that went down on *CSI* all the time, so it could be a legit plan. Of course, the people on *CSI* were all actors and there were no real bullets in the mix.

This was literally the most frightening thing she'd ever

done, but she'd do this twice to get her life back. To have choices again.

Her pulse thrummed in her throat as Noah moved out of sight with a reassuring nod, then started speaking through the earpiece.

"Now we wait," he told her.

Apparently he'd moved far enough away that she couldn't hear his actual voice any longer, just the electronic one in her ear. A minute turned into five. Ten. A million.

A car door slammed, making her jump. It echoed in the stairwell, which sat at the edge of the parking lot, but she couldn't see if it was the bank robbers from this angle. Not that she'd know them on sight, but she figured they'd look like hoodlums, sporting neck tattoos and wearing black jackets. Of course, that described Noah too, so what did she know?

No shady criminal types appeared in her line of vision, but her phone rang. She pulled it from her back pocket and glanced at it. Unknown.

Why was he *calling* her when he was supposed to be here? This was not the plan she and the robber had discussed. What was going on?

She hit the answer call button and held up the backpack in case he was watching her through binoculars, which Noah had told her might be the case. "Where are you? I have your money. Come and get it."

"Change of plans, sweetheart," the creep muttered. "Listen up, since you must be hard of hearing. We told you no cops and judging by the lineup on the rooftop, you invited all of them. So we're moving the party. To the resort. Meet me near the stables. Alone. If you tell anyone, the deal's off and I visit your parents next."

He ended the call before she could protest. The threat

to her parents was real—she believed that much. But she also believed this guy was playing for keeps. What might he do to *her*?

Her stomach squeezed so hard she thought she might throw up. How was she supposed to play this? Obviously she wasn't going to go to the stables without ensuring the police knew. But the bank robbers clearly had eyes all over her. They'd see her talking to Noah.

Unless she told him through the earpiece. Maybe the robbers didn't know she had a wire. So she covered her mouth like the call had upset her and relayed the caller's message.

Noah spit out a muffled curse. "We set up shop too late. They beat us here and saw everything. We're going to have to slim down operations."

"Are you out of your mind?" That was Josh's voice hitting her other ear, which meant he'd said it at top volume from somewhere behind her.

"Tell him it's fine," she murmured to Noah, even as her heart stumbled over Josh's obvious concern. This was why everything was so upside down—he couldn't keep acting like he cared unless he planned to do something about it. It was killing her. "He's got to calm down or we'll lose this opportunity."

Quickly, she and Noah worked out a plan for her to drive Josh's SUV back to the resort and park it in the lot, then take his golf cart to the stable. Noah and Josh would chopper in and have the concierge service pick them up at the helipad. It wasn't a perfect plan, but it would allow them all to arrive back at the resort around the same time, and the robbers would hopefully assume the helicopter passengers were guests.

Kelli's hands started aching two minutes into her drive. She couldn't unclench them from the wheel, or she feared she'd drive off the road. This wasn't a familiar vehicle and it was so big. But her moped was back at the resort.

She hated that Josh was no doubt freaking out. That she couldn't really talk to him in case the robbers were following her. It had to look like she'd left everyone at her apartment building, with no one the wiser.

Honestly, she was kind of freaking out too.

This change of plans worried her. Clearly the robbers knew they'd tried to set up a trap and hadn't fallen for it. What would Noah do to capture these men now that their careful ambush had been blown to pieces? Could he still arrest all of the men by himself? They didn't know how many there were, as far as she could tell.

The parking lot at Mariposa was dark. The security lights weren't on. Or something had happened to them.

She rolled into a spot, well aware the enormous SUV was crooked, but left it that way and climbed out of it, dashing toward the golf cart. Fortunately, she'd already known exactly where it was, diving into the driver's seat, muscles poised to feel someone grabbing her from behind.

Nothing happened.

She breathed as she started up the cart, hurtling toward the stables. She passed a few of the nighttime maintenance crew, the ones who emptied trash cans and handled repairs. Normally she'd wave but she couldn't risk anyone stopping to talk to her.

The stables weren't as dark, fortunately, courtesy of the moonlight. She'd never been to this part of the resort at night, but she suspected the security lights had been tampered with here as well.

Pulse throbbing, she rounded the building, praying Noah and Josh were nearby, preferably with the entire police department behind them with a borrowed SWAT team en route.

She didn't have to wait long. A hulking figure separated from the shadows, a gun drawn and trained on her. Her gaze narrowed to the slim barrel as he approached.

"I'll take that backpack nice and slow," he growled.

Creepy caller guy. She'd recognize his voice anywhere. "Can I throw it on the ground?"

Good grief, her voice had come out so high and squeaky, she sounded like a cartoon character.

"Sure, sweetheart. You knock yourself out."

She flung the backpack as far as she could behind him, which turned out not to be very far. It landed with a thunk near his black boots. He glanced down and started to bend to pick it up when a commotion sounded behind her.

Kelli swung around in time to see three more shadowy figures being hustled from around the side of the stables, all being held by uniformed officers. The rest of the robbers?

One of them broke free, drawing several more officers from behind the building. Shouts and a scuffle ensued as she held her breath. Surely these police people had training for this type of situation. But she wouldn't rest easy until all the robbers had been taken away.

Something hard bit into her ribs, then a rough hand manacled itself to her upper arm.

"You're coming with me, sweetheart."

Creepy caller guy—she'd forgotten about him still standing behind her. The hard thing must be his gun. Shoved into her ribs.

A bullet could tear through her abdomen at any second.

In slow motion, she watched Josh round the stable, his gaze locking onto hers. He froze, his expression going black as he absorbed the criminal behind her, his fingers wrapped around her arm.

"Let her go," Josh demanded, and creepy caller guy laughed.

"Not a chance. Follow me and I shoot her."

The creep backed away. No one advanced on him, not even Noah, who wheeled to a stop next to Josh, his chest rising and falling as if he'd run from somewhere else.

She couldn't take her eyes off Josh, shaking her head almost imperceptibly. Every muscle in that man's body was poised to take off from his starting position and come after her.

But if he did that, the creep might shoot him. She had a much better chance of reasoning with him if he thought everyone was following his instructions.

The creep kept backing away, taking her farther and farther from the stables. Fear became a live thing in her throat, worming its way down into her stomach with icy tendrils.

At least Josh hadn't followed them. She'd been watching and never saw even a hint of shadowy movement from the way they'd come.

Soon she couldn't see the stables any longer. The lights from the resort dimmed as the stars overhead brightened. Hushed, dark mountains loomed all around them.

How far into the desert would he take her before releasing her? He would release her, right?

She'd seen the backpack slung over the man's shoulders. Presumably he hadn't had time to verify it was actually money and hadn't realized yet that the authorities had faked it all. Probably once he figured out the backpack wasn't full of his stolen bank funds, he'd kill her. What did he have to lose? Nothing, at that point.

Her best bet was to get away before he figured out he'd come all this way for nothing.

"This is far enough," she told him, her voice shaky with adrenaline and stress. "You've got the money."

"Shut up. I'm thinking."

Because he realized there wasn't a lot of leeway in this plan of his to steal her away into the desert. He either had to let her go or shoot her—or the distant third option, keep her subdued with his gun while navigating the treacherous desert. In the dark.

This guy wasn't very smart, but she wasn't about to tell him that.

All at once, a sound like thunder erupted from behind them. Her captor's fingers wrenched from her arm. He cried out.

Suddenly free, she spun to see the magnificent figure of Josh on his horse. He'd roped the creep by the neck and yanked him away from her. Josh wound his end of the rope around the tab thing on his saddle, and his beautiful, beautiful horse leaned back, drawing the line taut.

The creep's hands scrabbled at the rope as he struggled to breathe. Josh slid from the saddle. The moment he hit the ground, she met him halfway, crashing into his arms as they closed around her like a vise. She didn't mind, her face buried in his shirt, which smelled so much like Josh that tears sprang to her eyes.

Safe. She was safe. And in his arms. The center of her chest near burst, it was so full.

"I have to let you go for like five seconds," he murmured, his lips in her hair. "Not because I want to. I have to get his gun."

That was a good enough reason to let him go too. She stepped back as he secured the gun in the waistband of his pants. A few dozen law enforcement officers on loan from surrounding cities flooded into the arroyo where the creep had dragged her. Noah jumped from the passenger seat of an ATV, his weapon drawn and trained on the robber, but the creep had fallen to his knees, still gasping for air.

Josh handed off the gun to one of the Sedona officers and a millisecond later, her knight in shining armor whirled her back into his embrace.

"Are you okay?" His fingers accompanied the question in a utilitarian survey of her face, tracing lines down her cheeks and along her throat.

Her skin could not get enough contact with his. She slipped one hand beneath his shirt, palm flat against his back and even that wasn't cutting it. "I'll be a lot better when we're not outside with a million eyes on us."

His lips tipped up in a semismile, but stark terror still lurked in the depths of his gaze. "He didn't hurt you?"

She shook her head, emotion clogging her throat. "He didn't get the chance. You showed up before he'd figured out what he wanted to do with me. You get the gold star for timing."

To his credit, he didn't say *I told you so* or mention the fact that he'd been against this sting operation idea from the beginning. Instead, he'd stood by and let her walk right into this dangerous situation because she'd yelled at him and told him he was awful for trying to take away her choices… and then he'd ridden through the dark desert to her rescue.

But he wasn't done making her feel important and seen and validated.

Before she could process his intentions, he captured her mouth in a fierce kiss in full view of everyone, no holds barred, no hiding behind anything. She couldn't do anything but hold on as this man filled her up with light and music, draining away everything else expertly. Instantly.

She clung to him, not even caring that things between them weren't resolved, that she had a lot of apologizing to do. This was the kind of kiss that scored you on the inside and you'd be a fool to end first.

But eventually his mouth lifted from hers as he kissed his way across her cheek to her ear, nuzzling it. "This is me owning my choices. I choose you. Always."

Her heart fell somewhere in the vicinity of her shoes as she tried to process what he was telling her. Had he done something to change things? Something irreversible like giving up Mariposa? Oh, no, he couldn't have. Could he?

Well, sure he could have, especially after she'd told him he needed to throw down or don't bother coming around her any longer.

"I don't understand what's happening, Josh," she said, searching his face for some clue that he hadn't actually trashed his entire legacy for her when she'd never meant for him to do that.

He just stared back at her as people swarmed around them. "We need to talk. Soon."

Chapter Twenty-Six

The Sedona police hauled away the robber in handcuffs. Kelli didn't have a moment to herself—or for Josh—as a paramedic checked her over, then tried to convince her to go back to the hospital with him.

As if. She needed to talk to Josh, not waste time in the ER over something minor like a forming bruise on her back.

Finally she satisfied the paramedic that she was fine, but then one of the officers corralled her next, pulling her to the side to talk through whether she needed counseling or other trauma resources. Probably she didn't reassure the woman by barking at her that she was totally good.

Kelli appreciated all the people here were trying to help. But they really weren't helping at all.

At some point, Josh personally supervised getting her situated into one of the ATVs so Noah could take her back to the resort. She'd have ridden on the back of Josh's horse, but he'd nixed that idea quickly because of how dark it was.

The stables were ablaze with light when she got back. Someone had obviously fixed whatever the robbers had done with the security lighting. All she wanted was Josh, but when she asked one of the officers, she found out he'd accompanied Noah to the police station to make a statement about how he'd subdued her kidnapper.

It was a long night without Josh's presence, and it was only then that she realized he didn't have to play bodyguard any longer. Had she lost her shadow for good? The thought made her sad. She'd liked the excuse to be near him more than she'd realized.

She collapsed onto the couch near the big window in the living room of her bungalow, the one that had the best view of Josh's house, but she must have fallen asleep waiting for him to come back from the police station. The next thing she knew, sunlight streamed into the room from the open blinds.

And someone was knocking on her door.

Josh. She'd recognize his knock anywhere. Her heart started smiling well before she swung open the door to admit him, stepping well aside so it was clear—she was inviting him in.

He didn't hesitate to cross the threshold, slamming the door behind him.

They had a lot to talk about, but she fell into his arms, letting his essence wash through her soul. This time, the kiss was long. Slow. Heavy. It weighed a million pounds because wrapped up in all of this was *something.*

What, she didn't know. A hello? Goodbye? Was she the one who was going to have to walk away before he did something stupid? What would she do if he'd broken the rules at her insistence when that wasn't the kind of person he was?

Good grief, she'd fallen in love with him because of his ethics. Because he did the right thing even when it was hard.

She pushed him back, nearly weeping with the effort it had taken to force him to stop kissing her.

"Can we just...talk, please?" she pleaded, squeezing her head in an attempt to keep it from exploding. Now that she knew what it felt like to have Joshua Colton show up for her, to *choose* her, she'd shatter into a million pieces if she had to give it up.

"Not my first choice, but yes," he said and sat down on the couch, perching right at the very edge with an earnest expression on his face. "Please, first of all, are you really okay? You didn't just say that last night, right? Tell me."

She smiled at the resurrection of their catch phrase from way back at the beginning.

"I'm fine." She sat on the couch too, lacing her fingers with his and holding his hand in her lap because she couldn't stand to sit here without touching some part of him.

It was like the kiss of last night unleashed something that made it impossible to ignore the things inside her that had Josh's name written all over them. The kiss of today had only intensified this feeling of everything between them being *more*.

But at what cost?

"Now *you* tell me why you're here. Inside." She jerked her chin at the door, which she'd had at least half the responsibility of opening to him. "You kissed me last night. Everyone knows about us now, or they will soon. What kind of disaster are we going to walk into today at work?"

"Well, for one, I have to retract my statement that we're not involved," he said with a slight eye roll. "But it kind of doesn't matter because I'm pretty sure the Sharpe merger is going through anyway."

"Are you going to be okay with that?" she asked cautiously because it wasn't exactly great news. At least not for Josh, and her soul hurt for him that he was being forced to sell off part of his birthright.

But at least it sounded like he was still involved in the daily business of the resort. If he'd done something to change his ownership of it to show he'd chosen her, surely they wouldn't still speak to him about decisions.

He shrugged. "It's a necessary evil, and I'd prefer to not have to even entertain this idea, but my father will not stop until he's destroyed Mariposa. If this merger saves it, I'm okay with it."

"Then you're still my boss," she said, disquiet rolling through her chest as she absorbed that he'd willingly stepped over the line, trouncing the rules under his heel.

But Josh shook his head, the corners of his mouth tilting up. "Not anymore. As of yesterday at three o'clock, the bar staff reports to Laura. The way it should have been in the first place. Sorry it took so long for all the paperwork to be wrapped up."

The blood rushed out of her head, and her knees would have given out if she hadn't already been sitting down. As it was, she had to duck her head to clear the black swirling through her vision.

"You…restructured the reporting hierarchy? For me?" she managed to gasp out as relief sang through her veins. "You're not my boss?"

"I haven't been for—" he glanced at his phone "—almost eighteen hours."

"And you couldn't have told me this last night?" She whacked him on the arm. "You could have slept here and I could have made you breakfast. We've wasted like seventeen hours and fifty-three minutes already."

He laughed and caught her as she launched herself into his arms, snuggling into the embrace she never wanted to leave. Miraculously, she didn't have to.

"Does this mean you're choosing me?" he murmured into her hair. "Because I want to be clear what's happening here. This is still a conversation."

His point winnowed into her heart and took up all the space. "Yes, yes it does mean that."

"Good. It would be very awkward to tell you I'm in love with you, only to have you say thank you and push me out the door."

She pulled back and met his gaze, wonder riding shotgun in her chest. "Oh, I can out awkward the best of them. Especially if we're going to be throwing around very big *L* words. This is for real? It doesn't feel like it's real. Say it again."

"I meant like. I'm very much in like with you." When she smacked him, he captured her hand and brought it to his lips, grinning as he glanced up at her from over her knuckles. "You heard me. I love you. This is me throwing all my cards on the table. If you're going to rip my heart out and stomp on it, I highly recommend you hurry up because Laura's about to text you."

"She is?" Kelli glanced around for her phone, which she frankly had forgotten existed now that she didn't have to sit around sweating over the next time the robber would call her up for another chat about the money she didn't have. "About what?"

"Okay, I'm dying here and you're looking for your phone," Josh said with a dramatic sigh. "Was my gesture not grand enough for your taste? Shall I hire a skywriter and scare up a string quartet?"

Oh, that sounded lovely. While she knew he was kidding—or at least she thought he was—she took pity on him and slid off the couch to kneel between his legs, taking his face in her hands as she brushed a thumb across his cheek. "I fell for you the moment you handed me that blanket at your house."

"The night we didn't sleep and sat out under the stars?"

Something beautiful spread through his gaze even as he cocked a brow. "That was all it took? A blanket?"

"I was halfway there after you pulled spinach out of your refrigerator."

"You should get out more," he advised her, turning his head to kiss her palm, which hadn't moved from his face. "But only with me. Now that we can make it official, I intend to ensure you don't share blankets with anyone else."

"You're the only man on the planet who keeps blankets on his patio," she told him with a laugh. "You're safe."

Her phone buzzed from the kitchen table where she'd apparently left it. Laura. Her new boss. It felt prophetic, since Laura had offered her the employment contract in the first place. She climbed to her feet, laughed as Josh yanked her back for a searing kiss and finally broke free to dash for the table, bobbling her phone into her right hand.

"She wants to see me," Kelli called to Josh, who had leaned back on the sofa, one leg bent up in a masculine sprawl that was so casually sexy, her mouth went dry.

"Yeah. I would be fine if you kept her waiting," he informed her with a lethal grin and patted the couch next to him. "I can think of a few things I would like to discuss with you as well, and none of them involve Laura or Mariposa."

"That's completely unfair," she moaned. "Making me choose between you and my new boss."

"What if I go with you?" he offered. "Then I can hold your hand the entire way and get started making sure everyone at Mariposa knows we're together. Especially Knox."

That tracked. She gave him that one because possibly she still owed him an apology for being a little self-righteous about his jealousy over Knox. "Sold."

True to his word, he held her hand as he drove her to L Building in his golf cart. It hit her then that she could go back to her apartment. The danger was over. The robbers had been arrested, which meant Valerie could come back to work too.

Everything was over. Except for Josh. Somehow. It was hard to believe.

Josh's thumb slid over hers and he glanced over, as if sensing she'd gone quiet for a reason. "Laura's a good boss, I swear. You'll love her. Not as much as me, but you can't have everything."

For how long would Laura be her boss though? A day? An hour? Was that what Laura wanted to talk to her about—to tell her Valerie had already set her return date?

Forlorn all at once, Kelli trudged through the lobby to the offices in the back, Josh's arm at her waist. Everyone noticed, but she didn't have the energy to deal with the stares and blatant whispering.

Laura was standing outside her office talking to Patsy, but she smiled when she saw Kelli, arching her brows at her brother. "I see you wasted no time."

"You're one to talk, future Mrs. Steele," he said with a smirk in the direction of her engagement ring. "Of anyone, I would think you'd understand that when you have something worth hanging on to, you grab on with both hands as quickly as you can."

As lovely as it was to hear Josh talk about her like that, she needed to rip this Band-Aid off sooner rather than later. "What did you want to see me about?"

"This jerk didn't tell you?" Laura said with a thrust of her chin toward Josh. "I'm offering you a permanent job at Mariposa. If you want to stay."

What? Convinced she'd misheard, she shook her head. "I'm sorry, did you say *permanent*? What about Valerie?"

Laura exchanged a look with Josh. "We feel it's better

business to keep a rock star bartender all the guests love, instead of bringing back one who left us in the lurch and didn't have the ethics to bring the stolen money to the police. If she'd done that, you'd never have been in danger. So please accept a 15 percent raise and an extra week of vacation for the trouble you went through on Mariposa's behalf as part of your employment package."

Kelli's brain switched to frappé mode as she tried to take in that everything she'd ever wanted had just dropped into her lap.

"I accept," she croaked out as fast as she could before someone changed their mind.

The hug Josh pulled her into had celebration written all over it. "I didn't say anything because I wanted it to be separate from any discussion about us. I wanted them both to be choices you could make without feeling they were tied together."

But they were tied together in the best way possible. She got to have her cake and eat it too. Which she did immediately by kissing Josh in full view of his sister.

She just laughed. "Welcome to Mariposa. And the family."

Epilogue

Kelli terminated the lease on her apartment, insisting that she could never sleep there again, knowing the robbers had been inside it, touching all her things. She stayed in the bungalow next to Josh's but the Coltons ended up needing that space with Laura's wedding on the horizon.

Plus she never spent any time there anyway.

It was too soon and probably raised a million eyebrows, but Josh didn't care. He asked Kelli to move in with him and took an unexpected amount of joy out of helping her arrange her things in his place. Best of all, she brought almost nothing with her, since she hadn't replaced her stuff after all of her possessions had been trashed by the robbers.

That meant he could shower her with gifts. Take her shopping. Toss some of his stuff so they could purchase things together to make it *their* house.

He kept the lounge chairs on the patio though. That was their favorite place to relax after dark, like they had been for the last hour or so. "Let's go to Flagstaff on our next day off. Check out that new furniture store."

"But I already have everything I want," she told him. "You're here, and everything else is just stuff."

It never failed to make him smile when she said things like that. "You're sure you're not unhappy that all that money you saved isn't going toward buying the house you've always wanted?"

Kelli took his face in both hands, a gesture she made when she wanted him to be still and pay attention to what she was saying. No chore on his part. He wouldn't have torn free for a million dollars.

"I didn't want a house," she told him, a wealth of emotions rising like the sun in her gaze. "I wanted a home. A center. A place to land after soaring into the heavens. That's what you are to me, every day. Wherever you are, that's where I want to be."

"But all that money is just sitting there," he protested lightly, unable to stop his heart from swelling as he checked all those things off on his mental list too. "You should do something with it that makes you happy."

"You could always up my rent," she suggested slyly, even though she knew bringing that up made him mad. "Charging me the same amount as my apartment is ludicrously cheap and you know it."

He didn't want her money and had more than enough of his own. But he also knew she appreciated it when he honored her independent streak, so he insisted that she pay him rent. Yesterday, she'd found out that he'd donated her first payment to an ocean cleanup charity.

That had been an argument and a half that had culminated with an apology on his part and then he'd ended up cooking dinner for her. The bath he'd drawn for her had ended up being a win for both of them, so he didn't count the hour they'd both spent wet and laughing as part of the apology like he'd meant it to be.

"Maybe I'll let you buy me a house off property somewhere," he suggested lightly, just to test out whether she'd go for the idea he'd been tossing around in his head.

Kelli whipped her head around and stared at him. "Leave Mariposa? What is this thing you're saying?"

He shrugged. "If the merger goes through, we should have enough cash to pay off Clive. But it's not a done deal. We might still lose the resort. I'm just thinking contingencies here. I don't mind the idea of being a kept man."

His gorgeous girlfriend shook her head. "We're not losing the resort. It belongs to me now too, in spirit anyway."

Maybe one day, he'd figure out how to propose to her without falling back into his idiotic ways and then she'd agree to change her name to Colton. He'd gladly split his third with her. She already owned every corner of his soul anyway.

"I appreciate your confidence," he told her, not at all sure how he'd gotten so lucky as to be sharing this journey with the only woman on the planet who got him.

"We'll figure it out. Together," she promised and scootched her lounger over so she could snuggle against his chest. "Now, it's your turn to say how happy you are. Tell me."

No problem. He'd gladly spend the next forever doing exactly that.

* * * * *

COMING SOON!

We really hope you enjoyed reading this book.
If you're looking for more romance
be sure to head to the shops when
new books are available on

Thursday 24th
April

To see which titles are coming soon, please visit
millsandboon.co.uk/nextmonth

MILLS & BOON

FOUR BRAND NEW BOOKS FROM
MILLS & BOON MODERN

The same great stories you love, a stylish new look!

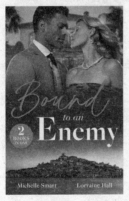

OUT NOW

Eight Modern stories published every month, find them all at:

millsandboon.co.uk

afterglow BOOKS

Afterglow Books is a trend-led, trope-filled list of books with diverse, authentic and relatable characters, a wide array of voices and representations, plus real world trials and tribulations. Featuring all the tropes you could possibly want (think small-town settings, fake relationships, grumpy vs sunshine, enemies to lovers) and all with a generous dose of spice in every story.

♫ @millsandboonuk
⊙ @millsandboonuk
afterglowbooks.co.uk

#AfterglowBooks

For all the latest book news, exclusive content and giveaways scan the QR code below to sign up to the Afterglow newsletter:

SCAN ME

(•(•)) Forced proximity

♠ Workplace romance

🗳 One night

✈ International

⧗ Slow burn

🌙 Spicy

OUT NOW

Two stories published every month. Discover more at:
Afterglowbooks.co.uk

LET'S TALK

Romance

For exclusive extracts, competitions
and special offers, find us online:

MillsandBoon

X @MillsandBoon

@MillsandBoonUK

@MillsandBoonUK

Get in touch on 01413 063 232

For all the latest coming soon, visit
millsandboon.co.uk/nextmonth